Harry Bowling was bo
left school at fourteen to supplement the family income as an office boy in a riverside provisions' merchant. Called up for National Service in the 1950s, he has since been variously employed as lorry driver, milkman, meat cutter, carpenter and decorator, and community worker. He now writes full time. He is the author of eleven previous novels: *That Summer in Eagle Street*, *Waggoner's Way*, *The Farrans of Fellmonger Street*, *Pedlar's Row*, *Backstreet Child*, *The Girl From Cotton Lane*, *Gaslight in Page Street*, *Paragon Place*, *Ironmonger's Daughter*, *Tuppence to Tooley Street*, and *Conner Street's War*. He is married and lives with his family, dividing his time between Lancashire and Deptford.

'What makes Harry's novels work is their warmth and authenticity. Their spirit comes from the author himself and his abiding memories of family life as it was once lived in the slums of southeast London' *Today*

Also by Harry Bowling

That Summer in Eagle Street
Waggoner's Way
The Farrans of Fellmonger Street
Pedlar's Row
Backstreet Child
The Girl From Cotton Lane
Gaslight in Page Street
Paragon Place
Ironmonger's Daughter
Tuppence to Tooley Street
Conner Street's War

One More For Saddler Street

Harry Bowling

HEADLINE

First published in 1996
by HEADLINE BOOK PUBLISHING

First published in paperback in 1996
by HEADLINE BOOK PUBLISHING

10 9 8 7 6 5 4 3 2 1

ISBN 0 7472 5197 5

Typeset by CBS, Felixstowe, Suffolk

Printed and bound in Great Britain by
BPC Paperbacks Ltd

HEADLINE BOOK PUBLISHING
A division of Hodder Headline PLC
338 Euston Road
London NW1 3BH

To the memory of Geoff Webster.
A courageous man.

Prologue

1923

Sister Beatrice gave out a deep sigh and shook her head sadly as she watched the young lad wolf down the hot potato soup. 'Cut the boy another slice of bread, Sister Consuela,' she said, and noticing the questioning look on the younger woman's pale face she added impatiently, 'hurry now, the poor mite's starving.'

Sister Consuela was aware that the supply of bread was running low and there would be no more forthcoming until the next foray down to the market, but when Sister Beatrice adopted that particular tone of voice she was not to be argued with.

Outside the heavy autumn rain fell in the cobbled yard and poured out from the broken guttering, cascading down over the ancient green stains on the grey stone wall. In the chilly convent refectory the young lad picked up the thick hunk of bread that Sister Consuela had placed in front of him and glanced up at the Sisters of Mercy with hesitation in his large dark eyes.

'Eat it up, child,' Sister Beatrice bade him kindly. 'Then it's a bath for you and we'll see what we can do about your feet.'

Jimmy Bailey unconsciously wriggled his toes and felt a nail press into the sore patch on the sole of his foot. He ignored the discomfort and broke the hard dry bread, dropping a piece into the remains of the soup. He felt tired and in awe of the two tall women with their white, flat faces and strange cloth hats, but the hot broth was beginning to work on his stomach and he felt less afraid as the warm glow rose up into his pallid face.

Father McCarthy came into the room and exchanged quick glances with the two Sisters before studying the lone figure who sat hunched over the soup bowl at the long pine table. 'I'm truly sorry to have to bring in another mouth to feed, Sister,' he said in his pronounced Irish brogue. 'Alas, there was nothing else I could do in the circumstances.'

Sister Consuela walked quietly over to the wide stone sink and set about washing the large pile of dirty crockery, leaving Sister Beatrice to admonish him.

'You know of our difficulties, Father,' the older woman said sharply. 'We have to rely on the kindness of the traders for donations of food and we have little to offer by way of clean clothes and footwear. The dormitory is full and we've two children sleeping in the meditation room as it is.'

Father McCarthy kept his distance, not wanting Sister Beatrice to get a whiff of his breath. She was not very tolerant of his fondness for a little tipple or two. 'I'm very sorry, but I was left with little choice,' he replied. 'St Mark's have taken in the other two children but the Mother Superior was desperate for help. If you could have seen the plight of that poor family, Sister, your heart would have been pained for them just as mine was. The children have no father and there was very little food in the house. The mother had taken to her bed with pleurisy and the children were trying to make her some broth with potato peelings, would you believe?'

'Nothing surprises me any more, Father, and my tears dried up long ago,' the nun told him with a harsh note in her voice. 'I resign myself to prayer these days.'

'I prayed too, Sister, when I saw the look of pain and suffering on the face of that poor woman,' the priest rejoined. 'I asked the Lord for guidance, for the grace of providence. I have to tell you that for a moment or two I felt that God had forsaken these poor wretches, but in my heart of hearts I know that he hasn't. He's working through us, and we can't fail him, can we?'

Sister Consuela dropped a plate and the noise of it shattering on the cold stone floor made Sister Beatrice jump sharply. 'Oh, do be careful with that crockery,' she said testily. 'There's little enough as it is.'

Sister Consuela bowed her head and Father McCarthy smiled at the rebuke. 'Never mind,' he said cheerfully. 'I'll go and see the Monsignor tomorrow. We need more funds from the charity coffers if we're to respond to the demands being made on us.'

Jimmy finished his soup and stared down at the empty bowl. He could not remember when food had tasted so good and it seemed ages since his stomach had felt so full.

'Come along, child,' Sister Beatrice said, giving the lad a reassuring smile.

Jimmy followed the nun along a stone-floored corridor, limping slightly as the nail bit into his foot. He could hear the swish of her clothing as she walked and was aware of the sweet aroma of incense hanging in the air. It was like a hospital, he thought, suddenly recalling the day his father had led him along a corridor like this one to the ward where his mother lay. It seemed so long ago and yet he could still remember clearly the feel of his father's arm around his shoulders and the hugeness of the man beside him. The kind eyes looked down at him and the mouth, half hidden by a thick moustache, split in a wide grin as they walked into the long ward. Jimmy remembered the noise his father's boots made as they walked down to the far bed and the smell of tobacco on the big man's breath as he bent down and lifted him up to greet his mother.

And there was that other day, in the little church by the river. The pews had been full and the hymn 'Eternal Father' had rung out into the cobbled lane as the congregation sang with a disturbing fervour. Jimmy was sitting upright on the hard wooden seat along with his sisters and glanced furtively at his tearful mother as she sat wringing a wet handkerchief in her long thin fingers. The booming voice of the vicar and the solemn fear of the grown-ups around him had made Jimmy frightened, and as the names of the drowned mariners were read out by the cold altar like a final calling and he heard his father's name pronounced he had burst into tears.

Jimmy could not remember who it was had carried him from the church out into the cobbled lane. He knew it hadn't been his mother; it had been a man and he remembered the strong arms around him and the soft voice urging him to be brave. 'Big lads don't cry,' the man had told him. The bad dreams had started then, when the waves washed over him and he felt himself sinking into endless water and he called out in the blackness, fighting for breath as his mother rushed into the bedroom to comfort him. He remembered his sisters sitting up in bed crying with him and his mother hugging him to her. 'Big boys mustn't cry,' she had told him. He wanted her now, to hold him and hug him tightly, but she couldn't. She was back in hospital, and his sisters had been taken by the nuns. He must be brave once more and let the lady in the swishing clothes see that he was too big to cry.

'There you are,' Sister Beatrice said, putting her hand into the hot water. 'If it's too hot give me a call, I'll be outside the door.'

Jimmy felt better at being allowed to bath himself and he sat down on the stone floor to take off his worn-out boots and his ragged clothes. Blood had congealed in one boot, and when he finally managed to ease it off he examined the hole the nail had made in the sole of his foot before climbing into the hot water.

In his office Father McCarthy eased his bulky frame in the padded chair and reached into the drawer of his desk to take out a bottle of Irish whiskey. He smiled sadly to himself as he recalled the look of horror on the young lad's face when told that he would be spending the next few days at the convent.

The boy had merely nodded in resignation but the look in those large dark eyes had spoken volumes. During the short journey by taxi from Rotherhithe to St Mary's in Dockhead he had tried to put the child at ease, offering some gentle words of comfort and encouragement, but he was not sure that it had done the trick. Maybe it would not be so traumatic for little Jimmy Bailey after all, the priest thought as he poured himself a large measure of the fiery spirit. From what Sister Beatrice had said it might well mean another one for Saddler Street.

Bill Curtis threw down the evening paper and sighed. 'I dunno, it's all bloody gloom an' doom in the papers these days,' he told Lottie. 'There's martial law bin declared in Germany an' there's trouble in Spain, an' I turned the page, an' what yer fink? It's all about the earthquake in Tokyo. It said there's fousands bin killed out there.'

Lottie looked at her husband with concern. 'Are yer feelin' all right, Bill?' she asked him. 'Yer bin a bit moody lately.'

'No I ain't.'

'Yes you 'ave.'

'Well, I ain't noticed it.'

'Why don't yer pop up the Crown fer a pint?'

'I ain't in no mood fer a pint,' Bill said tersely.

Lottie was not so easily fooled. It had been a quiet time along the river lately and she had seen the men standing around aimlessly on street corners when she went to the market. Bill had managed to get some work nevertheless and she had gone along to 'Uncle's' that Monday with the ruby ring her mother had bequeathed her, and the extra bit of money had kept the wolf from the door. Bill wasn't too happy about it though. He was a proud man who felt that it was the husband's duty to bring in the money, not rely on his wife using the pawnshop to make ends meet.

Lottie stood up and brushed her hands down her crisp, flowered apron. She was a short woman in her late fifties, with grey eyes and a small round face, and her greying hair was parted in the middle and pulled tightly into buns above her ears. She reached up and took down a small green vase, then sat down again to turn the contents out into her lap. 'There we are, go an' get yerself a pint,' she said, handing Bill a sixpence. 'A man needs a bit o' sustenance inside 'im.'

'Are you tellin' me yer food ain't good enough?' Bill said grinning, reluctant to take the money.

'Look, don't piss-ball about. Just take it,' Lottie replied.

Bill took the sixpence from her and got up from his armchair. 'I'll pay yer back, gel,' he said with a grateful smile. 'There's a bacon boat due in at Mark Brown's next week.'

Lottie heard the door open and then Bill's loud voice. 'Bloody 'ell, it's pissin' down.'

She knew that with the chance of going out for a drink her husband would not be deterred by the weather. 'Put yer cap on then, an' yer big coat,' she called out.

The fire was burning low and Lottie hummed contentedly to herself as she deftly sewed up the split seam of her cotton dress. It was too shabby to be seen out in but it was all right for working about the house, she reasoned. It was good to be able to find a few coppers for Bill. He hadn't complained when he handed over his pay packet this week and there had been no money left over for a pint of beer. As for the tally man – he would have to wait.

The sharp rat-tat on the door made Lottie start and she hurried along the passage with a look of concern on her face. Who could it be on such a night? she thought.

Her heart sank as she opened the front door and found the two Sisters of Mercy standing there with a small lad huddled between them. Jimmy Bailey stood just inside the parlour door grasping his wet cap in his hands as his temporary guardians spoke with Lottie.

'I know this is a terrible imposition, Mrs Curtis, but we are desperate,' Sister Beatrice explained. 'There's simply no more room at the convent. Jimmy is that much older than the others. He can fend for himself quite well.'

Lottie sighed in resignation. 'How long for?' she asked.

'We have no way of knowing at the moment,' the Sister replied. Then lowering her voice she said, 'The boy's mother was taken away with the fever today and there's no one else able to look after him. He's poorly nourished but apart from that he has a clean bill of health.'

'Well, that's somefing at least,' Lottie remarked.

'Can you manage him?' Sister Beatrice asked her.

Lottie turned to look at Jimmy who was staring along the passage at the fire. 'Yeah, I reckon so,' she said smiling. 'I can put Lucy in wiv Ellen an' the lad can 'ave 'er bed.'

'Are you sure you don't want to talk it over with your husband first?' the Sister asked tentatively.

Lottie gave the nun a knowing look. 'Come off it, Sister,' she said. 'Yer wouldn't bring that little lad out on a night like this unless yer was certain I'd take 'im in, now would yer?'

'You make me feel very sinful, Mrs Curtis,' Sister Beatrice replied. 'I'll pray for forgiveness, and I'll say a prayer for you and your husband. You are both righteous people.'

'While yer at it, Sister, yer might spare a prayer fer that little mite,' Lottie told her, nodding towards the weary young lad.

Sister Beatrice smiled at her and then turned to Sister Consuela. 'Come, Sister. I think we can leave in peace now,' she said, glancing back down at Jimmy. 'Goodbye, young man. Be good for Mrs Curtis.'

Lottie closed the door behind the two nuns and led the new arrival into the parlour. 'Are you 'ungry, Jimmy?' she asked him.

The young lad shook his head. 'The ladies gave me some soup, an' I 'ad a barf too,' he replied, his eyes open wide.

'Well then, yer better get some rest,' Lottie said smiling kindly. 'C'mon, luv, let's get yer ter bed. We'll need ter go quiet so's not ter wake the ovver two.'

* * *

The chimer on the centre of the mantelshelf struck the hour of ten and Lottie put down her sewing once more. Bill will be surprised when he finds out there's another child in the house, she thought. But as he said at the very beginning, 'They've only got little bellies an' it don't take much more ter feed anuvver one.'

Upstairs in the quiet bedroom Jimmy turned over on to his side and looked out from under the bedclothes at the dark night. It must be very late, he thought. His two younger sisters Lillian and Glenda would be asleep now, and his mother too. The nuns had frightened him but the lady seemed very nice. She even gave him a kiss on the cheek when she tucked him in.

Drowsy mumbling from the bed across the room brought a tear to the lad's eyes. Lillian and Glenda always mumbled in their sleep. He would be seeing them again very soon, he told himself. Jimmy felt the silent tear run down his face and he screwed up his eyes. His mother had told him, and the strange man outside the church had told him: big boys don't cry.

Bill Curtis let himself into the house and took off his saturated coat. 'I met Darbo up the Crown,' he said casually as he lowered himself into the armchair.

'Did yer? That was nice for yer,' Lottie replied. 'I've done yer a cheese sandwich an' there's a few gherkins left in the jar if yer want 'em.'

'Darbo was sayin' . . .'

'Bill.'

'Darbo reckons . . .'

'Bill, will yer listen ter me.'

The docker eased his position in the armchair and gave his anxious wife a big grin. 'Don't tell me. Yer gone an' took anuvver one in,' he said.

Lottie looked shocked. ''Ow d'yer know?' she asked quickly.

'Darbo come in the pub grinnin' all over 'is face,' Bill replied. 'When I asked 'im what the bloody 'ell was the matter wiv 'im, 'e said 'e'd just seen two nuns wiv a little kid knockin' on our front door.'

'What's so funny about that?' Lottie asked.

Bill tried to straighten his face. 'Darbo reckons they got yer taped at St Mary's. "Full up? Never mind. Send 'em all round to our Lottie. She'll take 'em in," 'e goes.'

''E's a lovely little lad wiv beetle-black eyes. It's so sad,' Lottie told him. 'Are yer sure yer don't mind, Bill?'

'All the same if I did,' he said wryly.

'If I thought yer'd object I'd refuse 'em, honest I would, luv,' she told him.

'Of course yer wouldn't. You ain't got the 'eart,' Bill said, getting up. 'C'mon, let's get off ter bed.'

'What about yer sandwich?' she reminded him.

'I ain't 'ungry. I'll take it ter work wiv me,' he replied. 'Let's creep in an' take a peep at that new little perisher.'

Lottie got up from her chair and kissed her husband on the cheek. 'You're a good man, Bill,' she said, sighing loudly.

'An' you're a soft touch, Lottie,' he told her. 'Darbo was right. I can just 'ear 'em. "Sorry, we're full, Farvver." "Never mind, Sister. One more fer Saddler Street."'

wiv 'im,' e said [illegible] however, two nights wiv a little kip [illegible] up our spare room.'

'What's to [illegible] about that?' Dulcie asked.

Bill tried to straighten his face. 'There's nothing else, [illegible] yer Emma [illegible] if yer don't mind. We'll [illegible] round to our Lorna, she'll take 'em in,' he [illegible].

'He's a lovely little lad [illegible] black eyes,' [illegible] said. [illegible] told him. 'Are yer sure yer don't mind, Bill?'

'[illegible] the same if I did,' he said [illegible].

'If I thought yer'd object I'd [illegible], honest I would [illegible] told him.

'Of course yer wouldn't, you ain't got the 'eart,' Bill said, getting up. 'C'mon, let's get yer off to bed.'

'What about yer sandwiches?' she reminded him.

'[illegible] I'll take 'em ter work wiv me,' he replied. '[illegible] [illegible] that new little [illegible].'

Dulcie got up from her chair and kissed her husband on the cheek. 'You're a good man, Bill,' she said, sighing loudly.

As [illegible] Dulcie was [illegible] were the [illegible] 'Never [illegible] One more for Saddler Street.'

Chapter One

1946

During the second half of the nineteenth century people had flooded into the riverside borough of Bermondsey to work in the tanneries, wharves, and new food factories that were opening up. The workers and their families were forced to live in disease-ridden hovels which were little more than encampments. Raw sewage flowed through the roughly carved ditches and rats infested the ramshackle dwellings. The men fought each other to grab one of the metal tokens tossed amongst them which entitled the holder to a day's work on the quayside, while others slaved away in the factories for a few paltry coppers. For them and their families, the ravages of hunger, empty bellies, deprivation and sickness were their lot, like a millstone around their necks.

From such living hell strong characters emerged, and they organised, challenged and fought for better working conditions and better housing. Trade unions sprang up and workers marched through the streets to protest. They were joined by the privileged, by crusading Christians, and people from the professions. The ranks were swelled by others, campaigners, moralists and ordinary working-class folk, all outraged by what they saw and what they experienced. Like a large snowball set rolling down a hillside, the clamour of protest gathered power as it grew ever larger until it became unstoppable.

Housing trusts and charities were set up, and a few farsighted people worked hand in hand with them to rid the borough of its stinking wooden hovels. By the end of the century brick houses had been erected, roads laid and an underground sewage system installed. From the sprawling chaos order was born. Trees were planted and the borough began to breathe again.

Saddler Street was like many of the other neat little backstreets of Bermondsey that had sprung up out of the cruel squalor of the past. For the people who lived in such backwaters theirs was a kind of inheritance, a legacy of the bitter struggles, suffering, and all too often early death. Like their neighbours, the people of Saddler Street were proud of their own little road, and it showed. It could be seen in the whitened doorsteps of the little two-up, two-down terraced houses, in the windows where crisp lace curtains hung, and it was reflected in the locals' faces and in their very demeanour. They held their heads high and walked proud, the men with their thumbs hooked into their braces and their cloth caps askew, and the women with their arms folded magisterially over fresh flowered aprons. For many the struggles of the past were still fresh in their memories and would remain so, and the younger folk were not allowed to forget the lessons of history.

Saddler Street ran off the main thoroughfare of Jamaica Road in Dockhead towards the River Thames. It had facing rows of houses and boasted two corner shops at the main-road end. On the left-hand side looking into the turning was Robey's, the newsagent's and sweetshop, and on the other corner there was a grocery shop owned by the Logan family. At the river end Saddler Street led into River Lane, which ran parallel to the Thames. The river itself was hidden by Allen's Wharf which rose above the backstreet, though the two crane arms pointing skywards behind the building were a constant reminder to the Saddler Street folk of its nearness.

At number five, Ann Johnson stood in the scullery stirring a large potful of stew. The late October weather had changed and there was now a distinct nip in the air. She had felt it that morning when she left the house at seven o'clock to go to her office-cleaning job at a provision merchants in Tooley Street.

Ann was a buxom woman nearing her fiftieth birthday, with pale blue eyes and fair hair that she wore short and shaped to her head. She had married Frank Johnson, a dock labourer, when she was just nineteen. Frank was twenty-one at the time and came from a large family. Within the first year of marriage their son, Alan, was born. Eighteen months later their second, Derek, arrived, and it was then that Ann Johnson's mother decided to make her views known. ''E comes from a large family 'imself so the chances are yer gonna be weighed down wiv an 'ouseful o' kids, unless yer put yer foot down,' Maggie Prentiss had told her.

Ann wasn't quite sure how to go about it. She loved Frank and was loath to spurn his advances. He was a kind and considerate lover and he made her feel good. She realised she would have to be careful, however, and was grateful for the fact that two years passed before their third child was born. Frank was ecstatic over it being a girl and he chose her name, Lana Louise.

While the boys favoured their father's dark looks and stocky build, Lana had her mother's colouring. Her hair was golden and hung to her shoulders, and her eyes were a deep blue. She developed into a strikingly attractive young woman who at twenty-five had undoubtedly broken a few of the local lads' hearts, Ann felt sure.

As she slowly stirred the contents of the iron pot on that Friday evening Ann's mind was troubled. Her son Alan and his wife Beth were expecting their first child and Beth had had a couple of scares during the early days of her pregnancy. As if that wasn't enough, Lana seemed to be serious about Ben Ferris, a local small-time villain whom Alan described as a no-good con artist. Derek had also added his opinion, though not in front of his sister, and as far as Ann Johnson could see her daughter was making a big mistake.

Like their father the two boys worked in the docks, and every Friday they stopped off to pay their union dues at the Crown and Anchor. Lana would be home soon from her job on the telephone switchboard of Baldwin and Meyers, a large insurance company near London Bridge, and there would be time for a quiet chat before the men arrived, Ann told herself.

Nearby, in a working-men's cafe in River Lane, two young men were in earnest conversation.

'I don't give two monkeys what Sammy reckons, the price is a dollar a pair,' Soapy Lomax growled. 'Yer've seen the commodity. They ain't yer everyday stockin's. They're first-quality Yankee nylons, as worn by all the film stars. If yer could buy 'em straight, which yer can't, they'd set yer back at least twelve an' a tanner a pair.'

Ben Ferris looked hard at the scruffy little individual with the darting eyes and felt like shaking him by the neck until he rattled. Soapy would be adding his usual cut, and buying in at five shillings a pair would leave no margin for a bargain price to the punters. Selling them at seven and sixpence a pair meant that they would not move very fast, and selling them in dribs and drabs brought added problems. There was always the chance of his house being turned over by the police. He had expected to buy in at three and sixpence and be able to sell the whole consignment of two hundred pairs to Sammy Goldbloom at six shillings a pair in one fell swoop.

'I got a fair idea who's got the gear,' Ben said, his dark eyes narrowing. 'I've a good mind ter go an' see 'im meself an' make 'im an offer fer the 'ole lot.'

Soapy's unshaven face broke into a sly grin. 'That's your prerogative,' he replied.

Ben realised that the bluff had not worked and he breathed out through his teeth. 'I tell yer what,' he said. 'Go back ter yer pal an' tell 'im I'll take the lot off 'is 'ands for four an' a tanner a pair, an' that's me final word.'

Soapy drained the cold tea from his mug and got up. 'I'll

be 'ere the same time termorrer, but I can't promise anyfing,' he said quickly.

Ben watched him leave and then went over to the counter. 'Give us anuvver mug o' tea, will yer, Joe?' he said.

The cafe owner smiled as he dropped the used mug into a sink full of suds behind him and picked up a clean one. 'Yer know who Soapy's frontin' for, don't yer?' he said.

'Who?' Ben asked quickly.

'The Carmichaels. Lol an' Freddy Carmichael came in 'ere yesterday round about four o'clock,' Joe Slavin told him. 'Then ten minutes later Soapy walked in. They was mumblin' away tergevver fer over an hour, an' all they bought was two mugs o' tea. I'd go out o' business if I 'ad ter rely on the likes o' them.'

Ben adjusted the cuffs of his white shirt and straightened the knot of his slim-Jim silver tie and he watched Joe pour his tea from a stainless-steel teapot. 'That's bad news,' he growled. 'I can't see Lol an' that boss-eyed bruvver of 'is movin' on the price.'

Joe scooped a heaped spoonful of sugar into the mug and added some milk. ''Ere, you ain't 'eard any more about that case o' tea, 'ave yer?' he asked as he pushed the mug towards Ben.

'I'm expectin' a delivery termorrer, Joe,' he replied. 'If so I'll bring it round, providin' me van's fixed by then.'

The cafe owner felt that he was being fobbed off and he gave Ben a quick look as he picked up the three pennies from the wet counter. 'What's the matter wiv yer van?' he asked.

'The bloody 'alf-shaft's gone,' Ben told him. 'The trouble is gettin' the spares. Toby at the garage said 'e might be able ter pick one up at the army surplus dump, but yer never sure wiv 'im.'

Another customer walked into the cafe and Ben took the mug of tea over to his seat.

The newcomer gave him a quick glance and then turned

to Joe. 'I'm lookin' fer Ben Ferris,' he said.

The cafe owner looked questioningly in Ben's direction and was relieved when the young man called the stranger over.

'What can I do fer yer?' he asked casually.

'I've got a message for yer from Mick Constantine,' the man replied. ''E wants yer ter meet 'im at the Crown, eight sharp.'

'I'll try an' be there,' Ben told him.

'I wouldn't be late if I were you,' the man said in a quiet voice. 'Mick ain't too 'appy at the moment. I thought I'd just tell yer.'

Ben sighed in resignation. 'I'll be there at eight sharp,' he replied.

The stranger turned and left without a further word and Ben bit on the inside of his cheek in consternation. From the tone of the man's voice Constantine was not going to extend his credit, he thought, and it looked very much like he would have to find the fifty pounds owing to the bookie by this evening. It was a tall order. Maybe Lana might be able to lend him the money. It would only be a short-term loan, until the silk-stocking deal was sorted out.

Joe Slavin had been busying himself behind the counter but he had heard every word and he shook his head slowly as Ben Ferris stood up and hurried out of the cafe.

Lana Johnson hurried home from work that Friday evening realising that her mother would take the opportunity of them being alone in the house to question her about Ben. News of his recent brush with the law had reached her ears and she had mentioned it that morning. Lana had made the excuse of being late and left the house, saying that she would explain when she got home from work.

'Is that you, Lana?'

The young woman smiled briefly to herself at the usual greeting. Her mother knew it could only be her at this time on Friday. 'It's turned cold ternight,' she said as she hung her coat in the passage.

'Can yer lay the table, luv?' Ann called out. 'This stew's takin' a time.'

Lana set about the task, thankful for the brief respite before the grilling. She was aware that her family was not very happy about her going out with Ben Ferris and her mother in particular had made it crystal clear that as far as she was concerned the man spelt trouble. Ben was a little wild in comparison with the usual young men in the neighbourhood, but he was nothing like the picture they all painted of him. He would settle down in time and want the things she wanted, like a home and children. In the meantime she would enjoy his company and live a little, despite the criticism from her family. They should try to see her side of it. Ben was good fun to be with and he had taken her to places she had never envisaged going to. The club they had visited in Soho and the race meeting at Epsom had made her realise that there was more to life than one night a week at the pictures and Saturday night at the Crown. Ben knew how to treat a girl and he made her feel good – how different from Tony Walsh, her previous boyfriend.

'Lana, when yer finished layin' the table will yer come an' give this stew a stir while I do the bread?' Ann called out.

The young woman walked out into the scullery and took the large wooden spoon from her mother. 'Lottie was tellin' me yesterday that that feller's poppin' in ternight ter fix 'er scullery winder,' she remarked.

Ann took a large Vienna loaf from the bread bin and set it down on the small table. 'Who, Jimmy Bailey?'

Lana nodded. ''E looks a real scruff.'

Lottie finished cutting the crust from the loaf and then looked up at her daughter. 'The feller might be scruffy, but I tell yer somefing. 'E's the only one o' those kids that Lottie took in who ever bovvers ter come an' see 'er. Never fergets a card on 'er birfday neivver. As far as I'm concerned 'e's a lot better than some I could name.'

Lana clenched her teeth and remained silent as she stirred the stew.

'Lottie told me that lad looks after 'is ole mum,' Ann went on. 'She's a sick woman by all accounts. It can't be very nice fer the poor sod.'

'Yeah, but 'e could smarten 'imself up a bit,' Lana remarked. 'The last time I saw 'im goin' in there 'e 'ad both pockets 'angin' off 'is coat.'

'P'raps the feller 'ad just come from work,' Ann replied.

'I saw 'im goin' in there a couple o' Sundays ago,' Lana told her. ''E was just the same then.'

Ann shook her head slowly. 'D'you know, Lana, sometimes yer give the impression o' bein' very unfeelin',' she said quietly. 'I know different, but if ovver people were listenin' to yer they'd be inclined ter fink bad of yer.'

The young woman sighed as she wiped the edge of the spoon on the side of the large iron pot. 'I didn't mean anyfing nasty, Mum,' she replied. 'I just don't reckon it's right fer a young bloke ter let 'imself go the way 'e does.'

'Yer gotta remember, the feller's just come back from the war,' Ann reminded her. 'Gawd knows what 'e went frew. It could 'ave a bearin' on the way 'e is.'

''Ow old would yer say 'e is?' Lana wondered.

'Lottie told me 'e was seven years old when she took 'im in. That was in nineteen twenty-three. That'd make 'im firty.'

''E looks older than that.'

'Well, anyway, 'e's a good sort ter fink of the ole lady the way 'e does,' Ann remarked as she set about cutting up the rest of the loaf.

Lana turned the gas down low under the pot and replaced the lid. 'That's about ready,' she said.

'Are you off out ternight?' Ann asked her.

'Yeah, but I've promised ter go in an' see Lottie first,' she replied quickly, sensing what was coming. 'I wanna make arrangements ter do 'er nails for 'er some time this week. She told me 'er feet are playin' 'er up again.'

Ann was not to be put off. 'I would 'ave thought it was about time you 'ad a night in,' she remarked. 'Yer've bin out every night this week.'

'Ben's takin' me ter see a show up West,' Lana told her.

Ann put the bread knife back in the table drawer and then turned to face her daughter. 'What was all this I 'eard about Ben gettin' pulled in by the police?' she asked.

'It was nuffing really,' Lana replied. 'It was over some lead that went missin' from the roof o' that church in Abbey Walk. Someone told the police that they saw Ben an' a couple o' blokes unloadin' some lead in Ben's yard last Friday night so they called ter see 'im.'

'An' what 'appened?'

'Well, they called round this Monday, an' by that time the yard was empty, so they've got nuffing ter go on.'

'Did 'e 'ave the lead?' Ann asked.

Lana gave her mother a hard look. 'Ben might be a bit of a chancer but 'e's not about strippin' church roofs, Mum,' she said sharply.

'Did 'e tell yer that?'

''E didn't 'ave to.'

'Yer seem ter put a lot o' trust in that bloke,' Ann replied quickly. 'I only 'ope yer don't end up gettin' 'urt.'

'Look, Mum, I know yer don't like the feller,' Lana countered, 'but Ben's never treated me badly, an' 'e's straight wiv me. As a matter o' fact 'e was unloadin' lead in the yard that night, but it didn't come off the church roof. The fellers who bought it were demolition men. They sell lead an' copper ter Ben. It's a regular deal 'e's got wiv 'em. There's nuffing dishonest about it.'

'Yer not tellin' me Ben's squeaky clean, are yer?' Ann retorted. 'The bloke's got a right ole name by all accounts. From what I 'ear 'e's got 'is 'ands in everyfing.'

'Yer shouldn't believe all you 'ear, Mum,' Lana told her. 'A lot of it is just plain jealousy. They'd like ter be able ter dress like 'e does an' go ter the places we go to. I could do a lot worse than Ben, believe me. If yer listened ter ovver people they'd say that Tony Walsh would make an ideal 'usband fer a gel, but I know different. At least wiv Ben I know where I stand.'

Ann did not reply for a while as she busied herself buttering the bread. Finally she looked up at her daughter. 'Lana, you're not sleepin' wiv 'im, are yer?' she asked.

The young woman's cheeks flushed and she shook her head. 'Of course not,' she replied.

Ann looked relieved. 'I just want yer ter give it time before yer get too serious,' she said quietly. 'Don't be in too much of a rush. Just remember there's two sides ter most fellers. The side yer've yet ter see is the side that only shows when the wrappin's come off. I'd die a death if you ever got pregnant an' was left stranded.'

Lana smiled. 'Don't you fret over Ben, Mum,' she told her. 'I know what 'e's really like, an' when you get ter know 'im yer'll find out 'e's not nearly as bad as 'e's painted.'

'I just 'ope so,' Ann said. 'I really do.'

Ben Ferris looked into the mirror and studied his reflection for a few moments before walking out of the bedroom of his flat above the yard in River Street. His dark wavy hair was combed back from his forehead and the day's stubble shaved smooth with a sharp razor. His dark-grey pinstripe suit fitted him well, the coat hanging straight from a broad pair of shoulders. His black patent-leather shoes shone and the dark-blue tie he wore was knotted neatly over a pale-blue shirt.

Ben had a worried expression on his handsome face as he hurried down the stairs and let himself out the front door beside the yard. In ten minutes he was due to meet Lana at the bus stop in Jamaica Road, and in ten minutes he was also due to meet Mick Constantine in the Crown public house. Mick would no doubt get angry at being stood up, but he could be made to see the sense in waiting another twenty-four hours for his fifty pounds, Ben reasoned, especially if a five-pound note was added as interest. He was feeling hopeful. Word was out that Gerry Knowland had made a nice little profit on a warehouse job in Rotherhithe, and when they met up at Rivellino's in Soho tonight there would be plenty of time to ask him for a little favour.

Chapter Two

Jimmy Bailey woke up early that Friday morning and rolled over on to his back, focusing his bleary eyes on the wide crack in the ceiling directly above his head. He tried to remember whether or not he had been up during the night. As he roused himself properly he realised that for the first time in a long while he had gone through the night without being woken by the rasping cough coming from the next room.

Jimmy sprang out of bed and quickly gripped the bedpost until the sudden giddiness left him, then he hurried into his mother's bedroom. She appeared to be sleeping soundly and he leant over her to reassure himself that she was all right before going down into the scullery to put the kettle on.

For a few minutes the young man sat hunched at the table, thinking about the day ahead of him. On Monday morning the man at the labour exchange had sent him along to Kimble's transport firm in Long Lane, but the transport manager there had seemed unimpressed by the fact that he was interviewing an experienced driver who had spent the last three years of the war ferrying supplies and ammunition along the treacherous mountain roads of southern Italy, often under fire. He had been more concerned with pointing out that Kimble's Transport Contractors were non-union and troublemakers would not be tolerated.

Jimmy had been eager to get away from the temporary job

he had taken at the sausage factory and he nodded acquiescently, whereupon the bowler-hatted manager opened his desk drawer and took out a bunch of keys. 'Go an' see the mechanic an' 'e'll sort a lorry out for yer,' he said, 'then come back ter the winder an' I'll sort out yer day's work.'

Jimmy found the elderly mechanic to be as grumpy as the manager. 'There she is,' the man growled, pointing over to an ancient-looking seven-ton Bedford parked in the corner of the shed. 'The bloody fing's clapped out. Yer'll 'ave ter mind those bald front tyres. If yer get into a front-wheel skid yer'll never get out of it.'

Jimmy was eager to get started and he jumped into the cab to start the engine, only to be stopped by the mechanic. 'Yer 'ave ter crank the bloody fing or yer'll run the battery down,' he told him.

The new driver did as he was bid, and after some difficulty he managed to get the vehicle running. When he finally reported back to the office window the transport manager handed him collection and delivery notes which required him to pick up a five-ton consignment of New Zealand cheese from King George the Fifth Docks in east London and deliver it to a large wholesale warehouse in Kent.

That evening Jimmy had gone home tired but contented with the fact that he had at least broken the ice at the new job. What he didn't know was that Kimble's other drivers were not particularly cheerful and obliging first thing in the morning, and fortunately for the transport manager here was a new man who did not question the work. By Thursday evening the rest of the drivers had come to realise that Jimmy Bailey had been given a very unfair baptism of fire.

As the young man sat waiting for the kettle to boil he realised that he had made a big mistake in accepting the daily work requirements without protesting. 'I'm sorry ter say, pal, but that big-nosed bastard's got yer card marked,' Bill Baston had told him. 'Yer should 'ave 'ad a moan straight away about the work yer bin given. It's too late now.'

Jimmy wondered just what was in store for him as he got up and poured the boiling water into the warmed teapot, but there was no time to dwell on it. His mother was coughing loudly and he knew that she had woken up and would be waiting for her morning cuppa.

'I don't fink I slept a wink last night,' she complained as he handed her a mug of tea and two slices of lightly toasted bread coated thickly with marmalade.

'You sure yer gonna be all right?' he asked with concern.

'All the same if I ain't,' Mary Bailey replied with a long face. 'Yer'll be at work anyway.'

'I s'pose I could take the day off,' he suggested.

'Nah, you go orf ter work, I'll manage, some'ow,' she told him. 'Anyway, yer sister's callin' in later. She'll 'elp me get dressed.'

Jimmy arrived at the transport yard at exactly seven-thirty and joined the line of drivers waiting by the office window for their instructions.

'If yer fink I'm pickin' that load o' rubbish up yer got anuvver fink comin',' Bill Baston told the transport manager sharply.

''Ere, do this load then, an' don't be all day about it neivver,' the manager growled.

The driver seemed happy with his revised orders, and as he walked away from the window he gave Jimmy a big wink.

When the young man reached the window the manager passed some notes through. 'This'll be a change,' he said, with a ghost of a smile on his angular face. 'It's a light load.'

Jimmy began to feel better as he swung his lorry left into Tower Bridge Road on that bright morning and headed for the bridge. Forty sacks of turkey feathers would be no weight at all, and the delivery to Hoxton would not take him very long, he thought. There would be time for a pull-up at a transport cafe and he could still get back to the yard reasonably early.

When he reached the London Docks and reported to the

collections office he was greeted with an inquisitive look from the clerk. 'Have you ever collected turkey feathers before?' the man asked him.

Jimmy shook his head, 'Nah. I'm new to the firm,' he replied innocently.

'That would figure,' the clerk said smiling.

'Is there any problem?' Jimmy enquired.

'Well, it's not a problem as such, but there'll most likely be a delay getting you loaded,' he was told. 'You see, our men get paid on tonnage and there's no weight in feathers. We have to get a scratch gang sorted out and there's usually a bit of argy-bargy over the bonus payment with the union official. Nothing for you to worry yourself about though.'

Jimmy nodded, beginning to understand that the day was not going to be as straightforward as he had imagined.

'If you'll wait over by number five shed I'll try to get things organised,' the clerk told him with a friendly smile.

The morning slipped by slowly and the shed remained locked. Jimmy sat in his cab, becoming more and more disenchanted with his new job, and by three o'clock that afternoon he was beginning to get anxious. Maybe they had forgotten all about him. Perhaps he should go over to the office and complain. Maybe the dockers had turned down the work and no one had thought of telling him.

Jimmy was suddenly jerked into action by a loud voice calling out. 'Oi you! Get yer lorry backed up ter the shed.'

At four o'clock that Friday afternoon Jimmy Bailey drove his lorry out of the London Docks with a thankful sigh. He made for Whitechapel and turned left into Commercial Street which led towards Hoxton, but before he was halfway down the long thoroughfare he started scratching his neck, his arms and his face. The itching was quickly becoming worse and soon it was almost unbearable. His back had started itching too, and his legs, and the young man cursed as he realised why. The turkey feathers were obviously lice-infested. No wonder he had been given the job.

Waldman's Feather Dusters Ltd. was just about to close when Jimmy pulled up at the entrance and he found the manager there to be almost as obnoxious as his own transport manager.

'Fine bloody time ter come,' the man growled. 'Where yer bin, sittin' in a bleedin' coffee shop all afternoon?'

Jimmy was by this time in a great deal of discomfort and he looked the manager square in the eye. 'As a matter o' fact I've bin stuck at the poxy docks all day waitin' ter get loaded,' he replied sharply.

The manager hustled his men and they quickly pulled the sacks from the tailboard and dropped them into large wickerwork baskets on wheels. The delivery note was signed without comment and Jimmy hurried back into his cab, desperate to get back to the yard and then home to get rid of the terrible itching that was by now afflicting every part of his body.

Stanley Bowditch had been with Kimble's transport concern for over twenty years now and he had risen from ledger clerk to assistant transport manager by the time war broke out. Being in his late forties he was not eligible for call-up, and when the transport manager enlisted in the army he filled the post. Disliked by the rest of the office staff and detested by the drivers, Stanley spent his working days being as unpleasant as possible to whoever he could. In the new driver he had found the perfect victim, or so he thought.

The tap on the window made Bowditch glance over from his desk and when he saw the new driver standing there he decided to ignore him for a few minutes. The repeated tap was sharper however, and the manager mumbled to himself as he reached for his bowler hat and got up. He was in the habit of donning his hat whenever he went to the window. It accentuated his authority, he felt. 'Where 'ave you bin all day?' he asked as he slid the glass panel to one side. 'I 'ad anuvver delivery fer you ter do this afternoon.'

Jimmy took a deep breath and breathed out slowly, trying to contain his rapidly rising temper. 'I was stuck at the docks till four, an' anuvver fing . . .'

'Don't you use that tone o' voice ter me, sonny,' Bowditch cut in quickly. 'The mechanic's waitin' ter go 'ome so get that lorry inter the yard, an' quick about it.'

The young man's eyes narrowed as he stared at the transport manager. 'What about me wages?' he asked.

Bowditch leered at him. 'Wages? We work a week in 'and 'ere,' he said, a malevolent glint in his eye.

As his temper reached breaking point Jimmy forgot all about the agonising red patches that were itching terribly, and with a quick movement he reached up and grabbed the brim of the manager's bowler in both hands and pulled down hard. The stiff brim ripped away from the rest of the hat and ended up hanging limply round the man's neck.

'Get 'im off, somebody!' Bowditch screamed as he found himself being pulled through the window.

The two clerks behind him ignored his plea for assistance, both grinning at the man's predicament.

'I'm comin' in on Monday sharp,' Jimmy growled, his face inches away from the manager's, 'an' if my money's not ready I'm gonna take it out on your face, understood?'

Bowditch could only nod and then he was shoved backwards, falling into a heap beside his desk. Jimmy threw the lorry keys through the office window and strolled out of the yard.

When he arrived home he saw that his mother was dozing peacefully in her favourite armchair in the parlour and he hurried into the scullery and bolted the door. He stripped off completely and washed himself all over with a bar of Sunlight soap and cold water, rubbing the lather into his thick dark hair. When he had finished Jimmy wrapped the large bath towel around his loins, gathered up his work clothes and stuffed them into a pillow case. They would have to be fumigated, he realised. The man at the public baths in Spa

Road would do it for a small payment.

The evening was chilly now and Jimmy shivered as he got dressed. He found an old cardigan in his bedroom cupboard. He had meant to darn the elbows but it would do to wear while he was at Lottie's, he thought.

'Is that you, Jim?' his mother called out.

'Yeah, I'll be down in a minute,' he told her.

'I fancy a nice piece o' skate an' chips,' she announced when he walked into the room.

Jimmy hid his irritation. 'I promised ter do a little job fer Lottie Curtis, Ma,' he replied. 'I won't be a few minutes there then I'll get the fish an' chips on me way 'ome.'

'Long as yer not too late,' she replied testily.

Lana Johnson took a last look at herself in her dressing-table mirror before she hurried down the stairs. She looked in the parlour and saw that her father was dozing in the armchair. Ann sat facing him, her head buried in the evening paper. 'I'm off, Mum,' she said. 'Where's Derek?'

''E's in the scullery, 'avin' a wash.'

'Don't wait up, I've got me key,' Lana told her.

'Don't you be too late,' Ann warned her.

The young woman hurried from the house just as Jimmy Bailey was letting himself in next door. Their eyes met briefly and Jimmy gave her a quick smile. Lana noticed the tatty cardigan he was wearing and saw that the elbows were holed, and she sighed sadly to herself as she set off to meet Ben Ferris.

Chapter Three

Lottie Curtis had a toothless smile on her lined face as she eased herself back to set the rocking chair in motion. 'I wish I'd bin there,' she cackled. 'I'd 'a' told the nasty bleeder what ter do wiv 'is job. It's a bloody disgrace what they get away wiv. Non-union, that's why. My Bill, Gawd rest 'is soul, always used ter say yer nowhere wivout unions. Mind you, in 'is day they 'ad ter fight fer a day's work at the docks, till the unions stepped in.'

Jimmy could hear Lottie going on in the parlour and he smiled to himself as he put down the screwdriver. 'I can't 'ear yer out there, Aunt Lottie,' he told her as he came back into the room.

'It doesn't matter,' the old lady replied. 'I was just finkin' aloud.'

The young man sat down facing her and watched the movement of the rocker for a few moments. The creak-creak sound had always fascinated him. He could never quite make out where the noise was coming from.

'I shouldn't 'ave lost me temper, Aunt Lottie,' he said quietly. 'I gotta start all over again on Monday lookin' fer a job.'

The old lady chuckled. She remembered the cold wet night when he had stood on her doorstep between the nuns as though it were only yesterday. The lad had obviously been frightened but he had not cried like some of her other charges, and in the two years she and Bill had looked after him he had never given her any cause to regret taking him in. He was a good boy, was Jimmy, so thoughtful and considerate of her needs.

Jimmy watched the old lady as she gazed distractedly into the low fire. She seemed to have aged considerably these last two years. Her hair was now snow white but she still kept it tidy, pulled into two buns, one on each side of her head covering her ears. She was still the same old Lottie: full of fire and spirit and sharp as a new pin. Her long bony fingers gripped the arms of the rocker tightly, the skin white at the knuckles, and Jimmy smiled wistfully as he recalled her sometimes heated conversations with Bill. The two had obviously been devoted to each other, but Lottie had her own opinions on most things and she would not be swayed.

Jimmy leaned back in the armchair and crossed his legs. There was one particular evening, he recalled, when Bill had arrived home slightly the worse for drink and Lottie had berated him for setting a bad example to their children – Lottie had always referred to him and the two girls as her children. Bill's excuse was that he had had to attend an important union meeting at the Crown and Lottie wanted to know all that had gone on. Jimmy remembered sitting between Lucy and Ellen on the settee while the interrogation dragged on, with Bill seeking to justify the union involvement and Lottie questioning him at every turn. The whys and wherefores were above their young heads but at that age it was exciting to be able to sit up later than usual.

'Yer look worried, boy,' Lottie said suddenly.

Jimmy realised that the old lady had been studying him too while he was staring down at the rungs of the old rocking chair and he gave her a big smile. 'I was just finkin' o' that night you an' Uncle Bill 'ad that big row about the union,' he told her.

'Yeah, I remember that night well,' Lottie replied chuckling.

'It wasn't exactly a row though, lad, it was more a discussion. Me an' Bill was always discussin' fings. Mind you, I did go on at 'im that particular night. Ter tell yer the trufe, that was the only night I can ever recall 'im comin' 'ome the worse fer drink. I really lambasted 'im over settin' a bad example an' 'e was very sorry. I was worried about you an' the two gels gettin' frightened. It used to terrify me when my farvver came 'ome drunk. Mind you, 'e was different ter my Bill. 'E used ter knock me muvver about in drink.'

'I wonder 'ow them two gels are gettin' on,' Jimmy remarked.

'Gawd knows,' Lottie replied. 'I ain't 'eard anyfing of 'em fer years. As a matter o' fact I used ter keep an eye on their progress frew the church, until ole Farvver McCarfy passed away. Then there was nuffing. I did 'ear tell that Lucy married a businessman an' moved out to Essex. As fer Ellen, last I 'eard of 'er was when Farvver McCarfy called round ter say she'd bin nicked fer shopliftin'. I broke me 'eart that day, I can tell yer. I never would 'ave thought it, not of 'er. She was such a lovely child. It just goes ter show yer.'

Jimmy uncrossed his legs and sat up straight in the armchair. 'I've took that lock ter pieces, Aunt Lottie, an' I freed it wiv oil,' he explained. 'I just gotta finish screwin' it back now.'

'Yer a good lad, Jim,' the old lady told him. 'While yer finishin' that I'll put the kettle on.'

'I'll do it for yer,' Jimmy said quickly.

'Nah, you leave it ter me,' Lottie insisted. 'I gotta get up now an' then or me joints are gonna seize up, like that bleedin' lock.'

The young man went out into the scullery followed by Lottie, who hummed to herself as she lit the gas under the large copper kettle. 'By the way, 'ow's yer muvver?' she asked.

Jimmy sighed deeply as he turned to face the old lady. 'She seems to 'ave lost the will ter go on, if yer ask me,' he told her. 'Me sister Glenda calls round most days, an' Lillian pops in too, when she gets time, an' they both feel the way I do. There don't seem ter be any fight left in 'er.'

'It's a bloody shame,' Lottie remarked. 'Mind yer, she's 'ad 'er share o' sufferin'.'

'I do what I can,' Jimmy told her, 'but as yer know there's certain fings only the gels can do.'

'I'm sure she appreciates yer, none the more fer that,' the old lady said kindly. 'There's plenty wouldn't do what you do. By the way, did yer tell 'er yer got the sack?'

'Not yet,' Jimmy replied. 'That reminds me, I've gotta call in at Ole Joe's for some fish an' chips so I'd better get movin'.'

''Ave a cup o' tea first,' Lottie urged him, 'the kettle's just comin' up ter the boil.'

Thirty minutes later the young man arrived home with the news that Ole Joe's had sold out of skate.

'That's frew 'angin' about at Lottie Curtis's,' Mary Bailey complained.

'I got yer a nice piece o' rock salmon, Ma,' Jimmy told her.

'Yer know I ain't too keen on rock salmon.'

'I'll go up ter Bacon's, they might 'ave skate.'

'Nah, never mind, I'll 'ave it, ovverwise I'm gonna be too tired to eat anyfing.'

Jimmy sighed in resignation as he unwrapped the fish and chips on to the plates.

'Didn't yer get no wallies?' Mary asked him. 'Yer know I'm partial to a wallie.'

'They was sold out, Ma.'

'Bloody fine shop that is. Fancy bein' sold out o' wallies.'

'There's yer knife an' fork, Ma. Eat it up before it gets cold.'

'All right, all right, I ain't a kid. Where's the bread?'

''Ang on, I'll cut some.'

'I dunno,' Mary sighed. 'If only this back would ease up I'd do fings meself. At least they'd get done properly.'

Jimmy swallowed a piece of fish and felt it stick in his chest. He felt uncomfortable trying to eat while she was ranting on.

'By the way, the tally man called this afternoon an' I couldn't pay 'im,' she remarked. 'I told 'im ter call back termorrer.'

'Well, yer better tell 'im ter call back on Monday afternoon,' Jimmy said sharply. 'I didn't get no wages.'

'No wages? Why?'

'You 'ave ter work a week in 'and there.'

'Yer gotta be stupid acceptin' a job like that,' Mary grumbled. 'Fancy takin' the job. Didn't they tell yer?'

'As a matter o' fact they didn't.'

'Well then, you can make a complaint at the labour exchange.'

'I've already put a complaint in,' Jimmy told her, his mouth creasing in a lopsided smile. 'They'll be ready on Monday mornin'.'

'Are yer sure?'

'Don't worry. I'm sure,' he told her.

Ben Ferris leaned back in his chair and smiled reassuringly at Lana. 'It's all right, really,' he told her.

'Ben, if I 'ad that sort o' money I'd willingly lend it to yer, yer know that,' she said, searching his eyes.

'Look, I've just said it's all right,' Ben replied with a note of irritation in his voice. 'Gerry ought ter be OK fer a tap.'

Lana looked across the dimly lit room and saw Gerry holding Mandy tightly to him as they danced to a slow foxtrot. 'Gerry's new girlfriend seems nice,' she remarked.

Ben nodded and hid a grin. Mandy had had more men than most but still put on that childlike air. She was currently keeping company with Mick Constantine, and if that villain ever found out that Friday night was not hair-wash and ironing night as she had told him, then Gerry Knowland would most likely end up in a concrete overcoat at the bottom of the Thames.

The band finished playing their number and Gerry slipped his arm around Mandy's waist as they walked back to the table.

'Waiter? Same again,' he said, giving his partner a suggestive wink.

Mandy looked at Lana. 'I need ter spend a penny,' she told her.

As soon as they had left the table Ben leaned over towards his friend. 'Gerry, I feel embarrassed to ask yer, pal, especially as yer footin' the bill ternight, but I'm desperate. I owe Mick Constantine an' 'e's puttin' the screws on.'

Gerry took a cigarette from a silver case and lit it from the red candle burning in the centre of the table. 'What's the damage?' he asked casually.

'A pony.'

Gerry's expression did not change as he took out his wallet and counted off the large white five-pound notes. 'Fifty o' the best,' he said, handing the money over.

'I'll pay yer back next week, that's fer sure,' Ben told him gratefully. 'Yer've saved me a lot o' grief, Gerry ole mate.'

The waiter arrived carrying a tray of drinks and Gerry flipped a five-pound note on to the tray. 'That's all right,' he said, waving the change away.

Ben sipped his fresh gin and tonic, feeling envious of his friend's good fortune. Gerry was a smart operator, he realised. He was always loaded, and there always seemed to be an attractive young woman drooling over him. He had it all. He was tall with fair wavy hair and blue eyes, well over six feet in height with the build of an athlete, though Ben had to admit that as far as he knew the only athletics Gerry ever performed were between the sheets.

Gerry took a deep drag from his gold-tipped Sobranie and lifted his head to exhale a cloud of smoke towards the stucco ceiling. 'Yer might be able ter return the favour and tear up the debt at the same time,' he said quietly.

'I'm listenin',' Ben said.

Gerry leaned forward over the table, his eyes narrowing. 'Tell me, 'ow much d'yer know about Mick Constantine?' he asked in a low voice.

Ben shrugged his shoulders. 'I know 'e's got a lot of influence an' 'e controls the local bookies. I also know that 'e's got 'is grubby fingers in a lot o' pies.'

Gerry took another deep drag on his cigarette. 'Mick Constantine made 'is pile from black-market dealin' durin' the war an' I 'appen ter know that 'e's still in the business, although it's more of a sideline these days.'

Ben watched another cloud of smoke spiralling towards the ceiling before he lowered his eyes. 'What's 'is racket now?' he asked.

''E's gone in the property business,' Gerry told him with a look of distaste on his face. 'Apparently 'e's bin buyin' up lease'olds an' free'olds on 'ouses left, right an' centre. 'E's turnin' 'em inter furnished flats an' chargin' exorbitant rents.'

'What about the tenants livin' in those places?' Ben asked quickly. ''E can't chuck 'em out just like that. There's a law against it.'

Gerry laughed bitterly. 'Mick Constantine's never let the law worry 'im so far,' he replied. ''E's got a team of aggravators who go round makin' life unbearable fer the poor sods, especially the elderly ones. By the time those monkeys of 'is are finished, people are only too glad ter get out.'

Ben looked angry. 'If I wasn't so sure I'd get worked over I'd let the bastard whistle fer that fifty quid I owe 'im,' he growled. 'As if 'e needs it.'

Gerry smiled briefly, then his face grew serious. 'Let me tell yer a little story,' he said. 'There's a row o' six 'ouses in Rovver'ithe which are in bad repair. The lease'old's run out an' Constantine's bought it. The tenants are all elderly folk. As a matter o' fact four out o' the six 'ouses are occupied by ole ladies livin' on their own. Now Constantine knows that 'e can't raise the rents 'cos they've bin fixed by law, so 'e's come up wiv an offer of a few bob fer the tenants ter get out.'

'But where could they be expected ter go?' Ben asked frowning.

Gerry shrugged his shoulders. 'Who knows? Old people's 'omes? Wiv relatives? Anyway, one ole couple 'ave moved out already, an' two o' the ole gels 'ave gone as well. The rest are stayin' put, but their lives are bein' made a misery. The no-good bastard's put in a team o' so-called builders ter do repairs ter the roofs and that. They're all bodged-up jobs o' course, an' in the process they're puttin' the poor soddin' tenants under as much pressure as they can. You know the score. Water cut off all day, tarpaulins over the roofs wiv the rain pourin' in, feet goin' frew the ceilin's. There's bangin' an' 'ammerin' all day long an' mess everywhere, an' in the end it just gets unbearable. An' that's just what's 'appenin' in Rovver'ithe.'

Ben looked at his friend quizzically. 'Where exactly do I fit in ter all this?' he asked.

Gerry caught sight of the two young women approaching the table and he rolled his eyes in their direction and winked at Ben. 'It'll 'ave ter keep fer the time bein',' he said quickly. 'We'll talk about it termorrer.'

The tall, swarthy, broad-shouldered man in the camel-hair overcoat ordered another Scotch and glanced up at the clock behind the bar. It was eight-thirty. 'Del, can yer send Baz round?' he asked, brushing his hand over his short-cropped dark hair.

The barman slipped his head into the public bar and caught the eye of the lean figure lounging against the counter. 'Mick wants yer,' he said.

When Baz came into the saloon bar Constantine summoned him over to a corner table.

'I want yer ter pay a call fer me termorrer, Baz,' he said quietly. 'Take the Varley boys wiv yer an' give Ben Ferris a pastin'. Not too severe, mind yer. I just want 'im marked up a bit, enough ter remind 'im that a debt's a debt an' it's gotta be paid on time. Just tell 'im that.'

Baz nodded dutifully and left the table without a word.

Mick Constantine watched him go and then picked up his drink, a satisfied smile forming on his thick lips.

Chapter Four

Lana Johnson was laden down with groceries as she walked quickly back to Saddler Street. The handles of the canvas shopping bag were beginning to cut into her hands and she could feel the muscles tightening up in her shoulder. It was a long trek through St James's Road to the market in Southwark Park Road but she preferred to go there on Saturday mornings rather than stand in the queue at Logan's, Saddler Street's corner shop. Fred Logan was a decent enough bloke, she thought, but inclined to take his time serving. His wife Lily was not much quicker, and she did like to catch up on the week's gossip whenever possible. To stand behind Bella Wickstead in the queue was to kiss the rest of the morning goodbye. The large, amiable Bella from number one could talk the hind legs off a line of donkeys, Lottie always said, and the old lady was right. Bella knew everything that was going on in the little turning and she was always eager to share her information with whoever was unfortunate enough to be around.

Lana crossed the wide Jamaica Road and turned into Saddler Street just as Bella was coming out of Logan's. ''Ello, luv, 'ow are yer?' the buxom woman said, smiling as she put her shopping bag down by her front door.

Lana hid a sigh of irritation. ''Ello, Bella,' she replied. 'I'm all right, fanks, or I will be, when I've dropped this shoppin' off indoors.'

Bella ignored the hint. ''Ere, I know yer must be busy, but I gotta tell yer,' she began. 'Phil Moseley's bin nicked.'

'Phil Moseley?' Lana queried.

''Im from number ten. The one wiv the bald 'ead an' wonky eye,' Bella went on. 'Apparently 'e's bin takin' bacon out the docks an' the 'tecs pulled 'im up in Tooley Street yesterday. I saw 'is wife this mornin' while I was gettin' Chas's fags an' paper. She did look worried. White as a sheet she was an' I could see she'd bin cryin'. 'E could get six months fer pilferin', 'specially if 'e comes up in front of ole Muvver Camelford. She can't stand dockers.'

Lana put down her heavy shopping bag and rubbed her sore hands together. 'It's a shame. I expect it must be 'ard tryin' ter feed that tribe of 'is,' she said sympathetically.

'Are you an' Ben still goin' out tergevver?' Bella asked. 'I ain't seen much of 'im round 'ere lately.'

'Yes, we are,' Lana said defensively.

'Nice feller Ben,' the big woman remarked. 'I remember the day 'e come 'ome from the war. 'E did look bad. It was 'is back, wasn't it?'

'Yeah, it was a shell splinter, at Dunkirk,' Lana told her.

''E looks all right now, though.'

'Yeah, 'e's fine.'

'I s'pose you two are gonna tie the knot before long, ain't yer?' Bella prompted.

'I expect so,' the young woman replied, wondering how to get away without being too rude.

'Mrs Conroy at the end 'ouse told me 'er boy's gettin' married next month,' Bella said, nodding her head down the street. 'It's a bit of a rushed affair. The gel's two months gone.'

Lana picked up her shopping bag. 'Well, it's nice talkin' ter yer but I gotta get goin',' she said with a sigh. 'Lottie Curtis is waitin' fer 'er dinner an' it's in the bag.'

'I 'ave ter say it's very nice the way you an' yer mum look after that ole lady,' Bella went on unabashed. 'There's many wouldn't take the time you do. She's a lovely ole gel.'

Lana smiled as she tried to back away. 'Yeah, she is. Oh well, I'd . . .'

''Ere, before yer go. 'Ow's Alan's wife?'

'She's fine.'

'Yer mum was tellin' me she's 'avin' a bad time carryin' the baby.'

'It's just mornin' sickness.'

'She should be careful. She doesn't look very strong.'

'Beth's as strong as they come,' Lana said emphatically.

Bella spotted Sadie Pugh from number eight coming along the street and she grinned cheerily at Lana. 'Well, give 'er my regards, luv,' she said quickly as she turned away.

Lana hurried into number five and dropped the shopping bag down in the passage. 'I've just bin waylaid,' she said, collapsing into the armchair.

Ann Johnson smiled as she picked up the teapot from the hearth. 'I saw yer frew the curtains. Bella means well, I s'pose, but it's best not ter tell 'er too much.'

Lana watched her mother pour out the tea. 'Bella asked me 'ow Beth was,' she said, a smile forming on her face. 'She said you told 'er Beth was 'avin' a bad time carryin'.'

'Well, I just mentioned it in passin', but I . . .'

'It's all right, Mum. I know Bella means well, I s'pose, but . . .'

Ann handed her daughter a brimming teacup and gave her a wry smile. ''Ere, drink this an' shut yer face.'

The two women sat quietly for a while then Ann looked directly at her daughter. 'You got in late last night.'

'We went over ter that club in Soho,' Lana told her.

'You should be careful goin' over there,' Ann warned her. 'I read a bit in the Sunday paper about the prostitution an' gamblin' that goes on in some o' them clubs. The paper said them sort o' places are owned by gangsters.'

'Not Rivellino's, Mum,' the young woman reassured her. 'It's a respectable place ovverwise I wouldn't go in there. Besides, Ben's wiv me. 'E wouldn't let anyfing 'appen. We just sit at a table wiv friends an' 'ave a few drinks. There's usually a band playin' an' we dance. Nuffing terrible goes on.'

'I s'pose it's all right if you enjoy it,' Ann remarked, 'but just be careful, that's all I'm sayin'.'

Lana finished her tea and carried the shopping bag into the scullery. It was supposed to have been an enjoyable night out, she reflected, but it had been spoiled. At first it was Ben not seeming to believe her about the money. She had been straight with him and told him that he could borrow the twenty pounds she had saved up, but he appeared to think she was lying to him. And that wasn't all – there was something else going on too. The men had seemed more than a little conspiratorial, and whatever scheme they were hatching was still preoccupying Ben when he saw her home. Normally they would slip into the darkened doorway of the wharf in River Lane and enjoy each other's embraces, but last night he was different. His kisses lacked fire and his caresses seemed half-hearted.

Something was brewing, she felt sure, and it did nothing to assuage the turmoil she felt inside of her. She was twenty-four and there was no firm commitment forthcoming from Ben. She wanted a husband, a home and children, not to be paraded as Ben's woman. He had been understanding at first and promised to save hard to buy her an engagement ring, but they were just empty words. Ben was a gambler, a chancer who chased quick money and usually ended up dragging the floor. Unfortunately he was a charmer too. He could be so loving and tender, and that was the problem. On the two occasions she had told him it was over between them he had been smoothness and charm itself. He had pleaded and cajoled her and made her feel as if she was doing something very terrible in breaking off with him. Her family were right about him, she knew, but the bigger part of her loved him and eclipsed the side of her that despised his weakness, his unreliability and all the other traits that were Ben Ferris.

* * *

Baz Smithson was lean and hard as nails and he had a record for violence. Usually he would do Mick Constantine's bidding with a length of lead piping, a chopper if the situation warranted it, or a cut-throat razor. The two men he had recruited on the order of his boss were equally vicious. Nipper Varley was short and stocky, with a sadistic streak to his nature, while his elder brother Sid was a head taller, dim-witted and strong as an ox.

The three men sat drinking mugs of tea in Joe Slavin's cafe in River Lane and Baz was doing the thinking. He knew that Ben Ferris frequented the cafe and it would be no hardship to escort him out to a quiet place nearby and work him over. If he failed to show then they would be obliged to visit Ferris's flat above the yard. The disadvantage there was that their victim might spot them and make things difficult. He would most likely phone for help and there was no way of preventing this. The phone lines ran overhead and none of them was equipped to clamber up a telegraph pole. Better to hang fire and see what turns up, Baz told himself.

Joe Slavin had had a chequered career, interrupted by two years in Wandsworth for warehouse breaking. He had many friends in the underworld, all of whom trusted him completely. His word was his bond and many a message had been sent via the cafe owner when other, more conventional means had not been possible. Joe could also be trusted to shut his ears to what was going on around him, and for that reason alone many a confidential meeting took place in the shabby establishment which had a reputation for strong tea and good wholesome food.

Baz Smithson knew of Joe Slavin's reputation and he was confident that he would ignore whatever went on at the place that morning. What he did not know was that the cafe owner recognised him and his cohorts and had guessed their intentions after overhearing Sid Varley mumble Ben's name. He had seen the look Baz gave the dimwit and it told him all he needed to know. Joe had a genuine liking for Ben Ferris, and at that very moment he was thinking hard about how best to warn his friend without making it look obvious. For a start he could not leave the cafe, and there were no customers in there that morning he knew well enough to pass a message to.

The clock on the wall behind the counter showed ten-thirty and Joe bit on his lip as he filled mugs with tea for two dockers who had just walked in.

'Got any soft rolls, Joe? Me teef are givin' me gyp,' one of the men said.

Joe leaned below the counter to take out a fresh batch from the large metal bin and suddenly he had an idea. He pulled out two rolls and grimaced at the docker. 'That's the last two, Bert,' he said in a voice loud enough to carry. 'The bloody delivery man's let me down this mornin'.'

'I only want two,' Bert replied. 'Stick a bit o' cheese in 'em, will yer?'

'Comin' up.'

'Make it snappy, Joe, we've only got ten minutes.'

As soon as he had taken the rolls over to the table Joe went over to his phone and dialled a number. 'Is this the Empire Bakery?' he asked. 'Well, it's Joe Slavin 'ere. What's 'appened ter me bread an' rolls this mornin'? No, I ain't 'ad a bloody delivery. Yer better get yer poxy finger out or I'll be takin' me trade somewhere else. Well, yer better speak ter someone who can 'elp an' then ring me back soon as yer can.'

A few faces smiled over at the angry cafe owner and he pulled a face. 'Bloody firm's a disgrace. That's twice this month they've cut me out.'

'P'raps they're tryin' ter tell yer somefing,' one of the dockers joked. 'Yer pay yer bill on time, don't yer, Joe?'

Before Joe could answer the phone rang again. ''Ello,' he said quickly. 'No, I can't. I usually 'ave three dozen. Yeah, that's right, three. Well, yer better 'urry up, there's not much time. I shut at one o'clock on Saturdays. Well, yer better, or it's curtains fer your firm, understood?'

One hundred yards along River Lane Ben Ferris put down the phone. He had been having a leisurely lie-in that morning, until the garbled message about bread and rolls. Ben knew that the cafe owner got his bread delivery from the baker's in Jamaica Road and his mind began to race. The order to phone back gave him time to think and he slipped out of bed and doused his aching head under the cold tap. Then he picked up the phone again and dialled Joe's number. 'Can yer tell me who's in the cafe?' he asked. 'Never mind, 'ow many are there? I got yer, three. OK, I'll sort somefing out.'

Joe's cryptic reply told Ben enough and he hurriedly threw on some clothes and went down the flight of stairs to the street, where he swiftly unlocked and opened the adjoining yard gate and went inside. On one side of the yard there was a square trap door by the high brick wall and Ben quickly pulled it open. The cellar below was reached by a stepladder and it had once been used to store leather by the saddler who traded from the yard. Ben had sometimes used it as a store but at the moment it was empty. He hurried down into the damp dark and switched on the light. Bolted to a bench in one corner of the cellar was an old electric grinder which the saddler had left behind. It had a soft wire attachment which he had used to burnish the brass saddle buckles, but Ben had another use for the device. He crossed his fingers as he switched on the power and grunted with satisfaction as the motor started up and gained speed. The hum grew loud and Ben hurried back up into the morning sunlight.

Baz Smithson looked at his two confederates and nodded towards the door. 'C'mon, you two, we can't wait no longer,' he announced.

The three men hurried along River Lane and when they neared the yard they saw that it was open.

'That's a stroke of luck,' Nipper Varley said.

'Be careful, we don't wanna advertise we're callin',' Baz warned them.

They entered the yard and immediately heard the hum of machinery. Baz motioned silently towards the open trap door and then took out a length of lead piping which he had tucked inside his belt. Nipper Varley held a cut-throat razor open, its blade bound with bandage up to the last half inch at the top. A quick slash from the weapon would open the victim's cheek and leave a permanent scar. Sid Varley carried a crowbar which he too had secreted in his belt and the three climbed down into the dimly lit cellar. Sid was the last in line and as he ducked his head below the edge of the opening he felt a boot in his back. The swift shove sent him careering into the other two and they landed in a heap on the stone floor. Before they could find their feet the trap door slammed shut and they heard a bolt being slid into place.

Baz cursed loudly as he struggled to his feet and walked over to shut off the motor. 'We've bin took on,' he growled. 'I'll do Ferris bad when I get to 'im, mark my words.'

Sid Varley had climbed up the ladder and was thumping on the trap door to no avail, and Nipper was searching for something to force it with.

'The bloody fing won't budge,' Sid shouted.

'Keep tryin', you bloody idiot,' Baz screamed at him.

'Oi, that's my bruvver yer shoutin' at,' Nipper told him sharply.

Baz did not relish the idea of having the Varley brothers turning on him and he held up his hands. 'All right, let's fink this fing out, lads,' he said in a quiet voice.

Ben Ferris strolled into Joe Slavin's cafe and winked cheekily at him. 'A mug o' tea on the quick, Joe,' he said. 'I gotta see someone pronto.'

At ten minutes past eleven Ben stepped into the saloon bar of the Crown and Anchor and ordered a pint of bitter. 'Is Mick Constantine due in?' he asked cheerfully.

'Yeah, 'e should be, but then on the ovver 'and, maybe not,' was the barman's unhelpful reply.

Ben sipped his drink and prayed that he would be able to square it with the big man before his henchmen freed themselves. The clock moved round towards twelve and still there was no sign of Constantine. Ben got up to get another pint and as he watched the barman pull down on the beer pump he felt a tap on his shoulder.

'You look remarkably . . . er . . . fit an' well,' the gang boss said in his ear.

Ben smiled as he turned to face the swarthy man in his camel-hair overcoat. 'Your boys are locked in my cellar,' he told him. 'I thought it best. They looked really mean an' if they'd 'ave got ter me I wouldn't 'ave bin in no fit state ter call in an' pay me debt, now would I?'

Constantine's eyes narrowed as Ben took out his wallet, removed eleven white five-pound notes and placed them down on the bar counter. 'There's an extra five quid there fer interest I must 'ave accrued, and I appreciate your patience, Mr Constantine,' Ben said with mock seriousness.

The gang boss stared at Ben for a moment or two and then he banged his fist down on the counter and roared with laughter. 'Yer got 'em locked in the cellar, yer say?' he spluttered.

'Yeah, an' I'd appreciate it if yer could send someone round ter let 'em out,' Ben told him. 'I daren't.'

'We'll 'ave a drink first an' then I'll come wiv yer,' the big man said, wiping his eyes with a silk handkerchief. 'This I wanna see.'

Chapter Five

Early on Saturday evenings the riverside backstreets became quiet. Fred Logan closed his grocery shop at six o'clock and soon after Albert Robey put the shutters up at his corner shop. The wharves along River Lane were deserted and the cranes abandoned for the weekend. Children were pulled off the street for their tea, and as the sun dropped down over the rooftops the autumn shadows lengthened. Later the street would come back to life once more as folk made their way to the local pubs or merely stood chatting on doorsteps, but for the moment it was quiet.

At number five Ann Johnson cleared the table and left the dirty crockery standing on the wooden draining board in the scullery. There was time later for washing up. The family was gathered and there were things to talk about.

'I've bin all right this last couple o' days,' Beth was saying. 'Last week though I couldn't keep a fing down.'

Alan nodded. 'She's got this fing about peaches now. Tinned peaches.'

Ann smiled at his expression. 'You men wouldn't understand,' she told him. 'Women get these fancies while they're carryin'.'

Alan patted his wife's hands. 'It could be worse, I s'pose. At least peaches are good for yer.'

Ann looked at the two of them sitting together on the settee under the parlour window and thought how well matched they were. Beth was fair-haired, with deep-blue eyes and a pretty face. She was inclined to chubbiness and had a happy-go-lucky attitude. Alan on the other hand had a swarthy complexion like his father, with large dark eyes and well-groomed thick dark hair. He was serious-minded and devoted to Beth, who at twenty-six was three years his junior.

Like Derek, who was twenty-seven and still single, Alan was a stevedore, and along with his younger brother he had volunteered for the army at the outbreak of the war only to be informed that dock workers were exempt. The two young men had been disappointed but resigned themselves to the fact, and for a time they found themselves working on ships in Bristol and Liverpool when most of the freighters were diverted away from the badly blitzed London docks. Now working at the Surrey Docks in Rotherhithe, Alan was becoming more and more involved in the trade union, and as a shop steward was hoping for elevation on to the executive committee.

Frank Johnson leaned back in his armchair and eyed his two sons. He had worked in the docks since he was twenty, and now at fifty-two his bulk was spreading. He liked nothing more than to visit the local on Saturday nights, and tonight with Alan round he was hopeful of the two boys joining him. 'D'yer fancy a pint at the Crown?' he asked them.

Alan looked at Beth quickly and she smiled at him. 'Why don't yer?' she said. 'It'll make a break.'

Derek stroked his chin thoughtfully. 'I was gonna go down New Cross dogs later, but the way my luck's bin lately a drink might be a better idea,' he said.

'Well, that's settled then,' Frank replied with a grin of satisfaction on his wide face.

Lana came into the room and smiled at Beth. ''Ow yer feelin' now?' she asked.

'I've got rid o' that mornin' sickness, fank goodness,' she replied.

'I must say yer lookin' well,' Lana told her. 'An' that dress really suits yer.'

'They're all goin' out ternight,' Ann said as her daughter sat down on the arm of the settee next to Beth.

'That'll be nice,' Lana replied. 'Where yer finkin' o' goin', the Crown?'

Derek nodded. 'Are you an' Ben likely ter pop in there?' he asked.

'We usually do on Saturday nights,' Lana told him.

Frank and Alan exchanged a quick glance of disapproval but Derek was more accommodating. 'That'll be nice. A family get-tergevver. Why don't you two come as well?' he suggested, glancing at his mother and Beth in turn.

The younger woman looked at Ann without much enthusiasm and Ann shook her head. 'We'll 'ave a nice cup o' tea instead,' she replied. 'I ain't seen Beth all week. We can 'ave a nice chin-wag.'

Lana got up. 'Well, I'd better start gettin' ready,' she announced.

As soon as she had left the room Frank turned to Ann. 'She's wastin' 'er time wi' that Ben Ferris,' he growled. 'I can't understand it. A gel like 'er could take 'er pick o' the blokes round 'ere, an' she 'as ter get 'erself 'iked up wiv a no-good . . .'

'Frank, there's no point in goin' on about it,' Ann cut in. 'She's old enough ter know what she's doin' an' nuffing we say'll make any difference. She may 'ave ter learn the 'ard way, but she'll learn, sooner or later.'

Beth looked from one to the other and saw the tension in their faces. ''Ere, while I fink of it, did yer know that Phil Moseley got nicked,' she said quickly. ''E was caught wiv an 'ock o' bacon under 'is coat.'

Alan shook his head slowly. ''E should 'ave known better. We warned 'em all about pilferin'. Those 'tecs from Dock'ead nick are always on the prowl in Tooley Street. Besides, 'e could lose 'is ticket.'

'I don't fancy 'is chances if 'e comes up in front o' Muvver Camelford,' Derek remarked. 'That ole cow's got a down on us blokes.'

Alan's face broke into a grin. 'I was tempted the ovver day,' he said. 'We was unloadin' tinned fruit an' I saw these lovely big cans o' peaches.'

Beth looked horrified. 'Don't you ever dare. I'd never get over it if you got nicked, 'specially on my account.'

'Don't take no notice,' Derek told her. ''E's windin' you up. 'Ow's 'e gonna get a bloody great case o' peaches under 'is coat?'

Frank was beginning to get fidgety. 'Are we gonna make a move then?' he asked.

'Yer can bring us back a nice milk stout, an' a couple o' packets o' crisps,' Ann told him, winking at Beth.

'There's nuffing else yer'd like, is there?' Frank growled. 'Like a carton o' jellied eels, per'aps?'

'That'd be nice,' Ann replied.

Lana made her way to Ben's flat in River Lane, realising that she and her young man were probably being discussed back at her house right that minute. Ben wasn't liked by her family and for that reason she insisted on calling for him, sooner than have him knock for her and be asked in. There was always a strained atmosphere whenever Ben met up with her family in the Crown and she was not looking forward to this evening. To give him his due Ben did try to defuse the tension on such occasions but that only seemed to make things worse.

The autumn night was drawing in as Lana reached Ben's flat and rang the bell. 'Oh my good Gawd!' she gasped as he opened the door to her. ''Ow did yer get that?'

The area around Ben's right eye was beginning to discolour and there was a cut on the bridge of his nose, which he had covered with a strip of plaster. He looked sorry for himself as he stood back to let her in.

Lana hurried up the steep flight of stairs and sat herself

down on the comfortable settee. Ben followed her into the room and sat down in the armchair facing her. 'Yer'll never believe this,' he said.

'Try me,' she replied, unbuttoning her emerald-green coat.

Ben told her the full story, how Joe Slavin had warned him by phone, and how he had managed to bolt the three henchmen in the yard cellar, and all the while Lana listened intently.

'Anyway, Mick Constantine stood back while I opened up the trap door,' Ben concluded, 'an' 'e told the three of 'em ter wait by the gate. Yer should 'ave seen the look on their faces as they came up out o' that cellar. Then Constantine turns ter me an' says, "Ben, I gotta 'and it to yer. Those idiots are never gonna live this down," an' I just nodded. Then 'e turns away an' suddenly spins back an' clocks me one. It took me by surprise an' I went down. I couldn't get up an' retaliate, not wiv 'is men standin' there, so I just stayed where I was. Constantine bent down over me an' said, "That's a reminder not ter get flash." As if I would.'

'No, of course not,' Lana said sarcastically.

Ben gingerly touched the bridge of his nose. 'I'm gonna look a right sight ternight,' he grumbled.

'Would yer sooner stay in?' Lana asked him.

'No, I gotta make a show at the Crown,' he told her. 'Gerry's gonna be there. 'E wants to 'ave a quick chat.'

'An' what am I s'posed ter do in the meantime?' Lana said sharply.

Ben reached forward and took her hands in his. 'Look, love, I won't be more than a few minutes. Gerry can't stop anyway, 'e's meetin' Mandy an' they're goin' up West. 'E just wants ter fix up a meetin'.'

Lana pulled her hands away from him. 'I don't like yer gettin' involved wiv 'im, Ben,' she said. ''E's playin' a dangerous game cartin' that Mandy around. You told me last night that she's Constantine's woman, an' if it ever gets out Gerry's dead.'

Ben shrugged his shoulders. 'What Gerry does an' who 'e

sees is none o' my business,' he replied quickly.

'Yeah, but will Mick Constantine see it that way?' she asked him.

'The way I see it, that no-good whoreson deserves ter be two-timed,' he growled. ''E's set Mandy up in a flat over in Poplar an' 'e only goes there when 'e feels like it. 'E treats 'er like a little whore, so why shouldn't she see Gerry?'

Lana sighed with exasperation. 'She's entitled ter see who she likes, but I just feel as though yer gonna be drawn inter somefing yer can't get out of,' she told him. 'Let's face it, yer've already 'ad a warnin'.'

Ben touched his nose once more with the tips of his fingers. 'All right, I'll promise ter be careful,' he said. 'I just wanna find out what Gerry's got in mind. It could be a good deal.'

Lana shook her head slowly. 'I don't fink yer'll ever learn,' she sighed.

Ben stood up and went over to her. He reached out and took her hands, coaxing her out of her chair, and when she stood up he held her close to him. 'I'm mad about yer, Lana,' he whispered, his lips against her long fair hair. 'I love the way yer worry over me. It shows me 'ow much yer really care.'

Lana felt the warmth of his body and his hands caressing the small of her back. It was so easy to forget about everything when he held her like this, but she had to try and talk some sense into him. Gerry Knowland had some scheme going and whatever it was she didn't want Ben to be part of it.

'Let's go ter bed, darlin',' he said hoarsely, his body moving sensuously against hers. 'We can meet Gerry later.'

Lana drew her head back to look him in the eye and pressed the flat of her hands against his chest. 'Now listen, Ben. I don't want you gettin' in deeper than you already are wiv Gerry,' she said urgently. 'I tell yer straight, that man spells trouble, ter you an' ter me.'

'There's no danger ter you, Lana,' he said, sighing deeply with irritation. 'Yer've got this bee in yer bonnet about Gerry.

If there's a chance ter make some big money I'm gonna take it. I don't wanna scratch around fer small stakes until I'm an old man. I wanna make it big, an' soon. I wanna face the likes o' Mick Constantine an' be respected, not treated like somefing that's just crawled out o' the woodwork.'

'That's a laugh,' Lana retorted bitterly. 'Respected by the likes o' Constantine? That man don't know the meanin' o' the word. I've seen 'im struttin' around the neighbour'ood patronisin' people an' pattin' kids on the 'ead when it suited 'im, an' I've 'eard plenty about 'im too, like the way 'e got Joey Swindley cut up over gamblin' debts, an' the way that shop burnt down in the Ole Kent Road 'cos the owner stood up to 'im.'

Ben turned from her and walked over to the window, then he swung round to face her, his eyes flaring. 'Yer know the trouble wiv you, Lana?' he said angrily. 'Yer listen too much ter what yer bruvvers an' yer farvver say. Yer gotta understand. There's always gonna be losers in this world, an' I don't wanna be on that list – I wanna be somebody. I don't wanna spend the rest o' me workin' life in some factory or on a quayside in all weavvers.'

'I understand, Ben, I understand only too well,' Lana flared back at him. 'In your world it's OK ter step on whoever gets in yer way as long as you get where yer goin'. In your world it's OK ter rob, scheme an' beat up anyone who messes wiv yer, just as long as it gets yer ter the top o' the pile. Well, that's not my world. I want a man who's willin' ter work fer me an' the kids, whatever the job. I'd be just as proud o' my man if 'e was a dustman or a roadsweeper out o' necessity. At least it'd be honest toil. At least it wouldn't mean walkin' all over whoever it was who get in yer way.'

Ben's shoulders sagged and he reached out to her. 'Look, Lana, yer gettin' yerself all screwed up. It's not like that at all.'

The young woman stepped back a pace. 'Don't try an' sway me wiv yer charm, Ben,' she said quietly. 'Yer too good at it an' I'm on me guard. You go an' see Gerry Knowland ternight an' spend as much time wiv 'im as yer want, but don't expect me ter sit there while you an' 'im plan yer big money-makin'. I'm goin' off 'ome.'

'Lana . . .'

'Don't try an' stop me, Ben. Just fink on what I've said.'

He stared at her as she made for the door and then his anger flared. 'Piss off 'ome then, I don't care,' he shouted after her as she hurried down the stairs. 'Yer've bin a pain in the arse lately.'

Lana slammed the front door behind her and hurried along River Lane, her eyes misty with angry tears. A chill breeze played on her face and the dark shadows of the tall wharves stretched ahead of her. She passed Saddler Street by, not wanting to face her mother and Beth until she had composed herself. Better to walk it off, she thought, and she turned into a narrow lane by Shad Thames and then emerged into the wide Jamaica Road. A brisk stroll took her to the junction with Tower Bridge Road and she turned left, walking away from the illuminated white stone bridge, past the vinegar factory and down to the deserted market. She glanced up at the large billboard as she walked by the Trocette Cinema and saw that there was an old film showing. She wanted to go in and sit in the darkness while she thought things out, but the film was one she had seen over and over again. It always made her cry and tonight she could not face it.

As she passed the entrance Lana saw Jimmy Bailey step into the bright foyer and walk up to the ticket kiosk. His hair was brushed back from his forehead and he was wearing a dark blue raincoat. He had not seen her and she walked on, suddenly feeling akin to the young man. He looked a lonely figure, and he no doubt felt that way. Most young men were grouped together in pubs on Saturday nights, or with their ladyfriends in the back rows of cinemas. Not Jimmy Bailey though. He was like her – at a loose end with no one to talk to, about to sit through *Now Voyager* on his own.

Lana crossed the wide thoroughfare and turned into Grange Road. It was a long walk home from here but she needed the time, and with a quick movement she brushed a solitary tear from her cheek.

Chapter Six

Ben Ferris sat sipping his beer in the saloon bar of the Crown and Anchor in Dockhead while he waited for Gerry Knowland to arrive. The argument with Lana and her running out of the flat had upset him and he was determined to get drunk that evening, as soon as he had spoken with his friend.

He looked around him and could see no sign of Constantine. It wasn't unusual, he thought. To his knowledge the gang boss did not often use the pub on Saturday nights. Baz and a few of his pals would no doubt be in the public bar but Ben did not envisage any trouble from them. Constantine would no doubt have warned them off. The Crown and Anchor was his local pub and he would not tolerate any of his men getting out of hand there.

At eight-thirty on the dot Gerry walked in and ordered a drink. He spotted Ben sitting at a far table and waved out, pointing to his frothing pint of bitter. Ben shook his head and Gerry walked over. 'What 'appened ter you?' he said.

'I fergot ter duck,' Ben answered.

'Anyone I know?'

Ben shook his head.

'Suit yerself,' Gerry replied, getting the message. ''Ere, 'ow long 'ave yer bin cuddlin' that pint? It looks a bit flat.'

'I'm pacin' meself,' Ben told him. 'I'm due fer one almighty piss-up.'

'Where's Lana?' Gerry asked.

'We 'ad a few words,' Ben replied. 'She's stoppin' in ternight.'

'Oh I see, so yer gonna get tanked up.'

'That's about the strength of it.'

Gerry sipped the froth from his pint and pushed it back while he made himself comfortable. 'Constantine not bin in?' he asked.

Ben shook his head. ''E wouldn't be on 'is way ter see Mandy, would 'e?'

Gerry laughed aloud. 'She's not entertainin' ternight, not that ponce anyway. She told 'im she's goin' 'ome ter Brighton ter see 'er ole muvver.'

'An' 'e swallered it?'

''E trusts the gel,' Gerry said, still grinning widely.

'It's just as well, fer yer sake,' Ben told him. 'I just 'ope 'e don't get the word than you an' Mandy are tergevver.'

'I'm pretty careful where I take 'er, as yer know,' Gerry replied. 'Mick Constantine ain't got many friends in Soho. In fact Mandy told me that 'e won't go near the place fer fear o' gettin' sorted out. The Malts rule the roost over there an' they're out ter crucify 'im.'

'That may be so but it's still a very dodgy game yer playin',' Ben warned him.

Gerry took a swig from his glass and dismissed his friend's fears with a shake of his hand. 'Look, I ain't got time ter dwell on what that no-good bastard might or might not do. I'm meetin' Mandy at nine sharp an' we've got fings ter talk about.'

'I'm listenin',' Ben said.

'I was tellin' yer last night about those 'ouses in Rovver'ithe that Constantine's involved wiv,' Gerry began. 'Well, what I didn't get the chance ter tell yer was that my old Aunt Ginny lives in one o' those places. She brought me up after me farvver pissed off an' me muvver went back on the game. She's a lovely ole dear too – salt o' the earth, an' now in 'er last few years she's got all that aggro ter put up wiv. She's eighty-six years old, fer Chrissake.'

'Look, I understand,' Ben cut in, 'but at that age wouldn't she be better off in an ole people's 'ome anyway?'

'What, my Aunt Ginny? Never. Not while she's got a breath left in 'er body,' Gerry said firmly. 'She's like a lot o' the ole dears of 'er generation. They 'ad it really 'ard in their younger days an' they've grown as tough as ole boots. They've got their pride too. It burns inside 'em. Nah, my Aunt Ginny an' 'er ole neighbours are gonna stick it out.'

'Yeah, but 'ow long can they put up wiv it?' Ben asked him.

'They won't 'ave ter put up wiv it fer much longer, if I 'ave anyfing ter do wiv it,' Gerry assured him. 'I'm out ter fix that dirty bastard Mick Constantine fer good.'

Ben stared intently at his friend. 'You ain't finkin' o' toppin' 'im, are yer?' he murmured.

'Constantine's made a lot of enemies an' if 'e does get topped it won't be me who's responsible,' Gerry said quietly. 'I'm out ter finish 'im in anuvver way, but ter do that I need all the info I can get. I need someone who can get inter his circle an' find out more about the workin's of 'is mob.'

'An' that's where I come in,' Ben said.

Gerry nodded, clasping his hands and pressing his thumbs together as he glanced briefly around the rapidly filling bar. 'I was sayin' Constantine's made a lot of enemies, well, there's a lot goin' on be'ind the scenes that you probably don't know about. D'you remember that load o' salmon what got nicked in February?'

Ben nodded. 'Yeah, I remember. Weston's Wharf in Shad Thames.'

'It was Darkie Samut's doin',' Gerry told him. 'I know 'cos I bought the bulk of it.'

'Yeah, I 'eard from a good source that it was the Malts who pulled that stunt,' Ben replied.

'A week after the break-in the law came sniffin' round the arch I was rentin',' Gerry went on. 'I got a feelin' somebody 'ad shopped me. Anyway, I was clean. They couldn't find any tins o' salmon, but a few days later the Ministry o' Food inspectors paid me a visit an' I ended up gettin' done wiv not 'avin' the necessary permits fer some o' the straight stock I was storin'. I was bailed to appear at Tower Bridge Court in March, but before the case come up I got a call from the big chief at Dock'ead nick who told me that they knew I'd 'ad the salmon an' if I shopped whoever 'ad sold it ter me they'd see I got off wiv a nominal fine. The copper told me it was the Malts they were really after. Anyway I engaged Tom Manley, the solicitor from Jamaica Road, to 'andle the case an' 'e was absolutely first class. Darkie Samut put me on to 'im as a matter o' fact, after I'd told 'im the score.'

'So yer told the law ter get stuffed then,' Ben said.

'Too true, in a more subtle sort o' way,' Gerry said smiling. 'Anyway, my defence was that I didn't realise that permits 'ad gone astray until I was asked ter produce 'em an' my guess was one o' the casual workers I employed must 'ave nicked 'em. The upshot was I got a seventy-pound fine. The Malts 'ad a whip round an' raised the money ter pay it. They was more than grateful. They knew that I'd stood a good chance o' goin' away fer six months or more an' I didn't shop 'em.'

'Yeah, I remember you bein' in some sort o' trouble,' Ben remarked, 'but I didn't know just what it was all about.'

'I expect you're aware that Constantine's bin squeezin' the Malts,' Gerry continued. ''E's run their bookies out o' the area an' installed 'is own crowd, an' what's more, 'e's comin' down 'eavy on their local shops. The ole protection racket. The Malts are up in arms an' Darkie Samut's took control. Me an' 'im 'ave 'ad a long discussion an' I made 'im aware of what Constantine's gettin' up to in Rovver'ithe. Like I explained, I got a stake in what's 'appenin' down there. Me an' Darkie 'ave joined forces, an' it's important we keep on top o' what's goin' on. That's why we need all the info we can get.'

'So yer thought o' me,' Ben said.

'We need someone who doesn't 'ave any connection wiv the Malts, fer obvious reasons,' Gerry told him. 'Besides, I can trust yer.'

'Well, I'm pleased about that,' Ben said with a smile.

Gerry glanced up at the wall clock behind the counter and stood up. 'We'll need ter talk more about this,' he said. 'Can yer pop in the Dewdrop in Long Lane? Say eight o'clock termorrer evenin'? The pub's as quiet as a morgue. It'll suit us fine. I wouldn't want Constantine or any of 'is monkeys seein' us two gettin' too cosy.'

Ben nodded. 'Enjoy the evenin', Gerry. As for me, I'm gonna get well pissed now.'

Gerry looked at his friend with concern. 'Remember ter ferget what we've bin discussin', till termorrer,' he told him.

'You can count on it,' Ben said.

Jimmy Bailey had ironed his clean shirt and he set about trying to darn the elbows of his only coat. Darning was something he could never seem to master. He had seen his army mates darn their socks expertly but his attempts always ended up a mess. With a puff of exasperation he finally gave up. Once he got a regular job he would be able to buy a cheap sports jacket and maybe a decent pair of grey trousers, he told himself, but in the meantime he would have to manage. The boiler suit would do for work over his well-worn trousers now that the cold was setting in, and he could always wear the raincoat if he went out anywhere in the evenings. Pity about the suit hanging up in the wardrobe. It had fitted him perfectly before he was called up, but his shoulders had broadened out and now it was far too tight.

'I should get Glenda ter do that for yer if I were you,' Mary Bailey told him. 'She's good at darnin'. I'd do it meself if I could but me fingers are too stiff.'

'It's all right, Ma, I'm gonna get a new one next week,' Jimmy said as he hung the coat behind the door.

'That one'll still do yer a turn if yer get yer sister ter darn it,' Mary persisted. 'There's no sense in goin' out wastin' money, there's ovver fings ter fink about. We need that wireless fixin'. I miss Saturday Night Theatre an' I like to 'ear the news. As it is I dunno what's goin' on.'

'It's all in the papers, Ma.'

'Papers? Yer know I can't read the papers. Those glasses o' mine ain't no use at all,' she complained. 'I'll 'ave ter try an' buck up an' go ter get me eyes tested again.'

Jimmy sat down in the armchair and tried to get interested in the tattered-looking western novel someone had given him at the factory, but he could not settle. He put it down with a sigh and took up the evening paper, only to realise that he had already been through it. 'I'll make us a cup o' tea,' he said as he got up.

'I don't want any tea,' his mother told him. 'That last one set me stomach off again. I fink it was too strong. Never could abide strong tea.'

Jimmy sat down in the armchair once more. She could be very trying at times, he thought, but she was a sick woman and easily upset. He would have to remain patient and bite his tongue when she led off at him. It would be terrible to row with her and then live to regret it. The doctor had told him in confidence only a few weeks ago that her heart was weak and that the constant coughing wasn't helping her.

'Why don't yer go out somewhere instead o' mopin' around the place,' Mary said irritably. 'Yer could go to the pub, or the pictures. Take the ten-shillin' note out the jug. Yer can replace it when yer get yer wages.'

Jimmy nodded. 'Are yer sure yer'll be all right?' he asked.

'Go out, fer Gawdsake,' Mary said, sighing loudly.

The young man slipped his raincoat over his tatty cardigan and stepped out of the house in Abbey Street, turning left into the quiet Tower Bridge Road. The pubs would all be busy tonight, he realised. Better if he went to the pictures. As he passed the Trocette Cinema Jimmy noticed that *Now Voyager* was showing and he decided to try the Globe Cinema by the Bricklayer's Arms. He glanced over at the shuttered shops as he walked along and saw that the rubbish from the stalls had been cleared away, leaving the busy daytime thoroughfare looking strangely different at night. When he reached the small picture house he found the brass stand placed in the entrance which indicated that the house was full. The Old Kent Picture House opposite was showing a war film and the young man decided that it would have to be the Trocette.

The elderly commissionaire stood by the lighted entrance in his grubby light-blue uniform with yellow epaulettes and announced to everyone who might be interested that there were seats in all parts. Jimmy gave him a brief smile as he reached the entrance and then suddenly out of the corner of his eye he saw a young woman coming towards him. It was Lana Johnson. Lottie had spoken to him about her in glowing terms and he had passed her in the street on one or two occasions when he visited the old lady. It would be nice to introduce himself, he thought, but she might become frightened being approached by a strange man on the street. Anyway, he wasn't feeling confident enough dressed the way he was, and he averted his eyes.

The film was a sad and tragic love story, and quite a few of the women in the audience had their handkerchiefs up to their faces. Jimmy slumped down in his seat between two young couples and felt the drama weighing heavily on him. He wanted to get up and leave but decided against it. Instead he let his mind wander from the sad lovers on the silver screen to Lana Johnson. Was she going to meet someone, he wondered, or was she alone too? Maybe she was here in the cinema, her handkerchief held up to her face with tears forming in her eyes.

Paul Henreid looked longingly at Bette Davis as she uttered the final words, and as the closing music grew louder the audience let out anguished sighs and stifled sobs. Jimmy left the cinema feeling depressed, and as he made his way home to Abbey Street he mused about the way he was living his life and the uncertain future that stretched emptily before him, and he thought again of the young woman from Saddler Street.

Chapter Seven

It was Sunday morning, and Frank Johnson lounged in the doorway of the scullery holding a mug of tea in his hand. Outside heavy rain falling on the deserted street was being swept along by a gusting wind, and the docker pulled a face. 'We've gotta expect this sort o' weavver now,' he remarked. 'After all it's almost November. Christmas'll be on top of us before we know it.'

Ann was busy peeling the potatoes and she looked up frowning. 'Don't remind me, Frank, fer Gawdsake,' she growled. 'There's so much ter do at Christmas, what wiv the presents an' worryin' about the food.'

Frank rubbed a large gnarled hand over his paunch and burped loudly. 'I read in the paper this mornin' there's gonna be a glut o' turkeys this year. It'll make a change from chicken.'

'Yeah, an' I fink I'll let you queue up fer it,' Ann told him. 'They were queuin' from seven in the mornin' last year at Massey's. The shop didn't open till nine o'clock.'

Frank scratched his chest thoughtfully. ''Ere, I meant ter tell yer, Ben Ferris was in the Crown last night. Well sloshed, 'e was.'

'Did yer speak to 'im?' Ann asked.

'Nah, 'e was in the saloon bar. We saw 'im stagger out as we was leavin'. I was surprised our Lana wasn't wiv 'im.'

'They've 'ad a bust-up, I fink,' Ann told him. 'She came in

early last night an' I could see she was upset.'

'Did she say anyfing?'

'Not a word.'

'Didn't you ask 'er?'

'No, I left it to 'er. If Lana wanted ter talk about it she would.'

'That bloke's a bloody waste o' time,' Frank growled. 'I'd like ter see 'er give 'im the elbow once an' fer all. 'E'll never amount to anyfing.'

'Mind, she'll be down soon,' Ann warned him. 'I wouldn't want 'er to 'ear us talkin' about 'im.'

Frank nodded. 'Stick the kettle on again, will yer?' he asked her. 'I wanna get a shave before Alan calls round.'

Ann filled the kettle and lit the gas, then she set about washing the peeled potatoes. 'If Ben's in the pub terday I don't want you or the boys sayin' anyfing to 'im,' she told him. 'After all, it's none o' your business.'

Frank was about to reply when he heard the landing floorboards creak and footsteps on the stairs. ''Ello, gel,' he said as Lana walked into the scullery.

She gave him a wan smile and looked at her mother. 'Any tea in the pot, Mum?'

'Yeah, 'elp yerself, luv.'

Frank exchanged a quick glance with Ann and then went back into the parlour. Ann hummed to herself as she swilled the potatoes around in the pot, and when she had put them over the gas she sat down at the table facing her daughter. 'You an' Ben 'ad a bust-up?' she asked quietly.

Lana nodded. 'I'm finishin' wiv 'im,' she replied. 'I know I've said it before, but this time I'm determined. I'm bangin' me 'ead against a brick wall tryin' ter get 'ome to 'im. I don't wanna go on leadin' the life we're leadin' now. I wanna look forward ter the future. I want what ovver gels 'ave got, a place o' me own an' a couple o' kids.'

'If it's meant ter be, it'll 'appen,' Ann said sagely.

'Not wiv Ben it won't, Mum,' Lana replied. ''E'll never be

able ter save 'is money like ovver fellers. One day 'e's flush an' the next 'e's borrowin'. I'm tryin' ter save but it needs 'im ter make the commitment as well.'

'Yer farvver an' the boys saw Ben last night as they was comin' out o' the Crown,' Ann told her. ''E was well drunk.'

'It doesn't surprise me,' Lana retorted. 'That's Ben's answer to everyfing.'

Ann shrugged her shoulders and made to get up. 'I'd better start cookin' the breakfast,' she sighed. 'Alan'll be round soon.'

'I'll do it,' Lana volunteered. 'Once we've got breakfast over I wanna pop in ter do Lottie's feet.'

Ben Ferris opened his front door to see Soapy Lomax standing there. 'I thought you was gonna pop in the cafe yesterday,' he said irritably.

'I looked in there but yer wasn't there,' Soapy replied.

'Yer could 'ave left a message.'

Soapy moved his weight from one foot to the other. 'Yer can 'ave the lot at four an' a tanner a pair,' he said.

Ben shook his head slowly. 'I've changed me mind. It's gotta be four bob a pair or yer can stuff 'em.'

'Out o' the question,' Soapy said indignantly.

'All right, it's up ter you,' Ben said with a shrug of his shoulders. 'I'll be seein' Lol Carmichael later. I'll 'ave a word wiv 'im.'

Soapy looked surprised. ''Ow did you know it was the Carmichaels?' he growled.

'I was 'avin' a guess, but you just confirmed it,' Ben said with a grin.

The scruffy-looking individual bit on his lip while he did some mental arithmetic. 'All right, but yer 'ave ter collect 'em yourself. Petrol coupons cost money,' he moaned.

'Sorry, pal. No can do. Me van's busted.'

'You drive an 'ard bargain.'

'So do you,' Ben told him.

Soapy's miserable face brightened somewhat at the

compliment. 'I'll 'ave 'em round in an hour,' he said, turning on his heel.

Lana finished scraping the hard callus from the sole of Lottie's foot and gently eased her leg on to the floor. 'There we are, luv,' she said. 'That'll be a lot easier now.'

'Yer a good gel, Lana,' the old lady said thankfully. 'It was drawin' somefing terrible. I'll be able ter go dancin' now.'

Lana removed the bowl of hot soapy water and when she came back Lottie eyed her closely. 'Yer bin a bit quiet terday,' she remarked. 'Normally yer got a lot ter say fer yerself. Ain't yer feelin' too good?'

The young woman sat down facing her and sighed deeply. 'Me an' me feller's 'ad a few words. I ain't seein' 'im any more.'

'I knew there was somefing wrong,' Lottie said. 'I could tell. Never mind, luv, it's prob'ly fer the best.'

'There was no future in it, Lottie, fer eivver of us,' Lana told her.

The old lady stared into the low fire for a few moments then her rheumy grey eyes met Lana's. 'From what yer've told me about 'im, yer right,' she said quietly. 'Some men are very 'ard ter pin down. They wanna 'ave their cake an' eat it. It's all about responsibility, yer see. It frightens the life out o' some of 'em. A nice place ter live wiv little feet runnin' about is OK fer yer 'ome-lovin' sort, but fer ovvers it's a frightenin' prospect. Money's gotta be earned, there's food ter supply, an' clothes. It ain't easy fer a man ter take on those responsibilities.'

Lana nodded. 'I understand that, an' I know the worries it can cause, but it must 'ave bin much 'arder in your day, Lottie.'

'Bless yer, luv, it was a bloody nightmare at times,' Lottie told her. 'Me an' my Bill, Gawd rest 'is soul, we struggled along some'ow, like everybody else, but it was far from easy. At that time the men was all fightin' over a day's work on the docks. It was the same in ovver places too. All over the country people were strugglin' ter survive on a pittance, that's if they was lucky enough ter be workin' at all.'

'It must 'ave bin even 'arder fer you an' Bill, what wiv takin' in those children,' Lana remarked.

Lottie's old face creased in a toothless smile. 'The church was good to us. They brought the children round when there was nowhere else fer 'em ter go, but they gave me some money to 'elp wiv the food. It wasn't much, granted, but they brought shoes an' bits an' pieces fer the kids ter wear.'

''Ow many kids did yer take in, Lottie?' Lana asked her.

The old lady stroked her chin and thought for a few moments. 'The first was five years after my Sara died,' she replied. 'That would 'ave bin back in eighteen ninety-five. It was a little baby an' I 'ad 'er fer a couple o' weeks. There was so many more that I lost count. I only 'ad 'em fer short periods.'

'Was Sara yer only child?'

'Yeah. She died before she was two. It was the fever,' Lottie explained. 'I couldn't 'ave any more children so it was a blessin' to 'ave all those ovver little ones ter look after at times. It was the church, yer see. Ole Farvver McCarfy thought it'd 'elp me get over me loss. As a matter o' fact me first long-term fosterin' was a boy called Charlie Smedley. I got 'im in nineteen 'undred an' ten. I'll never ferget the look on 'is face when they brought 'im. Struck dumb 'e was. Two years I 'ad 'im. Then I 'ad nine more after 'im, all long-term. Mind you, as one left anuvver came. The most I 'ad at one time was three, but it was only fer a few weeks. I fostered right up until I was sixty, as a matter o' fact.'

'Ten children,' Lana said shaking her head. 'Do yer remember 'em all?'

'Yeah, 'course I do,' Lottie replied quickly. 'They was all my kids as far as I was concerned. I tried ter keep track of 'em after they left an' Farvver McCarfy used ter call round wiv news of 'em. 'E did that right up until 'e died. I sometimes fink 'ow nice it would be if one or two of 'em came round ter see me now an' then, but they never 'ave, except Jimmy Bailey that is.'

'I've seen 'im come in 'ere,' Lana told her.

''E's a very nice lad,' Lottie said, a sad smile appearing on her face. 'Bloody shame though. That boy 'as ter give up every penny indoors. 'Is muvver's a very sick woman. She's got two daughters an' they call in to 'elp out at times, but it's young Jimmy who bears the brunt. 'E does the washin' an' ironin' an' keeps the place clean. On top o' that 'e gets the meals ready too. There's not many would stand it.'

''As 'e got a girlfriend?' Lana asked.

'Love yer no,' Lottie replied. 'The poor feller never gets the chance ter meet anybody, what wiv all 'e 'as ter do.'

'When did yer take 'im in, Lottie?'

The old lady thought for a moment. 'It was back in twenty-three. The lad's farvver 'ad bin lost at sea an' 'is muvver was took off to 'ospital wiv the fever. Apparently the nuns at Rovver'ithe took in the two gels but there was no room fer Jimmy. Anyway Farvver McCarfy took 'im ter St Mary's Convent but they was full up as well, so that's 'ow I come ter get 'im. I'll never forget the sight o' that little mite standin' on me doorstep between the two nuns. 'E was just seven years old, wiv an angelic little face an' the most lovely dark eyes. It was a cold night, wiv the rain beatin' down, an' there 'e was, frightened, tired an' 'ungry. On top o' that 'e was fair worried over 'is muvver an' the two gels.'

While she was telling her story Lana bent down and picked up Lottie's fluffy slippers without taking her eyes from her face and placed them down in front of her. The old lady slipped her feet into them as she went on.

'My Bill was up the pub that night an' when 'e came 'ome I told 'im about the lad. 'E went up ter the bedroom and peeped in. Jimmy was snuggled up under the blankets an' the piller was wet wiv 'is tears. 'E was brave though. There was two little gels in the ovver bed an' I'd already told 'im 'e 'ad ter be very quiet so's not ter disturb 'em. 'E was cryin' silent tears – an' yer know what? My Bill shed a few silent tears too. That's the sort o' bloke my Bill was. 'Ard as iron on the outside but soft as butter inside.'

''Ow long did Jimmy stay, Lottie?'

'Two years I 'ad 'im, an' not a minute's trouble.'

'It's nice that 'e never fergot yer.'

'I don't fink any of 'em 'ave fergotten me,' Lottie said quietly. 'They just went back ter their families an' picked up their lives again. I couldn't expect 'em ter come visitin' afterwards. Though it would 'ave bin nice ter see 'em now an' then, even if it was only fer just a few minutes.'

'Did yer ever get any photos of 'em?' Lana asked.

'Yeah, I did as a matter o' fact,' Lottie replied. 'My Bill 'ad a box camera an' 'e was always takin' pictures o' the kids. I've got all of 'em in an album upstairs in me wardrobe. I'll remember ter dig it out an' next time yer call we can look frew it tergevver.'

'That'll be lovely,' Lana told her, glancing up at the clock on the mantelshelf. 'Well, Lottie, I gotta go now. It's bin lovely listenin' ter yer.'

'It's bin very nice fer me too,' the old lady replied. 'It took me back. They were all lovely kids.'

'An' they 'ad a lovely mum an' dad ter look after 'em,' Lana said, smiling at her.

'That's very nice o' yer ter say so,' Lottie chuckled.

Lana got up and went to the door then she turned and looked at the old lady. 'Tell me, Lottie. Just out o' curiosity. Was there one out o' those ten children who was that extra bit special to yer?'

'I loved 'em all, an' still do,' Lottie told her, 'but there is one. Some day I'll tell yer all about that little perisher.'

Lana let herself out and stood for a few moments on Lottie's doorstep, the germ of an idea forming in her mind.

'Mum? When did yer say Lottie's birfday is?'

'I told yer yesterday. Christmas Eve.'

'Yeah, I remember. I just wanted ter make sure I 'eard yer right.'

'Are you OK?'

'Yeah, I'm fine.'

Chapter Eight

It had rained for most of the night, but now on Monday morning a watery sun was climbing up into an uncertain sky and the pavements were beginning to dry out. Ben Ferris glanced through his net curtains at the street below, then drained the coffee dregs from his cup and grabbed his coat. When he reached the garage in Salmon Lane Toby Mason looked up from the headlight he was fixing and nodded over at the Morris van. 'I've sorted it out, Ben,' he said. 'I fitted a new wheel bearin' an' I've topped up the differential. Mind yer though, it's a bit of a wreck. I should get rid of it soon as yer can.'

'Fanks fer the good news,' Ben said, giving him a sarcastic grin. 'What's the damage?'

'Four pound seventeen an' a tanner, that's countin' the oil I 'ad ter put in,' Toby told him.

Ben handed over a five-pound note. 'Keep the 'alf a crown fer a drink,' he said.

'Fanks, pal. The keys are in the ignition,' Toby replied, going back to the job in hand.

Ben drove the van back to River Lane and parked it outside his yard while he went up to his flat for the large carton containing two hundred pairs of best-quality silk stockings. Ten minutes later he pulled up outside Gold Seal Suppliers in Tooley Street and hurried into the building. There was a small prefabricated office situated to the left of the large storage area and when the young man looked in Sammy Goldbloom jumped up from his desk with a large grin and held out his hand. 'Ben, my son. It's been a long time.'

Ben smiled as he clasped the outstretched hand in a firm grip. 'I've bin very busy, Sammy,' he replied. ''Ow's Golda?'

'She's very well and looking forward to Jacob's bar mitzvah,' Sammy informed him.

'Jacob?'

'Jacob. Our Rubin's firstborn.'

'Of course,' Ben said quickly. 'I used ter play ball wiv the little lad right 'ere in the ware'ouse. Yer mean ter tell me 'e's fourteen already?'

'Thirteen,' Sammy corrected him. 'Jacob is thirteen next week.'

''Ow time flies,' Ben said shaking his head.

The diminutive trader reached his arm up and laid it on the shoulder of the taller man. 'Let me show you round my warehouse,' he said smiling. 'We've made some changes since your last visit.'

Ben was grateful for the consideration. The typist sitting in the corner of the office was eyeing him up and down, no doubt with ears cocked ready. 'The business appears ter be doin' well,' he remarked as he saw the produce piled high on each side of the gangway.

'We try,' Sammy said modestly, his hands gesturing as though he was feeling for rain spots. 'Golda wants me to retire and hand the business over to Rubin, but the boy wants to be independent. And why not? I spent a sizeable sum putting that lad through the best Jewish school I could find, and he does well, but Golda's protective. She still treats him like a child. So Rubin's now a chartered accountant handling the accounts of some big firms, but does that impress Golda? She said he should count his own money, not other people's. She wants him to follow in my footsteps.'

Ben smiled at the pained expression on Sammy's face. 'Yer

could retire wiv dignity, Sammy, an' take up ballroom dancin',' he suggested. 'Yer still look pretty nimble.'

'I'm sure Oscar Rabin wouldn't agree,' Sammy laughed. 'Did I ever tell you I sang with Oscar Rabin's band once? Just a guest spot, but it went over very well. I was surprised Oscar never invited me back.'

They had reached the end of the long gangway, out of earshot of the packers and loaders who were milling around. Ben turned to face the smaller man. 'Sammy, I've got a good buy for yer,' he said quietly.

'And what would be a good buy for me?'

'Two 'undred pairs o' silk stockin's. Pure quality.'

Sammy smiled benignly. 'And what would I be doing with silk stockings? This is a wholesale grocery concern. Butter, yes. Cheese, yes. Even shoe polish and Fairy dyes, but stockings? Do me a favour, Ben.'

The young man took a flat packet out of his coat pocket and handed it to Sammy. 'Before yer turn me down just take a look,' he urged him. 'Now 'ave yer seen any better?'

The smaller man held the silk stockings up to the light and gently moved them between thumb and fingers. 'What are you asking?' he said suddenly.

'I've got two 'undred pairs in me van outside. You can 'ave the lot at six an' a tanner a pair,' Ben said casually.

Sammy smiled. 'At that price I'd be hard pushed to move them.'

Ben took the stockings back and gently eased them into the packet. 'Look, I tell yer what,' he said. 'I'll take six bob, but that's me lowest price. Bloody 'ell, Sammy, I'm givin' 'em away as it is.'

The trader stroked his goatee beard and pursed his lips. 'All right, my son, you've got a sale,' he said. 'Bring your van round the back and I'll get someone to take them off you. When you're done come in the office and we'll have a drink, unless you've signed the pledge.'

As Ben went out to the van Sammy beckoned his foreman

over and mumbled a few words in his ear, then after spending a couple of minutes checking some delivery notes he walked back into the office and looked over at his typist. 'Ursula, I believe it's your lunch break,' he told her.

The dark-haired young woman looked over her thick-rimmed glasses. 'Not till twelve-thirty, Mr Goldbloom,' she replied.

'Well, go now and take an extended break,' he said firmly.

Ursula did not like being left out of things and she flounced out of the office, giving Ben a sweet smile as he passed her in the doorway. Sammy motioned the young man to a seat and handed him a filled glass. 'That's single-malt Scotch,' he told him. 'Savour it. It should be savoured first, not swallowed like water.'

Ben smiled and made himself comfortable while his host counted out sixty pounds. ''Ere's ter many more deals,' he said as he took the money.

Sammy sniffed the spirit before taking a sip. 'I'm sorry to disappoint you, my old friend,' he said quietly, 'but I feel this little transaction may be our last.'

Ben frowned. 'Yer mean you really are retirin'?' he said quickly.

'Retiring is the wrong word,' Sammy corrected him. 'Let's say I'm going to be more gainfully employed.'

'Doin' what?' Ben asked him in surprise.

The trader leaned back in his chair and clasped his hands together, his face suddenly taking on a serious expression. 'The war is over now, my friend,' he declared, 'but for the Jewish people there can never be a true peace until our persecutors are hunted down and punished. Nor can we be content until the wandering ends.'

Ben nodded his head slowly, taken aback by the emotion in Sammy's voice. 'Your people are still sufferin', that's fer sure,' he said. 'From what I've read in the papers an' 'eard on the wireless there's fousands o' survivors of the concentration camps spread all over Europe.'

'The yellow star of David was made a mask of shame,' Sammy said bitterly. 'And now they're labelled "displaced persons". Abandoned, and unwanted still.'

'So is that what you meant by bein' more gainfully employed, 'elpin' those people?' Ben asked him.

Sammy afforded himself a world-weary smile. 'I'm a Zionist, Ben. Have been for many years now. You understand what I'm saying?'

Ben looked a little perplexed. 'Not exactly.'

'We want to build a Jewish nation in Palestine,' Sammy explained. 'The movement was established before the turn of the century. There are members in all parts of the world, and never has it been needed more than at this time. So to answer your question, yes. This is how I shall be helping these people, working within the Zionist movement.'

'Well, I wish yer well,' Ben said, feeling a little overawed by the sudden disclosure.

'Never fear, my friend,' Sammy said, his eyes alight with faith. 'It won't be very long before the Jewish people end their exile and stand on Zion, on the holy hill of Jerusalem.'

The young man drained his glass and immediately Sammy held out the bottle. Normally Ben would have refused the refill so early in the day, but today was different. 'Tell me, Sammy,' he said as the older man poured another stiff measure into the glass. ''Ave you actually sold your business?'

The trader nodded. 'This is classified, of course. I agreed the sale last week. I'm selling to a consortium of the Maltese headed by Darkie Samut.'

Ben whistled through his teeth. 'You never fail to amaze me,' he remarked.

'Amaze you? Why should it amaze you?' Sammy queried. 'I would have thought it made good sense, for me and for them. I do good business with Maltese shops in the area. Now they can have their own wholesaler. As for me, the price was very fair. Besides, it's a good thing to know a little about the buyers.

I understand from Darkie that things are not too good for them at present.'

'You know of the problems between the Malts an' . . .'

'Mick Constantine,' Sammy cut in. 'Yes, I know of the protection racket, and the trouble over the bookies' pitches. I also heard about the Rotherhithe affair. People talk to me. They trust me, Ben, and they confide in me. And why not? I'm Jewish.'

Ben took another sip from his glass. 'When are yer actually leavin', Sammy?'

'That depends on a number of things.'

'We must 'ave a farewell drink tergevver,' Ben suggested.

Sammy smiled and nodded. 'It'll be a sad day when I walk out of here for the last time,' he said. 'I've traded in Bermondsey ever since the early twenties, when I stood in the Tower Bridge Road market in all weathers selling eggs from a stall. I built this wholesale business up with a lot of goodwill and very little money, and now I have enough to retire on and live in comfort for the rest of my life. Along the way I've seen the changes that the war brought. I've seen people fall and people prosper, and I have to say that I don't like what's going on in the area now. People like Mick Constantine are no better than the Brown Shirt bullies who terrorised the German Jews in the early days. The only difference is the target. Yesterday the Jews, today the Maltese, tomorrow who knows? It was a German priest called Niemoller who once said something like, "They came for the Jews but we did nothing, then they came for the Catholics and we did nothing, then they came for me and there was no one left to do anything." Do you understand what I'm trying to say, Ben?'

The young man nodded quickly, touched by the passion in his voice. 'I understand, Sammy,' he replied. 'At least you'll be doin' somefing.'

'It's comforting to know that people are beginning to stand up to swine like Mick Constantine and his thugs. No matter how strong they are at the moment, their days are numbered,'

Sammy said, swallowing the last of his Scotch as though drinking his own private toast.

Jimmy Bailey watched from the cafe opposite until he was sure that the last of the lorries had left the transport yard, then he hurried over and took a deep breath before tapping on the office window. 'I've called fer me wages,' he told the surprised clerk.

'I . . . eh . . . I better go an' see Mr Thompson,' the young man answered hesitantly.

'Where's Bowditch?' Jimmy asked him.

'I'm afraid 'e's not in this mornin',' he replied.

Jimmy leant against the wall until the timid clerk returned to the window.

'Mr Thompson wants ter see yer,' he said.

Jimmy walked into the office and was shown into a side room. A gaunt-faced man wearing metal-rimmed glasses looked up at him. 'I believe there's been some misunderstanding,' he said in a reedy voice.

'Not as far as I'm concerned,' Jimmy replied.

'Our company policy is that all employees work a week in hand,' the manager explained.

'I wasn't told that when I was interviewed,' Jimmy said quickly.

'I'm sure Mr Bowditch would have done so,' the manager insisted. 'He's been with us for many years.'

'I don't care 'ow many years 'e's bin wiv yer,' the young man argued. 'I wasn't told, so I want me week's wages. Now.'

The manager adjusted his glasses and looked down at the square of blotting paper on his desk. 'If you're not satisfied with this job then you must put in your week's notice. That's all I have to say on the matter.'

Jimmy Bailey gritted his teeth and drew a deep breath. 'Now, you listen ter me fer a minute,' he said icily. 'If I walk out of 'ere without me wages I'm goin' straight round ter see someone at the Transport an' General Workers' Union. I'm gonna tell 'em about the dangerous poxy lorries your firm's got operatin', an' then I'm gonna ask ter see one o' the dock officials. They might be interested ter know that your drivers are goin' in the docks wivout union cards. What's more, I'm gonna tell the union people that you warn yer drivers they'll be sacked if they try ter join the union. Now 'ave I made meself clear?'

'Don't you be so insolent,' the manager spluttered, his eyes flaring. 'We never pressurise any of our drivers. They are at liberty to join the union if they wish to.'

'Well, I'm pleased to 'ear it,' Jimmy said, his eyes narrowing menacingly. 'After I've spoken wiv the union people I'm gonna come back an' wait outside the yard all day if need be, an' when the drivers finish work I'll be 'andin' out membership forms. That's all I 'ave ter say on the matter.'

The manager looked apoplectic as he tugged the desk drawer open. 'There's your wages,' he said throwing a packet across the desk. 'Take them and go.'

Jimmy saw the packet slide from the edge of the desk on to the floor and he clenched his hands into hard fists. 'Pick that up an' give it ter me, you ignorant pig,' he snarled, 'or I'll come round there an' shake the poxy life out o' yer.'

The manager hurriedly retrieved the packet and handed it over.

'Don't fink yer've 'eard the last o' this,' Jimmy growled as he snatched it from him. 'I'm still gonna see the union.'

As soon as the young man had left the clerk tapped on the door before looking inside. 'Are you all right, Mr Thompson?' he asked. 'I 'eard raised voices.'

'There'll be raised voices right enough, when Bowditch returns,' the manager growled.

Chapter Nine

Lottie Curtis held on to the stonework for support while she raked out the ash from the bottom of the fire, grunting as she bent down further to pick up a knob of coal from the scuttle in the hearth. She felt a giddiness come over her and she slumped down thankfully into her rocking chair. It was late afternoon and Lana would be home from work soon, she thought with a sly grin.

When she had recovered sufficiently Lottie got up from her rocker and turned on the wireless. The children's programme 'Toytown' was just finishing and then there would be theatre organ music for half an hour. Lana would be in by then, she thought as she made herself comfortable.

The melodic sounds lulled the old lady off to sleep, and when she opened her eyes once more she looked up at the clock and cursed to herself. It was nearly six o'clock. With an effort she got up out of her chair, and taking up a silver toffee hammer from an alcove shelf she gave the iron fire surround three sharp taps.

'It sounds a lovely idea but it's not gonna be easy,' Ann Johnson told her daughter as the family gathered around the parlour table.

'I dunno so much,' Lana replied. 'Apparently she's got lots o' photos, an' she seems very clear about dates an' years.'

Frank came in, closely followed by Derek, and they pulled up their chairs expectantly as Ann served up boiled ham with carrots and pease pudding.

'I'll need ter talk to 'er a bit more though,' Lana went on. 'Some of 'em might live miles away. It'll be very interestin' ter see what transpires.'

'Appertainin' ter what?' Derek asked her, winking at his father as he imitated Charlie Smedley the union official.

'I'd wanna know the ramifications,' Frank replied, grinning at his son.

'Shut up, you two, an' get on wiv yer tea,' Ann ordered. 'It soon gets cold.'

'Me an' Mum's bin talkin' about ole Lottie Curtis,' Lana told them. 'She's eighty on Christmas Eve an' I 'ad this idea about tryin' ter trace some o' those kids she fostered. It'd really please the ole lady if they turned up on the day.'

'I fink that's a really nice idea,' Frank remarked. 'It'll be a job though, unless yer got addresses. They could be anywhere. Some might 'ave bin killed durin' the war or just disappeared.'

'Well, I'm gonna try,' Lana said positively.

'The Salvation Army might be able to 'elp,' Derek suggested. 'They do a lot o' work tracin' people who've disappeared.'

'Look, you lot, I won't tell yer again,' Ann said raising her voice. 'Not so much chattin'. I'm not slavin' over a meal fer you ter let it get cold.'

The men looked at each other and pulled faces, and the rest of the meal was eaten quietly. Ann got up and gathered the dirty plates, and as she took them out to the scullery she heard the three metallic taps. 'Lana,' she called out, 'it's Lottie. Can yer slip in an' see what's the matter while I get these dishes in the sink?'

The young woman took down the key from its hook on the dresser and hurried next door. Lottie looked up with a big smile. 'I'm really sorry ter trouble yer, luv, but I need a new tap washer,' she told her. 'That bleedin' tap's bin drip, drip, drip all day.'

'I'm sorry, Lottie, but I've never changed a washer,' Lana said.

'Gawd love yer, I don't want you ter do it,' the old lady replied with a chuckle. 'I was wonderin' if yer might pop round ter Jimmy Bailey's place wiv a note. 'E'll fix it. 'E did me last one.'

''Course I will,' Lana told her.

Lottie slipped her hand down the side of her chair cushion and pulled out an envelope. 'I've wrote 'im a message,' she said. 'It's one o' the 'ouses in Abbey Street, near the Tower Bridge Road end. I can't remember the number but yer'll spot it. It's got a crinkly doorknocker.'

'A crinkly knocker?' Lana queried.

'You know what I mean,' Lottie grinned. 'It's one o' those twisty ones. I know 'cos Jimmy showed it ter me one day when 'e called in. 'E'd just bought it at the ironmonger's in Tooley Street. 'E said 'e was gonna fix it on that day 'cos the ovver one 'ad snapped.'

'Right, then. The door wiv the crinkly knocker,' Lana said, taking the envelope with the feeling that she would have to use a doorknocker or two before she found the right house.

As she turned to leave Lottie called her back. 'By the way, 'ave you an' yer bloke made it up yet?' she asked.

Lana shook her head. 'I've not seen anyfing of 'im,' she replied.

'Mind 'ow yer go, luv, an' fanks,' the old lady said, looking pleased with herself as she set the rocker in motion.

Ann Johnson shook her head. Frank stroked his chin, and Derek suggested it might be a claw knocker, but none of them was very much help.

Lana walked along the still busy Jamaica Road and turned into Abbey Street. A train rumbled over the arch as she passed through, and up ahead she saw a line of horse carts parked outside a transport yard. For the last third of the turning, rows of houses faced each other and Lana bit on her lip as she looked along them. The doorknockers were of various designs: lions' heads, claws, flat-iron shapes and one of a grinning devil, but none was crinkly.

A tall man wearing a red neckerchief answered Lana's knock. 'Who?' he said, screwing up his eyes.

'Mr Bailey,' Lana said again.

'Sorry. Never 'eard of 'im.'

The next household was more helpful. 'I fink yer mean Jimmy Bailey, luv,' the elderly lady said as she pulled her black shawl more tightly round her thin shoulders. 'What a nice young man. Looks after 'is ole muvver, 'e does. She ain't well, yer know. It's 'er 'eart by all accounts. I ain't seen 'er out fer years. Tell a lie, I did see 'er once. Not so long ago. I fink it was Easter. I know it was Easter 'cos she was buyin' an Easter egg in Pullin's. That's the shop in Long Lane.'

'That's Mrs Priday yer talkin' about,' a voice called out from behind her.

'Can yer tell me which 'ouse Jimmy Bailey lives in?' Lana said quickly.

An old man emerged along the dark passage. 'She gets a bit confused at times,' he said. 'Mrs Priday don't live in this turnin'. She lives in Weston Street.'

'I know she does,' the woman told him sharply. 'She wants Mr Bailey. Young Jimmy Bailey.'

'Bailey don't live in Weston Street,' the man replied.

'I know that, yer silly ole sod,' the woman grumbled. 'Take no notice of 'im. 'E dunno what 'e's talkin' about 'alf the time. Just cross over an' walk on until yer come ter the 'ouse wiv the funny knocker. I don't know the number but yer can't miss it. Just look fer the funny knocker.'

'The crinkly one?' Lana said in exasperation.

'Well, it's not crinkly, though I s'pose yer could say it's crinkly,' the elderly woman replied.

'Can yer point out which 'ouse it is?' Lana almost pleaded.

'Me eyes ain't too good. I can't see that far wivout me glasses,' she said.

'They're on the table,' the old man told her.

'What are?'

'Yer glasses.'

'Them's me readin' glasses.'

'Where's yer ovver glasses?'

'Gawd knows. See if they're by me bed.'

'Look, it doesn't matter, I'll find it,' Lana said in desperation.

'Can't you point it out to 'er?' the woman said.

''Ang on, I'll get me glasses,' the man replied.

Lana gave out a deep sigh, dreading to think that this was a foretaste of what she would come up against in her search for Lottie's children.

'Them's mine, yer dopey git,' the woman said irritably as her husband reappeared holding her glasses.

'I know that, yer silly mare. I was just bringin' 'em for yer.'

'They're me bleedin' readin' glasses.'

'Where's yer ovvers then?'

'I don't bleedin' know.'

The man puffed loudly, edged his way past his wife and pointed a bony finger towards the houses on the other side of the street. 'That's the one,' he said.

'Which one?'

'The last but one.'

Lana's shoulders sagged in relief. 'Well, fanks fer yer trouble,' she said, forcing a smile.

'It was no trouble, luv,' the woman told her, smiling warmly.

Lana hurried across the street and reached the last but one house, finally discovering what a crinkly doorknocker looked like. It was a semi-circular piece of wrought iron, twisted like a rope to represent the type of handles which were fitted to large medieval doors. She smiled to herself as she raised the knocker and brought it down firmly. After a while she heard the shuffling of feet and then the door was slowly opened.

'Yeah? What yer want?'

'Does Mr Bailey live 'ere?' Lana asked the thin woman

who stood with bowed shoulders in the gloom.

'Who wants 'im?'

'I got a message for 'im from Mrs Curtis,' Lana replied.

''E's gone out,' the woman said.

'Can yer give this to 'im when 'e comes back?' Lana asked her pleasantly.

'What's this, more work she wants done?'

'I really dunno.'

'Give it 'ere.'

Lana handed her the envelope and hurried back along Abbey Street. The elderly couple were still at their front door as she passed on the opposite side of the road, but she kept her eyes to the front, in case they beckoned her over.

Ben Ferris was deep in thought as he made his way to the Crown and Anchor in Dockhead. The conversation with Gerry Knowland on Sunday evening in the Dewdrop Pub had left him feeling a little more confident about the plan. Gerry had been at pains to point out that the Maltese had enough friends in the borough and they were becoming more organised. He had told Ben that he need not feel isolated doing what he had agreed. People would look out for him, and providing he was careful there would be nothing to worry about.

Ben felt a little less anxious after Gerry's assurances, and he had been further encouraged by the conversation he had had with Sammy Goldbloom. The man had opened his eyes and instilled in him a sense of excitement. He realised that his mission to become the ear in the enemy camp was a crucial part of the scheme to get Mick Constantine on the hook, and he could feel the adrenaline flowing as he pushed open the door and walked into the pub.

The saloon bar was almost empty and Ben took his pint over to a far table from where he could watch without making himself conspicuous. The large clock over the bar showed eight-thirty and beneath it the bored-looking barman stood polishing glasses. One or two customers came in, and then at nine o'clock a well-dressed man pushed open the door and swaggered up to the counter. 'Is Mick Constantine due in ternight?' he asked.

'I ain't seen 'im terday so I can't say whevver 'e is or not,' the barman told him. 'I could ask Baz. 'E might know.'

'Baz?'

'Yeah, one o' Mick's pals.'

'Nah, leave it,' the big stranger said. 'When yer see 'im tell 'im Tommy Carberry asked after 'im, will yer?'

The barman nodded and put the glass he had been cleaning on the shelf above the counter. 'Can I get yer anyfing?' he asked.

The man placed a ten-shilling note down on the counter. 'A Scotch, an' one fer yerself.'

Ben studied the stranger as he sipped his pint of bitter. His suit and shoes looked expensive and he carried himself well. His shoulders were broad and straight, and his dark, greying hair was combed back from his forehead. There was something about the man which intrigued Ben. He looked confident and at ease as he stood at the counter chatting to the barman. His hands were huge and his neck short and thick, suggesting great strength. Ben could not make out what they were saying, but occasionally the barman smiled broadly. The stranger seemed to be describing something and gesturing with his hands and Ben noticed how the ring on his finger flashed in the light. The man stayed for half an hour, and when he left Ben sauntered over and placed his empty glass down on the counter. 'Same again,' he said.

The barman nodded towards the door as he pulled on the pump. 'Did yer notice who that was?'

Ben shook his head. 'Nah, I wasn't payin' much attention, ter tell yer the trufe.'

'That was Tommy Carberry,' the barman informed him. 'I've seen 'im wrestle dozens o' times. They used ter call 'im the Butcher. 'E was askin' after Mick Constantine. I 'ope 'e's a friend of 'is an' not an enemy.'

Ben shrugged his shoulders, trying not to look interested. 'I should fink Constantine can look after 'imself,' he remarked.

The barman smiled and went back to polishing the glasses and Ben took his drink back to his table.

The evening seemed to drag by and there were very few customers. Ben drained his third pint and decided to leave. He was missing Lana and hoped she had had time to think things over. Maybe she had come to understand how things were. There was more to life than slaving away in some dead-end job with all the responsibilities of a house and family. She would come to see the sense in his thinking, he felt sure.

Chapter Ten

Lottie Curtis's advancing years prevented her from venturing very far from her house, though if the weather was favourable, and she was in the mood, she would go as far as the corner shop, or merely take some air at her front door. Sometimes she would accept an invitation from Bella Wickstead next door to go in for a cup of tea and a chat but the old lady found it very tiring. Bella never seemed to stop for breath and after a while Lottie herself would become breathless and fatigued merely listening to the woman's gabbling. Bella was a friendly neighbour however, and her husband Chas too, so she suffered the ordeal.

Lottie's other next-door neighbours, the Johnsons, were friendly folk too, but Ann Johnson did not invite her in to talk about all and sundry, and for that Lottie was grateful. One vociferous neighbour was enough, she thought. Ann and her daughter Lana were neighbourly in a more practical way and it was a comfort to know that a few taps on the adjoining wall with the toffee hammer would summon immediate help, should the need arise.

On Tuesday morning the sun was out and it felt quite pleasant to Lottie as she stood by her front door, keeping her eye open for Ann who would be coming home from her cleaning job soon.

''Ello, luv, 'ow yer feelin' this mornin'?' Bella asked as she stepped out of her house and spotted the old lady.

Lottie was feeling quite wicked in actual fact but could not say as much to her nosy neighbour. 'I'm fine,' she replied. 'It's a nice day.'

'I'm just off down the Blue. Is there anyfing yer want?' Bella asked her.

Lottie shook her head. She did need some sugar but it would mean another lengthy chat when her neighbour knocked with it. 'No, I've got it all in, fank you,' she said.

'Phil Moseley got off wiv a five-pound fine an' a warnin',' Bella told her.

'That was fortunate,' Lottie replied.

'Sure there's nuffing yer want?'

'No fanks.'

'By the way, did you 'ear about Peggie Wheatley? She's 'ad a boy.'

Lottie felt that this could turn into another of Bella's borough-wide reports and she took evasive action. Glancing quickly over her shoulder she pulled a face. 'I gotta go in, me kettle's boilin',' she said quickly.

Lottie stood behind her front door for a few moments then she came back out on the doorstep again, feeling even more wicked for deceiving her neighbour. There was no point in getting old unless you got more devious with it, she reasoned.

''Ello, luv. You're lookin' very sprightly,' Ann said as she came up.

Lottie smiled at the compliment. 'Ann, will yer tell your Lana I've dug the pictures out?' she said. 'Tell 'er ter pop in this evenin' if she can.'

'Yeah, 'course,' Ann replied.

Her task completed, Lottie went in with a satisfied smile and made herself comfortable in her rocker.

Ben Ferris had finally made the long-awaited contact with the lorry driver at a cafe in Tooley Street and a rendezvous had been arranged for that afternoon. The driver backed into a bombed-out cul-de-sac where Ben's van was waiting, and a chest of tea was quickly manhandled from the lorry's tailboard into the back of the van and both parties drove off happy. Joe Slavin was happy too as he poured out a complimentary mug of tea for Ben. He had despaired of ever getting the tea.

'I couldn't let yer down, Joe, not after the favour yer did fer me,' Ben said gratefully.

'I should be very careful in future, mate,' Joe remarked. 'Mick Constantine ain't one ter be played about wiv.'

Ben thought about the cafe owner's warning as he sipped his tea, knowing he was right. The gang boss was all-powerful in the area and it was generally accepted that he had spies almost everywhere. That was what worried Ben. If Constantine had managed to infiltrate the Maltese mob, it would put all the conspirators in great danger. The man was ruthless.

'Did you 'ear about the fire last night?' Joe called over. 'Castellano's barber shop in the Borough 'Igh Street got burnt out. Someone lobbed a petrol bomb frew the winder by all accounts.'

Ben pulled a face. 'Sounds ominous,' he said.

Joe Slavin was busy serving customers for a few minutes then he came over to where Ben was sitting. 'Last week Don Minto got a brick frew 'is winder an' a Maltese bookie got 'is face slashed as 'e was takin' bets in Watson Street,' he went on. 'It's gettin' bad. I can see it all blowin' up before long. There's bin new faces seen on the manor – Malts drafted in from Cable Street, from what I've 'eard.'

Ben put down his empty mug, suddenly reminded of the appearance of Butcher Carberry at the Crown. 'I'd be careful too if I were you,' he advised his friend.

'Don't worry, I don't know anyfing,' Joe said smiling. 'It's the only way ter survive these days.'

Lottie had busied herself about the house. She had dusted the parlour and shaken up the cushions on the armchairs and given the rocker cushion a careful shake before making herself a cup of tea. The fire was burning nicely and she had the kettle simmering over the coals. The table was covered with a fresh white linen cloth and in the centre she had placed a slim vase containing heather.

The old lady hummed contentedly to herself as she rocked to and fro, her eyes occasionally straying down to the tattered album at her feet. Lana would be in soon to browse through it, and about the same time Jimmy Bailey would arrive to fix her leaking tap, she hoped. How nice it would be if they liked each other, she thought. Jimmy deserved to have a nice girl to call his own and Lana would be lucky to have a young man who was so thoughtful and kind instead of that one she was currently going with. From what she had learned from Lana he was a selfish pig with no thought for what she might want.

At seven-thirty Lottie heard the key in the lock and then Lana walked in the parlour. Her hair had been well brushed and seemed to shine in the light, she thought. She looked clean and wholesome, with a cheerful smile on her pretty face.

'I'm so glad yer called in, luv,' she told her. 'I got this album out 'specially. Let me get yer a cup o' tea.'

'You stay there, I'll make the tea,' Lana volunteered.

The old lady smiled gratefully as she set the rocker moving. 'I fink Jimmy Bailey'll be round later ter fix me tap, that's if 'e got the message.'

'I dropped it in,' Lana told her, omitting the details of her experiences in Abbey Street the previous night.

'Did yer see the lad?' Lottie asked her.

'No, 'is mum came ter the door.'

Lottie looked disappointed. 'Never mind. I expect she gave 'im the message.'

When Lana had made the tea she slipped a cosy over the flower-patterned teapot and then drew up a chair beside the rocker. 'Can I see it now?' she asked Lottie.

The old lady smiled and motioned over to the alcove shelf. 'Pass me glasses over, luv,' she bade her.

Lana made herself comfortable beside her and leaned closer as she opened the album.

'That's Charlie Smedley, the one I was tellin' yer about,' Lottie said, brushing her hand over the faded photograph. 'Four years old, 'e was, when the Sisters o' Mercy brought 'im ter me. 'E wouldn't say a word. Everyfing was just a nod or a shake of 'is 'ead. The poor little mite 'ad bin struck dumb, the Sisters told me. Charlie 'ad stood there while 'is farvver beat 'is muvver somefing terrible. The poor woman was rushed to 'ospital an' it was two months before she could come 'ome. In the meantime I was lookin' after the lad.'

'Did 'e go back 'ome then?' Lana asked her.

Lottie shook her head. 'The woman was still in no fit state ter look after 'im. I 'ad 'im fer two years before 'is muvver took 'im back.'

'Did 'e never speak again, Lottie?'

''E did after a while, an' then 'e was never quiet fer more than a few minutes at a time,' the old woman replied with a smile. 'It was my Bill who got the first word out of 'im. Funny it was. Bill 'ad this camera, yer see. It was one o' those box cameras an' 'e'd saved up 'undreds o' those tea coupons. It must 'ave took 'im two years or more. Anyway 'e finally gets this camera an' young Charlie was fascinated with it. Every time Bill took a photo Charlie was round 'is ankles. I fink my bloke must 'ave photoed everyone in the street. 'E'd line 'em up an' say, "Smile", then click would go the camera. Anyway, one day Mrs 'Alliday came along wiv 'er two. Lovely kids, they were. Two little gels wiv ringlets down ter their waists. Bill was standin' on the step an' 'e grabs 'is camera. Mrs 'Alliday was pleased she was gonna be photoed an' there she was lookin' all serious wiv 'er arms round the two kids. I was a few doors away talkin' ter Mrs Sullivan an' I see my Bill 'and the camera over ter Charlie. "Look in the winder an' when yer ready tell 'em ter smile. Then yer press the red button," 'e said. Now I gotta tell yer, up until then Charlie 'adn't uttered a word. 'E was standin' there wiv great big eyes an' 'is little 'ands 'oldin' the camera, an' Bill ses, "C'mon, Charlie, they ain't got all day. Tell 'em ter smile."'

Lottie shook her head slowly at the memory. 'Charlie was only four years old an' Bill 'ad told 'im the word "smile" was a magic word that made the camera work. Anyway 'is lips moved an' Bill said to 'im, "Yer'll 'ave ter say it loud or the camera won't 'ear yer." So Charlie peeped inter the square winder, then plain as anyfing 'e ses, "Smile!". That was the first word I ever 'eard the little lad say. Well, after that it was just a question o' perseverance, an' when 'e finally went back to 'is muvver 'e was a regular little chatterbox.'

''Ow lovely,' Lana responded. 'It makes me wanna cry.'

Lottie nodded. 'Funny fing is, that was one o' the best pictures that ever come out o' that ole box camera.'

'What 'appened ter Charlie?' Lana asked.

''E went ter work in the docks, so I 'eard,' Lottie told her as she turned the page. 'Now there's a precocious little miss if ever there was one.'

Lana looked down at the photo of a beautiful child sitting upright in a chair. She was wearing a frilly dress with button-up boots and a straw hat set on the back of her head. Her hands were clasped in her lap and she had a serious expression on her oval face.

'Who's this?' she asked.

'That's Phoebe Morris,' Lottie told her. 'I got 'er six months after Charlie left an' she was wiv me fer over a year. That photo was taken when she was seven, a few days before she went back to 'er muvver.'

The conversation was suddenly interrupted by a knock on the front door and when Lana opened it she found Jimmy Bailey standing on the step. He looked startled.

'I'm . . . I've come ter mend the tap,' he stuttered. 'Is it all right?'

Lana gave him a smile. 'Go in. Me an' Lottie are just lookin' frew some old photos.'

Jimmy walked into the parlour and slipped off his blue

raincoat. 'I got yer message, Aunt Lottie,' he said quickly. 'I've brought a new washer.'

'You two ain't met, 'ave yer?' the old lady said. 'This is Lana Johnson who lives next door. Lana, this is Jimmy Bailey who I looked after fer some time.'

Lana smiled as she gave him her hand and Jimmy held it lightly. 'Pleased ter meet yer,' he said, his cheeks flushing slightly.

'Likewise,' Lana replied.

'Well, I'd better get on wiv it then,' the young man said, looking a little awkward.

Lottie smiled as he left the room. ''E's pretty shy,' she remarked quietly.

Lana sat down next to her, eager for the old lady to go on. 'You was startin' ter tell me about this little gel,' she said.

'I was sure she'd make 'er mark in life an' she certainly did,' Lottie resumed. 'She's Phoebe Francis the musical star. Francis is 'er stage name. She was one I could keep tabs on. There's often bits in the newspapers about 'er. She's bin to America too. Travelled quite a bit, she 'as.'

'She was in that musical "Showboat" up the West End,' Lana said excitedly.

'Phoebe's muvver 'ad a nervous breakdown after 'er 'usband left 'er an' the little mite was bein' neglected,' Lottie went on. 'She don't look neglected in that photo, does she?'

Jimmy walked back into the parlour. 'Er, sorry to interrupt, Aunt Lottie, but there's nuffing wrong wiv the tap,' he announced. 'It wasn't turned off enough.'

'It must be me wrist,' she replied. 'I don't seem to 'ave any strength in it lately.'

'Well, I s'pose I'd better be off then,' Jimmy said.

'There's no need ter rush off right away,' Lottie told him. 'Sit down an' 'ave a cup o' tea. Lana, pour 'im out one, will yer?'

Jimmy sat down on the vacant armchair facing the old lady

and smiled at her. 'I 'aven't seen that album in a long time,' he remarked.

'I dug it out fer Lana ter see,' she told him. 'I was tellin' 'er all about the little terrors I used ter look after. I'm gonna show 'er one o' you in a minute.'

Lana handed him a filled cup and passed him the sugar bowl. He gave her a brief smile and she noticed his even white teeth. His dark hair was neatly brushed back from his forehead and he was wearing a clean shirt that looked freshly ironed. His trousers were well-worn and his shoes were down at heel but his face had a well-scrubbed look.

''Ow much do I owe yer fer the washer?' Lottie asked him.

Jimmy shook his head. 'I found one in me toolbox.'

The old lady flipped the pages quickly and grunted with satisfaction. 'There 'e is. Jimmy Bailey at seven years old.'

Lana studied the photograph and then looked up at the young man. 'Yer can see the likeness,' she remarked.

Jimmy smiled at her. 'That was taken after I'd bin wiv Aunt Lottie fer a while. She'd fattened me up by then,' he told her.

Lana was intrigued by him calling the old lady his aunt. It was said naturally and it seemed to please her.

'Did yer get yer wages?' Lottie asked him.

'Yeah, there was no trouble,' he replied.

'I 'ope yer reported that firm ter the labour exchange,' she said quickly. 'Firms like that should be stopped.'

'Yeah, I told 'em,' Jimmy replied. 'The manager told me there'd bin a lot o' complaints about that firm. They're gonna send me after anuvver drivin' job termorrer.'

'I am pleased,' Lottie told him.

Jimmy looked embarrassed. 'Well, I'd better be off,' he said putting down his empty cup. 'I'll pop round again in a few days. Nice ter meet yer, Lana.'

The young woman gave him a big smile. 'Nice meetin' you too,' she replied.

Lottie sighed contentedly. She had done her bit, she thought. The rest was up to them.

* * *

Jimmy Bailey thought about the pretty young woman from Saddler Street as he walked home through the quiet evening streets. She was pretty and bubbly, with a nice smile and a friendly way about her. She was the sort of girl he would go for, if things were different.

As he reached his front door and slipped the key in the lock Jimmy knew immediately that something was wrong. A strong smell of gas filled the passageway and he held his breath as he rushed into the scullery. His mother was crouched on the floor, her head and shoulders inside the oven. He turned off the gas and dragged her out on to the stone floor, coughing and fighting for breath as he threw open the window and the back door. His head was beginning to pound as he held his mother under the arms and dragged her into the backyard. She appeared to be lifeless and all the colour had left her face. He quickly laid her on her back and leant his cheek down near her nose and mouth, then tried to get her breathing once more, but it was in vain. He fell back and groaned aloud. 'No! No! Oh God. No!' he cried out in anguish.

Chapter Eleven

The hour was late and the fire had burned low at the Johnsons' house in Saddler Street. Ann sat in the parlour chatting to Lana as she was putting her hair in curlers. 'Yer farvver don't like me wearin' these in bed but I don't fink I'll get any grief from 'im ternight,' she remarked. ''Im an' young Derek looked sold out when they came in. There's a fruit ship in an' they've bin workin' on extra bonus ter get it turned round quick.'

Lana arched her back in the chair and leaned forward to rest her elbows on the table, cupping her chin in her hands. 'Well, at least I've got two names,' she said sighing. 'Charlie Smedley an' Phoebe Francis.'

'Just fancy, ole Lottie lookin' after a famous star,' Ann said.

Lana watched as her mother wet the tips of her fingers and ran them along an unruly strand of hair. 'Dad or Derek might know Charlie Smedley, or one o' their mates might,' the young girl said, 'but I dunno about Phoebe Francis. I can't imagine 'er wantin' ter come ter Lottie's birfday party.'

'I s'pose yer could write to 'er,' Ann suggested.

'I'll 'ave ter look in the paper an' see where she's appearin',' Lana replied. 'I could write ter the theatre. They'd give it to 'er, surely.'

'Well, if yer don't try yer'll never know, will yer?' her mother said, looking sideways into the small hand mirror in front of her.

Lana stared down at a hole in the linen tablecloth for a few moments and a smile grew on her lips. 'Lottie's a crafty ole lady,' she said. 'I'm positive she got Jimmy Bailey round just 'cos I was there. She knew me an' Ben 'ad split up. She asked 'im round ter mend 'er leakin' tap but it wasn't leakin' after all. She 'adn't turned it off enough.'

'What's 'e like, this Jimmy Bailey? Ter talk to, I mean,' Ann asked.

''E seems all right,' Lana replied non-committally. ''E's very shy an' 'e seemed a bit awkward. Yer can see 'e finks the world o' Lottie though.'

'What d'yer mean, awkward?' Ann asked her.

'You know what I mean. 'E seemed uncomfortable.'

Ann smiled as she rolled the last of the loose strands of hair round the metal curler. 'P'raps 'e 'ad good reason ter be,' she remarked. 'Don't ferget you felt that Lottie was matchmakin'. I expect the poor sod felt the same way.'

''E's quite a nice-lookin' bloke,' Lana said, tracing her finger round the hole. 'Yer can see 'e's down on 'is luck though. 'E 'ad a nice clean shirt on but 'is shoes were run-down an' 'is trousers looked all threadbare.'

'Yer know the ole sayin', yer can't tell a book by its cover,' Ann reminded her.

'I'm sure 'e's a real nice bloke but 'e's not my type,' Lana replied.

Ann felt that it was too late to take it any further and she gathered up her curler box and the mirror. 'Well, I'm off ter bed,' she said yawning. 'Don't you sit down 'ere finkin' about what yer've gotta do or yer'll 'ave big circles under yer eyes termorrer.'

Lana heard the chimer strike the half hour before midnight as she slipped down under the bedclothes. The curtains were parted slightly, letting in the light from the street lamp outside, and she turned on to her back with her hands behind her head. She thought of Ben and how angry he had made her feel by his uncompromising attitude, and she sighed deeply.

There was no future for them together but she felt miserable without him. She remembered the feel of his hands on her body and how she always responded. He was a considerate lover and she was never left wanting.

Lana closed her eyes, picturing him above her nakedness, and her hands went to her breasts, her thumbs moving slowly over her hardening nipples. He was smiling down at her in that lopsided way of his, exploring her body, and she shuddered as her skin flushed with heat. She stroked her hands down to her flat belly and down the thickness of her firm thighs. She was wet with desire, ready for him and suddenly she clenched her hands into tight fists. It was stupid to dwell on his lovemaking. She had to be firm, resolved not to be taken in and seduced again by his persuasive charm.

Outside the street lamp flickered and the chimer sounded the witching hour, and in the front bedroom the young woman tried in vain to sleep.

As Baz Smithson walked along the deserted cobbled lane in Dockhead he felt the familiar twinge of excitement playing on his insides. He knew that Constantine would pay good money for this job, and besides, it would raise his status within the mob. He would have to be careful though. He had been banged up already for grievous bodily harm and he did not want to spend another spell behind bars. Being in the pay of a man like Mick Constantine meant taking certain risks, so he needed to make sure that he was swift and thorough in getting the job done. The firebombing of the Malt shops had gone off a treat and Mick had been appreciative in the way Baz preferred best, with ready money. Tonight's escapade was going to be a little more tricky however, and for that reason Baz had decided it was best if he got it sorted on his own. The Varley boys were handy enough, a bit too handy at times, and if they piled in they would probably make it a bit too messy.

Baz stopped for a moment under a gas lamp to glance at his wristwatch and he smiled to himself. The riverside pub would be turning out soon and there was time to settle himself in a dark doorway.

Toni Rossi had been in the merchant navy during the war and had settled down in Cable Street in London's East End after the cessation of hostilities to lead a less strenuous life. Cable Street ran parallel to the Thames and was home to many of Toni's countrymen but it was becoming overcrowded and he decided it would be nice to cross the river and open a shop in Bermondsey. Several people he knew had had the same idea and he felt that he would be among friends.

Toni was in his forties and had not married. His passion for gambling had frightened off one or two young women in the past and now he was resigned to his bachelor life. At least he could play cards with his friends when he wanted without having to face the music when he got home. He could also go to the greyhound race meetings whenever the fancy took him, which was very often.

Tuesday evenings were special to Toni, for he met with old friends to play pontoon in the Ship Inn. The stakes were never high and over time the players came out about even. It was the camaraderie which he enjoyed, and among his ex-merchant navy friends he could chat about the war, the convoys and foreign ports, about the women they had loved and lost and the women they had lusted after. They sat together round a table strewn with copper coins and every Tuesday evening the good friends got steadily inebriated.

Toni's grocery shop in a backstreet off Grange Road had prospered and he had recently bought a greyhound of which he had high hopes. He was a friendly man, but with a naivety that belied his experience of life, and he was prone to voicing his opinions, not caring whether they pleased or offended. He had been vociferous about the recent attacks on his countrymen and said that they should band together and fight back. His friends felt that his views were sound and commendable, but what worried them was where he expressed them. They knew the area very well and thought that the Crown and Anchor was the last place to sound off in a loud voice, especially in the saloon bar.

On Tuesday night Toni left his friends with a friendly wave and set off home. His mind was on a woman from his past, Magdalena, and he could picture her dark flashing eyes as she teased him and ran off along the hot dusty alleyways in Valletta. He was young and in love but she was spoken for, and a torrid glance from her smouldering eyes was all he ever got from her. He smiled to himself sadly, dreaming of what might have been when suddenly a flash of light exploded in his head and he stumbled forward on to his knees. Instinct told him to cover himself and his arms came up to protect his head from another blow. He could feel warm blood running down his neck and he prepared himself for the worst.

During the early hours of Wednesday morning the rain started. At first it was a trickle but by five o'clock it was torrential. Water gurgled down into the gutters and bounced off the cobblestones, and when PC Jones stepped into the wharf doorway to shelter from the downpour he cursed loudly. He realised that he had stepped in something sticky, probably some mangy dog's mess but when he shone his torch down he saw that it was blood. The door itself and the brickwork around it had been splashed, and PC Jones was experienced enough to realise that whoever had lost that much blood could not have got very far. Forgetting the heavy rain he made a search of the area but found nothing, and he took his helmet off and scratched his saturated head as he tried to work it out. Before he went off duty at seven o'clock he penned a report which the desk sergeant at Dockhead Police Station passed over to Chief Inspector William Penrose.

Heavy rain was still falling at ten o'clock that morning as the inspector sipped his coffee pensively. There was another report lying on his desk concerning a body found early that morning wedged against a stanchion beneath Chamber's

Wharf. The lighterman who had spotted the body had been able to make a positive identification and the inspector now awaited the forensic report.

'I'm counting on these two reports tying together,' Penrose told his subordinate, Detective Sergeant Don Hallam. 'According to the constable there was enough blood spilled in the doorway to form a deep puddle and it had crusted over. If the forensic boys come up with a blood match, which I think they will, then we've made a fair start.'

By midday the forensic findings were in front of the inspector and he summoned DS Hallam. 'The two blood groups match,' he told the detective sergeant. 'They've fixed a time too. The murder took place between eleven and eleven-thirty last night and the victim was dead before entering the water.'

'Why kill someone in a doorway and then carry the body down to the river?' Hallam queried.

'In the hope that his body would be washed downriver,' Penrose told him. 'Whoever was responsible wanted to shift the onus.'

'Well, it figures,' Hallam replied. 'We know there's been bad blood between the Maltese and Mick Constantine's mob for some time, and according to our informant it was beginning to get nasty. Now it has.'

The chief inspector nodded his head slowly. 'I saw this sort of thing escalate over at Hoxton before the war,' he said. 'Rival gangs were jockeying for pride of place and it got very messy. The razors came out and finally there was a killing. It all went very quiet after that. It might be the same in this situation, but I'd be willing to bet money against it.'

'Is there any mileage in pulling a few people in?' the sergeant asked.

'I think a friendly visit might be more appropriate,' Penrose replied. 'I'll go myself. It's about time the gang bosses and I became properly acquainted.'

* * *

Angelo Samut had spent the war in the armoured corps, having volunteered in 1940, and after his unit landed on the Italian mainland he rose to the rank of sergeant. Angelo got his nickname from his swarthy complexion which became even duskier while serving in the Middle East. He was a good organiser and a born leader, and his qualities were currently being utilised in the escalating troubles with the Constantine mob. Darkie Samut was nothing if not astute, and having heard about Toni Rossi's outbursts in the Crown he knew that his countryman would be targeted sooner or later.

Aside from his devious dealings, Angelo Samut was landlord of the Lord Nelson, a small pub behind the Old Kent Road, and it was there that the Maltese confederates gathered on a regular basis. It was there, then, that Chief Inspector William Penrose went to beard the lion.

'And to what do I owe the pleasure?' Darkie said amiably when the policeman introduced himself.

'I think you know why I'm here,' Penrose said, looking quickly round the saloon bar.

'I'm sorry but I'm at a loss,' Darkie replied. 'Maybe you can enlighten me over a drink.'

The chief inspector nodded. 'I don't normally drink before evening but I'll make an exception today,' he said smiling.

'Like you, I don't usually take a drink during the day, but in this case I'll make an exception too,' the landlord replied.

The few afternoon tipplers had drifted out of the pub and after Darkie slid the bolts over the door he joined the inspector at a table.

'It's my responsibility to police Bermondsey,' Penrose said as he studied his Scotch, 'and I'm given to understand that the welfare of the Maltese members of our community is, unofficially, your responsibility, so for that reason I decided it was time that we met.'

'I see,' Darkie said quietly, his eyes fixed on the inspector.

'There's something you should know,' the policeman continued. 'We fished a body out of the river this morning.

You'll no doubt read about it in the evening paper. The body's been identified and we're pretty sure of the motive for the killing.'

'You're telling me that it was murder?' Darkie cut in quickly.

'Yes, it was murder,' Penrose replied. 'The man had had his throat cut and was dead before going in the water. We know where the killing took place and we are assuming that the body was dumped in the river for a specific purpose. It wasn't done to wrong-foot us, or the site of the killing would have been cleaned up. It was obviously done to shift the blame, to keep the lid on the troubles.'

'Troubles?'

'Yes, troubles. I'm talking about the simmering differences between your countrymen and the Constantine mob,' Penrose told him.

Darkie Samut nodded his head slowly and his eyes became hard. 'These troubles you speak of. They're not of our making,' he said coldly.

'Maybe not,' Penrose countered, 'but violence breeds violence, and I won't tolerate it, not on my manor.'

'What should we do, suffer in silence?' Darkie asked him angrily. 'Should we sit back and let our shops be fire-bombed, our men get slashed with razors, our businesses be sent to the wall?'

'No, you come to us,' the inspector replied quickly. 'Let us deal with it. It's our job. It's not for you to take the law into your own hands.'

'Be sure I will,' Darkie told him. 'But we'll expect results, not promises.'

'I won't make rash promises,' Penrose said quietly, 'but I will assure you here and now that nothing'll be spared in bringing the perpetrators to justice. That's my only promise.'

'That's good enough for me,' Darkie replied. 'Can I give you a refill?'

'No, this'll do nicely,' the inspector said, draining his glass before getting up. 'By the way, we've not given out the full story to the press as yet. The victim will be named, but cause and place of death are being withheld for reasons of our own.'

'Well, it was an enlightening chat,' Darkie said with a smile, holding out his hand. 'Call again any time, Inspector.'

'I will, and I hope it'll be purely social,' the policeman said by way of warning.

Darkie Samut stood at the door of his pub watching until the inspector disappeared round a corner, then he hurried inside and relocked the door. 'It's OK,' he called out.

The heavily built man emerged from the back room with an ashen face. His head was swathed in bandages. 'What's news?' he asked.

Darkie smiled laconically. 'Baz Smithson's body's been found.'

Chapter Twelve

Jimmy Bailey sat hunched in the armchair facing Glenda, his younger sister. 'I blame myself,' he said in a voice choked with emotion. 'I went out an' left 'er on 'er own. It was all fer nuffing as well. I should 'ave bin 'ere wiv 'er.'

Glenda's eyes were red from crying as she looked over at him. 'Now you listen ter me, Jimmy,' she said firmly. 'No one could blame you fer what's 'appened ter Mum. She just wanted the opportunity. If it 'adn't bin last night it would 'ave 'appened some ovver time. She was ill an' in a lot o' pain. She'd 'ad enough. You mustn't blame yerself. After all, yer've done more than most sons would 'ave done. Me an' Lillian know 'ow good yer've bin.'

Jimmy felt the coldness of the parlour and he stared down at the ashes in the grate. 'I don't fink Mum ever got over losin' Dad,' he said quietly. 'We was just kids at the time an' all those years since she's bin on 'er own. I know she 'ad us, but it wasn't enough. I wish she'd 'ave married again. We wanted 'er to, didn't we?'

'It's not a case o' what we wanted,' Glenda replied. 'Mum never wanted anuvver man. Anyway it's no good sittin' 'ere goin' over the whys an' wherefores. At least she's at peace now, an' there's no more pain. That's the way we gotta look at it.'

Jimmy nodded. Glenda had always been the practical one,

and she made sense. Their mother had been a sick woman for years, and now her pain and suffering were finally over.

'What are yer gonna do now, Jimmy?' Glenda asked him.

He shrugged his shoulders. 'I was s'posed ter start a new job terday. I'll 'ave ter get down the Labour Exchange soon as possible an' explain fings.'

'I meant about the 'ouse,' she said. 'Will yer stay on 'ere?'

'I dunno,' he replied, still staring into the grate. 'I s'pose the landlords would let me stay on provided they got the rent every week, but it's a three-bedroomed 'ouse, an' it's not bin a very 'appy place since you an' Lillian got married.'

Glenda stood up and laid her hand gently on his shoulder. 'C'mon, we'd better sort these policies out,' she told him.

In the small riverside community it was inevitable that news would travel fast, and by early evening people were standing on their doorsteps discussing the two deaths.

'I didn't know the woman but I've often seen 'er boy callin' next door,' Bella Wickstead told Ann Johnson. 'What a terrible fing fer that poor sod ter find 'is muvver wiv 'er 'ead in the gas oven.'

Sadie Pugh from number eight walked over to join them. 'I s'pose you 'eard about Baz Smithson,' she said. 'Del Moody in the Crown told my Dan this mornin'. Someone from the pub 'ad ter go an' identify 'im by all accounts. They found 'im in the river by Chamber's Wharf. I said ter Dan it could 'ave bin an accident an' 'e laughed. 'E said Baz might 'ave 'ad the shakes shavin' but not enough ter cut 'is froat from ear to ear an' then chuck 'imself in the Thames. My Dan's a wicked git at times.'

Bella looked at the thin woman and her staring eyes and chuckled. 'Actually we were talkin' about Mrs Bailey in Abbey Street,' she said.

'Who, 'er whose son calls on Lottie Curtis?' Sadie queried.

'That's the one,' Bella replied. 'She put 'er 'ead in the gas oven last night. 'Er boy found 'er.'

'Good Gawd!' Sadie exclaimed. 'Whatever makes 'em do it?'

'She was very ill apparently,' Bella told her. 'Probably 'ad enough o' the pain if the trufe was known.'

Sadie stroked her chin and started to pull on a whisker. 'My Dan said that there's a lot o' speculation goin' on about that Baz Smithson,' she told them. 'There's a rumour goin' around that the Malts done it.'

'Best ter take no notice o' rumours,' Ann advised her. 'People get in a lot o' trouble spreadin' rumours.'

'Yer right there,' Bella agreed. 'Remember that turnout wiv Mrs Rigby?'

The other two women shook their heads and Bella drew breath. 'Ivy Rigby used ter live in those railway buildin's in Webb Street,' she began. 'She was a funny woman. They said she 'ad a screw loose. 'Er ole man worked at the gasworks in the Old Kent Road an' 'e was on shift work. Anyway, rumours started circulatin' that 'e was 'avin' it off wiv this woman in the same buildin's as them. 'E was always talkin' to 'er an' laughin' an' jokin' wiv 'er. There was nuffing in it, it turned out afterwards, but Ivy Rigby listened to all this gossip an' she led 'er ole man a dog's life. One day 'e was comin' 'ome from work an' 'e bumped inter this woman 'e was s'posed ter be knockin' off. They walked along the street tergevver an' Ivy spotted 'em from 'er winder. She came runnin' down the stairs wiv a chopper an' chased the poor cow up the street an' right frew the market screamin' out at the top of 'er voice what she was gonna do wiv 'er when she caught 'er.'

'Did she catch 'er?' Sadie asked wide eyed.

'I'm comin' ter that,' Bella said quickly. 'Anyway, one o' the stall'olders grabbed 'er an' took the chopper away from 'er an' someone else called the police. It all come out in court an' it was in the local papers. The outcome was, Ivy Rigby was bound over ter keep the peace, Ivy's ole man gave this ovver woman a wide berf an' it was all quiet fer some time. Then one night 'e come over queer at work an' they sent 'im 'ome early. 'E walks in the 'ouse an' what yer fink? 'E catches Ivy in bed wiv the ovver woman's 'usband. Apparently it'd bin goin' on fer years but no one knew about it.'

'What 'appened then?' Sadie asked her.

'Ivy's ole man kicked the bloke out an' then 'e give 'er a right pastin', by all accounts,' she continued. 'Both couples split up an' Ivy ended up marryin' this ovver bloke.'

'What about Ivy's ole man?' Ann asked.

'Everyone thought 'e'd get tergevver wiv the ovver woman, but she went off wiv Tubby Westmacott,' Bella chuckled, ''im who 'ad the veg stall in the Tower Bridge Road.'

'Did 'e ever get married again?' Sadie enquired.

'Nah. 'E finally topped 'imself,' Bella told her. 'They found 'im 'angin' from a beam in the gasworks durin' the Blitz.'

'Poor bleeder,' Sadie remarked. 'Mind yer, it wasn't a rumour about Ivy an' this ovver bloke, was it?'

'That's what I'm sayin',' Bella replied. 'It's always the wrong people who get scandalised.'

Sadie wasn't quite sure that she understood Bella's logic but she nodded dutifully anyway. 'Well, I'd better be gettin' in,' she said. 'I got a meat pie in the oven.'

Ann Johnson made her excuses too and Bella stood at her door for a while surveying the street in case there was any more news forthcoming.

On Wednesday evening Lana left the insurance-office building and walked quickly along Tooley Street towards Dockhead. Suddenly she felt a light tug on her arm and turned to see Ben Ferris.

'We need ter talk, Lana,' he told her.

'I think we said all there was ter say,' she replied brusquely.

'Yeah, I know, an' I've 'ad time ter fink about all what yer said,' he went on. 'I'm gonna change, Lana, I really am. I've missed yer, missed yer badly an' I've come ter the conclusion that I've bin wastin' me time duckin' an' divin'. I'm gonna get a decent job, one that's got a future, an' I'm gonna save up 'ard.'

Lana increased her pace but he took her arm again to slow her down. 'Look, I know yer must be fed up wiv all me promises, but yer gotta remember that was when we were tergevver,' he persisted. 'I didn't realise what it would be like wivout yer. I've bin really miserable, honest. Give us anuvver chance, Lana, an' I promise yer'll not regret it.'

The young woman caught the sad, pleading look in his eyes and her heart melted. 'I've missed you too, Ben,' she said, 'but I can't go on livin' wiv empty promises.'

'All right, maybe I did make promises I couldn't keep,' he said quietly, 'but I've come ter realise more than ever that nuffing's any good wivout you. Give me one more chance, that's all I need, an' yer won't be sorry. I love you, Lana. I'll never stop lovin' yer whatever yer say.'

Lana felt the warmth of his hand on her arm and she forced a smile. 'This is the last chance, Ben. I mean it,' she told him firmly.

Ben's face broke into a wide smile. 'Look, I've gotta sort a few fings out this evenin',' he said. 'Can we see each ovver termorrer? My flat, say eight o'clock?'

The young woman nodded. 'Termorrer at eight.'

Ben hurried off, turning once to give her a cheery wave, and Lana sighed in resignation. It would all start again now, she thought as she turned into Jamaica Road. Her mother would shake her head in disgust and give her a lecture on having some pride and determination, and her father would puff and blow and bury his head in the paper. As for her brothers, Derek never said much, but Alan would show his disappointment that the romance was on once more. Well, they could all think and act how they liked, she resolved. She was over twenty-one and it was her life. If she wanted to throw it away on Ben Ferris it was her choice.

Gerry Knowland had grown up in Bermondsey and

Rotherhithe and had learned very early on that there were those who worked and others who organised, and at an early age decided that he was better suited to organising. At seventeen he hired a barrow and rented a pitch in the Tower Bridge Road market, and as soon as he was established he found a friend to run it for him while he negotiated another pitch in Rotherhithe. Within five years he had six stalls, all selling fruit and vegetables which he bought in bulk from the wholesale markets at a large discount.

The aspiring young businessman got in with a bad bunch and soon he was in trouble with the police. He served eighteen months for receiving and another nine months for assault. Two months after his release war broke out and like many of his friends Gerry immediately volunteered. It was then that he discovered he had a heart murmur and was listed grade four. Feeling very worried he went to see his panel doctor who told him that many people were born with a heart murmur and lived to be a ripe old age.

The young man's disappointment at being turned down by the army was tempered by the opportunities he could see opening up and he went into buying and selling, often in the black market. He had built up a dubious reputation in Bermondsey but unlike Mick Constantine he had no ambitions to become a gang boss. In fact his devious dealings were more subtle and he prospered.

On Wednesday evening Gerry met with Ben Ferris in the Dewdrop pub and he was interested to learn of the new arrival in the area. 'I'd say that Constantine's recruited Butcher Carberry as a bodyguard,' he ventured. 'The man must be worried, an' more so wiv Baz Smithson gettin' topped.'

'Any ideas about who done it?' Ben asked.

'If I did, I wouldn't say,' Gerry replied. 'I fink we've both got our suspicions, an' it makes good sense ter leave it at that. By the way, I've got an idea that might 'elp yer get yer feet under our man's table. Try an' get ter speak to 'im soon as yer can. Tell 'im yer've got five cases o' shoulder 'ams. Two quid a case, no questions asked. If 'e wants 'em let me know an' I'll let yer 'ave 'em.'

'It might 'elp,' Ben replied. 'This job ain't gonna be easy.'

'No one said it would be, Ben, but just do yer best, an' be very careful, especially now,' Gerry told him. 'Constantine's gonna be on 'is guard.'

Lana had been shocked to hear about Jimmy Bailey's mother, and the conversation around the tea table was dominated by the tragedy and the killing of Baz Smithson.

'I've seen 'im in the Crown many a time but I never got ter speak to 'im,' Frank remarked.

''E was one o' Constantine's minders,' Derek cut in. ''Im an' the Varley boys were always tergevver.'

'I 'ope you don't go gettin' chattin' ter people like that,' Ann said quickly. 'It's best ter keep out o' their way.'

'They don't interfere wiv us,' Derek told her. 'If they picked on one of our lads from the docks we'd go round mob-'anded an' sort 'em out.'

Lana felt that it wasn't the right time to tell her family she had decided to go out with Ben again and she sought to get the conversation moving in another direction. ''Ere, I wanna ask yer somefing, Dad,' she said suddenly. 'Do you know someone in the docks called Charlie Smedley?'

Both Frank and Derek smiled. 'Do we? 'E's a union official,' Frank told her. 'Why d'yer ask?'

'As a matter o' fact, Lottie showed me a picture of 'im as a kid when I popped in last night,' she replied.

'Yer don't mean ter say Charlie was one o' Lottie's kids?' Derek cut in.

Lana nodded, smiling. 'If it's the same Charlie Smedley.'

'Well, there can't be too many o' that name about,' Frank said.

'Nah, Charlie Smedley's gotta be a one-off,' Derek muttered with a wicked grin.

'Can you ask 'im?' Lana urged them.

'Just like that? Bloody 'ell, luv, Charlie Smedley's a very busy man,' Frank told her.

'Can yer try, it's very important,' she persisted.

Frank nodded. 'All right, I'll try. When was the picture taken, any idea?'

'Nineteen twenty-four,' she told him.

'What about Phoebe Francis? 'Ave yer found out where ter write to?' Ann asked.

Lana smiled smugly. 'It's done. She's rehearsin' fer a new musical called "Summer Madness" at the Royal Theatre in the Strand. One o' the gels at work knew all about it, so I wrote the letter durin' me dinner hour an' posted it straight off. She should get it first post termorrer.'

'Did I 'ear yer say Phoebe Francis? "The" Phoebe Francis?' Frank inquired with eyebrows raised. 'Don't tell me she was one o' Lottie's kids too.'

'She was, yer know,' Ann told him.

'Yer got about as much chance o' gettin' 'er ter come to an ole lady's birfday party as I've got o' winnin' the pools,' Frank remarked.

'Well, I'm gonna try anyway,' Lana said firmly.

Frank got out of his chair and put his arm around her shoulders. 'I 'ope yer succeed, luv,' he said kindly. 'If anyone can do it, you can.'

Chapter Thirteen

On Thursday morning Frank Johnson and his son Derek stepped off the tram outside the gates of Surrey Docks and immediately spotted Alan talking to a group of dockers.

'What's goin' on?' Derek asked him.

'We've got a meetin' over mannin',' Alan replied.

'They're tryin' ter piss-ball about wiv the gangs again,' one of the group said.

'It's a bloody disgrace,' another declared.

Alan raised his hands for calm. 'Now listen, you lot,' he said quickly. 'We was talkin' till eight o'clock last night an' we're in again this mornin' so we're askin' yer ter stay out until we came back ter yer.'

'That's bloody nice,' Frank growled.

'When's that gonna be?' Derek asked his brother.

'Charlie Smedley's on 'is way from Millwall Docks. 'E should be 'ere any minute now,' Alan told him. ''E'll 'old a quick meetin' outside Canada Dock.'

Buggsy Chapman strolled up to the group and gave Alan a sideways glance, then he slipped his thumbs into his waistcoat pocket and addressed the men. 'Bloody troublemakers,' he hollered. 'We got too many Bolshy bastards runnin' this union. We'll all end up out o' collar one o' these days. They'll end up shuttin' the docks the way fings are goin'.'

'Piss orf, Buggsy, yer stupid bastard,' a docker shouted at

him. 'It's idiots like you who'd let the guv'nors walk all over yer.'

Buggsy ran his hand over his spiky ginger hair and pulled a face. 'It's no good tryin' ter talk sense ter you lot,' he growled.

'Sod off,' an elderly docker told him sharply.

Word travelled quickly through the lines of dockworkers that Charlie Smedley had arrived and there was a general movement towards the Canada Dock gate. Frank took Alan's arm as they joined in the crush from the main road. 'I wanna try an' 'ave a word wiv Charlie Smedley afterwards,' he said.

'What about?' Alan asked, looking puzzled.

'About our Lana's little scheme,' he replied.

'Lana? What yer talkin' about?' Alan queried.

'You tell 'im, Derek,' Frank said as he spotted his gang coming along.

The men milled around at the gate and pressed forward to hear what Charlie was going to tell them. Someone found him a box to stand on and then the union official held up his hand for silence.

'This union's always done right by you lads an' you've always backed us right up ter the limit,' he began. 'So last night when the dock employers laid down a few new rules about mannin' levels we told 'em ter get stuffed. This union is all about stickin' to its guns when it comes ter servin' our members' interests. We're not cap-in-'and servants bowin' an' scrapin' to our lords an' masters. If they wanna change time-honoured custom an' practice then they'll 'ave ter come up wiv 'ard cash, as well as improved workin' arrangements an' all the ovver ramifications o' the deal. Never again will we fight each ovver fer a day's work. Never again will they be able ter split our ranks an' bring in scab labour. We go ter work wiv dignity these days, an' when we decide to invoke our right ter wivdraw our labour we do that wiv dignity too. One out, all out.'

The loud roar of approval echoed down the winding dock road and Charlie Smedley held his hand up again. 'Now listen carefully, lads,' he went on. 'This demonstration of solidarity will no doubt be noted by the dock employers. There's four 'eavily laden timber boats waitin' fer berthin' an' there's a Noskie boat due in termorrer. The pressure's on the employers, an' when that Russian captain sees the bottleneck 'e's gonna create merry bloody 'ell. Wiv that in mind your union representatives are goin' back ter talk tough. We'll be tellin' 'em that the mannin' levels are status quo or no soddin' go, an' we'll be reportin' back ter yer wiv answers at two o'clock terday. I believe we'll win the day, but if we don't succeed then you men will decide the outcome, not us.'

Applause and shouts of encouragement rang out, and then Charlie raised his voice. 'Two o'clock at the assembly 'all, lads,' he shouted.

Buggsy Chapman walked away mumbling under his breath and one of the dockers nodded after him. ''E'll be well pissed by two o'clock,' he remarked.

'If 'e jumps up again an' shouts 'is mouth off like last time I'm gonna plant 'im,' another said.

Frank Johnson turned to Derek and smiled. 'C'mon,' he said, 'let's go an' get a cup o' tea an' a bacon sandwich.'

At midday Ben Ferris walked into the saloon bar of the Crown and Anchor and ordered a drink. He could hear a continuous buzz of conversation coming from the public bar and he caught the barman's eye. 'What's goin' on in there?' he asked.

'There's a stoppage at the Surrey,' he was told. 'It's bin packed out in there since we opened.'

Ben stood at the counter sipping his bitter and at ten minutes past the hour Mick Constantine came into the bar along with Butcher Carberry. He gave Ben a brief acknowledging nod and ordered drinks.

'What's that racket?' Carberry asked.

'Trouble at the Surrey by all accounts,' Ben told him.

'Lazy bastards,' Constantine growled. 'That lot'll go out on strike at the drop of an 'at.'

Carberry was eager to familiarise himself with the locals

and he turned to the gang boss and nodded towards Ben. 'Who's 'e?' he asked quietly.

'This is Ben Ferris,' Constantine replied. 'I was tellin' you about 'im.'

Butcher Carberry grinned widely, showing a gold front tooth. 'So this is the geezer who locked your boys in the cellar,' he said.

Ben smiled and looked at the gang boss, rubbing the bridge of his nose with his fingertips. 'It was all sorted,' he replied.

Constantine gave him a crooked smile. 'There was no 'ard feelin's.'

'None whatsoever,' Ben said quickly.

'You 'eard about Baz, I take it?' the villain queried.

'Yeah, I'm very sorry,' Ben told him.

'Baz was a good'un. Someone's gonna pay fer it, that's fer sure,' Constantine growled.

Ben took a sip from his glass. 'I wanted to 'ave a word wiv yer about a bit o' gear, Mick,' he told him, 'but I realise it's not the right time. It'll keep.'

Constantine's dark eyes bored into him. 'Business is business. It 'as ter go on,' he said. 'What yer got?'

'I got some shoulder 'ams. Two quid a case.'

''Ow many?'

'Five.'

Constantine did not show any enthusiasm. 'Come ter me wiv a lorryload an' I might be interested,' he replied. 'Five cases ain't werf the aggro.'

'Yeah, sure,' Ben said with a shrug of his shoulders. 'I can place 'em OK but I thought I'd give yer the first refusal.'

'That's very big of yer,' the gang boss said sarcastically. 'Who's sellin' 'em, the Carmichael boys?'

Ben shook his head. 'I don't do any dealin's wiv those scheisters.'

'Since when?' Constantine asked him.

Ben sensed that the villain had somehow got to know about

his last transaction and he was quick with an answer. 'Since the stockin's.'

'Do yerself a favour an' stay clear o' those two,' Constantine told him. 'They're in the frame fer a pull, an' when the cozzers start steamin' into 'em their bottles'll go all over the place.'

'Fanks fer the warnin',' Ben said appreciatively.

Butcher Carberry had been listening to the conversation and he turned towards Ben. 'So yer in the buyin' an' sellin' business,' he said with a mocking smile on his thick lips.

Constantine grinned. 'Ben's a jack of all trades, ain't yer, my son?'

The young man felt the anger rising inside him at the sneering remarks but he knew that rising to the bait would do no good. 'I s'pose yer could say that,' he replied calmly.

''E likes a flutter on the gee-gees, but sometimes 'e gets a bit reckless,' Constantine went on. 'At least 'e pays 'is debts.'

Carberry grinned at the young chancer. 'What about cards? D'yer like a game o' cards?' he asked.

'Yeah, when I can get a game,' Ben told him.

'We've got a poker session 'ere on Sunday night,' Butcher said. 'If yer fancy yer chances come along. Tell the barman what yer've come for an' 'e'll let yer frew the bar.'

'I might just do that,' Ben replied.

'We got some business to attend to so we'll see yer later,' Constantine told him.

Ben took the summary dismissal calmly though he was fuming inside. 'Yeah, I gotta get goin',' he replied.

Constantine watched the young man drain his glass and walk quickly out of the bar, then he turned to Carberry. ''E's a loser,' he said. 'Don't take no IOUs from 'im.'

''E don't feel right,' the minder remarked. ''E ain't the sort who'd be sniffin' round fer somefing, is 'e?'

''E could be,' Constantine told him. 'Get someone ter keep an eye on 'im. I don't trust 'im.'

The dockers from the Surrey filed into the large assembly

hall in Rotherhithe and took their seats. In front of them the deserted platform was already set up with a long trestle-table and chairs and a microphone. Frank Johnson and Derek arrived early along with some of their friends, and they sat down near the front. A buzz of expectation grew as the union officials walked in from the side of the dais and took their seats. Charlie Smedley sat behind the table microphone and he flicked it once or twice to make sure it was working.

'Righto, lads, simmer down,' he said, his amplified voice resonating throughout the packed hall.

'Give us the bad news, Charlie,' one of the wits called out.

Charlie's face broke into a smile, then he pulled out his tobacco tin, a sure sign to all those who knew him well that the union official had something important to say.

'Are we gonna get on wiv it or not?' a loud voice called out from the back.

'Shut yer noise, Buggsy,' someone told him.

When Charlie had finished rolling a cigarette he slid his tobacco tin to one side and looked around the hall slowly. 'Right then,' he began. 'It seems that we were bein' blamed fer the snarl-up on the river. The turn-round rate wasn't acceptable ter the employers an' in their wisdom they decided to institute extra gangs on a reduced bonus-share scheme. Now you all know that we told 'em ter piss orf. Our argument was that the bonus rate was set for the present mannin' levels, an' we're not in the business o' takin' the bread out of our mates' mouths, 'cos that's what it would mean. Secondly, we informed the employers that extra gangs workin' in the 'olds an' on the quayside constitute a danger ter life an' limb. If we're fallin' over each ovver we can't be expected ter watch out fer each ovver in the way we do now. Wiv the present mannin' levels we've 'ad two fatalities in the last year, an' in my book that's two too many.'

'Too bloody true,' a voice rang out.

'All right, lads, be quiet an' listen carefully,' Charlie went on. 'We made it quite clear ter the employers that we would not consider any changes to our workin' practices. We also made it clear that, like them, we're concerned about the backlog. After a lot o' wranglin' we've managed ter get the next four Saturdays. That should clear the snarl-up, an' the overtime'll come in nice an' 'andy, what wiv Christmas comin' on.'

'What's the catch?' a voice called out.

'Yeah, what's the catch?' another echoed.

'Now listen, lads,' Charlie continued. 'Yer know that ter get a bit o' jam yer gotta give up a slice o' bread. We get the Saturdays if we start workin' number six berf.'

A mumble of voices started and grew louder, and then Buggsy Chapman's voice was heard above the din. ''E's bent. They're all bloody bent.'

'Sit down, Buggsy,' someone shouted at him.

'Shut yer trap, Buggsy.'

The drunken docker stood swaying in the aisle, trying to focus his eyes. 'What they pay yer, Charlie?' he slurred as he staggered towards the dais.

'Take yer seat, Buggsy,' the official said calmly.

'Don't you tell me ter sit down,' the inebriate went on. 'I know me rights. I can speak.'

'Not while I got the floor yer can't,' Charlie grated.

'Who's gonna stop me?' Buggsy shouted, raising his fists.

'I will fer one,' a diminutive docker said, jumping up and making for the drunk.

Frank Johnson grabbed the elderly man. 'Take it easy, pop,' he said quietly. 'The silly git's pissed out of 'is brains.'

'What poxy brains?' the docker growled.

'Right. I'm callin' on the stewards ter remove that man from the hall,' Charlie's voice boomed out over the microphone.

Two burly dockers took the dissenter by the arms and he struggled as they frogmarched him through the rear door.

'Now maybe we can get back ter some sort o' sense,' Charlie

sighed. 'As I said, we 'ave ter give a bit ter get a bit an' that means we work number six berf.'

A hand flew up and Charlie pointed over. 'Yes?'

'I thought we'd banned workin' there fer safety reasons?' the docker queried.

'Yes, we did, but the employers 'ave agreed ter let the construction go on over the weekend,' Charlie replied. 'We 'ave their assurances that the quayside will be levelled by Monday mornin'.'

'Yeah, but the crane won't be ready,' the docker went on.

'It'll be ready by Monday week,' Charlie told him. 'In the meantime they'll bring in a mobile crane. OK, it'll mean the job'll take longer but the safety aspect won't alter. We'll change the gang daily so yer'll all 'ave a taste. Fer one day's 'ard collar yer all gonna get four Saturdays. I'd say that's a fair deal.'

Alan Johnson leaned over and whispered something to the official.

'Oh yeah, I fergot ter tell yer,' Charlie added. 'The employers 'ave agreed to up the bonus on number six as a token o' goodwill, an' we've given assurances that the turn-round times on that quay will be the same as the rest. It means yer gotta pull yer fingers out. OK?'

When the mumbling died down a little Charlie Smedley spoke into the microphone again. 'If there's no more questions we'll 'ave a show of 'ands. All those in favour of acceptin' our recommendations raise yer 'and.'

With one exception everyone's hand went up.

'All those against.'

The little docker who had tried to get at Buggsy put his hand up.

'Any abstentions?'

No one moved.

'Right then. That's two 'undred an' forty-seven for, an' one against.'

A docker who was sitting next to the little elderly one nudged him in the ribs. 'Oi. Why did you vote against it, Percy?'

he asked with a puzzled look on his face. 'You said you was all for it.'

'So I am,' the man replied.

'Well, what the bleedin' 'ell are yer playin' at?'

'It never does to 'ave unanimous results,' he explained. 'The employers'll fink we're like a lot o' sheep.'

The men spilled out into the cold autumn air, feeling happy that a strike had been averted. Charlie Smedley was happy too as he shook hands with various dockers.

'Yer did well, Charlie,' Alan told him.

'They're a sensible bunch o' lads at the Surrey,' he replied.

'Charlie?'

'Yeah?'

''Ave yer got five minutes?'

'Sure. What is it?'

'It's a bit personal.'

'Oh?'

'Does the name Lottie Curtis mean anyfing to yer?'

Charlie Smedley stopped dead in his tracks. 'Yer mean Aunt Lottie Curtis?' he replied with a startled expression on his face.

'I fink we'd better pop in the labour club fer a pint,' Alan told him. 'I got somefing ter discuss wiv yer.'

Chapter Fourteen

Frank Johnson slumped down in his favourite armchair by the warm fire and sighed with contentment as he rubbed a large hand over his middle. 'That was very welcome,' he told Ann.

She leaned back in the armchair facing him and kicked off her shoes. 'Anyone'd fink yer'd bin 'ard at it all day long,' she said with a mocking smile. 'I dunno, you blokes seem ter walk out fer the least little fing. It's a good job us wives an' muvvers don't all decide ter go on strike.'

Frank gave her a wide grin. 'Yeah, but we treat you right, an' that's the difference,' he replied. 'Anyway it wasn't a strike, it was a stoppage.'

'Strike, stoppage, it's all the same,' Ann persisted. 'Yer lost a day's pay.'

Frank drew himself up in the armchair and leaned forward to make his point. 'Yer gotta remember that we've 'ad a long 'ard fight ter get better workin' conditions in the dock industry, luv. You know that as well as anybody,' he reminded her. 'We've gotta make sure that it don't all get taken away. It's always the same. Fings are runnin' smoothly an' then some new Jack-the-lad of a manager pops up an' decides that 'e can make savin's which'll put 'im in a good light wiv the bosses. People on the outside don't always understand that an' they tar all us trade unionists wiv the same brush. We're all lazy good-fer-nuffing gits who don't wanna do any collar. I'd like ter see some o' them 'ave ter do what we do.'

Ann smiled disarmingly. 'I was only windin' yer up, Frank,' she told him. 'I know it ain't easy. I've seen you an' our Derek come 'ome some nights fair worn out an' soaked ter the skin.'

Frank was satisfied and he leaned back in his chair once more. 'To change the subject, Lana was pleased about ole Charlie Smedley, wasn't she?' he said. 'Did you see 'er face light up when we told 'er Charlie 'ad promised ter be there?'

Ann nodded. 'I bet 'e was taken aback, wasn't 'e?'

Frank smiled at the recollection. 'When me an' Derek walked in the labour club fer a pint after the meetin' we saw our Alan chattin' ter Charlie in a corner. Anyway, Alan beckoned us over an' we 'ad a nice little confab. Charlie's eyes filled up as 'e was talkin' about ole Lottie. 'E remembered ole Bill Curtis an' the camera. It was just like our Lana told us.'

'Did 'e say why 'e never kept in touch?' Ann asked him.

Frank shrugged his broad shoulders. 'Charlie just said it was one o' those fings. 'E went back ter live wiv 'is muvver an' there was a lot o' growin' up ter do. 'E told us that they moved quite a lot an' then there was the war. 'E was surprised the ole lady was still alive.'

Ann sighed sadly. 'Kids tend ter take so much fer granted, don't they?' she remarked. ''Alf the time they don't realise the sacrifices made.'

'Yeah, yer right there,' Frank agreed.

Ann moved her feet away from the heat of the fire and ran her fingers over her chin. 'Lana was tellin' me before you an' Derek came in that she's back wiv Ben.'

Frank puffed loudly. 'I don't fink that gel knows 'er own mind,' he growled.

Ann shrugged. 'That's what I told 'er, but she said that Ben 'ad promised ter change. She said that this was gonna be 'is last chance.'

'A leopard never changes its spots,' Frank replied. 'She'll learn the 'ard way.'

'I wouldn't like ter see 'er get 'urt,' Ann said. 'She can be so trustin' at times.'

'Yeah, well p'raps it's time you an' 'er 'ad a good chat,' Frank suggested. 'She might take notice o' you. I can't talk to 'er.'

'An' why not?' Ann retorted. 'You're 'er farvver after all.'

'C'mon, luv, I can't talk about that sort o' fing.'

'What sort o' fing?'

'You know what I mean,' Frank said grimacing. 'Like if she's sleepin' wiv 'im or about precautions.'

'Well, I should 'ave thought it was obvious they're sleepin' tergevver,' Ann said quickly. 'The gel's not a kid. She's twenty-five an' 'e's a few years older. As fer precautions, I 'ad a good talk to 'er about that ages ago.'

Frank looked bemused. 'I dunno what ter fink,' he sighed.

'Well, if *you* don't I'm sure *I* don't,' Ann concluded, puffing despairingly.

''Ere, changin' the subject,' Frank piped up, 'what response d'yer fink Lana's gonna get ter that letter she sent off?'

'Gawd knows,' Ann replied. 'I can't see Phoebe Francis turnin' up in Saddler Street fer an ole lady's birfday party, can you?'

Frank shook his head. 'I don't s'pose she'll even bovver ter reply.'

'We'll just 'ave ter wait an' see,' Ann told him. 'Anyway I gotta pop in next door an' see Lottie. I promised Lana I'd break it to 'er about Jimmy Bailey's muvver.'

'P'raps she's already 'eard,' Frank said.

'I don't fink so,' Ann replied. 'It's bin too cold fer 'er ter stand at the door terday, unless Bella Wickstead's knocked wiv the news.'

Frank nestled down in his comfortable armchair. 'I'm gonna 'ave a bit o' shut-eye,' he announced. 'Derek wanted me ter go up the Crown ternight but I wasn't up to it. Anyway they're only playin' darts.'

'You ain't got a chill comin' on, 'ave yer?' Ann asked with concern.

'Nah, I'm just too warm ter move,' Frank told her.

The stage director walked quickly to the wings with his hand held to his forehead in a show of petulance and then he spun round to face the dance troupe. 'For God's sake, Sophie,' he whined. 'Space. Think space. This is supposed to be a musical, not a sex orgy. If I wanted you to mount Felix I'd have said so.'

The tittering stopped suddenly when Miles Lester stamped his foot down hard on the boards. 'Now come on. The show opens next week and you still look very ragged. Let's try this once more, shall we? And Jennie, change places with Margo, will you? Now try to remember the scene. The Count has just announced his betrothal and the village is very proud that he has selected one of their own. The village maidens dance through the streets in celebration. Just now you looked like you were all in mourning. Big smiles please, ladies, and Sophie, remember to keep your distance from Felix. He's supposed to be the burgomaster of Frensdorf and a nasty piece of work. All right, darling?'

The long-legged chorus girl flashed her white teeth and fluttered her eyelashes. 'Yes, Mr Lester.'

The director shook his head in despair and minced over to the pianist with his hand on his hip. 'Julian, we'll take it from the beginning once more. Introduction when you're ready, dearie,' he urged him, turning to face the dance troupe. 'Positions please,' he ordered, clapping his hands.

As the pianist tickled the keys and the line of scantily clad maidens danced in single file from the back of the steps, Miles Lester closed his eyes and pressed his fingers to his temple in anguish. 'Felix, the Count's rejected your daughter and you're supposed to be overwrought. Why are you grinning like a bloody idiot? What are you, a masochist?'

The pianist was not sure whether to continue or not and neither was Margo who was leading the troupe. The dancers tripped and stumbled into each other which sent the director into another of his stamping tantrums and he finally collapsed against the piano, holding his head in his hands.

'You did that on purpose, you bitch,' Jennie hissed to Margo.

'What was I supposed to do, dance right out of the theatre?' Margo growled.

'Oh, go and get screwed,' Jennie countered.

Felix meanwhile was being sensitive. 'It's the red footlight, Miles. It's placed too far to one side. It's lighting me up all wrong,' he moaned.

'A smile's a smile, Felix, and I don't care if the footlight's down the other end of Southend pier in the pissing bloody rain.' Miles shuddered with indignation. 'Think of something terrible, for pity's sake. Your cat's been run over, you've got the clap you so richly deserve, you've lost your handbag. Improvisation, please.'

The assembly looked up at the sound of the auditorium door opening and closing and they all stood in reverence as the tall, elegant woman dressed in an ankle-length fur coat and cossack hat swayed down the aisle on the arm of Sonny Edelmann, who was impeccably dressed in a grey suit and matching fedora, his shoes partially concealed beneath sand-coloured spats. They reached the orchestra pit and Phoebe Francis smiled sweetly at Miles Lester and the rest of the cast in turn.

'Welcome to our star and the producer of "Summer Madness",' the director said with an exaggerated sweep of his arm.

The resulting applause was quickly stilled by Phoebe as she held up her hands. 'Please, boys and girls. Don't let us distract you from your rehearsal,' she purred. 'I'd just like to say that Mr Edelmann and I do appreciate you staying on this evening to accommodate us. I'm sure that you will join with me in thanking our producer who has kindly agreed to grace us with his presence this evening.'

The cast applauded once more and Phoebe smiled indulgently. 'Mr Edelmann would like to say a few words.'

The impresario bowed stiffly to the troupe. 'I'm sure beyond any doubt whatsoever that "Summer Madness" will wow the public and critics alike,' he told them. 'What's more, it will make everyone recognise once more the incomparable talent that is our own Phoebe Francis.'

The cast applauded yet again and smiled graciously as Phoebe milked the feigned adulation. Sonny Edelmann took her hand and held it out as though she were taking a curtain call.

'Swanky bitch,' Margo whispered to Jennie.

'Syphilitic ponce,' Jennie contributed.

Felix fluttered his eyelashes at the impresario and sashayed over to his position at the side of the stage. Miles Lester hurried over to him, giving the audience of two a quick smile en route.

'Mess this up, Felix, and I'll neuter you, so help me,' he said out of the corner of his mouth, signalling the pianist to begin.

The rehearsal resumed and Miles Lester was in transports of ecstasy as the whole scene went off without a single hitch. The producer nodded in tune with the music, his lecherous eye on Margo Kellerman, the lead dancer, while Phoebe Francis sat rigid, a fixed smile on her beautiful face, her mind on other things. Only a few days ago the newshounds had gathered to interview the star of the eagerly awaited new musical, and she had been most forthcoming.

'Miss Francis. Is it true that you spent the whole of your childhood in India?'

'Yes. My father was in the Colonial Service.'

'Miss Francis. What about your mother?'

'My mother was governess to the children of the Maharajah of Jaipur.'

'Miss Francis. Is it true that the Maharajah wanted to marry you?'

'Yes, that is true.'

'Why did you refuse him?'

'I was already in love with a young subaltern in the Indian Army.'

'But you never married?'

'We became engaged to marry but two months later he was killed in a skirmish on the North-West Frontier.'

'Miss Francis. Have you any plans to marry now?'

'That would be telling.'

Phoebe had given out just enough details of her fictitious life to whet the appetite of the press, and the possibility of a romance with Sonny Edelmann made them eager for more disclosures. One particular Sunday paper already had an article ready for publication linking her with the impresario and other papers were out to upstage it. It was all very pleasing to the publicity-conscious West End star, until the letter had dropped through her door stamped with a Bermondsey postmark.

Felix was in top form as he danced the solo and Sonny warmed to him, but Phoebe hardly noticed. Damn the woman, she thought. Damn and blast the impertinence. She would have to ignore it, of course. Sonny was loaded, and he was paying her a lot of attention. He would be horrified to discover that her early life was much less glamorous than he had been led to believe. It was unthinkable that she could even consider the request under the circumstances. The old lady was eighty, for God's sake, and she would most likely be senile at that age, dribbling in a chair. She would just forget the letter and concentrate on the matter in hand: snaring Sonny Edelmann before someone else did.

A gusting wind carried spots of rain as it swept through the Bermondsey backstreets, and people banked up their fires and placed mats against their front doors. In the cosy flat in River Lane Lana moved over slightly on the settee as Ben came and sat down close to her.

'Do yer wanna go out or shall we stay 'ere?' he asked.

'It's up ter you,' she replied.

Ben sought to ease the tension by putting his arm around

her shoulders but she remained rigid. 'I'd sooner stay in,' he said, smiling at her. 'It's nice an' cosy by the fire.'

Lana felt the pressure of his hand on her arm and she let him pull her to him. His lips were close to hers and she could smell his aftershave and the peppermint on his breath. She closed her eyes as she submitted and felt the soft caress of his lips as they met hers. The kiss was tender at first but then as he leant over her it became urgent. She brought her hand up and ran her fingers through the thick dark hair on the back of his neck as her excitement grew. It was hard to resist him, she sighed. His lovemaking thrilled her and his hands upon her body made her feel ecstatic. She had vowed to be cool, to let him see that she meant every word she had said but now nothing mattered, only the warmth of his lovemaking that stoked the fire in her belly. She was his to love and she moved her body to accommodate his searching fingers as he reached inside her thigh. She felt him shiver with pleasure as he felt her stocking-top and above it her smooth skin. She should call a halt, she thought, make him wait and suffer a little more but she found it impossible.

'I've missed yer badly,' he whispered into her ear.

The feel of his lips as he nibbled her neck sent shivers of pleasure along her spine and she pushed her hips forward, urging him to explore her completely.

'I want you, Lana,' he gasped, the tips of his fingers touching her wet lips.

She shuddered to feel him and groaned in reply, 'I want you too.'

Ben tried to slide her skirt up over her thighs but she stopped him. 'Not 'ere,' she said breathlessly.

He stood up, his face flushed with expectancy and he took her hands in his, pulling her up to him. They kissed, sucking shared pleasure with their open mouths and then Ben broke away from her embrace, his arm around her waist as he led her into the bedroom.

Outside the wind was rising and large spots of rain spattered against the window as the lovers embraced, helping each other to undress with a clumsy urgency. Lana undid her bra and as it fell to the floor she pulled his head down on to her naked bosom. His lips found her hard nipples and she breathed out a deep sigh as he knelt down in front of her, his lips parted, licking her flat belly with his tongue. She passed her fingers through his hair as they fell back on to the bed, arching herself as he pulled off her knickers. She felt his swollen sex against her and she thrust forward impatiently. Her body was crying out for him and she knew he could not contain himself much longer. He came into her quickly and she wrapped her legs around his waist, twisting hard against him as he made love to her.

'Oh God!' she cried, feeling him more deeply and completely than she had ever felt him before.

Ben's thrusting grew faster as the moment of fulfilment drew near and then when he heard her groan and felt her muscles tighten around him his passion suddenly exploded.

'Was it good?' he whispered as they lay together in the darkness.

'The best ever,' she sighed.

A gust of wind sent rain sheeting against the windowpane and a flash of lightning split the night sky. The loud roll of thunder made Lana jump and she buried her head in Ben's chest. He was unreliable, unpredictable and often infuriating, she thought, but at this moment, as his arms encircled her and his body pressed against hers, it was of little importance. She felt safe, secure and happy, and this was all that mattered.

Chapter Fifteen

Gerry Knowland looked long-faced as he listened to a tearful Mandy Brophy.

'I've got no choice,' she sobbed. 'Mick set me up in the flat an' 'e's bin good ter me. What am I s'posed ter do, give it all up, put meself back on the street? God Almighty, Gerry, I don't wanna go back ter that life again.'

'There's no need to,' he told her, squeezing her hand across the table. 'I'll look after you. We can slip away from London fer a couple o' weeks.'

'Then what?' she replied sharply. 'Talk sense, Gerry. 'E'd find me an' then I'd suffer. An' what about you? Just fink about it sensibly. Mick would find out about us as sure as God made little apples.'

Gerry forced a grin at her cute turn of phrase. 'Me an' you are seein' each ovver already an' 'e 'asn't found out so far,' he said positively.

'Yeah, but we've bin discreet an' 'e's not 'ad any reason ter suspect me. I'm there for 'im most o' the time,' she reminded him.

'Turn 'im down, Mandy,' he urged. 'Don't sell yer soul ter that no-good bastard.'

Mandy dabbed at her eyes, happy with her performance. It had been a hard slog getting Mick Constantine around to her way of thinking. He had shied away from talk of marriage until his estranged wife filed for divorce. He had always thought that they might get back together one day and had refused to take steps to end the marriage, despite the fact that he and his wife had been separated for over five years.

'I can't, Gerry,' she told him.

'What about us?' he asked.

'We can still meet occasionally, after a while,' she replied. 'Nuffing need change.'

'You won't be 'appy bein' married to 'im, Mandy,' he told her. 'It's OK now while 'e treats you like a tom. Livin' wiv 'im all the time is gonna be a different story.'

She shrugged her shoulders and blew hard into her handkerchief. 'I'm gonna go along wiv it, there's no ovver way,' she said, pulling her hands away from his.

'I just 'ope this marriage don't bring yer a lot o' grief, Mandy,' he sighed. 'Constantine's made enemies an' one day someone's likely ter get 'im, minders or not.'

The shapely young woman ran her hand over her loose blonde hair and stood up. 'I must go now,' she said anxiously. 'I'll be in touch as soon as it's safe.'

Gerry squeezed her hand in parting and then watched from his table in the Soho coffee house as she hurried out. He thought about last night in the small Bloomsbury hotel and now he understood the reason for her strange behaviour. She had been tense and different, and she had obviously agonised over telling him there and then about her decision. She was a vibrant woman, but still a child in many ways. She needed the sort of protection and cosseting that Mick Constantine was able to provide. His money paid for her flat and provided her with expensive clothes, but Gerry felt sure that it could never buy the villain her love.

He paid the bill and walked out into the raw air. Sometimes things are done for the best, he reasoned. The rivalry between the Maltese and the Constantine gang was becoming dangerously charged up and he had to keep a clear head, which an affair with the gang boss's woman made difficult at the best of times.

Lottie Curtis dabbed at her eyes with a small lace handkerchief and shook her head sadly. 'What a terrible fing to 'appen,' she said. ''E'll blame 'imself fer not bein' there.'

Ann Johnson nodded. 'I'm sure 'e will, but it would 'ave 'appened some time or anuvver,' she replied. 'The woman's mind was made up an' she just needed the opportunity. Anyway there's no use you upsettin' yerself over the feller. 'E's a man now an' dyin' is part o' livin', as my ole mum used ter say. Jimmy'll be OK. I expect 'e'll be round ter see yer soon.'

Lottie gave her next-door neighbour a smile. 'Yeah, 'e'll be round ter see me soon,' she said. 'Your Lana told me she'll pop in again soon as well. I was showin' 'er all me snaps. She was askin' lots o' questions about those kids o' mine an' she seemed really interested.'

Ann hid a smile. If all went well the old lady was going to have a very big surprise on her birthday. At least one of the children she fostered had promised to be there, and there was still the letter Lana had sent to Phoebe Francis. 'It's November the first terday. It'll be Christmas before we know it,' she remarked.

'I'll be eighty on Christmas Eve,' Lottie said proudly.

'That's right, so yer will,' Ann replied casually.

'They brought Freddie Williams ter me on Christmas Eve,' Lottie told her. 'Now let me see. It was after Phoebe left. Yeah, that's right. It'd be nineteen thirteen, 'cos she went back to 'er muvver in the April o' that year.'

'It's wonderful 'ow yer remember all their names,' Ann said with a smile.

'Well, they was like me own, an' yer never ferget yer kids' names, do yer?' Lottie chuckled.

'Not unless yer name's Slosher Barnard,' Ann replied grinning. 'Remember 'im? The one who lived at number nine.

That ole goat used ter come 'ome from the pub well sloshed an' chuck 'is own kids away from the door. 'E thought they belonged ter somebody else.'

'Yeah, I remember 'im,' Lottie said nodding. 'My Bill gave 'im a good 'idin' one night. Right outside Slosher's front door it was. That was over kids. Bill was walkin' past an' 'e saw Slosher clout one 'is kids round the 'ead. Bill couldn't stand kids gettin' clumped, 'specially round the 'ead. Anyway 'e gave 'im a mouthful an' Slosher told 'im ter piss orf or 'e'd get the same. Yer couldn't say anyfing like that ter my Bill an' get away wiv it. Bill ups an' gives 'im one an' Slosher gives 'im one back so Bill set about 'im. Knocked 'im out cold 'e did. Slosher's wife came out an' chucked a bucket o' dirty water over 'im as 'e lay there, then she chucked the empty bucket at Bill. She was as scatty as 'er ole man.'

'I wonder what 'appened ter that family,' Ann remarked.

'They got chucked out at the finish,' Lottie told her. 'Couldn't pay the rent. I s'pose some poor cow got ter foster the kids. I was glad it wasn't me. They was a wild lot, the Barnards.'

'You was tellin' me about that lad yer took in on Christmas Eve,' Ann prompted her. 'What was 'is name, Williams?'

'Yeah, that's right, Freddie Williams,' the old lady replied. 'Smashin' little kid 'e was. Stayed wiv us fer a year. Blimey, that was a Christmas that was. Bill wasn't gettin' much work an' the money was really tight. At least the Sisters from St Mary's brought a few presents fer the boy an' we scraped a few bob tergevver. If yer'd 'ave seen 'is face. I don't fink 'e'd ever 'ad a present given 'im before.'

'Why was 'e sent ter yer?' Ann asked her.

'The lad's muvver died an' the farvver was away at sea,' Lottie explained. 'A year later the farvver married again an' 'e took little Freddie back. Grew up a lovely young man. Terrible fing it was.'

Ann saw the sad, faraway look in the old lady's eyes. 'What 'appened?' she asked.

'Young Freddie joined the navy at the outbreak o' war. 'E went down wiv the *Prince o' Wales* out in the Far East,' she said with a deep sigh. 'I got a photo of 'im in me album. 'Ere, I'll show it ter yer.'

Ann saw her reaching down by her rocking chair and she quickly picked the thick album up for her. Lottie took out a pair of glasses from her apron pocket and put them on before turning the padded cover. ''Ere we are,' she said. 'That's Freddie.'

'Who's the little boy standin' be'ind 'im?' Ann asked. 'Is 'e one o' your lads too?'

Lottie nodded fondly. 'That's Samuel. Samuel Selby. I got 'im just before Freddie left. Now that little mite made a success of 'is life. 'E's a barrister. I sometimes read bits in the paper about 'im. A couple o' months ago 'e was in a case at the Ole Bailey. Two years I 'ad 'im. It was the same ole story o' misery – muvver ill an' took in the infirmary, farvver unable ter cope wiv all the kids. I don't fink they wanted 'im back if the trufe was known. When she got better Sammy's muvver called round ter see me. Asked me if I could keep 'im a bit longer. It turned out ter be a year later when the boy finally went back ter live wiv 'em. Mind you, it was the church people at St Mary's who 'ad the final say.'

Ann had made a mental note of all Lottie had said but she could see that she wouldn't be learning very much more that evening. The old lady looked tired as she closed the album.

'Let me put it down beside yer, luv, an' I'll make yer a nice cuppa before I go,' she said kindly.

The old lady smiled. 'That'll be very nice,' she said as her eyelids drooped.

The weather was cold and flakes of snow dotted the purple robes of the Sisters of Mercy as they shivered on the doorstep. 'But there's no more room at the convent and we're desperate, Mrs Curtis.'

'Go. Leave this very minute or I'll fetch my 'usband.'

'Would you turn a child away on Christmas Eve?'

The young lad smiled between his protectors, his sunken eyes bright with fever and his cheeks hollow and pale. 'I could sleep in the stable,' he said in a tiny voice.

'You shall sleep in a warm bed with feather pillows and a soft eiderdown,' the proud woman told him. 'There's always room for one more in Saddler Street.'

Jimmy Bailey had been very busy making arrangements for his mother's funeral and sorting out her affairs, and he realised that he would have to get himself a dark suit and a white shirt. The Provident man was helpful in allowing him another cheque, despite the fact that there was still money owing on the previous one that his mother had taken out for new bedding. Lillian had cashed the two small insurance policies but these barely covered the funeral expenses, and Jimmy knew that it was going to be a tight squeeze from now on. The funeral had been arranged for the following Thursday, and as soon as it was over he would have to see about getting a job.

When he had finished his mug of tea the young man went out into the scullery and stood there for a few moments, staring down at the stone floor by the gas stove. He could still see his mother's lifeless body huddled there and he shuddered. I've got to pull myself together, he thought. There was still a lot to be done, and the house was looking very shabby. There would be friends and neighbours calling in to pay their respects and there wasn't a clean cup and saucer in the place. The parlour curtains were grubby too, and there was dust everywhere.

The knock on the front door startled him and he opened it to see Glenda standing there.

'I couldn't get round before, Jim,' she said. 'The little one's gone down wiv a sore froat an' 'e's very fretful. I 'ad ter wait till Bernie came in before I could leave 'im.'

Jimmy smiled at his petite younger sister and stepped back to let her in. 'It's all right, Glenda. I was just lookin' round ter see what I should do first,' he said. 'Sorry about the state o' the place but yer know 'ow it is.'

She went through and sat down in the cold parlour. 'Why 'aven't yer got a fire?' she asked him. 'Yer not out o' coal, are yer?'

'Nah, I wanted ter clean the grate first,' he told her. 'It needs black-leadin'.'

'Sod the black-leadin'. This place needs some warmth,' Glenda told him sharply. 'You light the fire an' I'll make us a pot o' tea. I need ter talk to yer.'

The cold, dreary afternoon suddenly felt less depressing as Jimmy walked away from the window and sat down in the tattered armchair. Glenda's red hair was always well groomed and her expressive green eyes seemed to radiate happiness, and even at this sad time her face was full of life.

'Don't let that tea get cold,' she told him.

He sat watching the flaring sticks under the coals for a few moments as he sipped his tea, then he looked up at Glenda. 'I was s'posed ter go fer a job terday but I couldn't manage it,' he said with a wry expression on his face. ''Ow's Bernie by the way? Still drivin' fer a livin'?'

'Yeah, 'e's fine,' Glenda replied. 'That's one o' the reasons I called round. They need a driver at 'is firm an' 'e's spoken fer you. It's a decent job, Jimmy, an' the pay ain't that bad, considerin'. They even get a uniform. Bernie looks right smart in 'is.'

'That's good news,' Jimmy said, his face brightening. ''Ow should I apply, by letter?'

'Nah, yer don't need ter do that,' she told him. 'Bernie said ter call in ter the firm next Friday. The transport manager knows the score about the funeral. 'E's expectin' yer between two an' three.'

Jimmy nodded enthusiastically. 'It sounds promisin',' he said.

'Yer'll get the job, no sweat,' Glenda said smiling.

'I'll 'ave the dark suit. I could go ter the interview in that, couldn't I?' he suggested.

'Just as long as yer don't go in that blue mac,' she replied quickly. 'Yer look a bit iffy in that.'

'Well, fanks very much,' Jimmy said with a grin.

Glenda moved forward in her chair. 'Now listen, Jimmy, the ovver reason I called round was this.'

'What is it?' he asked as she passed him an envelope.

'Open it.'

'Christ, there's twenty pounds 'ere,' he said quickly.

'It's yours,' she told him.

'I don't understand.'

'It's the money from the policy me an' Bernie took out on Mum.'

'But it's yours.'

'We want you to 'ave it.'

'I can't take this,' he said firmly.

'Yer've got to,' Glenda replied. 'Bernie won't like it if yer don't. Yer know 'ow funny 'e gets at times.'

'But it's not right,' Jimmy argued.

'Now, you listen 'ere,' Glenda said in a determined voice. 'Those ovver two policies'll cover the funeral expenses an' this is extra. If anyone needs it, you do. Just look at yourself. You ain't got a coat ter go out in except that ole gran'farvver's raincoat. Yer shoes are fallin' ter pieces an' you ain't got a decent shirt. Gawd knows what people must fink of yer.'

'The money's bin tight an' there was a lot o' debts ter settle,' he said quietly.

'Exactly. And fer that reason me an' Bernie decided that your need is greater than ours,' she told him. 'Besides, it's a little token of our appreciation. Me an' Lillian could turn our backs on this place, but you couldn't. It was you who 'ad ter get up in the night ter see ter Mum. It was you who 'ad ter get meals, clean the place an' give up yer own free time ter care for 'er. All right, me an' Lillian did what we could, but it's nuffing compared to what you've done fer Mum over the years. You're thirty years of age an' there should be someone in yer life, Jimmy, but what chance 'ave you 'ad? Take the money an' rig yerself out. Go out an' get yerself a nice gel.

See a bit o' life an' start to enjoy yerself. If anyone deserves it, you do.'

The young man's eyes filled with tears and he turned away in embarrassment. Glenda stood up and went to him, gently touching his arm. 'You always looked after us when we were kids, 'specially when Mum was ill,' she said in a soft voice as she patted his back supportively. 'Now we're all grown up there's nuffing ter say we can't give a little bit back.'

Outside the weather was deteriorating, but in the parlour the fire burned brightly and a cheery warmth filled the room.

Chapter Sixteen

The November Sunday started cold, with a wet mist drifting in from the river, and as fires were lit and smoke poured out from countless chimneys the white mist became a yellow fog, soot-laden and sulphurous. The Bermondsey backstreets echoed with the sound of footsteps as people went to church and later to the pubs, but by mid-afternoon it was quiet, the silence broken only by the occasional muffled sounds of foghorns and tug whistles.

At number five Saddler Street Frank Johnson dozed in his favourite armchair beside a warm fire, a discarded *News of the World* at his feet. Derek sat facing him, his legs sprawled out and his head forward on his chest as he slept off the effects of the lunchtime drink and the large roast dinner. Their combined snoring and occasional grunts sent Ann and Lana out into the scullery to talk and the older woman puffed loudly as she sat down at the table. 'There's no chance o' gettin' near that fire wiv them two splayed out in there,' she said.

Lana smiled as she pulled another chair up to the table. 'So what d'yer reckon I should do then?' she asked.

'Well, if I were you I'd write 'im a letter, the same as yer did wiv that Francis woman,' Ann replied.

'Yeah, I s'pose that'd be the best bet, though she's not bovvered ter reply yet,' Lana remarked.

'Yer gotta give 'er time,' Ann told her. 'After all, she must be kept pretty busy wiv that new musical. I was readin' about it in yesterday's paper. They reckon it's gonna be a smashin' show.'

Lana nodded. 'Yeah, I can understand she must be busy, but it wouldn't take a minute ter drop a few lines an' say yes or no.'

'Anyway yer might 'ave more luck wiv this Selby bloke,' Ann said encouragingly.

'Where would I get 'is address from?' Lana asked her.

'It could be in the phone book, but I doubt it,' she replied. 'I fink all them barristers 'ave offices over the Temple. Inns o' Court they're called, I believe.'

'In that case I'll write to 'im ternight,' Lana said positively. 'That'll make one promise I've got an' two in the balance.'

'Countin' Freddie Williams who died in the war, an' Jimmy Bailey, that's five yer know of, so that leaves anuvver five ter find out about,' Ann said.

Lana nodded. 'I'm gonna pop in ter see Lottie later an' if she's up to it I'll get 'er chattin' again,' she said. 'I'll 'ave ter be careful not ter seem too nosy though, or she might smell a rat.'

'She would do,' Ann replied. 'There's no flies on our Lottie.'

Jimmy Bailey left his house in Abbey Street and walked towards Dockhead through the thickening fog. Normally he would have had his well-worn raincoat on, but today he had confidently left it behind. He had taken Glenda's advice and rigged himself out at Burton's, the men's outfitters at the Elephant and Castle who called themselves the fifty-shilling tailors. He had bought a dark grey worsted suit and two shirts, one white and the other blue, as well as a pair of lightweight black shoes. He had also bought a slim-Jim tie with a blue and black diagonal stripe. There was money enough for a cardigan as well and a visit to the barber shop on his way home, and as the young man made his way to Saddler Street he was feeling more self-confident than he had in a long time.

As he walked along the backstreet and stopped at number three Jimmy fiddled with the knot of his tie, tugged on his shirt cuffs and then glanced down at his polished shoes before raising the knocker. He was expecting Lottie to make some remark when she opened the door but he was taken aback to see Lana smiling at him.

''Ello, Jimmy. C'mon in,' she said.

When the young man walked into the cosy parlour Lottie got up from her chair and took his hand between hers. 'I'm very sorry to 'ear about yer mum, Jimmy,' she said softly. 'It must 'ave bin a terrible shock ter find 'er that way.'

The young man nodded slowly. 'The only comfort I've got is that at least she's out o' pain,' he replied.

Lottie held on to his hand until she had manoeuvred herself back into her rocking chair, then she looked him over. 'My, my, you do look smart,' she told him, turning to Lana. 'Doesn't 'e.'

The two young people exchanged glances and Lana noticed the sudden flush of his cheeks as he dropped his eyes.

'It's nice an' warm in 'ere,' he said quickly as he undid his coat. 'It's gettin' very foggy outside.'

'When's the funeral, son?' the old lady asked.

'Next Thursday,' he told her.

She dabbed at her eyes and sniffed loudly. 'I'd like ter go but I know I wouldn't be able ter manage it.'

'It's all right, Aunt Lottie,' he said as he bent over and patted her hand. 'I know yer'll be finkin' of us.'

Lana felt a warmness towards the young man as she stood there watching him. His appearance had surprised her. The suit fitted him perfectly and his blue shirt was freshly ironed, with the tie neatly knotted. His dark hair was combed back from his forehead and his clean-shaven face glowed with the heat of the room.

'Lottie was just gonna show me that album again,' she told him.

'Jimmy's seen it dozens o' times,' Lottie remarked. ''E can

get 'imself a cup o' tea while we 'ave a look.'

Outside the late-afternoon gloom had settled over the deserted street and the fog began to shift and swirl as a light breeze stirred. Inside the house Lana sat beside the old lady in an upright chair, occasionally glancing over at Jimmy as the pages of the album were carefully turned and another episode revealed.

'That's Freddie Williams, an' that little one in the background is Samuel Selby,' Lottie said. 'Freddie was killed in the war an' Samuel's a barrister now. I was tellin' yer mum about these two men when she popped in the ovver night.'

Lana was eager to learn about the rest of the children and she pointed at a photograph of two youngsters standing together in the street. 'Who are these, Lottie?' she asked her.

'That's Alice Critchley an' Morgan Jones,' the old lady replied. 'Two lovely little kids they were. I got them after the First World War was over. It was the followin' year as a matter o' fact. Nineteen nineteen. I couldn't do any fosterin' durin' the last two years of the war, yer see, 'cos I was on war-work at the Woolwich Arsenal. Fillin' shells I was. Bloody dangerous job.'

'They look 'appy enough,' Lana remarked, trying to prevent the old lady from wandering off the subject.

'Yeah, they were an 'appy couple o' souls,' Lottie went on. 'Always tergevver they was. Two an' a 'alf years I 'ad 'em. Sad fing was, they left the way they came, wivvin days of each ovver. The place was always so quiet after me children left. They say yer shouldn't get too attached ter fostered kids but it's easier said than done. I got ter love those little mites just like they was me own, an' ter tell yer the trufe I wouldn't 'ave wanted it any ovver way.'

''Ow old are they 'ere?' Lana enquired.

'Alice was five an' Morgan seven,' Lottie told her. 'Morgan was Welsh. 'Is farvver was a miner who got killed in a pit accident an' the boy's muvver brought 'im ter London. She went inter service at some posh place in Finsbury. The man o' the 'ouse got 'er pregnant an' she was forced ter go ter one o' those backstreet abortionists. Bloody butchers, that's all they were. Nearly died she did. That's 'ow I come ter get young Morgan.'

'What about Alice?' Lana prompted.

'Every child I got was out o' some sort o' tragedy or the ovver, an' Alice was no exception,' Lottie explained. 'That little mite's muvver was a prostitute. One night she took a man 'ome an' 'e cut 'er up. Terrible state she was in, by all accounts. Alice was in the ovver room when it 'appened. All the time she was wiv me she 'ad nightmares over it. She most likely still does if the trufe's known.'

'I don't s'pose yer know where they are now?' Lana asked.

Lottie screwed her face up. 'Both them kids lived in Bermon'sey an' I used ter see 'em from time ter time before the war started,' she replied. 'I 'eard that Morgan went in the army an' was captured by the Japs when Singapore fell, but I never 'eard anuvver word. 'E could be dead fer all I know.'

'What about Alice?'

'She got a job in a clothes factory an' then I 'eard she joined up as an army nurse at the outbreak o' war,' the old lady said as she stared down sadly at the photograph. 'There again, I never knew what 'appened to 'er.'

'I fink that's absolutely terrible,' Lana said in anger, glancing quickly over at Jimmy. 'All those children yer looked after an' not one of 'em ever bovvered ter visit yer afterwards, apart from Jimmy of course. I can't understand it.'

The old lady smiled indulgently. 'I used ter fink like that at one time,' she said quietly, 'but it was Farvver McCarfy who explained it all very nicely ter me. 'E said that when the children first came ter me they'd all suffered in one way or anuvver an' they were all frightened an' worried about what was gonna 'appen to 'em. In time, wiv love an' care, they all recovered enough ter pick up their lives wiv their families, an' they looked on me as yer would a port in a storm. Fer them ter come back an' visit me in their young years would 'ave bin a painful reminder o' why the nuns first brought 'em. In the fullness of time, wiv their own children growin' up around 'em, p'raps they remember me wiv love. I can't ask fer no more than that.'

Lana felt a lump rising in her throat and she stole a quick glance at Jimmy Bailey. He looked very sad and she could see the love for the old lady shining in his dark eyes. 'I'm sure they all remember yer wiv love, Lottie,' she said simply.

'Yeah, of course they do,' Jimmy said giving her a smile.

Lottie closed the book and set the rocking chair moving. 'I'm feelin' a little tired,' she told them. 'P'raps we can talk some more anuvver time.'

Lana stood up and gently took the album from the old lady's lap. 'We'll let ourselves out, luv,' she said quietly.

The two young people stepped out into the damp evening air and saw that the fog was clearing. Jimmy turned to Lana and gave her a shy smile. 'It was nice meetin' yer again,' he said. 'I felt I should call in after what 'appened wiv me muvver.'

'I am sorry,' she replied. 'It must 'ave bin awful findin' 'er like yer did.'

The young man shrugged his shoulders. 'As I told Lottie, at least 'er sufferin's over.'

Lana felt at a loss for words. 'I'm sorry if I took up all Lottie's time. There was a good reason.'

'No, it was nice fer me just ter sit listenin',' he said quickly.

The young woman realised that she had to take Jimmy into her confidence and soon. Time was moving on and there was much to do if Lottie's birthday was to turn out as she planned. 'Look, I need ter talk ter yer, Jimmy,' she blurted out. 'Are yer pushed fer time?'

He shook his head and smiled pleasantly. 'That's somefing I 'ave got plenty of,' he quipped.

'Would yer like ter pop in fer a few minutes?' she asked.

He nodded. 'Yeah, sure.'

'Take no notice o' me dad an' bruv,' she told him as she let herself in. 'When I left they was snorin' their 'eads off in the parlour.'

Jimmy followed her into the scullery where Ann was doing the *News of the World* crossword.

'Mum, this is Jimmy Bailey,' Lana said.

''Ello, luv. Sorry to 'ear about yer mum,' Ann said getting up quickly, self-consciously brushing her hand down her clean apron.

Jimmy smiled appreciatively. 'I 'ope this ain't inconvenient,' he said.

'I asked Jimmy ter pop in, Mum,' Lana explained. 'I wanted ter tell 'im about what we've planned for Lottie.'

'What *you've* planned, yer mean,' Ann corrected her with a smile.

'Sit yerself down an' I'll put the kettle on,' Lana told the young man.

'I'll leave yer two ter chat,' Ann said as she picked up the *News of the World*. 'I 'aven't read this yet. I'll take it upstairs wiv me.'

Lana sat down facing Jimmy while she waited for the kettle to boil. 'I've 'ad this idea about makin' Lottie's birfday a bit special,' she began. 'What I thought o' doin' was trying' ter find all those people who Lottie took in an' askin' 'em ter come to 'er birfday party. What d'yer fink?'

Jimmy was grinning. 'What a good idea,' he said nodding his head. 'She'd be over the moon ter see 'em all again.'

Lana glanced over at the kettle and then leaned forward over the table. 'Look, I've already started searchin',' she told him. 'Lottie took in ten children in all. Charlie Smedley works in the docks an' 'e's promised ter come. I've written to Phoebe Francis as she's now called, an' I've also written to the barrister bloke. What's 'is name? Oh yeah, Selby. Lottie also told me mum that one of 'er children was killed in the war.'

'That was Freddie Williams,' Jimmy cut in.

'What about those two gels who were stayin' wiv Lottie at the same time as you?' she asked him.

'Lucy an' Ellen,' he replied. 'Lottie told me Lucy married a businessman an' Ellen got done fer shopliftin'. That's all she knows.'

'It's not a lot ter go on,' Lana said, rubbing her chin.

'I don't mind 'elpin' yer, if yer want me to that is,' Jimmy offered.

'I'd be grateful fer any 'elp I can get,' she told him as the kettle started to sing.

The young man watched as Lana poured a little boiling water in the china teapot and swirled it round before making the tea. 'As soon as the funeral's over I'll be able ter do whatever I can,' he said enthusiastically.

Lana covered the teapot and sat down at the table once more. She had been pleasantly surprised by the sudden change in the young man's appearance and she felt guilty for what she had said to her mother about him. He was certainly attractive, with a shy smile and lovely warm eyes. His manner was very apologetic and thoughtful, and he seemed mature beyond his years.

As she got up to pour the tea her mother came into the room carrying the unfolded newspaper. 'Take a look at that,' Ann told her.

As Lana read the article her face took on a look of anger. 'The lyin' bitch,' she exclaimed. 'So much fer that letter I wrote. She won't bovver ter reply now, that's a dead cert.'

Jimmy picked up the newspaper from the table and when he read about Phoebe's fictitious childhood he smiled slyly. 'I fink she might be persuaded ter come after all,' he remarked.

'Yer mean we use a bit o' blackmail?' Lana replied, her face breaking into a smile.

'Yeah, that's if we can find some way ter prove she stayed wiv Lottie,' he told her.

'We've got proof. The photo,' she said excitedly.

'I don't wanna put a dampener on yer plans,' Ann cut in, 'but the woman could deny it was 'er in the photo. After all it was took a long while ago. It'd be very 'ard ter prove.'

Lana passed around cups of tea and then sat quietly thinking for a few minutes. 'I know what I'm gonna do,' she said suddenly.

'Tell us then,' Ann said, glancing quickly at Jimmy.

'I'm gonna cut that article out an' send it to 'er,' Lana said positively. 'An' what's more I'm gonna put a letter in wiv it tellin' 'er that we've got a very clear an' unmistakable photo of 'er when she was a kid stayin' wiv Lottie Curtis. That should put the cat amongst the pigeons.'

'You mind what yer doin',' Ann warned her. 'That could really be seen as blackmail.'

'I'd 'ave thought it was more like gentle persuasion,' Lana replied, winking at Jimmy Bailey.

Sounds of recovery were coming from the parlour and Jimmy stood up. 'Well, I'd better be off 'ome,' he said. 'If there's anyfing I can do just let me know. I'll be callin' in on Aunt Lottie soon or yer can reach me at 'ome. Yer know where I live.'

As soon as he had left Ann turned to her daughter. 'Do I remember someone sayin' 'ow scruffy 'e was?' she remarked mockingly. 'I thought 'e looked really smart. Attractive too, an' what a pleasant young man 'e seems.'

Lana gave a deep sigh as she slumped down at the table.

'An' what's that sigh for?' her mother asked her.

'I was just finkin'. This could turn out ter be a bigger job than I thought,' Lana said dejectedly.

'Well, you took it on, an' yer gotta see it frew now,' Ann said plainly. 'I agree it won't be easy, but just remember that it'll be all the sweeter when Lottie sees 'em all on 'er birfday.'

'If they bovver ter come,' Lana growled.

'They will, luv. I've got a good feelin' about this,' Ann told her.

Chapter Seventeen

Joe Slavin had been kept busy at his cafe for most of the day, but in the late afternoon there were only a couple of lorry drivers sitting in one corner chatting over mugs of tea and he had time to have a word with Ben Ferris. 'Well, I fink yer did the right fing,' he remarked. 'If yer'd got involved in a card school wiv those monkeys they'd 'ave skinned yer. I know what they're like. They pull in a stranger wiv a few bob who's a bit gullible an' play as a team. Yer can't outbid 'em. The stakes go sky-'igh an' before yer know it yer signin' yer life away on slips o' paper.'

Ben looked moodily into his half-empty mug. 'I gotta get meself sorted out, an' quick,' he confided to his old friend. 'I got Lana on me back about me duckin' and divin' an' I'm in debt ter Gerry Knowland. What I need is a stroke o' luck. At the moment I feel as though everybody's pissin' all over me.'

Joe ran his hand over his close-cropped spiky grey hair. 'If I was you I'd get out o' their clutches before it's too late,' he said. 'Yer've 'ad Mick Constantine's boys after yer, an' yer still sniffin' round 'em like a bloody lapdog.'

'Yer don't understand,' Ben replied angrily. 'I'm returnin' someone a favour, an' that's the strength of it. It ain't as though I like the company.'

'Some favour,' Joe said scathingly. 'Yer'll end up wiv a lot o' grief if yer start runnin' wiv Constantine's mob.'

Ben looked across quickly at the two lorry drivers and then leaned forward over the table towards Joe. 'Gerry Knowland bailed me out,' he said in a low voice. 'I was in ter Constantine fer fifty quid. So it's Gerry I'm doin' the favour for.'

'I see. So yer sniffin' out info on Gerry's be'alf,' Joe replied. 'Yer puttin' yer life on the line fer a paltry fifty quid. Yer gotta be more stupid than I took yer for.'

'Gerry's bin a good pal ter me,' Ben told him.

'Don't get me wrong,' Joe said quickly. 'I reckon Gerry Knowland. 'E's a good sort, but 'e's also a shrewd operator. 'E's inclined ter manipulate people. Just fink about it. Constantine leaves 'im alone an' 'e gets no grief from the Maltese neivver. Gerry Knowland's got a lot o' friends amongst the costers an' 'e does business wiv some powerful people, that's the reason. But I got a gut feelin' it won't stay that way fer much longer.'

'What d'yer mean?' Ben asked him.

'You know the old Chinese proverb,' Joe replied. ''E who stands in the middle o' the road gets 'it by traffic from both sides. An' that's what's likely to 'appen the way fings are shapin' up round 'ere lately.'

Ben smiled cannily. 'Yer don't know the full story,' he told him. 'Gerry's lined up wiv the Malts.'

'I might 'ave guessed,' the cafe owner replied. 'That makes your position even more precarious. Get out while yer can, Ben, before someone pulls the plug on yer.'

'I'd like to, I really would, mate, but I'm in ter the tune o' fifty quid,' Ben said dolefully.

One of the drivers got up and strolled over to the counter. 'Give us a refill, Joe, will yer?' he said.

The cafe owner went round the counter and filled two fresh mugs from a large metal teapot, then he disappeared into the back room for a few minutes. When he came back to Ben's table Joe threw down an envelope. 'Do me a favour an' square Knowland,' he said quietly. 'Yer can pay it back when they've all stopped pissin' on yer.'

* * *

When Lana arrived home from work she found a letter waiting for her and she opened it expectantly. Ann stood watching and saw her daughter's expression change.

'She wants ter see me,' Lana said excitedly.

'Phoebe Francis?'

'No less.'

'Where? When?'

'At the Royal Theatre,' Lana told her, 'termorrer night.'

'Don't yer feel nervous?' Ann asked her.

'Not really. I'm just excited,' she replied. 'It'll certainly be an experience.'

'It's a pity yer didn't wait a day or two longer before sendin' that second letter off to 'er,' Ann remarked.

'I dunno,' Lana replied. 'At least it lets 'er know I've read the article. Besides, there was nuffing to upset 'er in the letter. All I said was that I 'adn't 'eard from 'er an' I'd appreciate an early reply.'

Ann smiled and shook her head slowly. 'Yer gotta understand, luv, those sort o' people are like prima donnas. They don't take kindly ter bein' told what ter do.'

'I fink it's a question o' common courtesy ter reply ter letters, 'owever busy you are,' Lana persisted. 'Anyway I'm not gonna be overawed by 'er. I'm only concerned that she 'as the decency ter show up at Lottie's birfday party, if only fer a little while.'

Ann saw the determined look in her daughter's eyes and she merely nodded in reply.

Mist was rising from the valley and drifting across the spacious grounds of Harpenden Manor as Samuel Selby struggled with his bow tie. 'Blast it,' he cursed as he saw the result of his efforts in the ornate bedroom mirror.

'Come here, darling, let me fix it for you,' Claudette said, giving him a condescending smile.

'I wish you'd put me out of my misery, darling,' he said,

suddenly feeling his throat constricted as Claudette pulled on the tie. 'I don't like surprises.'

'Don't be an old misery,' she replied. 'I think you'll enjoy this evening, despite your aversion to social gatherings.'

Samuel sighed in resignation. It was bad enough being summoned to the Bartrams' like a recalcitrant schoolboy, without having to listen to inane chatter from their quaint friends. 'I rest my case,' he said despairingly.

Claudette patted his broad back and moved away to complete her make-up. 'By the way, darling, don't forget to congratulate the Warmleys on the birth of their grandson,' she remarked. 'Oh and do remember to ask Lord Tinsley how his garden is coming along. He's had it relandscaped.'

'Anything else I should remember not to forget?' Samuel said sarcastically.

'You might make a point of spending a few minutes talking to the Scotts,' Claudette told him. 'They are fans of yours after all.'

Samuel smiled to himself as he slipped on his dinner jacket. Brendan and Margaret Scott were embarrassingly gushing in their appreciation of his efforts on their behalf. He had recently represented Brendan in a civil action against a national newspaper and secured for him a substantial settlement. 'Will do, dearest,' he answered.

Claudette stood up and twirled round. 'Well, how do I look?' she asked.

'Ravishing,' Samuel said smiling.

'Come along, Sam, let's have a very dry martini before the car arrives,' she suggested.

Fifteen minutes later the chauffeur-driven Daimler turned out of the Selbys' drive and purred along the winding country lanes, its headlights cutting through the evening mist. Claudette sat stiffly in the comfortable seat, her angular face a shadowy cameo beneath auburn hair that was expertly arranged on the top of her head, and she wore pearl earrings and a matching pearl pendant around her thin neck. Now in her mid-forties, Claudette was the only child of Lord and Lady Bartram, and after a disastrous marriage to an industrialist very much her senior she had succeeded in snaring the eligible Samuel Selby, two years younger than her and rapidly growing in professional eminence. Already he had defended one ex-cabinet minister and two members of the gentry, as well as the Scotts, and Claudette was happy to shine in his limelight.

Samuel Selby had no political ambitions, although his wife dearly wanted him to enter Parliament. He was content to spend the next five years establishing himself in the top echelon of his profession, and after ten years at the Bar he would be qualified for appointment to the bench as a high court judge. He had made Claudette happy and thus endeared himself to the Bartrams, which pleased him immensely. His only worry stemmed from the knowledge that Lord Bartram was a political animal, and a very strong instinct told him that tonight was the occasion when, with Claudette's connivance, the old boy would in his inimitable manner broach the subject of his own political career.

The car drove through the gates of Wheatlands and pulled up outside the stately home. Inside an ensemble was performing Tchaikovsky's String Quartet in F major and groups of people stood around chatting together, the men dressed in dinner suits and the women resplendent in long evening dresses and flashing jewellery. Claudette made her usual dramatic entry, her hands held out as she greeted the other guests with a gracious smile. Samuel walked in her wake, occasionally nodding and smiling, hoping to reach the Bartrams themselves with a minimum of fuss.

'Very good to see you, my boy,' Lord Bartram said in a loud voice. 'When you can free yourself why don't you join me in the study for a quiet snifter? A chap can hardly hear himself think out here, eh?'

'Of course, sir,' Samuel said dutifully.

The evening was young, the wine and champagne flowed

freely and Claudette was hardly able to contain her excitement at the thought of Samuel's political career. At first it would all be very pedestrian, but he was certain to be offered a shadow cabinet post, then when the Labour Government fell at the next election the sky would be the limit: travel, the excitement of meeting heads of state, dinners at Buckingham Palace, the Guildhall and Chequers, and as the wife of the feted Prime Minister the flashlight bulbs would pop and she would smile serenely, a star in her own right.

'Good Lord, you don't really think that this country can flourish under a socialist administration, do you?' Lady Helminth was going on. 'Granted, there was a certain anger expressed at the polls, but it was all based on past experiences. Despite what the *Daily Worker* said, Winston would never have ordered the troops to fire on the miners, nor did he say that the working classes would only store coal in their baths if they had them.'

'I thoroughly agree,' her companion replied. 'I should think Winston is absolutely devastated at the way he's been treated after leading this country to victory. It's a downright disgrace.'

Samuel had spent some time with the Scotts and he had asked after the Warmleys' grandchild, before seeking out Lord and Lady Tinsley to inquire about their extensive garden. Now it was time to face Claudette's doting father, and he feared the worst.

'Do come in. Take a seat. A brandy?' Lord Bartram said in staccato fashion. 'Try one of these Havanas.'

Samuel made himself comfortable in a leather-upholstered chair, a generous brandy in one hand and a large cigar in the other. He watched in anticipation as his host moved over to his huge desk and seated himself in the high-backed chair.

'Tell me, Samuel, have you considered entering Parliament?' Bartram asked bluntly.

Samuel stared at the distinguished, grey-haired figure of his father-in-law and noted the slight twitch of his waxed moustache. 'No, I hadn't given it a thought,' he replied.

'You should, dear boy,' Bartram said in a clipped voice. 'I have some influence and I can virtually guarantee you a safe seat in this shire. Jack Bromilow is very ill and I'm sorry to say that he's not expected to recover. The selection process will be just a formality if you put your name forward, and with the by-election already pencilled in for next February you would very soon be taking your seat as the Member of Parliament for Hawarth East.'

Samuel remembered shuddering with horror on seeing a nature film about Africa in which vultures tore at the bones of a deer. At this precise moment he felt that same revulsion as he listened to Bartram picking over the bones of a not-yet-deceased human being. It was all cut and dried: the by-election planned while Jack Bromilow still had breath in his body. 'I'm afraid I must decline the offer,' he replied firmly. 'I have other plans.'

'You should not be too rash, Samuel. Give it some thought,' Bartram went on. 'I know from speaking with Claudette that you have ambitions to go on the bench one day, but you are still comparatively young. You could return to the Bar if things did not work out politically.'

'I will give it some thought,' Samuel replied, 'but I doubt that I shall change my mind.'

Lord Bartram grunted loudly in displeasure and drained his glass in one gulp. 'I think that my daughter is going to be very disappointed,' he remarked. 'She was counting on your acceptance.'

Samuel bit back on an angry reply. Claudette had taken it upon herself to map out his future without consulting him. It was unforgivable and he would have a sharp word with her before the night was out. 'She'll get over it,' he replied coldly.

The guests began to leave and Claudette remained composed as she stood by the door bidding them goodbye. She had spoken with her father and learned the worst, and there would certainly be some harsh words for that inconsiderate husband of hers.

When the last of the guests had gone the Selbys took their leave. They remained silent in the car taking them home, but both were ready to explode the moment the front door closed. Samuel had intended to tell Claudette about the letter he had received from Bermondsey but he realised that it would now have to wait.

Chapter Eighteen

Ben Ferris had arranged to meet Gerry Knowland at the Dewdrop pub on Tuesday evening, and he was anxious to square the debt and make it clear that he was no longer prepared to get involved in any intrigue. Gerry would understand, he told himself as he hurried towards the pub. If he didn't it was just too bad. As Joe Slavin had said, he could well be putting his life on the line the way things were.

Gerry was not in the pub when Ben arrived but there was a message waiting for him.

'Gerry said ter meet 'im at the Lord Nelson,' the barman told him, ''E said yer'd know where it was.'

Ben hurried through the quiet evening streets feeling irritated. What was so important that Gerry couldn't wait five minutes, he wondered. Joe Slavin was a shrewd character. He had summed it up perfectly when he said the word 'lapdog'. That was how Ben felt right now, but things were going to change. He was finished with all the bowing and scraping. He would stay clear of gambling and concentrate on getting some money together. There was always money to be made. It was a question of being in the right place at the right time.

Gerry was standing at the counter and he greeted Ben with a grin and put his arm around his shoulder. 'Darkie, I want yer ter meet my ole mate Ben,' he said to the publican. 'Ben, this is Angelo Samut. Everyone calls 'im Darkie. I dunno why though,' he added with a wink at the Malt.

Ben watched while Darkie pulled two pints of bitter and then as soon as the publican was called away to serve another customer he turned to Gerry. 'I need ter talk ter yer,' he said urgently.

Gerry picked up his beer and nodded over to a vacant table.

As soon as they were seated Ben reached into his coat pocket. 'First of all I wanna fank yer fer bailin' me out wiv Constantine,' he said, putting an envelope down in front of his friend. 'That's the fifty oncers I owe yer an' I wanna . . .'

''Ang on a minute,' Gerry cut in. 'There's no need fer this. I told yer ter ferget it. We got a deal, remember?'

'That's what I wanna talk ter yer about,' Ben said quickly. 'I want out, Gerry. I can't afford ter get involved in all this business, it's too risky. Besides, I got Lana ter fink of. She's talkin' marriage an' kids.'

Gerry looked at him with amusement. 'It's OK, I understand,' he said amiably.

'I don't see anyfing funny about it,' Ben replied. 'I'm serious, Gerry.'

'I'm sorry, but I just can't see you changin' shitty napkins an' goin' off ter work in the mornin's, that's all,' Gerry told him.

'I'll manage,' Ben answered moodily. 'Anyway, I'm gonna concentrate on buyin' an' sellin'. I've got me van workin' again an' I can fill me yard wiv gear. I'll survive.'

'Yeah, I can picture it,' Gerry said with a smirk. 'Yer'll be barely scrapin' a livin' dealin' wiv the likes o' the Carmichael bruvvers an' that soapy git who works for 'em. Wise up, Ben. They're small-time no-'opers.'

'I've got ovver contacts,' Ben said defensively. 'I just gotta cultivate 'em.'

Gerry leaned forward over the table. 'Now listen ter me, pal,' he said in a serious voice. 'I've always made a point o' keepin' me distance from people like Constantine an' Darkie Samut. I reckoned that if yer tied in wiv people like that yer'd sold yer soul, yer'd always be at their beck an' call, but fings are changin' fast. I've realised I can't afford ter sit on the fence any longer. Mick Constantine an' 'is mob are out ter take control o' this manor. They're after outtin' the Malts an' then they'll come after the likes o' me. No one wiv their own business is gonna be safe, especially the one-man concerns, an' that'll include you. Yer'll do yer buyin' an' sellin' frew Constantine an' yer'll need permission ter shit, believe me.'

Ben looked confused. 'D'yer fink Darkie Samut's mob are any match for Constantine?' he asked. 'The Malt shopkeepers are bein' squeezed an' their places burned down, that's wivout the attacks on the bookies.'

'You remember the ole sayin', Ben. Enough's enough, an' too much ain't my idea of a feast,' Gerry remarked. 'Darkie's organised the Malts, an' 'e's bringin' people in from Cable Street. They're 'ard geezers who are used ter fightin' fer their bit o' space. Just remember what 'appened ter Baz Smithson. I 'appen ter know that Baz was out ter silence Toni Rossi fer shoutin' 'is mouth off in the Crown, but Rossi was bein' tailed by Darkie's boys, an' when Baz went for 'im they were ready. You know the outcome. Smithson ends up floatin' down the river wiv 'is froat cut. Make no mistake about it. Whatever Constantine tries now 'e's gonna be on a loser.'

Ben sat silently for a moment or two, then he nodded at the money. 'I'd still like yer ter take that dough,' he said.

Gerry shook his head. 'Yer pay me off an' owe somebody else. That's not good business, mate,' he said firmly. 'Pick it up an' don't feel bad about it. There's no need fer you ter feel under any obligation. All I want yer ter do is keep yer eyes an' ears open. Keep me informed on the least little fing you 'ear, 'owever unimportant it may seem. Yer gonna be on the winnin' side, that's fer sure. The Malts are businessmen, like the Jew boys. They're not villains. If yer put yerself in a good light wiv 'em they'll send business your way. Now put that money away an' fink about what I've said.'

Ben nodded and picked up the empty glasses. 'I'll get us anuvver drink,' he replied.

Lana smiled at the look of surprise on Jimmy's face as he opened the door to her. 'I 'ope yer don't mind me callin' round,' she said. 'I thought yer'd like ter know, I got a reply from Phoebe Francis yesterday. It was waitin' for me when I got in.'

Jimmy's face lit up. 'Would yer like ter come in?' he said.

Lana walked into the dimly lit parlour and immediately felt sad for the young man. He had obviously tidied the place a bit, but the curtains and tablecloth were drab and the room needed freshening up. There was a used dinner plate on the table, an empty mug standing in the hearth and the evening paper on the floor beside the fireside chair. 'There's the letter,' she said, handing it to him.

The young man read it quickly. 'Are yer goin' over there now?' he asked.

Lana nodded. 'I wasn't gonna trouble yer, bearin' in mind the funeral an' all, but I thought I should let yer know,' she said.

'I'm pleased yer did,' Jimmy replied. 'Would yer like me ter come wiv yer?'

'Only if yer want to,' she said smiling.

Jimmy slipped on the new black raincoat he had bought that day with the last of the money Glenda had given him and brushed his fingers through his thick dark hair. 'Let's go,' he said with a grin.

They turned into Tower Bridge Road and walked quickly to the nearby bus stop through the swirling fog. Lana had the collar of her fawn winter coat pulled up around her ears and she wore a scarf over her long golden hair. Jimmy stole a glance at her and her face looked flushed with good health, her eyes sparkling in the cold air.

''Ave yer just come from work, Lana?' he asked casually.

'Yeah, I've got a job as a telephonist at a place near London

Bridge,' she replied. 'It ain't bad, I s'pose. What about you? You was in the army, wasn't yer?'

'Royal Army Service Corps,' he told her. 'I was a driver, an' that's what I do in Civvie Street.'

A number one bus pulled up and they stepped aboard. Jimmy handed a sixpence to the conductor. 'Two ter Waterloo Station,' he said.

'Where did yer go durin' the war?' Lana asked him.

'I was in the Eighth Army in Norf Africa,' he replied. 'Then I was in Sicily an' Italy.'

''Ave yer got any bruvvers or sisters?'

Jimmy suddenly smiled broadly showing his white even teeth and Lana grinned.

'Sorry,' she said. 'I'm just a bit nosy really.'

'I got two younger sisters, both married,' he chuckled. 'Glenda's the baby o' the family. She's got two young children. Then there's Lillian. She's married to a builder over in Walworth, but she 'asn't got any kids yet.'

'Lottie told me yer dad was in the merchant navy,' Lana went on.

'Yeah, 'e was drowned at sea when I was just a nipper,' Jimmy told her. 'I never really knew 'im. I can only remember 'im vaguely.'

'I'm very sorry,' she said quietly.

'It was Mum really,' he remarked. 'It took its toll on 'er. I don't fink she ever got over it. There was never anyone else in 'er life.' He paused for a moment, staring down awkwardly at his hands. 'Now let me ask you a question.'

'OK, it's your turn,' Lana said smiling.

'What about your family?'

'Well, there's me mum an' dad. You met me mum. And I got two older bruvvers,' she told him. 'Derek still lives at 'ome an' Alan the elder one's married wiv a baby on the way. They're both stevedores. I've got a boyfriend too, but 'e's a bit of a nutter at the best o' times.'

Jimmy was quiet for a few moments then he glanced up at

her. 'I've seen yer a few times when I called round ter see Lottie,' he said. 'I fink it's very nice of yer ter look after 'er the way yer do. Lottie finks a lot of yer.'

'She's a lovely ole lady,' Lana replied. 'Anyway I fink it's nice o' you too ter visit 'er. She really appreciates it.'

'I 'ave a lot ter fank Lottie for,' Jimmy told her. 'I'd 'ave popped in more than I did but fer me mum. I couldn't leave 'er fer long.'

The bus swung into Waterloo Road and he gave the young woman a brief smile. 'You remind me o' Jenny,' he remarked. 'A gel I knew before I got called up. She was blonde an' she 'ad your colour eyes, though I 'ave ter say she wasn't quite as pretty as you.'

Lana felt herself blush a little. 'Was it serious?' she asked.

'We wasn't engaged, but we were goin' steady,' Jimmy replied. 'Ter be honest I don't fink she was all that keen on gettin' married, an' it's understandable. We were both pretty skint an' the war was loomin'. Anyway, we broke it off before I was called up, and she met someone else durin' the war and married 'im.'

The bus drew up outside Waterloo Station and the conductor announced the end of the line. Jimmy stepped off the bus in front of Lana and reached up to help her as she stepped down on to the pavement. The fog was clearing and they could see the lights ofWaterloo Bridge glowing up ahead.

'I wonder what she's like,' Lana said as they set off across the river.

'Well, we're soon gonna find out,' Jimmy replied.

Down below them the dark murky waters ran seaward, eddying and swirling round the stone supporting pillars of the bridge. Lights from the Embankment reflected off the water and a police launch chugged through beneath the centre span. In front they could see the sloping entrance to the Kingsway subway and the gradual curve of Aldwych.

'It's along 'ere somewhere,' Lana remarked as they reached the end of the bridge and turned into the Strand.

'There it is. See the sign?' Jimmy said pointing.

The end door of the foyer was open and when they stepped in out of the cold night air they spotted an elderly man fixing a light bulb.

'We got an appointment,' Lana told him.

He looked down from one to the other. 'Yer'll 'ave ter go inside, miss,' he replied. 'I'm only the electrician.'

They walked into the auditorium and saw a small group of people standing on the stage. A man holding some papers left his two companions and hurried down the side steps. 'You've come to see Miss Francis, I take it,' he said to Lana, his eyes flashing briefly to Jimmy. 'Are you both proposing to see her? She told me there'd only be one visitor.'

'We'd both like ter see 'er,' Lana told him.

'Very well, if you'll just follow me I'll inquire if she'll see you both,' the stage director replied, leading the way with a quick mincing gait. 'Mind the steps.'

Lana gave Jimmy a nervous smile over her shoulder as she followed the director on to the stage and into the wings. They found themselves in a long passageway and they exchanged a quick glance as the man knocked timidly on a door with a large silver star stuck on it. 'It's the stage director, Miss Francis,' he called out.

'Come in,' a high-pitched voice called back.

The director disappeared into the room and came back out smiling. 'Miss Francis will see you both,' he told them.

Phoebe Francis sat wrapped in a frilly dressing gown that reached down to her ankles and she had a towelling turban round her head. Her features were classical, and she waved an elegant white hand towards chairs placed strategically to one side of the long dressing table.

'I have both your letters here, Miss Johnson,' she said, glancing briefly at the young man. 'Are you husband and wife?'

'No, I'm this young lady's friend,' Jimmy replied. 'I was fostered by Lottie Curtis too.'

Phoebe looked at each of them in turn. 'I'm very sorry to

have to tell you that you seem to be labouring under a misapprehension,' she said with a frown. 'I just don't know this Mrs Curtis and I was certainly not fostered out to her. You read the article in the Sunday newspaper. As it said, I spent my childhood solely in India.'

Lana glanced quickly at Jimmy. 'I can understand the reason fer you denyin' it,' she said to Phoebe, 'but the ole lady 'asn't made a mistake. She showed us a photo of yer. There's no doubt at all. That picture was of you.'

'Well, I'm afraid I have to challenge that assumption. Old photographs can be deceptive,' the star said coldly. 'If I were you I would accept that you have made a mistake.'

'There's no mistake,' Jimmy cut in. 'That ole lady looked after you when yer muvver 'ad a nervous breakdown, an' if it wasn't fer the care an' attention she lavished on you yer might not be where you are now. Surely you could find the time just ter look in on 'er, even if it was only fer a few minutes? It wouldn't take much o' your time, an' it would really make that ole lady's day. It's 'er eightieth birfday, fer Chrissake.'

Phoebe's expression was unchanged. 'I'm sorry but I've said all I'm going to say on the subject,' she answered. 'Now if you don't mind, I have to get ready. I have a car coming for me very soon.'

Lana stood up and turned to the young man. 'C'mon, Jimmy, I can see we're just wastin' our time 'ere,' she said bitterly.

They stepped out into the cold night air and made their way back over Waterloo Bridge, feeling shocked and frustrated at Phoebe Francis's reaction.

'I can't believe it,' Lana said angrily. 'Like you said, if it wasn't fer Lottie that selfish, stuck-up cow might be workin' in some factory now.'

'Never mind, Lana, there'll be ovvers there,' Jimmy told her gently. 'We'll try our best ter get all the rest of 'em.'

They sat in silence during the bus ride back to Bermondsey, and when they stepped down in the Tower Bridge Road Jimmy shivered. 'C'mon, I'll walk yer 'ome,' he said, 'it's gettin' late.'

Lana felt strangely elated as she walked beside him through the quiet street. She had thought him pathetic once and criticised him uncharitably, but now she felt a glowing warmth towards him. He had compassion and feeling, and a quiet way about him that concealed a hidden strength and self-confidence.

'I'm sorry about that Francis woman,' he said as they neared Saddler Street. 'I know 'ow you were countin' on 'er comin' ter Lottie's do.'

'Never mind, Jimmy. Like you said there'll be ovvers there,' she told him, smiling.

When they reached her front door Jimmy looked around self-consciously and coughed. 'I, er, I 'ad a nice time this evenin', despite the kick in the teef from Phoebe Francis,' he said. 'I'll call round an' see Lottie after Thursday. Maybe I'll see yer then.'

'Goodnight, Jimmy, an' fanks fer yer support,' Lana replied.

She slipped the key into the lock and paused, watching the young man disappear out of the turning.

'Well? I'm waitin' to 'ear all about it,' Ann said eagerly.

'Phoebe Francis won't be comin' ter Lottie's birfday party, Mum,' Lana replied tersely as she slipped off her coat.

Ann looked surprised. 'Oh? I thought it was good news by the smile on yer face as yer walked in,' she said.

'Jimmy came wiv me,' Lana remarked. ''E's very nice, Mum. Anyway, about that nasty bitch . . .'

Chapter Nineteen

As the cold, damp November days slipped by Lana was becoming more and more disheartened. There had been no reply to the letter she had sent to Samuel Selby and no opportunity to further her plans for the reunion on Christmas Eve. Lottie had taken to her bed for three days with the flu and had been surviving on hot soup and bread provided by Ann Johnson. The old lady had recovered enough to sit in her chair for a few hours each day but she needed constant attention. Ann and Lana had kept the fire going and cleaned the house, something that Lottie was always very particular about, but when they took turns to sit with her during the evenings she tended to nod off in the middle of a conversation. Lana could see that there was no point pressing her about the rest of the children until she was feeling stronger, and the album remained closed at her feet.

The fire had burned low and Ann yawned as she picked up her mug of cocoa and took the skin off with a spoon. 'Well, I'm off ter bed,' she announced to Lana. 'I've gotta be up early an' I wanna pop in ter see 'ow Lottie is before I leave fer work.'

Lana said goodnight and stayed where she was, staring moodily into the dying fire as the embers dulled and the white ash sifted down into the ash pan. She sat hunched forward in the armchair with both hands round her mug of cocoa and sighed deeply as troubled thoughts tormented her. Ben was playing with her emotions and it was obvious he had no real intention of changing. There was always someone he had to see and big deals in the offing, but nothing ever seemed to come of it. He had been blowing hot and cold lately: very loving and attentive one evening and uninterested the next. There seemed to be something preoccupying him, and Lana felt that it was connected with Gerry Knowland. They were drinking together quite often and Ben would invariably clam up whenever she remarked on it.

The young woman sipped her cocoa, her thoughts suddenly turning to Jimmy Bailey. She had seen him only twice since the funeral and there had been little chance to talk much. On both occasions she had been busy tending to the old lady and Jimmy had spent all of one visit fixing strips of cord around the front and back doors to stop the draught. He had managed to tell her a little about his new job driving for a wholesale grocery firm, however, and she remembered feeling elated when he arrived and gave her a friendly smile. She felt disappointed too when he left early. He was getting to her somehow, making her feel confused and nervy, and it was affecting her relationship with Ben. She found herself comparing the two men, and when Ben did something that irritated her she would think of Jimmy and how comfortable she was in his company. It was wrong of her, she knew. Ben was her steady boyfriend and she should not allow herself to dwell on any other man; but somehow she couldn't help herself.

The fire had died and Lana raked the ashes before going off to bed. Outside the fog was dense and she heard the moaning, muffled sound of foghorns coming from the river as she pulled the bedclothes up around her ears. She felt tired and jaded but sleep would not come and she twisted over on to her back, trying hard to still her restless mind. Ben loved her in his own way, she was sure, but there seemed no urgency on his part, or even desire, to make the commitment she needed. He valued his freedom, chancing his arm and chasing the big one while she dreamed of marriage and children.

Lana turned on to her side and closed her eyes, trying to woo sleep by thinking of lying with Ben and picturing him in her mind as he caressed her and showered her with kisses. Instead she saw Jimmy, and remembered how pleasant it had been walking home with him through the quiet streets. She could see his smile clearly, and recalled how she had fantasised about him kissing her goodnight at the front door. She sighed deeply and gave in as her imagination ran rampant; she savoured the pleasure, a glowing warmth in her loins as sleep claimed her.

Samuel Selby added another log to the fire and then poured himself a brandy before settling back down at his desk to put the finishing touches to his summing-up speech. He felt that his arguments had been well founded and equally well presented, but it was difficult to gauge the attitude of the jury. However strong one's case might seem to be, the rhetoric of the prosecution and its appeal to prejudice could never be underestimated.

Richard Marsden was a villain, there was no denying that, and with his shifty appearance and gravelly voice it would be understandable if the members of the jury had become biased against him. But British justice insisted that one was innocent until proven guilty, Samuel reminded himself. It was up to him now to sum up with a speech that would stir the emotions of the twelve members good and true, allowing them to leave feeling proud to have participated in coming up with a just verdict.

Samuel took a sip from his brandy and thought how quiet it was. Claudette had been conspicuous by her absence that evening. Normally she would have been on hand, listening as he read passages from the speech he had prepared and ready to suggest a minor change here and there. This evening, though, she had stayed away from the study, reading a trashy novel in the lounge and no doubt seething inside at what she unreasonably saw as recalcitrance on his part. Not only had he been forced to defend himself in the face of a two-pronged campaign to steer him into Parliament; he had also been compelled to remind Claudette in no uncertain terms that he was not of aristocratic stock, and there was no shame in remembering from where one had come.

Samuel Selby leaned back in his chair and pressed his eyelids with his thumb and forefinger. It was done, honed to perfection, or as near as, dammit. Maybe now was the time to break the ice with Claudette, he thought, try to coax her out of her infernal sulk. The trouble was she was so immovable in this sort of mood. The last time it had occurred was when he forgot her birthday, and her sulks had lasted for more than a week.

The sound of the telephone ringing jerked Samuel from his reflections but before he could pick up the receiver it had stopped. Claudette must have answered it, he realised as he picked up his drink. A few minutes later the study door opened and his wife came in looking suitably sad. 'That was Daddy,' she said. 'He rang to say that Jack Bromilow died earlier this evening.'

'I'm very sorry,' Samuel replied. 'It *was* expected though.'

Claudette smiled sheepishly. 'Samuel, I'm sorry to have been so horrible,' she began slowly, 'but I was very upset that you refused Daddy. You know that I only want the very best for you, and you'd be so good for the party. Daddy feels that it wouldn't be long before you were offered a shadow cabinet post. You'd climb right to the very top in no time at all, I really mean that.'

Samuel bit back on an angry reply. She never stopped, he thought. The poor man had only just breathed his last and already Claudette was scheming again. 'I do understand how you feel, darling,' he said with control, 'and I do appreciate your wanting the best for me, but I still need a little more time to think about it.'

'You mean you are seriously considering it?' Claudette said, her eyes brightening.

'Yes.'

'Oh, darling, you will say yes soon, I know you will.'

Samuel gave her a brief smile. 'Just let's not be too hasty,' he told her.

Claudette moved round the desk and put her hand on his shoulder. 'Darling,' she said, frowning and pouting, 'you're not going to take any notice of that silly letter, are you?'

Samuel sighed with irritation. 'I'm so busy at the moment I haven't had time to think about it.'

'It's not that I have anything against working-class people,' she went on, 'but for someone like yourself to be seen fraternising with them might give the wrong impression to the local Conservative Association.'

'So that's why you were so cross,' he said. 'I thought you were worried I might catch something or learn some naughty swearwords.'

'That's not funny,' Claudette said sharply. 'You have to remember you're in the public eye and that last case won you a lot of acclaim. Those pictures of you in the newspapers will have been seen by people in Bermondsey too and the local papers would make capital out of it if they got the chance.'

'"The eminent Samuel Selby K.C. arrives for Lottie Curtis's birthday party",' Samuel declared in a stentorian voice. 'I can see it now.'

'Don't be so flippant, darling,' Claudette said. 'It doesn't become you.'

'Nor does being a snob, and that's how I feel in ignoring that letter,' Samuel told her curtly.

'You really are infuriating at times,' she stormed.

'I'm sorry but that's how I feel,' he replied bluntly. 'I can't help it.'

'Well, you can jolly well feel how you like. I'm not going to argue with you any more,' she said in a sour tone of voice. 'It's very late and you're due in court at ten, in case you've forgotten.'

Samuel sighed and slid back his chair. 'I'm finished here anyway. Will you be in court tomorrow, by the way?'

'I've not decided yet,' she told him.

'But you've been following this case and you promised to come.'

'I'm sure you'll be very eloquent as usual and the result will be as you expect,' Claudette said haughtily. 'Besides, I've been neglecting my friends. They enjoy my coffee mornings and so do I.'

Samuel got up from his chair and went to her. 'Darling, don't let's argue any more,' he said quietly as he slipped his arms round her waist.

Claudette felt the fire growing in her belly and she wanted him to crush her to him but she placed her hands on his chest and held him away. 'You've been very beastly lately,' she told him in her baby voice. 'I've missed you so much over the past two weeks.'

'I've missed you too, darling,' he replied. 'I've missed stroking you, I've missed your hot kisses and your sensuous hands provoking me. I've been in agony each night, not daring to touch you for fear of rejection.'

Claudette allowed him to pull her in tight to him. 'I lay awake for hours last night, darling,' she murmured as she felt his urgency. 'I willed you to reach out for me. I was very hot and I desperately needed your loving. I need it now, right this minute.'

Samuel felt the heat of her body and her hot breath on his cheek and he lowered his hands, feeling her tight bottom. 'Shall we play our little game tonight?' he whispered suggestively.

'It's rather late,' she said. 'Are you sure you won't be too tired in the morning? It's going to be a big day for you.'

'I'll phone you in ten minutes,' he said.

'Make it fifteen.'

The log crumbled in the hearth as Samuel poured himself a large brandy, then at the appointed time he picked up the phone. 'This is your lover, darling,' he said huskily. 'Is that husband of yours away? Oh splendid. My horse is saddled and ready and I'll fly to you. By the way, are you wearing those long, sensuous stockings? A girdle too? No, darling, don't. Leave your hair piled high on top of your head. Yes, I have the whip. No, I'll be very gentle. Bye, bye, darling. Be ready for your lover. Yes, he can feel the ache, the intense longing. Yes, I'm just about to climb into the saddle.'

Claudette put down the phone and turned off the lights, with the exception of one small bedside lamp. Its red glow was discreet, she thought, almost wicked, and she lounged back on the bed, her left leg raised in a provocative gesture, one arm behind her head as she awaited the pleasure of the young lord of the manor.

Chapter Twenty

Photographers from the local newspapers were on hand when Mick Constantine married Mandy Brophy at Camberwell Register Office on Friday morning and the gang boss smiled obligingly, wallowing in the attention. He was still smiling when the wedding party arrived for the reception at a nearby club owned by him; but had he known then that the main concern of the press was to familiarise their readers with the man behind the housing scandal in Rotherhithe, the smile would have disappeared and the diminutive photographers would no doubt have been left with wrecked equipment and more than a few bruises. For the time being, however, Mick Constantine looked forward to seeing his face on the front pages, and he joked with his minder Tommy Carberry as they took their places at the head table.

Mandy Brophy, now Mrs Michael Constantine, looked radiant in her navy blue two-piece which was edged with white satin trim like her wide matching hat, and she smiled serenely at the well-wishers who gathered around her. Deep down inside though she had no bridal feelings of romance or true love. She knew that it was a marriage of convenience. She had gone on to the streets in her early twenties and had the misfortune to become involved with a notorious pimp, who not only took more than his pound of flesh but delighted in brutalising the women. Mick had changed all that soon after meeting her in a Poplar pub. He had been attracted by her look of innocence and was shocked to discover later that the young woman he had wined and dined, and finally coaxed into his bed, was actually an experienced prostitute. His anger at having been so gullible was lost in an obsession with her childlike beauty, and he set her up in a comfortable flat, away from the harsh and dangerous street life and protected by his reputation. She was his woman now, there to cater to his sexual needs.

The Bermondsey gang boss had realised straight away that taking a woman off the East End streets for his own private use would cause certain problems, and he dealt with them in his usual fashion.

Unfortunately for Theo Podopolis, he had never heard the name Constantine and was unaware that the gang boss had interests on both sides of the river. He came looking for his woman and ended up in a dingy back alley with his head caved in.

Mick Constantine's new wife was an enterprising young woman who had seen the advantages in marrying him and was experienced enough to realise that he was not really a home-loving man. When his rose-coloured glasses came off he would be bound to seek other forbidden fruits and leave her to her own devices, and she would then be able to resume her passionate affair with Gerry Knowland, the only man she had ever truly loved.

Ben Ferris felt that Joe Slavin's working men's cafe was as safe a place as any to meet and discuss important matters, and it was there that he sat sipping from his mug of steaming tea as he listened to Gerry.

'The problem is, I can't just go round there like a bull in a china shop,' Gerry was saying. 'Fings are very dicey at the moment an' I can't afford ter show me 'and. Believe me, I'd prefer ter pay a few o' the lads ter rough those monkeys up an' frighten 'em off, but Constantine would only bring in more. Besides there's the ole people ter fink about. They'd be in the front line an' it'd only aggravate the situation. As it is I've managed ter get the papers interested an' I've given 'em a file on what's goin' on in Rovver'ithe. Both the *Souf London Press* an' the *Kentish Mercury* are doin' articles on it an' it's sure ter set the cat amongst the pigeons.'

'I can just imagine the look on Constantine's face when 'e reads it,' Ben said grinning.

'Yeah, so can I,' Gerry replied. 'As a matter o' fact the feller at the *Souf London* told me they were gonna cover the weddin', an' the *Mercury*'s bound ter be there too.'

Ben's face grew serious. 'I bin finkin' about that Baz Smithson killin',' he said. 'I can't see Constantine lettin' that go by the board. 'E's bound ter come back in some way.'

'Yeah, I bin finkin' about it too,' Gerry told him. 'Darkie's got a lot o' new faces 'angin' around in 'is pub. They're from over Cable Street, an' I wouldn't like ter mess wiv 'em.'

'I don't fink Mick'll try anyfing there,' Ben remarked. ''E'll be more likely ter pick on one o' the shops, or maybe waylay someone else. After all Darkie an' 'is boys can't be everywhere at once. It was just lucky that they were on 'and ferToni Rossi.'

When Joe finished serving some workmen he came over to their table. 'Mind what yer sayin'. One o' those geezers who's just come in is a mate o' the Varley bruvvers,' he said in a low voice.

Gerry gave the cafe owner an acknowledging wink and then leaned forward across the table. 'I've bin told about a load o' spirits that's due ter go missin' en route,' he said quietly. 'The lorry's comin' down from Scotland an' it'll be nicked well out o' London. I'm already in fer fifty cases o' Johnny Walker at a fiver a case. What about you?'

'Sure fing,' Ben said enthusiastically.

'It'll mean gettin' up ter St Albans. That's where it'll be stored,' Gerry told him.

'I got me van runnin' OK an' Tubby's let me 'ave five gallons o' commercial petrol so there's no problem,' Ben replied.

'I'll give yer a shout when it's in place,' Gerry said. 'It's all gotta be shifted wivvin two days at the most. It's ter do wiv the ware'ouse changin' 'ands apparently. Let me know 'ow many cases you can 'andle an' I'll pass the word on.'

Ben stroked his chin and he suddenly thought of Sammy Goldbloom. 'I'll take twenty,' he said.

Gerry nodded. 'Leave it wiv me,' he grinned. 'It'll be a nice seasonal commodity, won't it?'

Ben took a sip of his tea, remembering what Sammy Goldbloom had told him about selling his business to the Maltese. ''Ow close are yer wiv Darkie Samut?' he asked.

'Pretty close. Why d'yer ask?'

''As Darkie mentioned anyfing ter you about goin' in the 'olesale business?' Ben enquired.

'Yeah, as a matter o' fact 'e did, but it's all 'ush-'ush at the moment,' Gerry told him.

'Did yer know the Malts 'ave formed a syndicate an' they're negotiatin' ter buy the Gold Star grocery firm in Tooley Street?'

Gerry looked surprised. 'No, I didn't,' he replied. 'Darkie's bin very cagey as a matter of fact. 'Ow did you find out?'

'Sammy Goldbloom is an ole pal o' mine,' Ben told him. 'I've done quite a bit o' business wiv 'im. 'E told me in confidence so yer better keep it ter yerself or it'll queer my pitch wiv 'im.'

The workmen left the cafe and Joe came over to the two young men. 'That geezer I was tellin' yer about seemed ter be payin' you two a lot of attention,' he said.

Gerry shrugged his shoulders. ''E couldn't 'ear anyfing, Joe.'

The cafe owner smiled. 'Workin' in this poxy cafe is better than goin' ter the pictures sometimes,' he remarked. 'There's more intrigue in 'ere in one day than in ten spy films put tergevver.'

'Remember that film "Casablanca"?' Ben said grinning. 'You should put a joanna over there an' stick a neon sign outside that ses "Rick's Cafe". Yer'd double yer business overnight. "Of all the greasy spoons in all the world, you 'ad ter walk inter mine."'

'Yeah, but I ain't 'Umphrey Bogart,' Joe laughed. 'I wouldn't get ter service Ingrid Bergman. I'd end up wiv Marfa Ray.'

Gerry was looking thoughtful. 'Tell me, Joe, do those workmen come in 'ere regularly?' he asked.

The cafe owner shook his head. 'Nah, but like I said, one o' 'em drinks wiv the Varley boys. They use my local as a matter o' fact.'

'Which pub's that?' Gerry asked.

'The 'Orseshoe in Tower Bridge Road.'

'The pub next ter the Trocette?'

'Yeah, that's right.'

'I was just finkin',' Gerry said, turning to Ben. 'If the geezer tells Constantine we've bin chattin' tergevver 'e might start askin' yer questions. I know fer a fact 'e's curious about where I stand.'

'Yeah, an' 'e might pay you a visit too, Joe,' Ben warned him.

'Don't you worry about me,' Joe said with spirit. 'I'm like those wise monkeys. I see no evil, 'ear no evil an' speak no evil. In fact I say nuffing.'

The Marsden murder trial had attracted a lot of public interest, coming in the wake of a much-publicised police campaign to clean up the Soho area, and the Old Bailey's number three court was filled to capacity for the final day. Everyone sat eagerly awaiting the summing-up by the defence counsel, and in the public gallery above the defendant's family and friends stared down anxiously into the well of the court.

Richard Marsden, a market trader from Hoxton, was charged with the murder of an Italian immigrant, Dino Marinello, who had been stabbed through the heart in a back alley off Lisle Street. The defendant had recently been released from prison after serving two years for black-market offences, and was known to frequent the drinking and gambling clubs in Soho. Convinced of his innocence, however, Marsden's market friends and family had raised the money necessary to obtain the services of the best counsel available, and though worried about the strong case presented by the Crown they were nevertheless hopeful of an acquittal.

Samuel Selby K.C. sat passively in his wig and gown, his fingers drumming a tune on the table as he waited to address the jury. Occasionally he glanced up towards the cold sunlight in the high windows and thought about his long night of love. Claudette had been unbelievably passionate and it had been truly wonderful, but during an early breakfast that morning she had been strangely quiet, tending to avoid his eyes when he looked at her. It was as though their feverish lovemaking had been merely an interlude, a brief respite from the strange distance that had grown between them. He blamed her father, trying to use him as a surrogate for his own ambitions and twisting his daughter's mind to achieve his ends. Well, to hell with the bloody man!

A hush came over the court as Selby rose to his feet, his arm sweeping up from under his gown to grip his collar in a professional pose. He approached the jury, taking a deep breath and swallowing hard. A man's life was hanging in the balance, and he reproached himself angrily for allowing his mind to wander. For God's sake concentrate, he told himself.

'Members of the jury,' he began in a measured tone of voice. 'Above this famous old building is the figure of justice, blind to prejudice and appearances, holding the scales of judgement. It is a fitting symbol. Jurisprudence requires that the accused must be tried before a court of law in a spirit of impartiality and fairness, however the concerns of the day and the pressures of public opinion may seem to impinge upon and lay claim to the case. Justice must be done, not just be seen to be done. It is the gravity of solid evidence as opposed to airy supposition that should tip the scales, and this morning I am going to remind you of the facts of this case so that you may weigh the evidence fairly and impartially.'

The silence of the expectant court was broken by a stifled cough and Selby leaned on the polished rail of the jury box, his dark eyes moving along the line of jurors. 'Richard Marsden is no paragon of virtue, nor is he, by his own admission, an upright citizen,' he continued. 'In fact he has been at pains to make his criminal record known to you, despite being advised to the contrary and notwithstanding his right to withhold such information. Why, you might ask? The answer, members of the jury, is quite a simple one. My client is anxious for you to understand and believe that he is not a violent man. His offences, for all of which he has been suitably punished, have been of a non-violent nature.

'Are we to believe therefore, that on the night of June the sixth, Richard Marsden contradicted the habits of a lifetime and cold-bloodedly committed the heinous crime of murder? The fact is, my client found himself in the wrong place at the wrong time. He was drunk, and he stepped into an alley to relieve himself. An innocent act that finally brought him here into the dock to face a charge of murder.

'You have heard the evidence so eloquently put by my learned friend, that Marsden's hands, suit and shoes were found to be smeared with blood when he was stopped by the two police constables in Lisle Street. You have also heard the police report which stated that when apprehended the accused was staggering drunkenly and his speech was slurred. Is such a state of intoxication consistent with the commission of an act of murder performed with deadly expertise only minutes, perhaps even seconds earlier? Of course not. But let us move on. Forensic evidence stated that the blood found on my client matched that of the victim, Dino Marinello. You have heard too that the fatal stab wound was inflicted with a long, thin instrument, quite possibly a stiletto knife. The weapon, stiletto or otherwise, has never been found. Are we then to believe that my client, in a drunken state at the time, remember, managed to conceal it so ingeniously as to defy discovery, despite a thorough search of the area?

'Members of the jury. It was enlightening to hear Chief Inspector James stating in evidence that a stiletto is not the type of knife with which most villains would normally arm themselves. They are much more likely to use a flick knife or indeed a cut-throat razor, both of which could be easily concealed. A stiletto is an Italian dagger, and it so happens that on the night of the sixth of June there were five Italian nationals sitting around a table playing poker in the gambling club. Now you will also recall that Alberto Verruchio stated in evidence that he was one of the card players that night, and the only member of that group who spoke English. Verruchio testified that Dino Marinello left the table around eleven o'clock to get some air, and when he failed to return another of the card players went to look for him and found him in the alley lying in a pool of blood. Dino Marinello had died from a single stab wound to the heart.'

Selby stood up straight and walked slowly past the intent faces of the jurors. 'You have heard Richard Marsden's testimony under oath, that he went into the alley to relieve himself and stumbled over Marinello, landing on all fours beside him. Even in his drunken state he could see that the victim was in his death throes. His hands were clasping his chest and blood was pumping out from the wound. You heard my client say that the man's eyes were staring at him, pleading, and in his inebriated state he tried to stem the bleeding with his scarf, which was subsequently found across the body. Then when he realised that the man had died he panicked and staggered out from the alley, only to be detained by two passing policemen a few yards along Lisle Street.

'The act committed by my client that night was not one of murder but one of compassion, of mercy, as he saw the pleading look in the eyes of the dying man.'

Selby turned and walked back slowly to his original position and gripped the rail with both hands, leaning forward slightly for effect. 'Ladies and gentlemen of the jury,' he said in a tone of sober entreaty. 'What of the motive? My learned friend for the prosecution would have you believe it was a vendetta, a planned killing in an area where racial tension is at boiling point. Pure supposition. You have heard from Alberto Verruchio that he had never seen Marsden before the trial. Are we to give credence to the idea of a premeditated murder that depended on Dino Marinello taking an unwonted break for a breath of air and my client lurking around in the alley just in case he did? Are we to believe that my client planned the murder and before carrying it out drank himself into a near stupor, then dealt the death blow with frightful, expert precision? The answer is no. Have we to accept that my client set upon a complete stranger, an Italian immigrant who spoke no English, a fact that is on record? An animated argument between two people in two separate languages ending in murder? A drunken man answering a call of nature who just happens to have a stiletto on his person and uses it to inflict a fatal injury, then magics the weapon away? Of course not.'

Selby cast his eyes along the stern faces in the jury box. 'Members of the jury,' he concluded, 'my client does not deserve your compassion, nor your pity. He deserves your fair and rational judgement, your sensible appraisal of the facts of this case. I exhort you, ladies and gentlemen of the jury, to bring in the only verdict possible. Not guilty!'

A buzz of voices rose up and was silenced by the loud knock of the gavel as Samuel Selby took his seat.

In a marble alcove in the antechamber of the court Samuel sat gazing at the ancient frozen cracks of stone pillar. Something was troubling him, something he had pushed out of his mind for a long time, and he felt assailed by a terrible sadness. He could not get the figure of Richard Marsden out of his mind, standing there in the dock thin and shifty-looking, dressed up in a cheap suit with the collar too tight and an old-fashioned tie clumsily knotted at the neck. Trussed up for the kill. The man was innocent, there was no question about it, but whether the jury believed him was a different matter.

Prejudice will out, Samuel thought bitterly. Spawned in a mean backstreet, orphaned at seven years old and shunted from one family to another, what chance had the man had? In a children's home at nine and Borstal at fifteen, it had been downhill from then on. Walk down any back turning in London and you would find a Richard Marsden. There but for the grace of God, Samuel sighed to himself. Just another mother's son.

Just another mother's son.

It was well into the afternoon when the jury returned, and as the foreman rose Samuel Selby felt his insides twisted by a horrible, poignant sense of mortality as if he himself were standing in the dock.

'We the jury find the defendant . . . not guilty.'

Pandemonium broke out and cheering from the public gallery greeted the verdict. Richard Marsden stepped down and shook hands with Samuel, shocked with relief. Samuel turned on his heel and strode from the court, feeling like a man reborn. He knew what he would do now. As soon as he got home he would write a reply to the letter about Lottie Curtis's party, and then he would tell Claudette that he had no intention of standing for Parliament, now or ever, and anyone trying to persuade him was wasting their time. And if she and that arrogant father of hers didn't like it, then they could damn well lump it.

Chapter Twenty-One

Ann Johnson had spent much of the day working on a patchwork cushion which she had stuffed with down, and by early evening it was ready. 'I 'ope Lottie'll like this,' she said, holding it out in front of her.

'I'm sure she will,' Lana told her. 'It'll be nice an' soft fer 'er ter sit on. That ole one she's got now is as flat as a pancake.'

'There we are then, you can take it in to 'er ternight, unless yer goin' out,' Ann said as she took off her glasses and rubbed her tired eyes.

'Yeah, I'll be poppin' in later,' Lana replied. 'Ben's out again ternight.'

'Yer've not bin seein' much of 'im lately, 'ave yer?' Ann remarked, eyeing her daughter with concern.

Lana shook her head. ''E's bin sortin' out some business, at least that's what 'e said.'

Ann studied her daughter's face and caught the look of irritation. ''E'll never change. Duckin' and divin', that's all 'e knows,' she told her. 'Still, it's your life. I just 'ope yer know what yer doin'.'

'Don't worry, Mum, I've 'ad it out wiv 'im,' Lana said. 'Ben knows the score an' it's up to 'im.'

Ann gave her an indulgent smile. 'Just don't wait around too long, that's all. There's plenty more fish in the sea.'

Lana picked up the cushion, not wanting any further

discussion. 'I fink I'll take this in now,' she said.

'Don't ferget ter see what Lottie needs from the market termorrer,' Ann called out as Lana went out into the scullery to pick up the key.

Lottie Curtis gave the young woman a wan smile. ''Ello, luv, what yer got there?' she asked.

Lana sat down facing her. 'You look much better ternight,' she remarked. 'Mum sent this over for yer. She made it 'erself. She said it'll be more comfortable than that ole one yer sittin' on.'

Lottie pulled a face. 'I'm used ter this cushion, but it was a nice thought anyway,' she replied.

'Yer can still keep that ole one, but put this on top, it'll be more comfortable for yer,' Lana persisted.

The old lady did not appear too eager but she eased herself up on the arms of the rocker while Lana slid the new cushion under her.

'There we are, that's better, ain't it?'

'Yeah, it feels nice an' soft,' Lottie replied without much enthusiasm.

Lana guessed that the old lady was feeling a little depressed from the after-effects of her flu and she leaned forward eagerly in her chair. ''Ere, what yer fink? Our Alan's wife's bin ter the clinic an' they've told 'er it might be twins,' she said beaming.

'Gawd 'elp 'er,' Lottie replied. 'One's an 'andful, let alone two.'

'By the way, Mum said ter remind yer about the shoppin' list.'

'I'm all right, fanks. I ain't in need of anyfing.'

'D'yer want me ter put a bit more coal on the fire?'

'Nah, it's all right.'

'Would yer like a cuppa?'

Lottie's face remained impassive as she shook her head.

''Ave yer seen anyfing o' Jimmy Bailey?' the young woman asked in an attempt to buck her up.

''E said 'e was callin' round, but that was days ago.'

'Are yer tired, luv? Would yer like me ter go?' Lana said quietly.

'Nah, you stay fer a while if yer want to,' Lottie replied. 'Take no notice o' me, it's just the way I feel.'

Lana bit on her lip as the old lady took out a handkerchief from her apron pocket and dabbed at her eyes. 'I understand,' she told her kindly. 'Yer've not bin very well an' it's bound ter make yer feel a bit depressed. Anyway, now yer up an' about yer'll soon be yer ole self.'

Lottie smiled back at her and stuffed the handkerchief back into her pocket. 'This is a nice comfortable cushion,' she remarked. 'Yer mus' fank yer muvver. It was very nice of 'er ter fink o' me.'

Lana looked down and saw the album at Lottie's feet. 'D'yer fink I could 'ave anuvver peek at those photos?' she asked.

''Course yer can,' Lottie said, her eyes brightening.

Lana took up the album and placed it on the old lady's lap, then drew up a chair from the table. 'I love lookin' frew those ole photos,' she said smiling at her, 'especially when yer tell me all those stories about the kids.'

Lottie turned the pages. 'I told yer about Freddie Williams,' she said, 'an' this little mite,' pointing to the little lad behind him.

'Yeah, that's Samuel Selby,' Lana replied. ''E's the solicitor.'

'Barrister,' Lottie corrected her as she turned the page. 'Now there's a nice snap o' the two little gels that was 'ere when Jimmy arrived. That's Lucy, the fair one, an' that's Ellen wiv the ginger 'air. Lucy was five when that was taken. Last I 'eard of 'er she'd married inter money. The man 'ad some sort o' business. Local feller 'e was, so Farvver McCarfy told me. They got married in 'is church just before the war broke out an' apparently they moved out o' London when the Blitz started. Kent somewhere, or maybe it was Essex. I can't remember.'

'What about the ovver little one, Ellen is it?' Lana inquired.

Lottie suddenly looked sad. 'She got inter bad company

when she grew up. Farvver McCarfy told me she got nicked fer shopliftin', an' there was anuvver time when she stole some money from where she worked. I dunno the strength of it, but she got sent ter prison. I read about it in the paper. Mind you, she didn't 'ave much of a chance in life, poor little cow. 'Er muvver was no good. Always takin' in men when 'er 'usband was away. 'E was one o' them commercial travellers. 'E used ter go all over the country. The kids were badly neglected an' someone got on ter the police about it. Anyway they summonsed the muvver an' took the children away. That's 'ow I come ter get 'er.'

'Did she go back to 'er muvver?' Lana asked her.

Lottie shook her head. 'One night 'er farvver come 'ome unexpected an' caught 'is wife in bed wiv a seaman. 'E divorced 'er an' after 'e got a job workin' locally 'e took Ellen back. From what I 'eard 'is second wife wasn't much better. So yer see there's some excuse fer the poor cow be'avin' the way she did. Fer all I know she could be 'appily married wiv a tribe o' kids now, though I doubt it. Sad. Very sad.'

Lana watched as the old lady flipped the page and came to a blank sheet. 'I was just finkin',' she remarked. 'There's nine children yer told me about. I thought yer 'ad ten in all.'

Lottie's eyes took on a faraway look. 'Yeah, that's right, there was ten, but I never 'ad any photos o' the last one. 'E wasn't wiv me very long,' she replied quickly.

Lana wanted to ask more, but there was a look in the old lady's eyes that stopped her. Better to leave it for the time being, she thought.

'Well, what about that cup o' tea?' Lottie said cheerily.

Lana took the album from her lap and slid it down beside the rocker. 'You lean back an' close yer eyes fer five minutes an' I'll call yer when the tea's made,' she said kindly.

Lottie patted her hand. 'You're a dear,' she said smiling.

The young woman walked out into the cold scullery and filled the kettle. There was some more information to work on now, she thought, though the last of the children still remained unnamed. The job of locating the rest of them would be a mammoth task, however, and time was getting short.

Lana struck a match to light the gas but as she turned on the tap a roaring sound frightened her and she turned it off again quickly. Just then she heard a knock on the front door.

Jimmy Bailey's eyes lit up when he saw her. 'Long time no see,' he said smiling.

The young woman felt her heart surge and she gave him a warm smile in return. 'It seems ages,' she replied, appraising his donkey coat with the collar turned up and the white scarf knotted round his neck.

'Yeah, it does,' he said. 'Any chance o' comin' in?'

'I'm sorry,' Lana giggled, bringing her hand up to her mouth as she stepped back.

Jimmy strolled along the dark passage and put his head round the parlour door. 'Lottie's asleep,' he remarked as he followed her into the scullery.

'We've bin lookin' at the album again,' she told him. 'I've managed ter get some more info.'

''Ave yer 'eard from that Selby bloke?' he asked.

Lana shook her head. 'Not yet, an' some'ow I don't fink I will.'

'I shouldn't worry too much, there's time yet,' he said brightly.

The young woman stared at the kettle. 'Jimmy, could yer try lightin' the gas? There's air in the pipes an' it scares me in case there's an explosion.'

The young man laughed aloud as he took the box of matches from her. 'Where did yer get that ole wives' tale from?' he asked.

Lana watched as he turned the gas tap on and she stepped back a pace as she heard the roar. He turned the tap off and then successfully lit the low back burner. 'That should do it,' he remarked as he turned it off before lighting the one under the kettle. 'There we are, no trouble. That's got rid o' the air.'

Lana leaned against the old Welsh dresser and folded her

arms. ''Ow's yer new job comin' on?' she asked.

'It's OK,' Jimmy told her as he undid his coat and loosened his scarf. 'I got a new Bedford lorry an' they've supplied me wiv overalls an' this jacket. It's all local work so there's no nights away, not that I'm worried now I'm on me own.'

Lana felt sorry for him as he tried to disguise his sadness. 'It must be awful bein' on yer own,' she said.

'It's not so bad,' he replied. 'I go round ter see Glenda an' Lillian occasionally, an' sometimes they get me a meal. I'm gettin' used to it.'

Lana found herself staring at him intently as he spoke. His dark eyes were brightly alive and his thick dark hair was combed back neatly. She gazed at his square chin and small straight nose and realised how attractive he was. 'I'm glad yer called in ternight,' she said almost without thinking.

'I'm glad too,' he said quietly. 'I've missed yer.'

Lana felt her cheeks becoming warm and she averted her eyes suddenly, fussing with the teapot and caddie. 'I've missed you too,' she replied, feeling her throat suddenly going dry.

Jimmy sat down at the table. 'Tell me all about what yer found out,' he said with a disarming smile.

Lana spooned the tea leaves into the pot before pulling up a chair, and as she finished telling him what Lottie had said the kettle started to boil.

'I was just finkin' that maybe we could get in touch wiv the Far East Prisoners o' War Association,' he suggested. 'They might 'ave some info on Morgan Jones.'

'That's a good idea,' Lana replied as she filled the teapot. 'S'posin' 'e didn't survive though?'

'They still might be able ter tell us somefing,' Jimmy said. 'They've got records of all the men taken prisoner, so I 'eard.'

'I'll 'ave ter find an address ter write to,' Lana told him.

'Leave it ter me, yer've got enough ter be goin' on wiv,' he replied. 'I'll make a few phone calls.'

'That'll be great,' she said smiling.

The young man took out a tobacco tin and looked

inquiringly at her. 'Do yer mind if I smoke?' he asked.

Lana shook his head. ''Course not. Me dad rolls 'is own.'

Jimmy flicked off the lid and licked the tips of his fingers before pulling a cigarette paper from the packet. 'I used ter smoke tailor-made but I found this way I don't smoke so much. Besides, yer can't roll a fag while yer drivin' a lorry,' he said giving her a quick wink.

Lana sat quietly watching as he expertly rolled the paper and makings between thumb and fingers and then wetted the gummed edge of the paper with the tip of his tongue. 'I'm pleased yer got a decent job,' she remarked. 'Do yer like drivin' fer a livin'?'

Jimmy nodded. 'It's out in the open air, an' there's no one standin' over yer like in a factory,' he replied. 'I've 'ad factory jobs an' I used ter get so cranked up. The time drags an' there's foremen chasin' yer up all the time. It was terrible. Wiv a drivin' job I can pull up fer a cuppa when I like an' I get ter see different places. Actually though, if I told yer what I'd really like ter do yer'd prob'ly laugh.'

'Try me,' Lana said, her lips parting in a smile.

Jimmy lit the cigarette with a petrol lighter and took a deep drag, blowing a cloud of smoke towards the ceiling. 'I'd like my own business,' he said, looking a little self-conscious.

'What sort o' business?'

'Well, I'd really like ter be a smithy.'

'A blacksmith? That's a surprise,' Lana said as she got up to pour out the tea.

Jimmy smiled. 'When I was a kid there was a blacksmith's shop just off Abbey Street an' I used ter go there every chance I got,' he told her. 'At first the blacksmith used ter tell me ter bugger off, but I always went back an' peered round the door, watchin' 'im work. Then, when 'e realised I was genuinely interested, 'e let me stand inside the smithy. Joshua Blackwell 'is name was. 'E was a typical blacksmith, with arms like tree trunks an' 'ands like dinner plates. Joshua was a very gentle man though, considerin' 'is size, an' 'e taught me a lot. 'E was a farrier too an' there was always somefing different goin' on. One day 'e'd be busy shoein' 'orses an' the next 'e'd be making wrought-iron gates an' the like. Ole Joshua used ter let me work the bellows of 'is fire an' sometimes if 'e wasn't too busy 'e'd let me 'old a piece o' red-'ot iron in a massive pair o' tongs while 'e shaped it. I got ter love that man. 'E treated me like the son 'e never 'ad.'

'Wasn't 'e married?' Lana asked, intrigued.

'Nah 'e was a strange, lonely man,' Jimmy replied. 'I used to 'ave long chats wiv 'im as I got older. As a matter o' fact 'e actually showed me 'ow ter shoe 'orses. I got pretty good at it.'

'Is 'e still about?' Lana asked.

Jimmy shook his head sadly. 'I was eighteen when 'e died. I'll never ferget the day. I was in the smithy watchin' 'im bend this length o' red-'ot iron fer an ornamental gate an' 'e suddenly staggered back an' then dropped ter the floor. It was a stroke. 'E died in Guy's 'Ospital a few days later. I was 'eartbroken. It took me ages ter get over it. I couldn't understand 'ow a big, powerful man could keel over an' die just like that. 'E was only in 'is mid-forties.'

''Ow terrible,' Lana remarked.

Jimmy nodded slowly. 'So now yer know my little secret. Mind you, if I ever got enough money ter start up as a blacksmith I'd go on one o' them ex-service courses they're offerin'. I'd take a weldin' course. I'd make a go of it, I know I would.'

Lana saw the determined look in the young man's eyes and she smiled at him. 'I'm sure yer would,' she said.

Jimmy got up and looked into the parlour. 'She's still sound asleep,' he said when he came back.

The two sat sipping their tea and Lana looked thoughtful. 'Well, we've got two definites out o' the nine left,' she said after a while. 'There's you an' Charlie Smedley. We know fer certain that 'orrible Phoebe Francis won't be there, an' we're still waitin' fer Samuel Selby ter reply, though I don't 'old out much 'ope. So there's five more ter find. Morgan an' Alice, that's if Morgan's still alive , an' Ellen an' Lucy. As fer the fifth, that one's a bit of a mystery. I asked Lottie about 'im but she seemed ter clam up. It was really strange.'

'Yeah, I knew she took in ten of us in all but she's never spoken about the last one she fostered,' Jimmy replied. 'You said "'im". Did Lottie tell yer it was a lad?'

Lana nodded. 'We'll just 'ave ter concentrate on what we've got so far, I s'pose. I'll wait till Lottie's feelin' a bit better before I ask 'er again.'

Jimmy's eyes narrowed. 'I was finkin',' he said, rubbing his chin with his thumb and forefinger. 'Ellen got nicked fer shopliftin'. It might 'ave bin in the papers.'

'Yeah, but it would take ages to look through 'em,' Lana told him. 'If we 'ad a year ter go on it'd 'elp.'

'At least the parish records will tell us when Lucy got married, an' we'll find out the name of 'er 'usband,' Jimmy said positively. 'That'll be a start.'

'I'm really glad yer in on this,' Lana said, smiling gratefully. 'I don't fink I could do this wivout your 'elp.'

'I'm only too glad to oblige,' he replied, looking at her earnestly. 'Ter be honest, I fink it was a very nice thought ter make this birfday special fer Lottie.'

Lana smiled modestly. 'She's a lovely old lady, an' let's face it, we don't know fer sure if she'll see anuvver birfday.'

Jimmy got up and popped his head round the parlour door once more. 'She's stirrin',' he said.

Lana stood up to go to her, and as she passed Jimmy in the doorway their bodies almost touched. Their eyes met, and for a split second she saw something in his that made her spine tingle. Jimmy reached out his hand and gently touched her forearm. 'You go an' talk to 'er. I'll pour the tea,' he said quietly.

much.' [illegible] So that's five more for [illegible]. [illegible] and Alice [illegible] then [illegible] for the [illegible] I asked [illegible] the [illegible] for [illegible] was [illegible] strange.

'Yeah, I knew she took [illegible] of us in all but she never spoken [illegible] the last [illegible],' Jimmy replied. 'Now and then [illegible].'

I [illegible] nodded. 'We'll just [illegible] concentrate on [illegible] as far as the post. I'll wait [illegible] Lucas's [illegible] before [illegible] again.'

Jimmy's eyes narrowed. '[illegible],' he said, [illegible] his chin with his thumb and forefinger. 'Then you [illegible] around [illegible] might [illegible] in the [illegible].'

'Yeah, but it would take [illegible] to look [illegible] right [illegible].'

'At least the parish records will [illegible] us [illegible] find out the name of her husband,' Jimmy said [illegible]. 'That'll be [illegible].'

I [illegible] and smiling [illegible] 'I could do [illegible] without you [illegible].'

'That's what [illegible] to [illegible],' he replied, looking [illegible] 'but it [illegible] a very [illegible] daughters like [illegible] special [illegible].'

I [illegible] 'a [illegible] know for sure [illegible] ever [illegible].'

Jimmy got up and popped his head [illegible] the window [illegible] once more. 'She's [illegible] again.'

I [illegible] went [illegible] her and as she passed Jimmy in the doorway [illegible] almost touched. Their eyes met, and in a split second she saw something in his that made [illegible]. Jimmy reached out his hand and gently [illegible]. 'You [illegible] for [illegible] your [illegible] church.'

Chapter Twenty-Two

Westbrook Avenue was a long leafy backwater in Camberwell. It was far enough away from the main thoroughfares of the district to be quiet and secluded, yet convenient for businessmen and professional people who earned their living in the capital. The avenue had large, well-maintained Victorian houses with lengthy back gardens, and amongst its residents was one Michael Constantine.

At number sixteen Westbrook Avenue there had been an influx of visitors on Thursday evening and their hostess was kept busy serving drinks and sandwiches. Most of the visitors were unknown to her and she was feeling nervous as she passed amongst them. Mick had been in a foul mood all day and she realised that the meeting he had called for that evening was not a normal social gathering. He had made it clear to her that she should ensure all the guests were suitably welcomed and then make herself scarce while the meeting took place.

The last guest to arrive was a tall, thin man in his mid-forties wearing gold-rimmed spectacles and carrying a briefcase. He was smartly dressed in a dark suit and a belted mackintosh and his grey hair was flattened down with brilliantine. He blinked nervously as the gang boss pulled him to one side and conversed in whispers, then he accepted a drink from Mandy with a curt nod.

'Right then, let's get started,' Mick Constantine said peremptorily.

Mandy did as she had been told and left the large comfortable lounge for the seclusion of the kitchen where she sat down to scan through a fashion magazine once more. There was a two-piece costume which had caught her eye and she hoped that the meeting would go well and her new husband would emerge from it in a better mood than when he went in. The costume would do wonders for her, she could just see it, and she wanted to look her best for Gerry Knowland. He would have received her letter by now and she was praying that he could meet her in Brighton very soon as they had planned.

Constantine stood by the ornate fireplace with a glass of Scotch in his hand as he eyed the gathering. His face was dark with controlled anger and his powerful presence dominated the room.

''Ave you all read the report in the papers?' he asked. Profuse nods led him on. 'I fink it's a diabolical piece o' crap. A scandal they call it. I'm puttin' new roofs on an' new sinks in dilapidated shit-'oles an' they've got the nerve ter call it a scandal. If makin' run-down properties fit ter live in is a scandal then what do they call the borough council? Most o' the older properties they rent out are damp, bug-ridden 'utches. Why don't the papers latch on ter them? You're my legal representative, you tell me.'

Frederick Barnfield quickly cleared his throat, moved his briefcase back a few inches and crossed his legs. 'As a matter of fact they have,' he replied in a reedy voice. 'As it happens there's been a housing standards crusade recently by the local press. They homed in on bad maintenance and long delays in implementing repairs, and in reply the Bermondsey Borough Council spokesman gave a good account of himself in explaining their difficulties, lack of funds, skilled labour shortage, etcetera, etcetera. Apparently it satisfied the muckrakers, so now they're turning their attentions to private development and renovation.'

'Oh they are, are they?' Constantine retorted sarcastically. 'Well we'll just 'ave ter satisfy the muck-rakers too, one way or another.'

Barnfield reached down and unclipped his briefcase. 'I've prepared a statement for you, Mick,' he said, taking out a green folder. 'I've dealt with the main bone of contention, namely the inconvenience caused to the elderly tenants while repairs are being carried out, but I need to go over it with you as soon as possible. I've managed to stall the reporters thus far but they'll be pestering us for a statement very soon, that's for sure.'

Constantine nodded then turned towards a thick-set individual sitting near the window. 'Barry, what about those roofs?' he asked.

'We're waitin' on slates, guv, but there's tarpaulins up ter keep out the rain,' the works manager replied. 'Mind yer though, the weavver don't 'elp.'

Constantine afforded himself a smile. 'What about the plumbin'?'

'Terrible, guv. It's causin' us a problem, but we're sortin' it out.'

'I'm sure yer are,' the gang boss told him with a sly smile before turning to Nipper Varley who was slumped in his chair. 'Did yer get ter see Palmer?' he asked him.

'No problem,' Varley said smiling. ''E can supply all the muscle required. All 'e wants is a few hours' notice.'

'Good. What about the Malt bookies, Des?'

'They're all off our manor wiv the exception of Luigi Comino,' Des Wilshaw replied. ''E's operatin' from 'is own drum, that's bin the problem.'

'Get your boys ter warn 'im off politely, then 'ave a word wiv our friend at the station,' Constantine told him. 'We'll let the law sort it out for us in this instance. We can't 'ave private premises used fer gamin'. It gives the area a bad name.'

A ripple of tense laughter ceased when the gang boss raised his hand. 'Now ter the important matter outstandin',' he said, looking around the room slowly. 'I'm sure you're all upset about Baz Smithson, but none more than I am. Baz was on an errand fer me when 'e got topped an' I take this sort o' fing personally. The Ole Testament ses an eye fer an eye, but we gotta be patient. The cozzers are expectin' a backlash, an' if one o' the Malts gets done they're gonna come down 'ard on us. So fer the time bein' we're gonna 'ang fire. Nipper, go an' tell Mandy ter get off 'er arse an' get us all a drink.'

Tommy Carberry had been sitting quietly near the door and he took the opportunity to go over and whisper a few words in his employer's ear. Constantine nodded and then beckoned to Barry. The builder came over and glanced round quickly at the gathering before divulging his bit of information. 'I dunno if this means anyfing, guv, but one o' my lads told me 'e saw Gerry Knowland down the street we're workin' in,' he muttered. ''E was talkin' ter one o' the tenants there. Also Knowland's bin gettin' a bit fick wiv Ben Ferris lately. This lad saw 'em tergevver in a transport cafe in River Lane.'

'That cafe's run by Joe Slavin,' Constantine replied. 'Slavin's got a bit o' form an' 'e's well known locally. I just 'ope 'e's not encouragin' the wrong sort in 'is establishment. Get your man ter keep 'is eyes an' ears open. Give 'im a few shekels as an incentive, an' tell 'im there'll be a bonus fer any tasty info 'e can supply.'

As soon as the works manager walked away Tommy Carberry turned to Constantine. 'What's the starting price on this Knowland geezer?' he asked.

The gang boss looked thoughtful. 'Gerry Knowland's got interests in the market,' he replied. ''E takes money from at least 'alf a dozen stalls an' 'e's got a yard in Dock'ead. 'E's inter buyin' an' sellin', an' word 'as it a couple o' good lorryloads 'ave gone 'is way lately. The trouble is, Knowland plays 'is cards close to 'is chest an' it bovvers me. What was 'e doin' sniffin' around down Rovver'ithe? Why so cosy wiv Ben Ferris? Ferris is only a chancer. More importantly, who supplied 'im wiv all that bent gear?'

'The word is the Malts were be'ind the recent lorry snatches, an' also that load that got nicked out o' the wharf,' Carberry told him.

Constantine's face grew dark. 'I got a gut feelin' Knowland's plannin' ter line up wiv the Malts,' he growled. ''E's known ter go clubbin' it up West on occasions an' it's a known fact that the Malts run the clubs in Soho.'

'Why should Knowland wanna team up wiv the Malts?' the minder inquired. 'They're clannish, an' they certainly don't take kindly to outsiders musclin' in on their manor. Cable Street's a good example. Yer can't get in any o' their gamblin' establishments over there unless yer speak the lingo.'

The gang boss nodded. 'I bin givin' it a lot o' thought. I reckon Knowland's out to extend 'is business an' 'e's after a franchise wiv the Malts ter supply their shops. If yer look around the manor yer'll find a Malt grocery shop in every poxy backstreet. It's a bloody disgrace.'

Thick cigarette smoke hung in the air, and as Mandy circulated with fresh drinks everyone present took the opportunity to chat together, with the exception of Frederick Barnfield, who sat quietly studying the folder he had prepared for his client. There was more news that would worry Mick Constantine, he reflected, but it would have to remain under wraps until the general meeting was over.

Constantine brought the assembly back to order and the bookmakers' group put forward their plans to carve up the territory vacated by the Maltese. The manager of the Camberwell drinking club owned by the gang boss also gave his report and introduced two new minders he had recruited from a local boxing gymnasium, and Barnfield sat patiently waiting. Excluded from the meeting, a very irritated Mandy stood over the sink washing sticky glasses and fuming over having to act as a common waitress. The lounge would be in a filthy state by the time the gathering broke up and her nails would be ruined with all the cleaning and washing up. The only consolation was that Mick would be mellowed by the

Scotch and too tired to want anything other than sleep that night.

It was almost ten o'clock when the meeting ended, and as the room emptied Constantine went over to a drinks cabinet and took out a bottle of brandy. 'This is vintage stuff, Frederick,' he said, pouring a large measure into each of the two brandy bowls that were standing on a silver salver. 'Now, let me see that statement while yer get this down yer.'

The solicitor sipped his drink with relish and watched as Constantine scanned through the pages. Suddenly he saw the man's forehead pucker.

'What's this bit?' he asked. 'Liaison wiv tenants an' completion date ter be set? I can't 'ave that. It defeats the bloody object. Barry tells me the rest of 'em are finkin' o' movin' out anyway, an' that only leaves ole Muvver Percival. I can wait fer 'er if I 'ave to. The cantankerous ole cow's turned eighty-six, she won't last fer ever.'

Barnfield smiled patiently. 'Mick, it's just a public relations exercise. What we're doing here is mollifying the press. When you get the tenants together you can promise them anything within reason. The completion date can be unavoidably extended through no fault of the builders, and as for their complaints, get your man to jot them all down and tell him to be sympathetic. It works wonders. The papers'll be stymied for a while, and in the meantime other burning issues will be certain to come to the fore. The Rotherhithe housing scandal, as they call it, will be yesterday's news.'

Constantine nodded. ''Ow do I present this?' he asked.

'I've arranged for a reporter to be on hand for a response,' Barnfield replied. 'It might be better if you meet him on site, certainly not at this house. Under no circumstances agree to meet the tenants yourself. It might give out the wrong signals. Let your hirelings do the business.'

Constantine nodded. 'Another drink, Frederick?'

'No, I've a court appearance tomorrow morning and I need a clear head,' the solicitor replied.

'Anything else?' the gang boss inquired.

Barnfield studied his empty glass for a few moments before replying. 'As a matter of fact, there is one thing,' he said quietly. 'A colleague of mine has been engaged in drawing up documents for the sale of a very successful local business. It's rather complicated, in as much as the business is creditor to the buyer, or in this instance the buyers.'

Constantine showed his impatience by sighing deeply. 'Go on.'

Barnfield would not be hurried. 'It appears that the owner of the business, which is situated in Tooley Street, has agreed to sell out to a consortium, formed by a group of shopkeepers who have individually been financed by the same businessman. I'm speaking of the Gold Star wholesale grocery concern.'

'Sammy Goldbloom,' the gang boss growled darkly. 'An' don't tell me, let me guess. The shopkeepers are none ovver than our Malt friends.'

'Right in one,' Barnfield replied.

'Yer say it's a consortium?'

'That's right.'

'And the down payment's no doubt bin raised by those lorry snatches,' Constantine growled. 'It's bad news, Frederick.'

The solicitor nodded his head slowly. 'It'll put the Malts in a very strong position. If any of the grocery shops go to the wall the consortium can take over the business, then either sell it back or sell it on to another of their own. It's a good tactic. It keeps it all in the family.'

The gang boss sat down heavily in a chair and took a gulp from his glass. 'I've not 'ad much ter do wiv Sammy Goldbloom, but I know 'is pedigree,' he said. 'That Gold Star business 'as bin goin' fer years. The man must be stone rich. When's this changeover likely ter take place?'

'In about two weeks, I should say,' Barnfield informed him. 'It'll take that long to sort out all the legal complexities.'

'S'posin' I was ter go in there wiv a late offer?' Constantine asked.

Barnfield shrugged his shoulders. 'I don't know, to be honest. My advice would be to forget it. Remember you'd be inheriting debtors.'

'Exactly,' Constantine said smiling evilly. 'I can't fink of a better way ter get rid o' the Malts.'

'Well, I'm sure that they're contractually tied to the Gold Star business for their supplies, and I would hazard a guess that they pay off their debts on a percentage basis on goods delivered,' Barnfield explained. 'You would have to continue supplying them. It would be included in the terms of sale.'

'Yeah, but the prices wouldn't,' the gang boss replied quickly. 'Nor would delivery times. If shopkeepers can't supply demand then people go elsewhere ter shop. I'd root the bastards out in no time at all.'

'Well, if you do decide to make an offer, time's paramount,' Barnfield told him. 'I'd just like it to go on record that I have advised against this venture.'

Constantine's eyes narrowed. 'Why, Frederick?' he asked. 'Be straight.'

The solicitor stared down into the brandy bowl in his hand. 'So far your methods have been successful, Mick,' he said slowly, 'but a desperate man resorts to desperate measures, and if you allow them the opportunity to band together out of desperation you could find yourself juggling with live grenades. One slip and it's kingdom come.'

'I've got more than enough muscle on my payroll ter take care of any eventuality,' the gang boss told him. 'But I'm a businessman an' I'd like ter conduct my affairs in a businesslike way. It's much less . . . er, taxin'.'

'I would agree entirely,' Barnfield replied.

Constantine stood up and walked over to the drinks cabinet. 'Well, I won't delay yer furvver,' he said. 'I'll be in touch very soon, after I talk to our friend Sammy Goldbloom.'

Mandy heard the front door close and realised that it was

now time to carry on with her chores. She hurried into the lounge to see Mick slumped down in his chair, a glass of brandy in his hand. 'I was just about ter tidy up,' she said.

'Leave it, I've got some serious finkin' ter do,' he told her. 'Yer can do it termorrer.'

Mandy sighed in resignation and walked out of the room. It was about time Mick employed a housemaid, she thought. She would have to speak to him about it. It would have been nice to approach him about that two-piece in the magazine but now was definitely not the time. Maybe she could extract a promise from him later, when he came up to bed, if he wasn't too drunk.

now there to carry on with her chores. She hurried into the lounge to see Mick slumped down in his chair, a glass of brandy in his hand. 'I was just about to go up,' he said.

'Leave it. I'll get by without nothin' ter eat,' he told her. 'Ye can do it termorrer.'

Mandy sighed in resignation and walked out of the room. It was about time Mick employed a help-a-hand, she thought. She would have to speak to him about it. It would have been nice to approach him about that new piece in the magazine but now was definitely not the time. Maybe she could extract a promise from him later, when he came up to bed, if he wasn't too drunk.

Chapter Twenty-Three

Rain was falling from a leaden sky as Lana hurried along Abbey Street on Thursday evening and knocked on the last house but one. She could hardly contain herself as Jimmy Bailey opened the door. 'I 'ad ter come round,' she said smiling broadly. 'I got a letter from Samuel Selby.'

Jimmy stepped back to let her in. ''E's comin'?' he queried.

'Yeah. Read the letter,' Lana urged him. 'I'm so pleased.'

The young man took the envelope from her and brushed the evening paper off the armchair. 'Sit down,' he said, amused by the ecstatic look on her pretty face as he sat down facing her.

My Dear Miss Johnson,

I was very pleased to receive your letter of the 15th November and delighted to hear that Mrs Curtis is still very hale and hearty. It will be a privilege to attend her very special day and I have entered it in my diary. I look forward to meeting Lottie once more, and I'm sure that the occasion will evoke many childhood memories for me, mostly happy ones. Until Christmas Eve then.

Yours sincerely,

Samuel Selby.

Jimmy handed the letter back and grasped her hands in his.

'That's really wonderful,' he said beaming.

Lana's face was still flushed from the journey round but she felt her cheeks growing hotter and she slowly withdrew her hands from his with a smile. 'Mum gave me the letter as soon as I got in this evenin',' she told him. 'Ter be honest I thought 'e was gonna refuse. I'm over the moon, 'specially after gettin' nowhere wiv that Francis woman.'

The young man shared her elation. He stood up and went over to the sideboard. 'I've got some news too,' he said, handing her a slip of paper. 'Morgan Jones survived the war. 'Ere's 'is address. I got it from the Far East Prisoners of War Association.'

Lana looked at the piece of paper. 'Seventeen, Station Lane, Woodside, Essex,' she read out. 'That's a stroke o' luck too.'

'I don't work Saturdays,' Jimmy said suddenly. 'D'you?'

Lana shook her head. 'Whereabouts in Essex is Woodside?' she asked him.

'It's a village near Brentwood,' he told her. 'It's not very far really. We could get a train from Liverpool Street. It'll only be an hour by train.'

'Let's do it,' she said quickly.

'Shall I call for yer?' he asked.

'If yer like. Say about ten o'clock, or is that too early?'

'No, that'll do me fine.'

Lana bit on her thumbnail. 'I don't know 'ow we're gonna contact Alice though, nor the ovver two, Ellen an' Lucy.'

Jimmy dismissed her anxiety with a wave of his hand. 'Look, let's concentrate on findin' Morgan first,' he said. 'Don't ferget 'im an' Alice were inseparable, accordin' ter Lottie. They might 'ave kept in touch over the years, an' in any case Alice went inter nursin' durin' the war. We could make inquiries.'

'You're right,' Lana told him. 'I'm too impatient at times.'

Jimmy sat down on the edge of the armchair. 'Look, we could discuss this over a drink, if yer'd like,' he suggested.

Lana's expression grew regretful. 'I'm sorry, Jimmy, but I've gotta go out.'

He looked crestfallen. 'I'm sorry, I forgot yer was goin' steady wiv someone,' he said quickly. 'Maybe when yer got a free night. Just fer a drink an' a chat.'

'I dunno about steady,' she replied. 'But I'd love ter take you up on the offer, soon as I can.'

The young man smiled happily. 'I'll really look forward ter that,' he told her. 'I'll walk yer back 'ome.'

'There's no need, really,' Lana said quickly.

'Until Saturday then.'

'I'll expect yer at ten.'

Ben Ferris put down the phone with a satisfied look on his face. He had read in the previous evening's paper that a lorryload of Scotch whisky had been hijacked near York and he had been awaiting a call. The front doorbell startled him and he bit on his lip in consternation. That could be Lana. He had promised to take her to the musical *For Me an' My Gal*, with Gene Kelly and Judy Garland, and she was looking forward to it.

'I'm sorry I'm late,' she said as he opened the front door.

'It's OK. Come up a minute,' he said.

'Ain't you ready, Ben? We'll miss the start,' she said irritably.

'Look I'm sorry, Lana, but somefing's come up,' he replied.

She followed him up the steep flight of stairs. 'Don't tell me, yer gotta go somewhere,' she said sighing.

'I gotta meet Gerry in the Dewdrop at nine,' he told her. 'You can come wiv me. It shouldn't take long, but it's urgent I see 'im.'

'Look, I've told yer dozens o' times, I'm not sittin' on me own in a pub while you discuss business at the bar,' she flared. 'What d'you take me for?'

Ben looked dejected. 'You could wait 'ere for me. I should only be an hour at the most.'

'Yeah, I could, but I'm not goin' to,' she replied quickly. 'Ben, yer'll never change, no matter 'ow many promises yer make. It wouldn't be so bad if yer were gettin' somewhere, but yer not. At this rate we'll never 'ave enough money saved up ter get married.'

Ben's eyes widened in anger as he rounded on her. 'My ole dad worked in a tannery all 'is life, an' where did it get 'im?' he said contemptuously. 'I'll tell yer where, six feet under before 'is time. My muvver took in washin' an' scraped an' schemed ter put bread on the table, an' I might add there was little else to eat. Four kids an' no ole man ter keep 'er, 'cos 'e'd caught anthrax. Our Betsy got it right. She wasn't goin' in no dead-end job, she 'ad the sense ter marry a feller who 'ad a few bob. Me two bruvvers should 'ave learned the lesson as well, but what did they do? As soon as they left school they went straight inter factories. All right, Jack's a foreman but Bert's still workin' on a lathe in the same poxy factory 'e was in before 'e got called up. Both of 'em are married wiv kids an' strugglin' ter make ends meet on a pittance. No, Lana, that ain't fer me. I want a little more out o' life. I ain't gonna make the mistake they made.'

'You make me sick at times,' Lana said scathingly. 'What makes yer fink your two bruvvers got it wrong? They're married wiv kids, yeah, an' all right they're strugglin' ter pay the bills, but 'ave you ever asked 'em if they're 'appy or not? No, you're just assumin'. Are you 'appy duckin' an' divin', not knowin' from one day ter the next if yer gonna earn as much as a brass farthin'? Don't tell me you are 'cos I know yer not.'

Ben's shoulders sagged under the onslaught and he walked over to the window to stare out at the night. 'What's got into us, Lana?' he said quietly. 'We always seem ter be at each ovver's froats lately.'

'P'raps it just ain't gonna work, Ben,' she replied. 'We certainly can't go on like this.'

'Look, I've gotta get goin' in a minute,' he said. 'Don't let's leave it like this. I'll see yer termorrer. We can talk about fings calmly an' sensibly.'

'I can't see yer termorrer,' Lana said quickly. 'Yer know I 'ave ter wash me 'air an' do all me ironin' on Fridays.'

'I'll see yer on Saturday then.'

'I can't. We're goin' over to Essex. We got a lead ter foller up.'

Ben jumped. 'Who's we?'

''Is name's Jimmy Bailey. 'E was one o' the kids Lottie looked after an' 'e still comes an' sees 'er a lot. 'E's bin 'elpin' me.'

'Oh, I see. Very cosy. An' 'as this Jimmy Bailey pushed the right button?'

'D'you know, Ben, you can be so stupid at times,' she said disgustedly.

'Don't you call me stupid,' he said, coming towards her with a menacing face.

'What yer gonna do, whack me?' she raged. 'Go on then, if it'll give yer some satisfaction.'

Ben stopped short. 'Yer know I'd never lay a finger on yer. Yer just all screwed up.'

'Yeah, an' maybe I've got good reason ter be,' she countered.

'P'raps yer right. P'raps it ain't a good idea ter go on like this,' he said.

She nodded and walked to the door. 'I'll be seein' yer, Ben.'

'Yeah, take care.'

Outside the rain had ceased and the moon was peeping out from a gap in the clouds as the angry young woman hurried home. River Lane was deserted and silent, save for the sorrowful sound of a tug whistle echoing through the cobbled byway.

Joe Slavin lived alone above his cafe in River Lane and it suited him. The flat was cosy and comfortably furnished, and when the day was over he was content to retire to the room overlooking the lane and listen to the wireless or read. Joe preferred the classics, and his books were the only possessions he had managed to salvage from his disastrous marriage. Melody had taken him for every penny he had, but he was not bitter. He had learned a lot about life in his fifty-two years and understood that he had brought most of his troubles upon his own head.

'Hell hath no fury like a woman scorned,' he had quoted to Ben Ferris on one occasion when discussing his past life, though he was quick to point out that he had not exactly scorned her, merely mislaid her. He could have sworn that Melody had arranged to visit her ailing old mother in Brixton that evening, and he had taken the opportunity to bed one of the waitresses who worked at the restaurant he was managing in Peckham. Melody had not been at all pleased to find a much younger woman in her bed, as he had explained to Ben, and he was very lucky to escape in one piece, considering that his outraged wife was armed with a meat cleaver and threatening to neuter him. Joe had made it intact to a friend's house wearing nothing but a look of terror, and he realised that he had some serious thinking to do.

Melody's father owned the restaurant and he had lots of friends who coveted Melody and offered to avenge her honour, so when the news got back to Joe Slavin that half the young bucks in Peckham were out to impress her by beating him up he decided it was time to seek a safe haven. Bermondsey seemed a good idea. He had one or two friends there and they would most likely put him up until he sorted himself out.

When Joe Slavin arrived in the riverside borough he was dressed in borrowed clothes and was penniless, but he managed to locate one of his old friends, Charlie Best, who let him bed down on his sofa for a few nights. The good Samaritan was almost as badly off as his guest however, and out of desperation the two men joined forces to raid a fur warehouse across the river. Spotted by a vigilant night watchman, both Joe and Charlie were arrested on site and charged with attempted warehouse breaking, for which they were sentenced to two years' imprisonment.

Joe's fortunes took a turn for the better on release, and

through contacts made in Wandsworth and subsequent shady dealings he was able to amass enough money to set himself up in a little business, the working men's cafe in River Lane. His friend Charlie Best had been less fortunate and was currently serving another prison sentence, looking forward to release in the near future.

Joe was sitting by the dying fire still engrossed in D.H. Lawrence's *Sons and Lovers* when he heard a knock on his front door. Instinctively he looked up at the clock on the mantelshelf, and seeing that it was turned eleven he went over to the window and eased the curtain to one side. Down below he could see a broad-shouldered man at the door and he picked up the poker before hurrying down the steep flight of stairs. 'Who's there?' he called out.

'Open up, yer dozy git, it's Tommy Carberry.'

Joe slid the bolts back quickly and opened the door. 'Bloody blimey! If it ain't the Butcher 'imself,' he exclaimed, beckoning him in.

Tommy stepped inside the door and clasped Joe's hand. 'Long time, no see,' he said grinning. 'I know it's late, Joe, but as a matter o' fact I was casin' the place an' saw the light was still on, ovverwise I wouldn't 'ave knocked.'

'Come on up,' the cafe owner told him with a grin.

Tommy made himself comfortable by the fire and undid the buttons of his dark grey suit. 'It's bin a long while, pal,' he said, brushing his hand over his iron-grey cropped hair.

'Would yer like a drink?' Joe asked.

'Yeah, if yer've got any whisky.'

Joe went over to the sideboard and filled two small glasses from a bottle of Haig. 'Bloody 'ell, I can't get over it, seein' you again,' he said, handing Tommy his drink. 'It brings ter mind the night I see yer wrestle the Iron Duke. What a scrap that was.'

'Yeah, I almost pinned 'im twice,' Tommy replied, smiling nostalgically.

Joe sat down by the fire facing him. 'What's all this about

casin' the place?' he asked. 'There ain't much 'ere werf nickin'.'

Tommy shook his head. 'I was in company earlier ternight an' someone 'appened ter mention this cafe, then someone else said that you owned it. I wondered where yer'd disappeared to. Anyway I decided ter take a look fer future reference an' like I say, I saw the light on.'

'It seems I'm becomin' a bit notorious,' Joe said, sipping his drink.

Tommy studied his glass for a few moments. 'What d'yer know of Mick Constantine?' he asked suddenly.

'I know 'e's a big man in the area. The number one, some would say,' Joe replied.

'I'm workin' for 'im,' Tommy told him. 'I'm employed ter look after 'im.'

'Well, I'm sure yer will,' Joe said smiling. 'Was it Constantine who told yer this was my cafe?'

'Yeah, but I didn't let on I knew yer,' his old friend answered. 'I was at this meetin' at Mick's place over in Camberwell an' one o' the geezers marked Mick's card about the customers yer get in 'ere. 'E mentioned Gerry Knowland an' Ben Ferris in particular.'

'An' Mick's worried about Gerry Knowland, I take it,' the cafe owner replied.

'Yeah, yer could say that.'

'D'yer know 'em personally?' Joe asked him.

'I've met Ben Ferris,' Tommy replied. 'In the Crown as a matter o' fact, but I don't know Gerry Knowland.'

'Knowland's kosher, but 'e don't run wiv the crowd,' Joe explained. 'That's the reason fer Mick's concern. It's all tied up wiv what's 'appenin' on this manor at the moment. Anyway, you'd know all about that by now.'

'Between you an' me, Constantine's worried about Knowland linin' up wiv the Malts,' Tommy told him. 'As fer Ben Ferris, 'e's only a chancer, Mick's words.'

'Yeah, but I 'ave ter tell yer Ben's a friend o' mine,' Joe said quickly.

'I gotcher,' Tommy said smiling. 'Anyway, I thought I'd let yer know about the interest in your little establishment, so don't be surprised if Mick's boys come sniffin' round.'

'Fanks fer the tip-off,' Joe replied. 'You know me, I mind me own business. I wouldn't 'ave survived round 'ere fer long ovverwise.'

'It's important yer play it cagey, Joe. It's likely ter get very nasty before long,' the ex-wrestler warned him. 'Lofty Palmer's bin contacted ter supply muscle, an' yer know what that means.'

'Is that no-good bastard still around?' Joe asked. 'I thought 'e'd be out ter stud by now.'

'No, 'e's still runnin' the gym, in Camberwell,' Tommy replied. 'Palmer's team ain't ter be messed wiv neivver. Some of 'em even scare the shit out o' me, ter be honest.'

'Let's fill yer glass,' Joe said, reaching for the bottle. 'Tell me, 'ow come yer got 'iked up wiv Constantine?'

Tommy shrugged his shoulders. 'There's too many young bucks climbin' inter the ring these days an' they're all out ter make a name fer themselves. As fer me I'm finished wiv all that nonsense, but I gotta live. All right, I've put a few bob ter one side, but it won't last fer ever. So, when I got put in touch wiv Mick Constantine I was 'appy ter take the job.'

'Yeah, but yer know the full s.p. now,' Joe remarked. 'Do yerself a favour an' get out while yer can, Tommy. This sort o' fing ain't fer you. All right, anyone who can give the Iron Duke a good fight ain't ter be messed wiv, but this is different. It's not gonna be merely a question of a few slaps an' a warnin'. There's already bin one killin' on the manor an' the battle's not started yet.'

'Sorry, Joe, but I'm in up ter me neck now an' that's the way it's gotta be,' Tommy replied.

The cafe owner looked at his old friend with concern. 'Where yer livin' now?'

'Still in Camberwell.'

'It's gettin' late,' Joe said, glancing up at the clock. 'Yer welcome ter doss down 'ere ternight.'

'I might just do that,' Tommy said smiling.

Joe reached for the bottle once more. 'Let's 'ave a top-up,' he said. 'We got a lot o' chin-waggin' ter do.'

Chapter Twenty-Four

The steam train chugged slowly out of London and Lana leaned her head back against the seat and stared out of the carriage window. She could see the mist hovering over the green fields and frost silvering the bare trees and she glanced at the young man opposite her. 'Do you ever wish yer lived in the country?' she asked him.

Jimmy shrugged his shoulders. 'I've never given it much thought,' he replied.

They were alone in the compartment and Lana was grateful for the privacy. 'I've often wished I lived in a nice country cottage with roses round the door,' she said quietly. 'There'd be a stream runnin' down the bottom o' the garden an' we'd 'ave an apple orchard. I'd wrap up in the winter wiv a big woolly scarf an' take long walks frew the woods an' over the fields. I'd 'ave a dog too, an' on warm summer nights I'd go down by the stream an' just sit there in the quietness and dream.'

'What would yer dream about?' Jimmy asked, a smile playing on his lips.

'That would be tellin',' Lana said, her eyes sparkling.

'This cottage would be in a small village, o' course, an' there'd be a smithy at the end o' the lane,' Jimmy said, grinning mischievously. 'Yer'd 'ear the sound of iron an' when yer came by the blacksmith would stop work an' give yer a wave. 'E'd be dressed in a leavver apron wiv 'is sleeves rolled right up over 'is elbows, the muscles on 'is brawny arms standin' out like sparrers' kneecaps.'

'Yer've ruined it for me now,' Lana said quickly, her laughing eyes flashing at him.

'I'm sorry,' Jimmy said, still smiling.

The train pulled into Broxbourne Station and a distinguished-looking gentleman armed with a rolled-up umbrella glanced in at them and decided to go on to the next compartment. The train shuddered and moved off again, picking up speed as the station disappeared behind them.

Lana studied her companion and imagined him in uniform. 'It must 'ave bin terrible ter be called up an' 'ave ter fight in a war,' she remarked.

Jimmy's face became serious. 'It must 'ave bin terrible fer soldiers like Morgan Jones,' he replied. 'They were just slaves on that Burma railway. Apart from bein' brutalised an' starved there was all the disease – cholera, beri-beri an' jungle ulcers.'

'It don't bear finkin' about,' Lana said shuddering.

Jimmy looked at her intently. 'We 'ave ter be prepared fer a kick-back wiv this one, Lana,' he told her. 'The feller might be too sick ter make the journey. A lot o' these prisoners came 'ome on stretchers, an' their minds are scarred as well as their bodies.'

Lana gave him an understanding smile and returned her gaze to the window, watching the steam from the engine drift by and quickly dissipate amid the wintry landscape. She wanted to tell Jimmy about her split with Ben, but she held back. He might see it as a come-on, she thought. But then she wanted him to come on to her, to desire her enough to fight his corner and to hell with any opposition.

The train rattled as it pulled into Stanstead Abbots Station and a large woman with a flushed face opened the door of the compartment and ushered her three young children on board. She stepped on Jimmy's foot without seeming to notice, then as the train pulled out of the station she began to organise her brood. 'Sidney, let Gladys sit by the window. Beryl, don't fiddle with your plaits. Sidney, do as you're told. No, Gladys, don't pinch. Sidney'll change places, won't you, Sidney?'

The small lad moved next to Jimmy and stared up at him for a few moments. Gladys meanwhile had decided to write her name on the steamy window only for it to be quickly rubbed out by Beryl.

'If you don't behave yourselves I'm going to leave you with the porter when we get off the train,' the big woman threatened.

'Mum, can I have an apple?'

'Manners, Sidney.'

'Mum, can I please have an apple?'

'No.'

'Presently?'

'Yes, presently.'

Jimmy looked down at the lad and gave him a friendly wink then exchanged a smile with Lana.

'Was you a soldier, mister?' Sidney asked him suddenly.

'Yes, I was,' Jimmy told him.

'My dad was a soldier.'

'Sidney, don't pester the gentleman,' his mother said sharply.

'It's quite all right,' Jimmy told her.

'My dad was at Arnhem,' Sidney said matter of factly.

'Sidney, what did I just tell you?' the big woman said, then she turned to Jimmy. 'I'm sorry, but he's very proud of his dad. He was killed at Arnhem, you see.'

'I'm very sorry,' Jimmy said sincerely.

'I've come to terms with it,' the woman replied, looking at Lana. 'I haven't much option, really. Not with these three to bring up.'

The train shuddered to a stop at Woodside Station and Jimmy helped Lana down on to the platform. 'Good luck,' he called out to the woman as he shut the carriage door.

'You were talkin' about the scars o' war,' Lana said as they walked out of the station into a long, deserted lane. 'That poor family's certainly scarred.'

Jimmy nodded without comment and looked around him. He quickly spotted the road sign. 'Well, this is Station Lane,' he said, looking along the row of houses. 'Ah, there we are, number seventeen.'

They slipped the catch on the garden gate and walked up the concrete path, and Lana held her crossed fingers up as Jimmy reached for the doorknocker.

The tall thin man's hollow eyes stared hard at them. 'Yes?' he said sharply.

'Mr Jones? Mr Morgan Jones?' Jimmy asked him.

'Yes, I'm Mr Jones,' he replied.

'We're sorry ter trouble yer, but we've come from Bermon'sey an' we'd like ter . . .'

'Bermondsey?' the man cut in, frowning.

'Do you remember a lady called Lottie Curtis?' Lana asked him.

'Lottie Curtis? No, I don't know anyone of that name,' he replied quickly.

'Look, Mr Jones, can we come in fer a few minutes an' we'll explain,' Jimmy said.

The man hesitated for a moment or two, then he nodded. 'All right then, but just a few minutes. My wife'll be back from church soon.'

They followed him into the comfortably furnished lounge and waited for him to offer them a seat, but their reluctant host seated himself in an armchair and looked up at them curiously. 'You say you've come from Bermondsey,' he said.

'Yes.'

'What was the woman's name again?'

'Lottie Curtis.'

The man's face was blank. 'Sorry, I can't help you.'

Lana looked over at the settee. 'Can we sit down fer a minute?' she asked him.

Morgan nodded. 'Should I know this woman?'

'Lottie took you inter care when you was a child, in nineteen nineteen,' she told him. 'There was a little gel there at the same time an' you two were very close to each ovver, accordin' ter Lottie. Don't you remember?'

Morgan pinched his chin with thumb and forefinger. 'Can't say I do,' he replied.

Jimmy studied the man and made a quick calculation. Lottie had said he was seven years old when she took him in and that would make him thirty-four now. He looked at least ten years older, and he had the stoop of a much older man. His face was gaunt and his eyes sunken, and his fair hair was very thin and unkempt. Saddest of all, his memory seemed to have deserted him.

Lana leant forward in the settee and smiled patiently. 'Look, Mr Jones, I live next door ter Mrs Curtis, an' Jimmy an' I 'ave planned a birfday surprise for 'er. She'll be eighty years old on Christmas Eve an' we're tryin' ter contact all the people she fostered over the years. As you were one of 'em we thought yer'd like ter be there on the day.'

Morgan looked down at his clasped hands and seemed to be thinking hard. 'I've heard of Bermondsey,' he said in a quiet voice. 'It's on the River Thames. Tower Bridge. Yes, that's right, Tower Bridge. I've seen Tower Bridge. I've seen the Tower of London. It's as you go over the bridge. That's right, I remember now. I saw it when we were on the bus.'

Lana looked despairingly at Jimmy and then turned back to Morgan. 'Lottie would be very pleased ter see yer after all these years,' she said kindly. 'Would yer like ter come to 'er birfday party?'

'I don't get out much,' he replied. 'But I do remember that time we were on the bus. My wife was with me and we saw the Tower of London. I pointed it out to her. Can't quite remember what we were doing over there, Bermondsey, I mean. It was a long time ago, anyway.'

Jimmy tried to hide his sadness as he touched Lana's arm.

'Mr Jones, you said yer wife'll be in soon,' he reminded him. 'Can we wait an' meet 'er?'

'She's gone out, to the church,' Morgan replied in a flat voice.

'Will she be in soon?' Jimmy pressed him.

'Can't say, not really.'

'Maybe we could call back a little later,' Lana suggested.

'Won't do any good. She's at the church, you see.'

The young woman glanced quickly at Jimmy and caught the look in his eyes. 'Well, fanks fer lettin' us come in ter talk ter yer, Mr Jones,' she said, getting up.

Morgan nodded but made no attempt to see them out.

As they were walking down the passage the front door opened and a slim woman stepped inside carrying a laden shopping basket. She looked up and started. 'Who the devil are you?' she asked sharply.

'I'm sorry if we startled yer but Mr Jones let us in,' Jimmy said apologetically. 'Are you Mrs Jones?'

'Yes, I'm Mrs Jones. Is my husband all right?'

'Yes, 'e's fine,' Lana told her.

The woman glanced quickly towards the lounge. 'I'm home, dear,' she called out, then she turned to Lana. 'Perhaps you'd be kind enough to explain the reason for your visit. My husband isn't quite himself.'

'If we could 'ave a few minutes you'll understand our reasons fer callin',' Lana replied.

Mrs Jones showed them into a wood-panelled room with a bookcase to one side and a desk beneath the window. There were prints around the walls, and opposite a gas fire set on a marble plinth there was a settee and a leather-padded chair.

'This is my husband's study,' she told them. 'He's an accountant. Won't you sit down.'

'Mrs Jones, my name's Lana Johnson an' this is my friend Jimmy Bailey. We've come from Bermon'sey,' Lana told her as she joined Jimmy on the settee. 'Your 'usband was fostered out as a child an' the old lady who cared for 'im is nearin' 'er eightieth birfday. It's on Christmas Eve an' we came wiv an invitation.'

'That would be Lottie Curtis,' the woman replied, and seeing the look of surprise on her visitors' faces she added, 'I'm Alice.'

'Lottie told me you an' Morgan were inseparable,' Lana said smiling broadly. 'An' you ended up marryin' each ovver. 'Ow lovely.'

Alice nodded, smiling back at the young woman, then her face became serious. 'You tried to talk to Morgan but didn't get much response, I take it.'

'No, I'm afraid not,' Lana replied.

'Do you believe in fate?' Alice asked, looking from one to the other.

'I do,' Jimmy said nodding.

'It was fate that brought Morgan and me together again,' Alice professed. 'When we went back to our respective parents we saw nothing of each other. We grew up and went our separate ways, but I often thought about Morgan. He told me later that he often thought of me too. Anyway, when the war started I volunteered for army nursing, and unbeknown to me Morgan joined the army. In nineteen forty-one his unit was posted to India and from there he went to Singapore when the Japanese were pushing down through Malaya. Morgan was a second lieutenant with the Royal Artillery. He was captured and interned at Changi jail, and from there he was sent to work on the Burma railway.

'I don't want to dwell on what happened to him and thousands of other soldiers during that time,' Alice went on, 'but you have seen the way he is today. Anyway, when the survivors were finally freed they were flown to Bangkok and from there to Colombo. I was posted there to help with the rehabilitation of those poor men, and believe me I saw many terrible cases. One day a medical team carried a stretcher into the hospital and I was on duty at the time. I looked down on that stretcher and nearly died. He was a pitiable shadow of a human being weighing less than five stone, but I recognised him right away. I was too shocked to do anything, too shocked even to speak at first, and then Morgan looked up and smiled at me. He had recognised me too. It was destiny. We were always meant to meet again.'

'An' now you're tergevver fer always,' Lana said smiling.

'Yes, but fate had another hand to play,' Alice continued. 'Before Morgan was sent home we exchanged addresses and promised to write to each other when we got back to England. I wrote to him as agreed but over a month went by and still I hadn't heard anything, so I decided to look him up. The address I had was in Bedfordshire and when I arrived there I found that the house had a new tenant. I made lots of inquiries but they all came to nothing. I thought I'd never see him again, but as I said, fate intervened again. I remember it like it was yesterday. I was working as a nurse at the Charing Cross Hospital and one night I went off duty quite late. It was raining heavily and I went into a small coffee bar near the hospital until it eased up. While I was drinking my coffee I picked up an evening paper that someone had left behind, and an article caught my eye. Apparently a young man had been found wandering through Piccadilly in a dazed state and the police had picked him up. He was found to be suffering from amnesia. The only clue to his identity was a crescent-shaped scar on his forehead and another on his forearm. The report went on to say that he was recovering from hypothermia in Charing Cross Hospital, would you believe? When I recovered from the shock of reading that article I ran all the way back to the hospital and saw that it really was Morgan. He didn't know me at first but a few days later he regained his memory. The doctor who was treating him told me that his widowed mother had died while he was en route home, and the shock of that, added to his weak condition and fragile mental state, had simply proved too much.'

'What 'appened next?' Lana asked, intrigued.

'Well, I wasn't going to lose him again, so as soon as he

was well enough I proposed to him,' Alice said smiling, 'and we were married in July. We found this place and it's proved to be ideal for us. It's quiet and peaceful, and not too far from London. I help out at the church fêtes and coffee sessions on Saturdays and when Morgan's well enough he goes to the village pub. Unfortunately he's going through a bad patch at the moment, but it's only a temporary condition. On the plus side these lapses are becoming less frequent and his doctor told me that in time and with proper care he'll be back to normal, or as normal as anyone could be, considering what he's been through.'

'We'd love yer both ter come ter Lottie's birfday party,' Lana told her. 'Two ovver people 'ave promised ter come, an' there's Jimmy, 'e was one o' Lottie's children too.'

'So that's three you've got so far then,' Alice remarked. 'Well, you can make that five. Morgan and I would be honoured to come.'

was well enough I proposed to [illegible] as a [illegible] we were married in July. We found the place and it's proved [illegible] and [illegible] London. I [illegible] and [illegible] village. [illegible] he's going through a bad patch at the moment, but he's in a [illegible] condition. On the other side the [illegible] and the Doctor [illegible] that in time and with proper care he'll be back to normal, or as normal as anyone could be, considering what he's been through.

'We'd love you both, for some [illegible] party [illegible] promised to [illegible] too.'

'So that's [illegible]

'Will you [illegible] and I would [illegible] around [illegible]'

Chapter Twenty-Five

On Saturday morning Mick Constantine called in at the Gold Star Wholesale Groceries as arranged and was shown into the office.

'I'm pleased to meet you, Mr Constantine,' Sammy said, rising from his desk chair and extending his hand. 'I'm intrigued to know how you found out I intended selling the business.'

The gang boss took off his fedora and laid it on the edge of the large desk before sitting down. 'You're an old-established figure in the area, Mr Goldbloom, an' it's news,' he replied. 'Too important ter keep under wraps.'

'Old established, yes, but I'm tired too,' Sammy told him. 'On Saturdays I should be at the synagogue, but trade has been such that I haven't found the time.'

Constantine pulled open his camel-hair overcoat and stuck his thumbs in the pockets of his waistcoat. 'I'm a man who likes ter get down ter brass tacks, Mr Goldbloom,' he declared, 'an' my purpose 'ere is ter make yer an offer fer the business. Lock, stock an' barrel.'

Sammy caught sight of the gold watch-chain that was draped across his visitor's chest and he leaned back in his chair. 'I've already got a buyer,' he replied.

'From my information I understand that the papers aren't finalised as yet,' Constantine said, his face set.

'True, but a deal is a deal and it's a very good offer,' the little Jew replied, smiling. 'One I found hard to refuse.'

'I'm prepared ter better it,' the gang boss said quickly, leaning forward in his chair for effect.

'Do you know the price I'm asking?'

'Yeah.'

Sammy reached into his desk drawer and took out a box of cigars. 'I think it's only right to tell you that there is a problem concerning the sale,' he said, taking out a Havana and sliding the box towards Constantine. 'You see I've always made a point of looking after my customers. They're my bread and butter, after all. On occasions I've found it necessary to offer a bit of help financially. Quite a few of my corner-shop customers in this area are in debt to me, and any buyer would inherit that debt. It's all allowed for on paper and written into the contract of course, but it could prove to be an inconvenience, nevertheless.'

'I'm aware o' that,' Constantine replied.

'You seem very well informed.'

'I make it my business ter be.'

'And you still want to make me an offer?'

'I wouldn't be sittin' 'ere ovverwise.'

Sammy bit the end off his cigar and lit it with a gold lighter. 'What sort of offer are you thinking about, Mr Constantine?' he asked.

'I'll up it by two grand.'

The Jew dragged hard on his cigar and blew the smoke towards the ceiling. 'You see, the problem I have,' he went on, 'is that my son is a partner in a chartered accountancy firm and he's not interested in following his father into the family business. Therefore I need to realise the capital and invest a fair portion of it into something copper-bottomed which will be his inheritance. I'm talking about land, Mr Constantine. And to that end my solicitor and my accountant have been busy trying to find me some suitable properties. There are one or two likely sites coming on the market very shortly and I need the ready cash to jump in before someone else does. As a matter of fact I'm due to complete the sale of my business on Monday. Good as it is, your offer would incur too much of a delay while the new contract was being drawn up, and I can't afford the time.'

Mick Constantine puffed away on his own cigar and looked up at the spiralling smoke for a few moments. 'I understand the urgency, Mr Goldbloom,' he said quietly. 'I bought some properties myself a year ago an' the sellin' price 'as gone up by ten per cent, lookin' at comparable properties terday. I can only foresee the prices doublin' in five years' time, what wiv all these plans fer modern 'ousin' the politicians are talkin' about. Now s'posin' I include those properties of mine in the deal. Let's say at five per cent up on the price I paid for 'em. Yer wouldn't get a better deal anywhere. As a matter o' fact I could get my accountant ter go over the figures wiv yer on Monday an' my solicitor'll brief yer on the legal aspects o' the properties, location an' condition, etcetera. It would only mean puttin' off signin' fer one day at the most.'

'Tell me about the properties,' Sammy said, drawing on his cigar.

'I've got two rows of 'ouses in Rovver'ithe,' Mick replied. 'I'm almost finished renovatin' 'em, an' as a matter o' fact they're mainly empty. I was intendin' ter let 'em out as furnished flats.'

'What sort of money are we talking about?' Sammy inquired.

'Wiv five per cent added, seven fousand.'

Sammy rolled the cigar between his fingers for a few moments, his mind racing. 'Are you contactable tomorrow?'

'All day. There's my phone number,' Constantine replied, passing over a card.

Sammy slipped it into his coat pocket and then reached into his desk drawer. 'Are you a drinking man, Mr Constantine?' he said smiling broadly.

* * *

At number seven Saddler Street Irene Frost was doing the ironing on the parlour table and she gave her husband Wally a look of irritation as he sat slumped in the armchair. 'I 'ope you ain't gonna sit there snorin' all afternoon,' she said. 'That bloody coal scuttle needs fillin' an' yer promised ter fix that bedroom winder weeks ago. I'm sure it's that draught what's playin' me shoulder up.'

Wally sat up straight in the chair and rubbed his gnarled hands over his balding head. She's missing Caroline, he thought. She never used to get on to him so much when their daughter was living at home. Now she had married and moved away Irene was different. On the other hand it might be her change. How old was she? Forty, or was it forty-one?

Irene patted the curlers in her hair to make sure they were still there. 'While yer doin' that winder yer might look at the curtain rail. It needs a new 'ook,' she reminded him.

Wally sighed in resignation. 'Yeah, all right,' he replied, putting his slippers back on.

Irene put the flat-iron back on the coals, picked up the other iron and tested the heat by spitting on it. 'As if I ain't got enough on me plate, she's up to 'er tricks again,' she groaned.

'Who, yer sister?'

'Who else?'

'What's the matter wiv 'er now?' Wally asked, dreading the answer.

Irene's angular face took on a look of disgust. 'I bumped inter Madge Conroy an' Sadie Pugh down the market this mornin' an' Sadie told me that 'im on the fish stall told 'er that Bubbles 'as rented the big 'ouse in Paradise Street.'

'So?'

'Well, surely yer don't want me ter spell it out ter yer, do yer?'

'I'm not wiv yer.'

'No, you never are.'

Wally sat back in his chair and gave her a hard look. 'Now

are yer gonna stop talkin' in riddles an' tell me what's upset yer, or are we gonna play silly buggers all afternoon?' he growled.

'It's a two-storey, six-bedroomed 'ouse. What does she want wiv all that room?' Irene asked him.

'Search me.'

'Bubbles 'ad a nice little 'ouse round the corner from the place she's just moved into, an' she used ter sub-let the upstairs ter those two prossers,' Irene explained. 'Accordin' to 'im on the fish stall, she's took the two women wiv 'er. Now d'yer see?'

'Yer mean she's turnin' it into a knockin' shop?'

'What d'yer mean, turnin' it? She already 'as.'

Wally shook his head slowly. 'I dunno why yer gettin' yerself so upset about it,' he told her. 'After all, it's nuffing ter do wiv you what yer sister does. She ain't a kid any more.'

'That's not the point,' Irene replied quickly, still holding the flat-iron. 'I've always bin respectable an' I've brought me kids up the same, an' now everyone in Bermon'sey knows that my younger sister's a brothel madam. I felt sick wiv shame when Sadie Pugh told me, an' in front o' Madge Conroy of all people. It's like tellin' the *News o' the World* tellin' 'er anyfing. She loves openin' 'er trap, 'specially if it's scandal.'

'Well, I wouldn't lose no sleep over it,' Wally said calmly.

'Nah, 'course yer wouldn't. Men are all the same,' Irene led off at him. 'The place could turn into a shit tip an' yer wouldn't bovver. Women are different. We set ourselves certain standards an' it's a question o' pride. I don't want ole fish'ead down the market pointin' me out an' sayin' me sister's got a bawdy 'ouse. People'll fink I'm the same.'

'P'raps we should consider it,' Wally said smiling. 'Now the kids 'ave gone we could let their room out to a tom.'

Irene gave him an icy look and cursed as she felt the cold iron. 'Fill that scuttle up, will yer, or the bloody fire'll go out.'

Wally did as he was told, knowing just how far to go before his wife exploded. He didn't like the look of those two flatirons either. Irene was prone to throwing anything at hand when she blew up.

'There we are,' he said as he brushed his hands together. 'The fire's banked up, an' now I'm just off ter take a look at that winder. Can't say no fairer than that, can I?'

'An' don't ferget that curtain rail or everybody'll be gawkin' in when we go ter bed,' she called out after him.

Wally smiled to himself as he climbed the stairs. The vision of all the neighbours standing in the street gazing up at Irene in her curlers and long flannel nightshift amused him.

Down in the warm parlour Irene smashed the iron across the clothes, still fuming over what she had heard from Sadie Pugh. That in itself was bad enough, but what Ann Johnson had told her in confidence could make it even more degrading. Bubbles was brash, outlandishly dressed and no respecter of morals. She was prone to flirt with any man who took her fancy, married or not, and to top it all she was even more outrageous and reckless when she had a bucketful of gin inside her. Bad enough that she carried on in Paradise Street, without being invited to Saddler Street, and at Christmas of all times. Well, sister or not, no one would be able to say that Irene Frost was party to it. Bubbles's whereabouts would remain a mystery as far as this street was concerned and she would just have to miss the old lady's party.

The new Mrs Constantine boarded the train at Waterloo Station and stowed her small suitcase in the luggage rack before making herself comfortable in the first-class carriage. The ploy Gerry dreamed up had gone off a treat and Mick had been unusually sympathetic. Had he taken the trouble to notice the outdated postmark, however, it would have been a different story. As it happened he had taken the letter concerning her mother's poor health, quickly scanned it with a few grunts and passed it back with the comment that perhaps she should go down to Brighton to visit her, unaware that the poor woman had been dead for two years.

As the train pulled out of the station Mandy flipped open the fashion magazine and looked again at the two-piece she so dearly wanted. She had meant to show it to Mick but he had been too busy. Things seemed to be getting red-hot at the moment, and from what she had been able to gather by listening at the door while he was on the phone it appeared that he was buying another business. It had something to do with the Maltese and the properties he owned. Anyway it didn't matter. She was going down to Brighton for two nights with Gerry and that was a much nicer prospect to dwell on.

Frederick Barnfield gathered a sheaf of papers together and put them into a folder which he deposited in his briefcase. He was ready and prepared to carry out the instructions he had just received by phone and now there was time until Monday morning to reflect on other, more exciting matters. The latest letter he had received from his younger brother in Australia had been very encouraging. Desmond had finally settled in a pleasant suburb outside Sydney and was already established in a smart office. He had said in the letter that the details of the immigration programme were being finalised and soon there would be assisted passages for tradesmen and young hopefuls from the old country. Once the flood gates opened there would be plenty of business for the professions, and even as things stood at the moment Australia was certainly a land of opportunity.

Frederick smiled to himself as he re-read the letter. It was like preaching to the converted, he thought. He had been the prime mover in encouraging Desmond to take the decision to seek his fortune in the new country, and he was eagerly looking forward to joining him there very soon. He was a free agent after all: unmarried, professionally experienced and, he hoped, still with twenty years of work left in him.

For the time being, though, there were some tricky hurdles to clear, and perhaps his very life depended on there being no slip-ups. Mick Constantine was no fool. He had made a lot of money from gambling, his club, and other devious activities, but he had his Achilles heel: his pathological hatred for the Maltese. The villain was about to make a big mistake and Frederick Barnfield smiled to himself. He had warned against buying the Gold Star business, for the record, but he was the one who had sowed the seed in the first place by mentioning the Maltese consortium and its plans. Constantine would have expected to be kept informed anyway, but should he find out that his trusted legal adviser had accepted thirty pieces of Maltese silver to do just that, then Barnfield comforted himself with the thought that he would be safely aboard ship en route to a new life in Australia.

Chapter Twenty-Six

Lana casually slipped her arm through Jimmy's as they walked back towards Woodside railway station. The early afternoon was overcast, with the winter sun hidden behind grey cloud. 'Well, that was a turn up for the book,' she remarked. 'Two at once. I really feel 'opeful now. There's just those two gels Ellen an' Lucy ter find, an' o' course the mysterious last one that Lottie fostered.'

'Shame about Phoebe Francis,' Jimmy replied. 'She's the only one so far ter refuse ter come.'

'I'm tryin' ter ferget 'er,' Lana told him. ''Ow could anyone be so 'orrible?'

They reached the station and Jimmy spotted the station master busily raking over a patch of hard soil that served as a flower bed in summer.

'I'm afraid there's no train due for two hours,' he said in reply to Jimmy's question. 'It's a quiet line this, especially at weekends. You can wait in the waiting room, or you might like to get a drink and some lunch. The Ploughshare does a nice pint and a cheese and onion sandwich. Out the gate, turn left and it's about fifty yards down on the left. My cousin is the landlord but I'm not touting for him. It's the only pub in the village. Like I say, turn left and you can't miss it, unless you're totally blind,' he added with a friendly smile.

'Let's go,' Jimmy said, needing little encouragement.

As they neared the pub Lana took out a ten-shilling note from her handbag. 'Look, you got the tickets, let me buy the drinks,' she offered.

Jimmy shook his head and smiled at her. 'I wouldn't dream of it,' he said grandly.

They walked into the public bar and were immediately struck by warmth coming from the log fire burning brightly in an inglenook fireplace. The ceiling was supported with oak beams adorned with brass and copper pots and there was a long hunting horn hanging behind the bar. A few locals stood around chatting and one or two older men sat at tables.

'What'll it be, folks?' the ruddy-faced landlord asked them.

Jimmy looked at Lana and she hesitated. Usually when she went into a pub with Ben she drank gin and lemon, but today seemed special and she wanted to try something else. 'Eh, could I 'ave a port an' lemon please?' she said.

Jimmy settled for a pint of ale and glanced up at the chalked menu to one side of the counter. 'I dunno about you but I'm starvin'. What about a sandwich?' he suggested.

The heat from the fire and the warm sensation in her chest as she sipped her drink made Lana feel totally relaxed, and when she saw Jimmy tucking into the thick cheese sandwich she smiled with amusement. He too seemed totally at ease, and as she demurely tackled the thick crusty bread she caught his eye.

'Get stuck in,' he said winking encouragingly.

The day had begun with some uncertainty but now Lana felt warm, contented and strangely excited as she stole a glance at Jimmy. He was handsome in a rugged sort of way, she thought. He was uncomplicated and good to be with. He was caring and considerate, and she knew that rightly or wrongly she must somehow let him know about the situation between her and Ben.

As if reading her mind Jimmy wiped his mouth on a paper serviette and then looked at her intently. 'Lana, I want yer ter know that I like bein' in yer company very much,' he began slowly, 'an' I'd like ter feel that I can be a special part o' yer life, even if only as a good friend, but ter be perfectly honest I'd like ter be more than that. All right, I know that you've got a boyfriend already, but I need ter know if I'm in there wiv a chance.'

Lana was taken aback by his frankness and the sudden thrill left her insides fluttering. 'As a matter o' fact there's no boyfriend, not any more,' she told him, swallowing hard. 'We've decided ter call it a day.'

Jimmy looked surprised. 'I should be sayin' that I'm sorry, but it wouldn't be true,' he said quietly. 'I really would like yer ter walk out wiv me, an' I'd be grateful if yer'd fink it over.'

'I don't 'ave to,' Lana told him, smiling. 'I'd be 'appy to.'

They left the Ploughshare with half an hour to spare and strolled leisurely back to the station through the winter gloom. The train was fairly full and they had to share a compartment, but Lana enjoyed the feeling of closeness as they sat side by side, and she gave him a demure smile as he took her hand in his.

Ben Ferris drove out of Bermondsey early on Saturday morning and by four o'clock he was back home with fifty cases of Scotch whisky in the back of his van. Once he had parked it in the yard and securely locked the gate he went up to his flat and poured himself a stiff drink. It had been a bit of a nerve-wracking caper. The men at the farmhouse just outside of St Albans had been on edge as they helped him stow the contraband and couldn't get rid of him fast enough. Then there was the journey home with his overloaded van coughing and spluttering. If it had broken down it would certainly have attracted the attention of the police and there would have been some explaining to do. As it was he had made it, and the load was safely stashed away in the yard, but now he had to sell it as quickly as possible.

Ben slumped down in his armchair and stared moodily up at the ceiling. The whisky was a stopgap, but it wasn't going to make him rich. There was fifty pounds owing to Joe Slavin and he hadn't begun to work off the debt to Gerry. Maybe he could worm his way into Mick Constantine's good books if he offered him some of the whisky at a reduced price, he thought. Perhaps it would be more sensible to take notice of what Joe Slavin had said, though. The cafe owner had advised him to steer well clear of Constantine, and he was a wise old bird. Maybe he should do what Lana wanted and look for a decent job after all. It could be too late now though. There appeared to be someone else on the scene, or at least lurking in the background, unless it was just a ploy of hers to make him jealous. To hell with it. It was Saturday night and he had business to attend to. He would have a nod in the chair and then go to the Crown later. Christmas wasn't far off and there would no doubt be a few prospective buyers on hand.

Lana arrived home at teatime, and after telling her mother the good news about Morgan and Alice she mentioned that Jimmy Bailey had asked her to walk out with him.

'Well, 'e seems a very nice lad, an' at least 'e's got a steady job,' Ann remarked as they sat at the table. 'I could never see you an' that Ben Ferris makin' a go of it.'

'Are you an' this Jimmy feller goin' out ternight?' Derek asked her.

'Yeah, 'e's asked me out fer a drink,' Lana told him.

'Come up the Crown,' Derek suggested. 'Alan an' Beth said they'll be there ternight.'

'Yeah, why don't yer?' Frank piped in. 'I might even persuade yer muvver ter come too. We can make it a nice family night out.'

'I can't,' Ann replied. 'Look at me 'air, it's a mess. I couldn't go out lookin' like somefing the cat dragged in.'

'Well, I'm glad you said it an' not me,' Frank laughed. 'Why don't yer let Lana fix it for yer? It'd make a nice change ter go out fer a drink tergevver.'

Ann looked doubtful. 'I dunno.'

'Don't worry, I'll tong it for yer, Mum,' Lana said quickly. 'An' what's more yer can try my new shade o' lipstick. By the time I'm finished wiv yer you'll look like a film star.'

'An' ter show yer we all mean business, I'm volunteerin' ter do the washin' up,' Frank announced.

'Are yer sure yer feel all right, Frank?' Ann said sarcastically.

'Never felt better,' he replied, grinning.

'Well, in that case I'm gonna keep out of everybody's way an' sit in the armchair wiv the paper,' Derek ventured.

'You can give yer farvver an 'and,' Ann told him sharply. 'Let 'im wash an' you wipe. Last time 'e 'elped me wiv the dryin' 'e smashed two o' me best dinner plates.'

'Yeah, but there was an excuse that night,' Frank said grinning. 'That was when yer told me Beth was pregnant. I misunderstood what yer said. I thought yer meant it was you that was up the duff.'

'D'yer know, Frank, I 'ave ter say yer've got a lovely turn o' phrase,' Ann remarked with a despairing glance at Lana.

While the men were busy washing up Lana heated the tongs in the fire and began to brush out her mother's shoulder-length fair hair with a stiff brush.

'I've bin in ter Lottie this afternoon,' Ann told her. 'She looks a bit brighter than yesterday. I was beginnin' ter worry about 'er ter tell yer the trufe. Never mind, she'll be over the moon ter see all 'er kids again as she calls 'em.'

'I do 'ope we can find those two ovver gels,' Lana replied. 'There's nuffing to go on, though.'

'Would it be werf phonin' up 'Olloway?' Ann asked. 'It'd be a start.'

'The prison, yer mean?' Lana queried as she took the tongs out of the fire.

'Yeah, why not?' Ann said quickly. 'Remember the gel Ellen got done fer shopliftin'. She'd most likely 'ave gone there. They'll 'ave 'er address.'

'I don't fink they'd give out that sort of information,' Lana replied. 'After all, it could be someone out ter settle an old score.'

'Why don't we try an' find out a bit more from Lottie about when the gel was caught,' Ann suggested. 'It might 'ave bin in the papers an' they usually give the person's address.'

'That's an idea,' Lana replied as she set to work with the hot curling tongs.

'That ovver gel might be the 'ardest one of all ter find,' Ann went on. 'Apparently she left the area when she married.'

'Well, we can only do our best,' Lana said. 'I would like 'em all ter turn up on the day though. It'd really make it special fer ole Lottie.'

Ann winced as she felt the hot iron near her scalp. ''Ere, be careful,' she said quickly. 'I don't want a scorched bonce.'

Lana smiled. 'Don't worry, by the time I'm finished yer'll look like Bette Davis. She 'as 'er 'air tonged.'

Ann sat still, hardly daring to move in case the tongs slipped. 'Is Ben Ferris likely ter be in the Crown ternight?' she asked.

'Yeah, it's quite possible,' Lana told her. 'As a matter o' fact I did mention it ter Jimmy when 'e asked me ter go up there wiv 'im, but 'e said Ben would 'ave ter see us tergevver sooner or later, an' sooner's as good as later.'

'Just as long as 'e don't get stroppy,' Ann remarked.

'Nah, it's not 'is way,' Lana replied. 'Not unless 'e's really drunk.'

'Anyway, apart from Jimmy yer farvver an' Derek'll be there,' Ann said reassuringly.

Ben walked into the saloon bar of the Crown at seven-thirty on that Saturday evening and found it still comparatively empty. He was surprised to see that the landlord had made a very rare appearance, standing talking to Del the barman. Rumour had it that Patrick Monahan was merely a front man for Mick Constantine and spent most of his time running another pub in Walworth belonging to the gang boss.

Ben had only just taken his drink over to a table when the

Varley brothers walked into the bar. They were smartly dressed and they immediately got into conversation with the landlord. Something was brewing, Ben felt sure. Apart from Patrick Monahan being there, it was unusual for the Varleys to use the saloon bar. Maybe the man himself was going to make an appearance this evening.

As he sipped his drink Ben noticed that the Varleys kept looking in his direction and he guessed they were discussing him. He had not seen them since the cellar incident and he prepared himself for the inevitable confrontation. He did not have long to wait. Nipper Varley ambled over with his brother following behind.

'Well, well, if it ain't Mr Box o' Tricks,' Nipper said.

'Not really,' Ben said casually. 'I was just playin' safe.'

Nipper and Sid sat down at the table and stared at him. 'We're both friendly blokes as a rule, ain't we, Sid?'

The bigger of the two nodded. 'Yeah. As a rule.'

'An' ter show yer there's no 'ard feelin's I'm gonna buy yer a drink,' Nipper said. 'What'll it be?'

'If that's yer attitude I'll 'ave a pint o' bitter,' Ben replied humorously.

'Sid, get the man a pint,' Nipper told him.

As his brother loped over to the counter Nipper leaned back in his chair. 'Drinkin' alone. That ain't kosher on a Saturday night,' he remarked.

'Yeah, well sometimes I like me own company,' Ben replied cuttingly.

Nipper Varley ignored the intonation. 'Where's Gerry Knowland then?' he asked. 'You an' 'im usually drink tergevver, so I understand.'

'I don't see much of 'im these days,' Ben told him.

'Yer used ter be chummy though.'

'Yeah, at one time.'

Sid came back with the beer and put it down clumsily in front of Ben, who leaned back quickly as the froth spilt on to the tabletop.

'You an' 'im were tergevver in Joe Slavin's cafe the ovver day, so I was told,' Nipper went on.

'Yeah, so what?' Ben asked him sharply.

'Just makin' a point,' Varley replied calmly.

Ben finished his pint and took up the fresh one. He had already downed a few whiskies before he left the flat that evening and realised he would need to be on his guard. The Varleys might be out to goad him, or more likely try to loosen his tongue by plying him with drink. 'As a matter o' fact I just bumped inter Gerry in Joe's cafe an' we chewed the fat for a while,' he said casually.

Nipper nodded towards the counter. 'Pat's in ternight 'cos Mick Constantine's comin' in later. We're 'avin' a little celebration.'

'That's nice,' Ben replied. 'An' what's that in aid of?'

'Mick's grey'ound "Camberwell Pride" won the gold cup at New Cross on Thursday,' Nipper informed him.

'Broke the track record,' Sid butted in.

Ben smiled coldly. 'Well, that does call fer a celebration,' he said, getting up from his seat. 'What yer 'aving?'

'We're on gin an' tonics,' Nipper told him.

Warning bells were starting to ring fast and furiously in Ben's head and he took a few deep breaths as he walked over to get the drinks. The Varley brothers were not usually ones to socialise but they could drink like fish, and it was obvious they had been briefed to get as much out of him as they could. The night was young, he thought to himself, and it looked as though it was going to be a heavy session. Maybe he would be able to turn the tables. He owed Gerry Knowland and this might be the time to start repaying him.

Chapter Twenty-Seven

Ann Johnson was feeling happy as she linked arms with Frank and stepped out of the house. Lana had made a good job of her hair and it was nicely waved and set. She had also done her make-up for her and even Frank had felt moved to say how nice she looked. She wore her winter coat of emerald green, her favourite colour, with a white silk scarf that was loosely knotted at her neck. Frank looked smart this evening, she thought. He was wearing his navy-blue suit with a white shirt and silver tie. His short greying hair was combed neatly back from his forehead and he had used the aftershave that she had bought him for his birthday.

Lana and Jimmy brought up the rear, chatting away to each other as they stepped out into Jamaica Road. The Crown and Anchor was only a short distance away and Ann was looking forward to a chat with Beth. Frank was right, it was nice to get out occasionally on a Saturday night, even though the weather was not very enticing at this time of year. It was also nice to see Lana looking so radiant and happy. Jimmy Bailey had certainly made a difference, and she had said as much to Frank.

The saloon bar was filling up, and when they arrived Frank hustled Ann and Lana into a vacant corner spot before ordering the drinks. Jimmy accompanied him to the counter and glanced around while Frank was waiting to be served. Lana had said that Ben Ferris might be in the bar and would probably be drinking alone. There were three young men sitting together who appeared to be deep in conversation but he could not see anyone drinking alone, apart from a couple of elderly men. Lana had not been too keen to visit the place when he asked her out that evening, but as he had explained the Crown was their local pub after all and Ben would have to accept the situation.

'I do 'ope Beth ain't got one of 'er sick 'eadaches,' Ann remarked. 'It'll be nice fer 'er an' Alan ter get out. She won't fancy goin' out when she gets much bigger.'

Frank and Jimmy were talking about football and Lana was elaborating on the trip to Essex so no one saw Alan and Beth enter the bar until Alan touched his father on the shoulder. 'Room fer two more?' he said grinning.

Ann moved up to let Beth sit between her and Lana and immediately the three of them became engrossed in a lively discussion. Lana had purposely not glanced around the pub when she came in and she had not noticed Ben sitting in the far corner with the Varleys.

Ben had seen her and his face had taken on an angry look. He was feeling the effects of all the drink he had been plied with and he was already upset by Nipper Varley's probing into his business. Why had Lana brought her new boyfriend into the saloon bar? She had always preferred the public bar when she was with him. Was it to gloat over him, make him feel guilty? Well, to hell with her, and her boyfriend. He'd soon find out that she was only interested in marriage and babies. Maybe he was of the same mind, and if so they were welcome to each other.

'Did you say Derek was comin' up 'ere tonight?' Beth asked Ann.

'Yeah, but yer know what 'e's like,' she replied. 'It takes 'im hours ter get ready. I've never known a boy like 'im. 'E'll be late fer 'is own funeral.'

''Ere, Lana, I bin meanin' to ask yer, 'ow yer gettin' on wiv the Lottie business?'

The young woman told her about the progress she had made so far, and also about the response she and Jimmy had got from Phoebe Francis.

'Well, if it was me I'd threaten ter tell the papers that 'er story about 'er child'ood was a pack o' lies,' Beth said firmly.

'Ter be honest I was tempted ter do just that,' Lana replied, 'but then I thought ter meself, well, if she doesn't wanna come of 'er own free will then Lottie's well rid of 'er.'

'I dunno, some people can be really 'ard,' Beth remarked.

'Yeah, but there's also the ovver side,' Ann cut in. 'You take that Selby feller. 'E's a barrister an' 'e must be really busy, but 'e still agreed ter come.'

'Morgan an' Alice too,' Lana reminded her. 'That poor feller's really sick but Alice is gonna bring 'im.'

Derek came into the bar and ambled over to them. 'Sorry I'm late, I fell asleep,' he said sheepishly.

'What did I tell yer?' Ann said smiling at the two younger women.

Derek shrugged his shoulders. 'Well, I s'pose I'd better get the drinks in,' he told them. 'I don't wanna be talked about.'

Frank and Jimmy had got up and moved near the counter, not wanting to get drawn into the women's nattering, and when Derek joined them Frank introduced him to Jimmy. ''E's a Millwall fan so I guess that makes 'im one of us,' he said grinning.

Just then Mick Constantine made an ostentatious entry, flanked byTommy Carberry and a couple of well-dressed men smoking cigars.

'I see Flash 'Arry's arrived,' Frank commented.

'You know who that is wiv 'im, don't yer?' Derek said.

'No.'

'That's Butcher Carberry. 'E used ter be a top wrestler.'

'I s'pose 'e's watchin' Flash 'Arry's back,' Frank growled. 'Who's the ovver two?'

'They're bookies,' Derek told him. 'The fat one stands in Dock'ead Buildin's an' the ovver one's got a pitch in St James Road.'

'You're very well informed,' Frank remarked.

'It's a good policy ter know who's who in this neighbour'ood,' Derek replied, giving Jimmy a wink. 'Now you take Mr I'm It over there. 'E's got pubs, clubs, an' 'e runs the local bookies as well. I 'eard 'e's even got 'ouses fer rent. Baz Smithson used ter be 'is minder, till 'e got topped, that's why Butcher's wiv 'im ternight. As a matter o' fact there's bad blood between ole Constantine an' the Malts an' between you an' me I reckon 'e's runnin' scared.'

'You should get a job on *Crime Weekly*,' Frank told him. 'Now what about you puttin' yer 'and in yer pocket an' getting us all a drink. Jimmy's already bin in.'

The atmosphere in the far corner of the bar was getting decidedly hostile.

'I dunno about that,' Ben said in a slurred tone of voice. 'I reckon yer just 'ired muscle. You don't know any more than I do about the goin's on between Mick an' the Malts. Like I say, yer just 'ired muscle.'

'You just watch yer mouth,' Sid snarled. 'Don't sit there takin' the piss out of us.'

'All right, Sid, leave it out,' Nipper told him.

'Well, 'e wants ter be careful in future,' Sid replied, giving Ben a filthy look.

Ben waved his hand carelessly. 'OK, I stand corrected,' he said. 'Now what about a top-up?'

As he staggered towards the counter Nipper leaned across to his brother. 'Don't aggravate 'im,' he growled. 'We're s'posed ter be pumpin' 'im. We don't want 'im clammin' up.'

'Well, I fink it'd be better ter knock it out of 'im,' Sid scowled.

Ben found a gap and leaned on the counter for support, trying to focus his eyes properly. Suddenly he realised that he was standing next to Jimmy Bailey. 'Well, if it ain't the man 'imself,' he slurred.

Jimmy ignored him but Ben was not to be put off. He reached out and took hold of Jimmy's arm. 'Don't turn away when I'm talkin' ter yer,' he said. 'Me an' Lana are very good friends. In fact me an' Lana . . .'

'Look, why don't yer go an' sit down,' Jimmy told him quietly.

'I'm Ben Ferris. Ain't Lana told yer about me?' he asked, his eyes blinking.

'Yeah, she's told me about yer,' Jimmy replied, trying to keep his temper in check.

Frank and Derek had seen what was going on and they moved in between them. 'Now why don't yer do like yer bin told, Ben, an' piss orf,' Frank growled.

'This don't concern you, so stay out of it,' Ben told him sharply.

'Yes, it does,' the older man replied. 'Jimmy's in our company an' if yer aggravatin' 'im yer doin' the same to us. So piss orf while yer in front.'

'Yeah, why don't yer?' Derek told him.

Customers were beginning to take notice and move away in case a fight broke out. Mick Constantine had seen what was going on and he beckoned Nipper over.

'Take 'im outside,' he whispered, nodding towards Ben. 'I'm 'ere fer a comfortable drink, not ter witness a punch-up.'

Nipper grabbed Ben's arm but the young man pulled away and staggered. Sid immediately hurried over and between the two of them they hustled him out of the bar. The Johnson women had seen what was going on and Lana hurried over and took Jimmy by the arm. 'I didn't know Ben was in 'ere,' she said quickly. 'Those two ain't 'is friends, in fact they've got a score ter settle wiv 'im.'

Jimmy saw the look of concern on her face and he nodded. 'I'll see if 'e's OK,' he said, striding out of the bar.

Derek followed him out and as Frank went to join them

Ann grabbed his arm. 'Oh no, yer don't,' she said quickly. 'I don't want you gettin' involved. Those two are quite capable o' sortin' fings out.'

Frank looked anxiously at her. 'You don't know those sort,' he told her. 'They come tooled up.'

She sighed. 'All right, Frank, but be careful fer Gawdsake.'

Derek and Jimmy hurried along the street as the Varleys were dragging their intended victim into a narrow cobbled lane. They broke into a run and when they reached the entrance they saw Ben Ferris crouched on all fours with Sid Varley kicking out at him.

'Oi! What's goin' on?' Derek shouted.

'Piss orf, it's none o' your business,' Nipper yelled at him.

'We're makin' it our business,' Jimmy said quietly, walking slowly towards them.

Frank came running up and turned into the lane. 'OK, lads. The joke's over,' he said calmly.

Jimmy helped Ben to his feet only to be pushed away.

'I don't need you ter wet nurse me,' he growled.

'Get 'ome, Ben, an' fink yerself lucky,' Frank told him sharply. 'I dunno why we bovvered.'

Ben staggered off without another word and Frank turned to the Varley brothers. 'Now, why don't we all go back ter the pub an' let it rest,' he suggested.

Nipper nodded for Sid to follow him, and then he looked at Frank. 'This won't go down well wiv Mick, yer know,' he said quickly.

'Yeah, but what Mick's gotta remember is that a lot o' dockers use that pub,' Frank told him. 'We're a funny breed really, but we do tend ter stick tergevver. I'm sure Mick understands that.'

Nipper seemed about to say something but thought better of it and walked away with Sid trailing him.

'C'mon, lads, the beer's goin' flat,' Frank said grinning.

The three strolled back to the Crown through the cold night air and were met at the door by the women.

'I fink we'd better go 'ome,' Ann suggested.

'So I coax yer out an' then yer wanna go 'ome early,' Frank said, smiling affectionately at her. 'No fear. We'll do what we always do, wait fer the last bell.'

Lana pulled Jimmy to one side. 'I feel terrible about what 'appened,' she said. 'I shouldn't 'ave got you involved.'

'But I am involved, or at least I 'ope I am,' he replied, his dark eyes searching hers.

She smiled and squeezed his arm. 'Fanks, Jimmy,' she said softly.

Alan looked sheepishly at his father. 'I was just gonna come out an' she grabbed me arm,' he moaned. 'She wouldn't let it go.'

'Too bloody true,' Beth said quickly.

'No sweat,' Frank replied. 'There was no 'arm done an' I fink those two monkeys got the message. Not even Mick Constantine's gonna risk mixin' it wiv a couple of 'undred dockers.'

Derek was smiling as he brought fresh drinks over. 'These 'ave bin paid for,' he told them.

Frank glanced over towards the counter and saw the gang boss looking in his direction, raising his glass.

'Bloody 'ell, we must be celebrities,' he mumbled to Ann. 'Flash 'Arry buying the Johnsons a drink? I'll never live it down.'

Rain had started to fall as the family walked back to Saddler Street. Beth sat at the table in the scullery watching Lana and her mother prepare cheese and ham sandwiches while the men sat chatting in the parlour.

'Those Varleys was out ter give Ben a good pastin',' Frank was saying. 'They could 'ave killed 'im if we 'adn't shown up an' outnumbered 'em.'

Derek shook his head. 'Nah, Dad, they ain't that easily put off. Nipper's a mean bastard an' Sid's as strong as an ox. They would've took us on, that's fer sure, 'cept they were doin' Constantine's biddin'. That's 'is pub, remember, an' I 'eard that Ben Ferris 'as bin makin' a nuisance of 'imself lately. Constantine just wanted 'im worked over. 'E ain't lookin' fer a full-scale war, not yet anyway.'

'What's all this about war?' Ann said sharply as she came in carrying a plate of sandwiches.

The rain was still falling an hour later as Lana stood with Jimmy just inside her front door.

'I really enjoyed this evenin',' he told her.

'Yeah, it was very nice fer me too, but I'm sorry about what 'appened,' she said quietly.

The young man took her by both arms. 'Look, don't worry about it. It wasn't your fault,' he replied firmly. 'Ben was certain ter front me one day an' now it's over. There was no 'arm done.'

'Yeah, but I feel I put you at risk by tellin' yer about those Varleys bein' against 'im,' she went on. 'You 'ad no reason ter try an' 'elp 'im, an' I couldn't 'ave blamed yer if yer'd turned yer back on 'im, but yer didn't, Jimmy. It was nice what yer done.'

He smiled, his white teeth flashing in the darkness of the passage. 'I did it fer you, not 'im,' he said simply.

'Yes, I know yer did, an' that's what makes it all the nicer,' Lana replied. She looked up into his eyes. 'Me an' Ben are finished, Jimmy, an' that's the trufe, but I couldn't see 'im 'urt.'

The young man put his arms round her and pulled her to him. She did not resist as his lips found hers and her arms went around his neck as she savoured his warm kiss.

'I'm comin' round ter see ole Lottie termorrer night,' he said as they moved apart. 'Will I see yer there?'

'You try an' stop me,' she replied smiling.

Jimmy stepped out into the light rain and turned his coat collar up as he hurried off. Lana watched him walk to the end of the turning and returned his cheery wave.

Her family all looked at her as she entered the parlour.

'That Jimmy's a real nice bloke,' Frank said.

''E's got some bottle frontin' the Varleys,' Derek added.

'Yeah that's fer sure,' Alan said.

'Yeah 'e's OK, I s'pose,' Lana replied, trying to be casual as she took another sandwich from the plate.

Chapter Twenty-Eight

On Monday morning Gerry Knowland and Mandy Constantine travelled back to London on separate trains, and when she arrived back at her house in Camberwell at lunchtime Mandy assumed a suitable expression with which to face her husband. After such a wonderful, romantic weekend it was going to be difficult playing the part of a sad and worried daughter, she realised. To all intents and purposes she had only that morning left her very sick mother, and was expecting to be called back down to Brighton at short notice. The pretence was unnecessary, however, for Mick was not at home, and the young woman breathed a sigh of relief. By the time he arrived home he would no doubt have other things on his mind.

When Gerry arrived at Waterloo Station he took a cab to the Old Kent Road and called in at the Lord Nelson. Darkie Samut was looking very pleased with himself and he served his friend with a frothing pint of bitter. 'It's on the house,' he said.

'Good news, I take it?' Gerry inquired.

'Well, it seems that Gold Star Groceries is in the process of changing hands,' the landlord informed him.

Gerry sipped his pint with relish. 'He swallered it 'ook, line an' sinker then,' he said grinning.

Darkie nodded. 'I got a call from Barnfield. He's been

instructed to start the ball rolling. I also got a call from Sammy Goldbloom. He told me he's looking forward to his retirement.'

Gerry smiled at the news. 'That's a laugh. Sammy's gonna be busier than ever now,' he remarked.

'I've got to meet with Sammy in the next couple of days to sort out the re-financing,' Darkie said. 'I can just see Constantine's face when he puts the squeeze on the shopkeepers and they all settle up their debts.'

'Yeah, an' what about when they all tell 'im they're gonna be usin' a different supplier,' Gerry said grinning. 'This calls fer a little celebration. Give us anuvver pint, an' one fer yerself, mate.'

Irene Frost had had the whole weekend to dwell on the shame and disgrace hanging over her head in the shape of her enterprising sister, and she decided to go and see Sadie Pugh as soon as the woman got home from her office-cleaning job that morning. Sadie was a good sort and would respect a confidence, not like that Conroy woman who would take great delight in broadcasting the news to all and sundry.

At eleven o'clock Irene crossed the street and knocked on Sadie Pugh's front door, hoping that no one would notice her.

'You look a bit worried,' Sadie remarked as she let her in.

'I bin worried all weekend as a mattér o' fact,' Irene replied.

'Sit yerself down an' I'll make us a nice cuppa,' Sadie told her, eager to hear the story she knew was coming.

Irene folded her hands in her lap and took a deep breath. 'A couple o' weeks ago Ann Johnson told me in confidence that she an' 'er Lana were plannin' a surprise birfday party fer ole Lottie Curtis,' she began. 'Now I know that yer won't breave a word of what I tell yer to anybody. The Johnsons are tryin' ter trace all those kids that Lottie used ter look after.'

'That's nice,' Sadie said.

'Yeah, but the trouble is Bubbles was one of 'em,' Irene told her.

'Oh dear!'

'Exactly.'

'But do the Johnsons know?' Sadie asked her.

'I wouldn't fink so,' Irene replied. 'Yer see, Bubbles still uses 'er married name, although she's bin divorced fer years, an' she's only bin known as Bubbles since she went on the game. A lot o' people round 'ere know she's me sister, though, an' Gawd 'elp us I'm ferever tryin' ter live it down.'

'I shouldn't worry too much about that,' Sadie said supportively. 'Everyone calls 'er Bubbles. I don't even know 'er real name an' I don't s'pose there's many who do.'

'It's Ellen.'

'Well then, the Johnsons are gonna be searchin' fer a gel called Ellen, ain't they?' Sadie replied. 'The only fing you gotta worry about is if anyone round 'ere knows it was Bubbles who Lottie Curtis looked after.'

'I shouldn't fink so,' Irene told her. 'It was twenty-odd years ago an' there's bin a lot o' new families moved in the street since then. The only one I'm worried about is Madge Conroy. She's bin livin' in the street fer donkey's years.'

'Well, apart from you an' me, no one outside the Johnsons knows about Lottie's party, so I shouldn't give it anuvver thought.'

'Yeah, p'raps I'm bein' a bit silly, but the thought o' Bubbles prancin' down the street in one o' those fancy dresses she wears makes me cringe wiv shame,' Irene groaned. 'I just couldn't bear the embarrassment of it all. Fair enough, people know she's me sister, but I don't want 'er comin' round 'ere advertisin' the fact.'

Sadie agonised over whether or not to tell her about Preacher Jack but the boiling kettle interrupted her thoughts and she got up to fill the teapot. She felt sorry for her neighbour, though she failed to understand why the woman was so obsessed with what her sister did. After all, she wasn't her sister's keeper. As long as she lived a respectable life why worry about anybody else, sister or otherwise?

Outside the weather was cold and damp, but in the tidy parlour the fire was burning merrily and Irene started to feel a little less worried. Sadie was right, she thought. It was very unlikely that anyone would realise Bubbles was little Ellen, the sweet child Lottie had cared for. 'This is a nice cup o' tea,' she said appreciatively.

'It's Brooke Bond's,' Sadie told her. 'I save the coupons.'

Irene wiped her cup along the edge of the saucer and took another sip. 'My Wally finks I'm bein' silly about it,' she remarked.

'Yeah, but men don't understand 'ow we fink,' Sadie replied. 'They'd live in shit if we let 'em. Can you ever imagine 'em changin' the curtains or cleanin' the winders? They're lazy gits the lot of 'em!'

'Yeah, yer right there,' Irene said, smiling self-righteously. 'The only fing they're interested in is the old 'ow's-yer-farvver. They're never too tired fer that.'

'Too true,' Sadie replied nodding. 'Mind you, though, I fink that as they get older they only do it ter prove they still can.'

'Ter be honest, I'd sooner 'ave a nice cup o' tea,' Irene confided.

Sadie felt that she didn't like tea that much but she didn't want to contradict Irene. 'Yeah, me too.'

'Well, I'd better be goin',' Irene said getting up. 'Fanks fer the tea an' the chat, luv.'

Sadie stood up and followed her neighbour out into the passage. 'I wasn't gonna tell yer,' she said, 'but yer'll 'ear it from 'im on the fish stall anyway. Preacher Jack's playin' up again.'

'That's all I want,' Irene groaned. 'Last time 'e started 'is tricks Bubbles put 'er dog on 'im an' she got took ter court. It was in the papers.'

'Anyway try not ter worry, luv. It'll all come out in the wash,' were Sadie's parting words.

* * *

Not more than half a mile away in Paradise Street, Ellen Madigan, alias Bubbles, was busy filling the vases in her salon with paper flowers. She was a buxom thirty-two-year-old, with blue eyes and blonde hair that was a mass of tight curls. She had first found herself on the wrong side of the law at nineteen, when she was arrested and fined for trying to smuggle a dress out of an Oxford Street store. That little experience was not enough to discourage her, and for a further offence she was sent to prison for nine months.

Life in Holloway made her realise that shoplifting was too risky a business and there were other ways of making some quick money that were less likely to land her behind bars. A street girl she befriended inside gave her some good advice about working the streets, and on release Bubbles found herself a patch near the docks. She followed the oldest profession in the world for more than ten years, and then decided that it was about time she put her experience to good use. When the large house became vacant she felt that it was her big opportunity, and after talking to some of the other streetwalkers who worked the area she took a gamble and rented the place.

As she busied herself with her chores Bubbles hummed away contentedly. It was important that the customers were given a good impression when they came in. The rooms had to be welcoming and relaxing and she had had them all nicely wallpapered and painted, with erotic pictures hanging over the beds and low lights for effect. Her girls were all hand-picked from the regulars who frequented the dock area. It was a good setup, she thought. They were all free from predatory pimps and could practise their trade in comfort and security, and any uncooperative customer would be politely persuaded to see the error of his ways by Moses, a huge, dumb ox of a man who was totally loyal to Bubbles.

Trixie was one of Bubbles's most popular girls and when she popped her head into the salon the madam pulled a face. 'You must 'ave 'ad a busy night, yer look awful,' she remarked.

'Yer'd better get yer 'air done at Marie's.'

'I've just seen Mad Jack from me winder,' Trixie said, ignoring the criticism. ''E's standin' outside.'

'That man's beginnin' ter be a pest again,' Bubbles growled. 'I dunno why they don't keep 'im in that nut'ouse.'

'Shall I tell Moses?' Trixie asked.

'Nah, 'e'll soon get fed up an' move off.'

'Well, I'd better get goin',' the young girl replied, 'or I won't get me 'air done terday.'

Bubbles had a contract with Marie's hairdressing salon which allowed her girls to have their hair taken care of at a reduced rate, and she insisted that they take advantage of the arrangement. As Bubbles had warned them, 'A gel goin' out lookin' like a rat-bag only attracts rats.'

Outside the big house Jack the Preacher stood on the wet pavement clutching a Bible. He was wrapped up in a tatty overcoat and woollen scarf, with a trilby pulled down round his ears and a wild expression on his unshaven face.

'Gather round, you sinners,' he called out to a passing woman who was carrying a laden shopping bag.

'Piss orf, yer silly ole bastard,' she mumbled.

Preacher Jack took a deep breath as he prepared to deliver his sermon for the day. It was a diatribe on the evil pleasures of the flesh, and where better to inveigh against the fires of lust than here, he told himself.

'The evils of the world flourish everywhere,' he began in a booming voice. 'They are amongst us all, even here in this fine Catholic borough, here in that house you see before us.'

Two passing dockers stopped to listen, and one or two children came up to stand at a safe distance for fear of being chased by the madman.

'View the house of carnality if you will,' he went on, waving his hand theatrically. 'There in that den of iniquity the sinner damns himself to the fires of hell with his licentious behaviour. He consorts with nefarious women who are the handmaidens of the devil himself. Turpitude running wild in our midst, unabated and unchecked.'

'What the bloody 'ell's 'e talkin' about?' one of the dockers asked.

'Oi, Jack, speak in plain English, will yer?' the second docker called out.

'Peruse the books, study the language, my friends,' the preacher shouted back at them. 'Even in this, the greatest language of all, it is hard to find words that describe fully the evils perpetrated in that house of Satan.'

'I thought it was just a knockin' shop,' the docker told him, grinning widely.

'And they mocked, rending the vestments,' Jack declaimed. 'Better it be put to the fire now like the blasphemers of old while there is still salvation at hand. To delay will set the devil amongst us.'

A few more curious folk had gathered and Preacher Jack responded with fervour. 'You, sir,' he said pointing, 'will you stand back and let the devil ride his monster in our midst?'

The shabbily dressed old man who was being addressed shrugged his shoulders. 'Yeah, if yer like,' he replied.

'You, madam. Will you just be content to stand and watch as those handmaidens of the fiend ply their evil trade?'

'Yeah, of course I will, I don't s'pose they can show me anyfing I don't know already,' the old lady replied with a chuckle.

Suddenly an upstairs window in the house flew open and Bubbles leaned out. 'Now piss off, Jack, or I'll send Moses out after yer,' she shouted down.

'Heed the warning and seek salvation,' the preacher called out, pointing his bony finger at her.

'Yer got one minute,' she shouted.

Jack waved the Bible at her. 'Look for the word of the Lord,' he ranted. 'Repent and be saved before the hourglass is broken and the sands of time trickle down into the pit.'

'Right, yer've 'ad yer chance,' Bubbles told him.

Jack stood there as the window came down hard and then

he set off without another word, watched by the amused gathering. Fronting the devil was one thing, but standing up to Moses was a more daunting prospect.

The children skipped after him, chanting at a safe distance.

'Two, four, six, eight,
who do we appreciate.
Preacher Jack,
ole rotten 'at.'

The man shook his fist at them as he turned the corner and the children walked back to play five-stones outside the den of iniquity.

Chapter Twenty-Nine

A December fog was thickening as Lana left her office and hurried down the long flight of steps from London Bridge Station to Tooley Street. She was keen to get home before the fog became too dense and anxious to call in on Lottie later that evening. Time was running short and all efforts to trace Ellen and Lucy had failed. The prison authorities had refused to give out any information on Ellen, and when she had surreptitiously brought up the subject with Lottie the old lady had been unsure about when Father McCarthy had actually told her of Ellen's misdemeanour. Without much to go on Jimmy had visited the *South London Press* offices and searched through back numbers of the paper, but he had found nothing.

They had not had any better success with Lucy. St Mary's Church had a record of her marriage and had been able to supply her erstwhile address in Bermondsey, and also the Balham address of her husband, but visits to both of these had proved fruitless. To all intents and purposes the Thompsons had disappeared completely. Lana remembered how depressed she had felt after trying their old houses, and how Jimmy had raised her spirits by telling her of another idea he had. Tonight he was going to call round and she was hoping that he might have had some success.

As she set off along by the railway arches Ben Ferris stepped out of a doorway a few yards ahead and her heart sank. Twice recently he had waited for her as she came home from work and each time he had asked her to go back to him. The last occasion had ended with a row and Lana prayed that this time he hadn't been drinking.

'I 'ad ter see yer again, Lana,' he said as she drew level. 'We gotta talk.'

'I thought we'd talked enough, Ben,' she replied.

'A little chat won't 'urt,' he persisted as he walked along beside her.

'Yer wastin' yer time, Ben,' she said quickly.

'Yer don't really mean that, do yer?' he asked. 'Yer just sayin' that 'cos yer still mad wiv me.'

'I'm not mad at yer, not any more, Ben.'

'Well, there's 'ope yet then.'

'Not fer us gettin' back tergevver there's not.'

'You don't really intend ter stay wiv that feller, 'e's not your type,' Ben said, reaching for her arm.

Lana pulled away. 'I'm 'appy wiv 'im, Ben, so yer better get it inter yer 'ead.'

'Yeah, but yer don't love 'im, not the way yer love me.'

'You can fink what yer like, it won't make any difference,' she told him sharply.

'Look, what if I told yer I've changed,' he replied. 'Really I 'ave. I've paid Joe back the money I owed 'im an' . . .'

'Joe?'

'Yeah, Joe Slavin who owns the cafe in River Lane,' Ben started to explain. ''E leant me the fifty quid I owed Gerry so I could square 'im up, but Gerry wouldn't take it. So I paid Joe back.'

Lana sighed in irritation. 'This is just gettin' stupid,' she said, rounding on him. 'So yer still owe Gerry Knowland the money.'

'No. 'E told me I'd repaid the debt by gettin' 'im certain info.'

'What are you now then, a spy?' Lana replied with sarcasm.

'Now, listen ter me,' he said as she moved off once more. 'I got a load o' whisky an' I've sold it all apart from a few bottles. It got me straight an' now I can see me way clear ter gettin' some money tergevver. I'm goin' inter buyin' an' sellin' in a big way, Lana. All I need is a bit longer. Yer'll be proud o' me.'

There was a note of desperation in Lana's voice as she answered him. 'Yer've got to understand, Ben, what we 'ad was good while it lasted, but it's past, gone fer ever. I want different fings out o' life than you. What I want you can't give me. I'm not blamin' yer, 'cos I've 'ad time ter fink it all out. Yer not the marryin' kind, Ben, an' I'm not the sort o' gel who's content ter be seen as some bird yer got in tow, someone ter show off ter yer friends. There's someone else in me life now, someone who makes me very 'appy, an' one day when yer finally come ter terms wiv the fact that me an' you could never make a go of it tergevver yer'll be content, an' 'appy fer me too.'

They had reached Dockhead and Ben took her arm quickly, stopping her. 'I'll never be content wivout you,' he said sharply, 'so don't try ter preach the gospel ter me. One day yer'll come back, when yer realise what yer bin missin'. An' yer can tell that bloke o' yours ter keep out o' me way, or I might do somefing I'd regret.'

'It was a good job I never told 'im that at the Crown,' Lana replied angrily. 'If it wasn't fer Jimmy yer might not be 'ere now.'

Ben scowled. 'I could 'a' took care o' fings.'

'Not the way I 'eard it,' she said quickly.

'I'm not listenin' ter this,' he replied. 'Just remember what I said, that's all.'

Lana watched him walk away and disappear into the Crown and she carried on home feeling angry and upset.

Jimmy Bailey had collected a consignment of sultanas from the West India Dock and when he arrived back in the early afternoon he was pleased to see a space on the loading bank. As the last cases were trucked from his lorry by the warehousemen the transport manager came over to him. 'Get yer vehicle washed down, Jimbo, an' then yer can shoot off,' he told him.

Jimmy drove his lorry into the garage opposite and set to work with a vengeance. He wanted to follow his hunch and get to the town hall before it closed, and with a bit of luck he would be a lot closer to finding the whereabouts of the elusive Ellen.

While he was drying off the paintwork on the lorry with a leather, his brother-in-law Bernie came up. 'Ole Kenwood's in a good mood terday,' Bernie remarked. ''E told me I could go after I washed me motor down.'

'Yeah, me too,' Jimmy replied. 'I'm chasin' it up so I can get ter the town 'all before they shut.'

Bernie smiled. 'Still tryin' then?'

'Too true,' Jimmy told him. 'Time's gettin' short but we're not givin' up yet.'

''Ere, gis that leavver an' I'll finish off while you wipe the wheels,' Bernie said obligingly.

The two worked with a will and then as Bernie squeezed the leather out he looked over at Jimmy. ''Ere, I was just finkin',' he said. 'That ovver one yer was tellin' me about. The one who married a businessman. Couldn't yer find out 'is name an' address an' what sort of a business 'e was in from the marriage lines?'

'I've already found out,' Jimmy replied. ''Is name's John Thompson an' 'e's a builder from Balham, but 'e's moved away an' no one seems ter know where.'

'Well, 'ave yer bin frew the phone book? 'E might be in there under 'is own name.'

'I've already done it.'

''Ave yer thought o' phonin' a few builders in Balham?' Bernie persisted. 'Someone might know of 'im.'

'That's an idea,' Jimmy said.

'Righto then, if yer in a 'urry park the motor outside an' I'll put it away later,' Bernie told him.

Jimmy hurried off, grateful for Bernie's help and when he arrived at the town hall he crossed his fingers as he hurried up the wide flight of steps.

Lottie had been feeling perky and she decided she would take the opportunity to have a tidy-up. Lana and Jimmy would be calling in this evening and she was determined to have the place looking shipshape. First she did the dusting, carefully polishing the ornaments and pictures that were disposed about the parlour. Afterwards she tackled the armchairs and settee, shaking up the cushions and rearranging them to her satisfaction. Her breath began to get short and she sat down in her rocking chair, realising that perhaps she had overdone it. It was tidy anyway, she thought. Later she would take those old coats down from behind the door and bank up the fire. For the moment though she would just sit quietly and get her strength back.

The creak of the rocker and the gentle rhythm lulled the old lady into a calm, reflective mood and she let her mind wander. They were nice children: Lana was thoughtful and caring, and Jimmy too. She was pleased that they got on so well. Maybe her little ploy in sending the girl to his house with the note had helped. Lana seemed different lately, more lively since parting from the other young man. From what the girl had told her about him he certainly wasn't the one for her. Yes, she and Jimmy made a nice couple. Strange how they had harped on about that album of hers, and all the questions they had asked her about her children. Every time they called in she had been obliged to tell them something or other. Still, young people seemed very inquisitive these days, and good for them.

As Lottie rested she caught sight of the album on the shelf by the window. It was nice to have that reminder, she thought to herself with a smile. Nice to look through it on occasions and remember the days gone by, the hardships and the happy times too. It was a good thing that Bill bought the camera. He had captured it all – well nearly all. Ten children and nine photographs to look back on. Shame about the other little mite. His photo would have been with the rest had he not disgraced himself. Bill had been right to punish him. Another man would have taken a belt to him but that was not Bill's way. He was a kind, gentle man with not a hard bone in his body. Instead he refused to take the boy's picture, saying that naughty boys never came out on film. The little chap knew he'd done wrong and tried so hard to mend his ways, but misfortune always seemed to follow him.

The little old lady smiled sadly at the memory. Bill had promised the lad that he would consider taking his photo and putting it along with the rest if he could keep out of trouble for two weeks, but it had been hopeless. A vase got broken, then there was that trouble over Mrs Brabon's cat. They said he was the one who tied the tin cans to its tail and they were probably right, though the lad swore it wasn't him. It didn't help matters when a week later Mr Jones's mongrel arrived home with a black stripe painted along his pure white fur. Once again the fingers pointed at him and Bill decided that until his behaviour improved dramatically the boy would not get to see his photo in the album.

Strange how things turn out, she sighed. He was a good lad at heart and so tenderhearted too, but like many of the other children in the neighbourhood there was little help for him and he was forced to carve out his own future the best way he could. At least he had come back to see her often during his growing years, and as a young man too, until that bad day, that awful day. How nice it would be to have the power to turn back time, to take back the awful words said in haste. To speak the words that should be said, but never are.

The rocking stopped as Lottie dwelt on the last of the children the nuns had brought to her. All that had happened, all that had been said didn't matter now. Words had been spoken in anger and frustration at the time – but he was still her favourite, and always would be, despite his character, despite everything.

Sadie Pugh considered herself to be a reliable, tactful and discreet person, but she had to admit that there were times when things that should not be said were. There were times too when certain things happened which provoked serious discussion, during which confidences were sometimes compromised. One such occasion arose when Madge Conroy tugged on Sadie's arm at the market and caught her off guard.

'Preacher Jack's bin at it again, by all accounts,' she announced.

'What's 'appened?' Sadie asked her.

''E's s'posed to 'ave stuffed a rag soaked in paraffin frew Bubbles' letterbox an' chucked a match in after it, accordin' ter the fish man.'

'Good Gawd!'

'Would've burned the place down but fer the bloke who lives there,' Madge went on. ''E gave chase an' caught 'im. Gave 'im a good pastin' so the fish man told me. Blacked both 'is eyes 'e did. Anyway 'e's bin put away.'

'Who, the man that whacked 'im?'

'Nah, Jack the Preacher. 'E come up in court an' they sent 'im ter the looney bin again.'

'Best place.'

'Yeah, if they keep 'im there.'

'They will, won't they?'

'The fish man reckons 'e'll be out in a couple o' months.'

'Good Gawd!'

Madge grinned evilly. 'Wait till I tell Irene Frost,' she remarked. 'She'll raise the roof.'

'I shouldn't tell 'er if I were you,' Sadie urged. 'She's worried sick over that sister of 'ers.'

'Why should she be upset? Bubbles is big an' ugly enough ter take care of 'erself,' Madge replied.

'It's not that,' Sadie explained. 'It's the shame she feels.'

'Pity,' Madge said unfeelingly. 'It ain't Irene's fault what 'er sister is.'

'Nah, but she's frightened Bubbles'll come round the street showin' 'erself off an' chattin' up the men,' Sadie went on.

'Well, I dunno what you fink, but I'd say there ain't many fellers in the turnin' wiv a jump left in 'em,' Madge said smiling. 'So I dunno what she's worried about.'

'She's a funny woman,' Sadie replied. 'Yer see she's got this fing about bein' upright an' respectable. I mean she even does 'er step twice a week, an' she's always changin' 'er curtains in case people fink she's dirty in the 'ome. And now there's all this business wiv Bubbles. It's all about family pride, yer see. Irene don't like the idea o' people knowin' 'er sister's on the game.'

'But they do know, so it's 'ard luck,' Madge said quickly.

Sadie Pugh stopped to think for a few seconds. Her neighbour was being very uncharitable and it did not become her. Madge was a good person behind her façade and maybe if she was told in confidence the fears that Irene Frost harboured, then perhaps she might be a little kinder towards her. 'The problem is, Madge, the woman's got good reason ter feel worried,' she began.

'Whatever for?'

'Well, if I tell yer mustn't breave a word about it 'cos I bin told in confidence meself.'

Madge nodded and Sadie continued, 'Lottie Curtis is eighty this Christmas an' . . .'

Chapter Thirty

Unlike her neighbours from a few doors away, Madge Conroy had no qualms about passing on valuable information, even though it might be confidential. The only consideration was whether she would get it in the neck as a result. In this case it certainly wouldn't harm Sadie Pugh, she decided, as long as her identity was not divulged, and it wouldn't harm Ann Johnson. She would be only too glad to discover the whereabouts of Bubbles Madigan. The only person it might adversely affect would be Irene Frost, but it certainly wouldn't do her any harm. She was taking the whole thing too seriously in any case.

After weighing it all up very carefully Madge Conroy decided that she should go and see Ann Johnson straight away. It was the Christmas season, the season of goodwill, and she would at least have played her part in making the old lady's birthday party one to remember.

'Look, Ann, yer know I ain't one ter stand gossipin',' she said as she made herself comfortable in the Johnsons' parlour. 'An' ter be honest, I never pry into ovver people's business.'

Ann nodded, smiling with barely concealed amusement at the most loose-tongued gossip in the street. 'Go on, Madge,' she urged her.

'Well, as a matter o' fact I 'eard from a certain person who got it from anuvver person that you an' your Lana are plannin' a nice surprise fer Lottie Curtis on 'er birfday,' Madge continued.

Ann nodded once more, making a mental note never again to tell Irene Frost anything in confidence. 'Yeah, that's right, but the old lady mustn't know at any cost. I 'ope this person told yer that,' she said quickly.

'Of course she did,' Madge replied. 'Actually it's a bit awkward to explain. She wouldn't 'ave told me anyfing at all about Lottie's party, but while we was tergevver down the market we found out somefing from the fish man an' we decided ter put our cards on the table.'

Ann knew she was going to get a headache if she tried too hard to make sense of what Madge was prattling on about. 'What exactly did yer find out?' she sighed.

'Somefing ter your advantage an' I fink yer should know.'

'Know what?' Ann nearly screamed.

'The whereabouts o' one o' them fostered children,' Madge said triumphantly.

'Which one?'

Madge Conroy drew a deep breath as she rested her hands on her large handbag. 'The one called Ellen,' she answered, 'though she don't go by that name any more. They call 'er Bubbles now, an' I 'ave ter tell yer that she's not a respectable woman.'

'Oh?'

'She's on the game.'

'What the woman does is 'er business,' Ann replied quickly. 'All we're interested in is whevver or not she'll come ter the birfday party. Where does she live?'

'She runs a brothel in Paradise Street,' Madge told her. 'It's the big 'ouse on the left.'

'An' yer say she's called Bubbles?'

'Yeah, Bubbles Madigan.'

'Well, fanks fer comin' ter tell me,' Ann said, feeling somewhat mollified. 'Can I get yer a cup o' tea?'

Madge Conroy shook her head. ''E'll be in soon an' I gotta

get the tea ready,' she replied as she got up to leave. 'There's just one fing though. Don't let on to 'er next door.'

'Who, Irene Frost?'

'Yeah, 'cos she'd only get upset,' Madge told her. 'Bubbles is 'er sister an' they ain't spoken fer years.'

Ann made herself a strong cup of tea and sat sipping it gratefully while she thought about the intrigue. She began to have visions of furtive neighbours slipping in and out of each other's houses wearing dark glasses and capes to hide their identity, with shadowy figures resembling Sidney Greenstreet and Peter Lorre skulking around in the fog.

Ten minutes later Lana came home from work and her mother greeted her with a big grin. 'What's the weavver like now?' she asked pointedly.

Jimmy Bailey scraped together the last forkful of his egg and beans and then wiped a thick slice of bread around the plate. Lana would be pleased with the results of his trip to the town hall, he thought, glancing at the sheet of paper lying beside him on the table. The man at the town hall records office had been very helpful, digging out old voters lists and supplying him with the address of the Building Trades Federation.

Jimmy washed and changed, slipped on his donkey jacket and scarf and stepped out into the gathering fog. As he walked quickly along Abbey Street his mind centred on the young woman who had recently come into his life. He had fallen hopelessly in love with her. But what of her? Did Lana really feel love for him? That night in the Crown and Anchor she had been very concerned abut Ben Ferris, which was understandable, but was that all it was, concern? Was she still romantically attached to him, secretly yearning perhaps to try again? Maybe he should ask her about it, he thought briefly. No, it was too soon. Better to be patient and let things develop naturally.

As Lana showed her young man into the parlour Derek looked up from the paper he was reading. 'Wotcher, mate. Yer don't fancy a trip ter the local brothel, do yer?' he said grinning.

'Take no notice of 'im, 'e's got 'is funny 'ead on ternight,' Lana said with a baleful glance at her brother as she took Jimmy's coat and scarf and hung them up behind the door.

'If they ask yer ter promise yer'll do somefing say no, categorically no,' Frank added.

'I'd wanna know the ramifications,' Derek muttered.

Jimmy looked puzzled by the mysterious banter and he glanced at Lana for some guidance.

'We'd better go in the scullery,' she told him. 'It's no good talkin' in front o' those two.'

The young man listened quietly while Lana told him about Bubbles and then he grinned knowingly. 'So it's gotta be a trip ter the local brothel after all.'

'I'll trust yer,' Lana said with a smile.

Jimmy took out the slip of paper from his pocket. 'I've bin busy too,' he said. 'There's the names o' the families who were livin' in the street back in nineteen twenty-three. If any of 'em still live 'ere we might be able ter get some info on Lucy from 'em.'

Lana scanned the list. 'The Conroys are still livin' 'ere,' she told him. 'The Moseleys too. I'd better let Mum see this, she'll know better than me.'

When Ann Johnson came into the scullery carrying a bundle of washing Lana showed her the names.

'The Buckmans at number fifteen,' she said. 'I can 'ave a word wiv Clara Buckman an' Nell Moseley termorrer. As fer Madge Conroy, I don't fink it's werf askin' 'er. She would've told me if she knew anyfing more.'

'I'll phone up the Buildin' Federation termorrer too,' Jimmy said. 'Thompson might be a member.'

'Well, we're doin' all we can,' Lana remarked. 'I just 'ope it all works out.'

Ann got up and took a bag of sugar from the dresser. ''Ere, give this ter Lottie when yer go in there, Lana,' she told her. 'Ask 'er if there's anyfing she wants fer termorrer. I've already bin in there twice terday. As a matter o' fact, I noticed she still 'ad that tatty ole cushion under the new one I made fer 'er, an' when I suggested she should get rid of it she nearly bit me 'ead off. Yer gotta tread carefully at times when they get ter that age. The ole gel's got attached to it, I s'pose. I should'a known better.'

Mick Constantine had spent the whole day acquainting himself with the Gold Star workforce and he had spelt out clearly to the sales manager that certain changes were being made. From today the price tariff supplied to the Maltese shopowners would show an increase of ten per cent on all groceries and provisions, and the manager was instructed to tell them that should they refuse to pay the increase then the outstanding loan would have to be paid in full forthwith.

'I just can't believe it,' Saul Kosky told his reps after Constantine had left. 'Sammy would be horrified. A lot of those shopkeepers are Sammy's friends.'

'Surely he made some provision in the transfer papers,' remarked Ira Greenbaum, the Bermondsey sales representative. 'I need to know. I'll get plagued with questions when I call on the shops.'

'The trouble with Sammy was, a lot of his deals were done with a shake of the hand,' Kosky told him. 'It might have suited him at the time but look where it's left us.'

'And look where it's left the shopkeepers,' Greenbaum replied quickly. 'They can't be expected to stump up for that sort of increase. It'll put them out of business.'

Saul Kosky knew only too well that without a contract to control the loan repayments Constantine could make his own rules. He had picked a good time too, right on Christmas. Sammy should have known better. 'Well, there's nothing we can do about it,' he said, scratching his bald head nervously.

'What's this Constantine like?' Ira asked.

'In a word, ruthless,' Saul replied. 'He made it clear to me in no uncertain terms that I'd be expected to build up the trade both sides of the river and he'd be going over the orders weekly.'

'It seems a strange way of doing things,' Ira said scornfully. 'We'll lose all the Maltese trade for a kick-off.'

'That would appear to be the general idea,' the manager replied. 'Constantine doesn't want their custom, only their shops.'

'Well, I've got to go round scratching for orders tomorrow,' Ira reminded him. 'What do I tell them? How do I explain it?'

'You don't, except to say that there's been a change of ownership,' Kosky replied.

The rest of the sales team had little to say. While sympathising with their Bermondsey colleague they had a living to earn too, and they were grateful their tariffs had remained unchanged.

Darkie Samut signed the surety and passed it back to Sammy Goldbloom as they sat in the small room behind the saloon bar of the Lord Nelson.

'Well, that covers you for any non-payments, Sammy,' he said.

'I'm much obliged,' the little Jew replied. 'I'd love to be there when Mick Constantine realises he's been taken for a ride.'

Darkie looked serious. 'A cornered rat can be dangerous,' he said quietly. 'We'll need to be on our toes from now on.'

'I'll be well out of the line of fire by tomorrow,' Sammy told him, 'but you'll still be here. Just make sure you stay prepared for any eventuality.'

Darkie afforded himself a smile. 'I've got a strong team over from Cable Street and this pub is never left unguarded, Sammy,' he replied. 'If Constantine comes here mob-handed then we go to his club in Camberwell, it's as simple as that. The same applies if he tries to get rough with the shopkeepers. We'll torch his warehouse.'

Sammy nodded. 'Constantine's not the sort of man to let

it go, though,' he warned. 'He'll be determined to come back at you in some way or another.'

'We'll be ready, don't you worry,' Darkie said smiling.

Sammy got up to leave and held out his hand. 'I wish you luck,' he said.

Darkie Samut clasped his hand in a tight grip. 'It's been very nice knowing you, Sammy, and good luck with your venture.'

'It can't fail,' Sammy replied. 'It's written in the Scriptures. I just pray I live long enough to see the birth of the new State of Israel. Shalom, my friend.'

Joe Slavin liked to close up his cafe by five-thirty in the evening, which gave him half an hour to wash the last of the dirty crockery, mop the floor and have a general tidy-up before the six o'clock news came on the wireless. He knew through long experience that after the wharves and warehouses closed at five there was little trade to be had, apart from the wanderers and drifters who ambled past the cafe on their way to the men's hostel at Dockhead. Once in they were the devil's own job to get rid of, and for that reason the cafe owner endeavoured to keep strictly to a regular closing time.

At ten minutes past five Ben Ferris came into the cafe and ordered a cup of tea. Joe could see that his old friend was decidedly under the weather and he gave him an inquiring look as he took down the large chrome teapot from the top of the urn. ''Ave you bin knockin' that whisky back again, Ben?' he asked.

The young man shrugged his shoulders. 'I kept a couple o' the bottles back,' he replied. 'It's always a good tonic fer whatever ails yer.'

'Are you ailin'?' Joe asked as he filled a mug with tea.

'Fings are not all that rosy at the moment, Joe,' he was told. 'I got a few deals in the offin' but nuffing concrete, an' yer can't get rich on spec.'

'D'yer want somefing to eat? I'm closin' shortly,' Joe reminded him.

Ben shook his head. 'Nah, this'll do. I'm s'posed ter be meetin' Gerry 'ere but 'e's obviously late.'

'Well, 'e'd better 'urry up. Like I say . . .'

'Yeah, I know, yer closin' shortly.'

Joe got on with the mopping, aware that Ben was not in a very friendly mood this evening. 'So yer got rid of all the spirits then,' he remarked.

Ben nodded. 'Yeah, no problem. I could do wiv anuvver load, 'specially this time o' year.'

Gerry Knowland walked into the cafe at that moment. 'Sorry, Ben, I got delayed,' he said, nodding a greeting to Joe. 'Is there time fer a cuppa?'

''Ang on a minute while I put the bolts on,' Joe told him. 'It's gonna be foggy ternight an' there'll be a queue at the doss'ouse. Trouble is they fink they can use this gaff as a poxy waitin' room.'

Gerry sat down in the bench seat facing Ben and looked at him closely. 'Are you all right?' he asked with concern.

Ben ignored the question. 'Gerry, I'm sorry I ain't bin in touch but fings 'ave got a bit on top of me lately,' he told him.

'Yeah, so I 'eard.'

'Yer know about the business in the Crown then?'

'Yeah, I 'eard.'

Ben ran his hand over his two-day growth of beard and sighed dejectedly. 'I've not bin much use to yer, 'ave I?' he remarked.

Gerry shrugged his shoulders and glanced quickly over at Joe who was mopping the floor. 'It can't be 'elped,' he said casually.

'Nah, but that's not the point,' Ben argued. 'I'm still obliged to yer fer that fifty quid an' I don't like debts 'angin' over me 'ead.'

'I told yer ter ferget it,' Gerry replied testily. 'Yer did what yer could an' yer brought us the news about Butcher Carberry workin' fer Constantine.'

'Don't patronise me,' Ben said bitterly. 'Everyone tries ter patronise me. I can do wivout it, fank yer very much.'

Joe squeezed out the mop into a bucket and then looked over towards the table. 'I'll be in the back room,' he told them. 'I got some fings ter do.'

Gerry watched as the cafe owner disappeared into the store room then he rested his elbows on the table, a hard look on his handsome face. 'Now listen ter me, Ben,' he insisted. 'No one's patronisin' yer. All I'm sayin' is I'm not callin' in yer debt. As far as I'm concerned, it's cleared.'

Ben sagged in his seat. 'I ballsed it all up, didn't I?' he said. 'Instead o' rowin' meself in wiv Constantine's mob I ended up gettin' 'em on me back.'

'Yeah, well that's in the past,' Gerry replied. 'Fings are movin' very nicely at the moment an' that no-good bastard's got plenty ter worry about.'

Ben raised his eyes. 'Yer don't 'ave ter tell me, I sussed it all out,' he said bitterly. 'Constantine's bought Sammy Goldbloom out fer a start.'

''Ow did yer find that out?' Gerry asked him.

'I went ter see Sammy about 'im buyin' some o' the booze I 'ad an' I was told 'e wasn't there any more,' Ben replied. 'Then as I was leavin' I saw Tommy Carberry standin' outside the office, so I made a few inquiries. I can't understand fer the life o' me why Sammy would sell ter Constantine of all people, not after what 'e told me.'

'About sellin' ter the Malts?'

'Yeah. It don't make sense.'

Gerry smiled slyly. 'That Maltese consortium was never on the cards,' he explained. 'It was put about purposely ter get ter Mick Constantine's ears. All the Malt shopkeepers in Bermon'sey were financed by Sammy, an' Constantine was made aware of it frew certain channels. 'E saw that if 'e acquired Sammy's business 'e could force the Malts out by makin' it impossible fer 'em ter meet the payments 'e'd set. What 'e don't know is that Sammy Goldbloom 'as refinanced all the Malts wiv Darkie as guarantor an' now fer the first time they're free ter trade elsewhere. They're not tied ter Gold Star any more. All right, Constantine won't go bust. Sammy 'ad a good trade across London, but at least 'e won't be able ter drive the Malts out an' take over their shops.'

Ben had grown angry as he listened. 'Sammy told me 'e was sellin' out ter the consortium,' he replied. 'Was that why 'e told me? Did 'e expect me ter go mouthin' off ter Constantine?'

Gerry shook his head slowly. 'No. Sammy was just bein' sensible. What we were up to was a closely guarded secret. What else could 'e 'ave told yer?'

Ben snorted. 'You could 'ave told me, Gerry,' he said crossly. 'Instead yer made out you was surprised when I told yer Sammy was sellin' ter the Malts. I'm yer friend, yer could'a told me.'

'I couldn't,' Gerry replied. 'I 'ad ter play me cards close ter me chest.'

'Yeah, like you always do.'

Gerry smiled disarmingly. 'There was a lot at stake,' he said quietly. 'Sammy's business was well established an' 'e knew that the askin' price would stretch Constantine, so 'e put a tasty little bait on the line. Sammy told 'im 'e was lookin' fer properties to invest in, knowin' that Constantine owned those 'ouses in Rovver'ithe. Anyway, it worked. The bastard was 'ooked. They were part o' the deal an' Sammy's now the proud owner, fer the time bein'.'

'What d'yer mean, fer the time bein'?' Ben asked.

'Sammy's not interested in that sort o' property,' Gerry told him. ''E's gonna invest in the Middle East. The 'ouses in Rovver'ithe are gonna be sold off to an 'ousing trust, which'll give the tenants security an' low rents. As a matter o' fact, Constantine 'ad ter complete the repairs ter the tenants' satisfaction before Sammy would sign on the dotted line, so yer see there was more at stake than met the eye, Ben.'

Joe Slavin came out of the back room looking worried. 'Did yer tell anyone yer was callin' in 'ere this evenin', Gerry?' he asked.

The young man shook his head. 'Nah, why?'

'Yer remember that geezer I warned yer about the ovver day?' Joe went on. 'Well, 'e's standin' across the street an' it looks ter me as though 'e's clockin' the place.'

Gerry smiled calmly as he prepared to leave. 'I fink the big man's runnin' scared,' he said.

Joe Slavin was too late for the six o'clock news that night, and when Gerry and Ben Ferris stepped out into the fog River Lane was deserted.

''Ow's fings wiv you an' Lana?' Gerry asked as they walked towards Ben's flat.

'We've split up,' Ben told him.

'I'm sorry to 'ear it,' Gerry replied. 'Is there a chance yer'll get back tergevver again?'

Ben shrugged his shoulders. 'I dunno. There's someone else on the scene.'

Gerry looked closely at his friend and saw the dejection in his eyes, as if a light had gone out. Ben's shoulders were hunched over and he had his hands buried in his pockets. He was shuffling along with his overcoat collar pulled up around his ears. With his unshaven face and dishevelled hair he looked a sorry sight as they turned out of River Lane and away from the river, unaware that they were being watched.

Chapter Thirty-One

Jimmy Bailey turned into Paradise Street and glanced up at the big house in front of him. He could see the boarded-up window and the scorch-marks on the surrounding brickwork and he hesitated. It was one thing to go inquiring at a normal house, he thought, but this was something else. Lana had told him with a cheeky grin to be careful and Derek had warned him about one or two of the women who worked there, saying that their reputation for kinky carryings-on was a major talking point in the pubs he used.

Jimmy took a deep breath, climbed the few steps to the front door and rang the bell.

'Come along in, young man. Yes, that's right – go in there,' Bubbles said accommodatingly. 'I'm sorry about the state o' the place but we 'ad a little problem wiv Mad Jack the Preacher. 'E tried ter set us alight. Do yer know Mad Jack?'

Jimmy shook his head. 'As a matter o' fact I've, eh, I've come ter . . .'

'Look, there's no need ter feel worried,' Bubbles told him with a big smile. 'Just take a seat an' I'll be wiv yer in two shakes. There's some magazines there yer might find interestin'.'

Jimmy watched Bubbles leave the room and then looked around. There were comfortable seats placed here and there on the plush carpet and a sickly smell of cheap perfume hung in the air. Vases of paper flowers and lurid-coloured cushions were scattered about the place. Pictures of nude Greek maidens carrying urns adorned the walls and in the centre of the salon there was a low coffee table covered with magazines and papers. Suddenly the door opened and a tall, shapely woman came in.

''Ello, young man. I'm Trixie. What's your name?' she asked, smiling to display a row of large white teeth.

'Jimmy Bailey,' the young man replied. 'Look, I've come ter . . .'

'Ooh, I know what yer come for,' Trixie said, smiling seductively as she took his arm. 'C'mon, I want yer ter meet the ovver gels. Yer can take yer pick 'ere, yer know. We don't stand on ceremony.'

Jimmy felt himself being urged firmly into the passage and he tried to resist. 'Look, yer don't understand, I need ter get . . .'

'All in good time,' the woman said, smiling even more broadly. 'Meet the gels first an' then yer can tell me all about it. Is there anyfing yer particularly like? Yer know what I mean?'

Four young women who were lounging in armchairs flashed their teeth and flickered their eyelashes as Jimmy was pushed into their midst and he stood red-faced as they appraised him.

''Ello, darlin'.'

'Is it yer first time, luv?'

'Never mind, we don't bite, unless yer like it.'

Jimmy smiled to cover his embarrassment and the fourth woman stood up and came over to him.

'What a lovely smile. What's yer name, lovey?' she asked, sidling up to him.

'Now come on, ladies, give the lad a chance,' Trixie said sharply. 'Any preference, luv?'

'As a matter o' fact I wanted Bubbles,' he replied quickly.

'I'm sorry but she don't do it any more,' Trixie told him. 'She leaves it to us these days. Age, yer see. It catches up wiv us all in time.'

'No, I wanted ter see 'er about somefing,' Jimmy replied. 'It's personal.'

'Yer can get as personal as yer like wiv me, luv,' the woman leaning against him remarked with a huge wink.

Trixie took his arm. 'Give the feller a break, gels. We'll be back in a minute.'

Jimmy let himself be led back to the salon and he breathed a sigh of relief as she hurried away.

Bubbles was sitting in her comfortably furnished front room on the first floor and she looked up from the newspaper when Trixie entered. 'Anyfing wrong?' she asked her.

'I dunno, 'e looks OK but I don't fink 'e's come 'ere fer a bit o' the ovver,' Trixie replied. ''E wants you.'

Bubbles frowned. After Mad Jack's attempt to burn the house down she was feeling very vulnerable. A report in the newspaper she had in front of her stated that the Preacher had absconded from the mental hospital where he had been sent for tests prior to being sentenced. ''E's not one o' them religious maniacs, is 'e?' she asked.

'Nah, I don't fink so,' Trixie chuckled.

'All right, send 'im up, but get Moses ter stand outside the door just in case,' Bubbles told her.

Ten minutes later Jimmy Bailey stepped into the street with a big smile on his face. Bubbles Madigan had said that she would be delighted to attend Lottie Curtis's birthday party, and added that maybe it would be nice to visit her estranged sister beforehand in an effort to heal the rift between them.

'Psst! Over here,' an urgent voice called out.

Jimmy had only gone a few yards before he saw the shadowy figure lurking in a doorway opposite. He crossed the street towards it and a tall man stepped out into the light of a gas lamp.

'I saw you enter the house of the devil, young man, and I saw you leave,' the man said in a rebuking tone.

'Who are you?' Jimmy asked.

'My name is Jack Ezekiel Dangerfield, known in these parts

as Jack the Preacher,' he replied. 'The middle name comes from the prophet Ezekiel and Jack from my late father, himself a paragon of virtue in a land of Malakites. I saw the smile of satisfaction on your face as you left that den of iniquity and I woe betided myself to see yet another life destined for the fires of hell. Repent, you sinner! Cast out the devil and repent, for Salvation is nigh.'

'Look, pal, I could explain but I fink I'd be wastin' me time,' Jimmy told him, hiding a grin. 'Anyway, I'll fink about what yer said.'

'Nay. Harken, sinner, and hear the word from the book of Ezekiel,' Mad Jack ranted on. 'It is said in the scriptures, "Son of man I have made thee a watchman unto the house of Israel: therefore hear the word at my mouth, and give them warning from me".'

'OK, I've got the message,' Jimmy replied, attempting to walk away.

The Preacher reached out and took him by the arm. 'Before you leave, a further message. "Yet if thou warn the wicked, and he turn not from his wickedness, nor from his wicked way, to save his life; the same wicked man shall die in his iniquity; but his blood will I require at thine hand." So beware the fires, friend. The spinning circles of swords. Heed the warning.'

Jimmy dragged himself free and hurried off smiling. Things were moving and Lana would be pleased to hear his good news. There now remained only two of Lottie's children to be found: Lucy Thompson and the mysterious last of the old lady's brood.

Saul Kosky sat back in his chair and ran his hand over his face. Twenty-five years he had been in the grocery trade, he sighed to himself. From sales rep to sales manager, and in all that time he had never found reason to wish he had chosen a different profession, until today. Sammy Goldbloom had gone and the new owner looked more like a gangster than a businessman. His knowledge of the grocery business was nil and that in itself was bad enough. As hard as Sammy was at times, he at least had made decisions, had taken some of the pressure off his staff and praised them when they did well. The new owner had started by antagonising the Maltese shopowners and the results were waiting on the desk for him. Four shopkeepers had refused to meet the new prices and had phoned in to cancel their standing orders. More would certainly follow and the trade in Bermondsey would drop to zero.

Ira Greenbaum came into the office and flopped down in a vacant chair. 'I give up,' he growled. 'What am I supposed to be, a miracle worker? "Mario, listen," I told him. "Don't be hasty. Phone in and ask to speak to the boss himself. No, not Kosky, the big boss." You know what he said? "You can tella your boss to get stuffed," and other things about his mother. I tell you, Saul, they won't stand for it.'

Saul put up his hands to calm his salesman. 'You don't need to tell me, Ira,' he said irritably. 'I've got four cancellations here already.'

'What's going on, Saul?'

'They're fronting the boss, that's what.'

'Are they mad?' Ira exclaimed, holding out his hands. 'The boss will foreclose on them. Are they willing to lose their businesses?'

Saul shook his head slowly. 'I've been sitting here for the past hour trying to fathom it all out,' he said. 'The only conclusion I can come to is that the shopkeepers have managed to get refinanced.'

'And they'll take their trade elsewhere,' Ira added.

'Four already have, remember,' the manager replied, holding up the slips of paper.

'What can we do about it, Saul?'

'Well, I'll tell you what you can do about it, just stay out of the way when Constantine comes in,' Saul urged him. 'As for me I've got to face him, and I'll tell you something else.

Very soon there'll be a vacant post for a sales manager at Gold Star Groceries. I've already replied to three adverts for a position as sales manager. I just hope I hit lucky before I'm fired.'

Ann Johnson stroked her chin as she sat at the scullery table. 'You say there was no John Thompson registered with the federation?'

Jimmy nodded. 'The man I spoke to told me that most o' the reputable builders belonged ter the federation. Eivver Thompson never bovvered ter join or 'e's not a builder. After all, 'e could 'ave just made out 'e was in the buildin' game.'

'I don't know where we go from 'ere then,' a dejected Lana groaned.

'Nell Moseley wasn't any 'elp, so all we've got ter go on is what Clara Buckman told me,' Ann replied. 'She said she thought Lucy was the one whose muvver 'ad a stroke an' used ter walk wiv a limp. I fink she got it right, 'cos she remembered that Lottie was carin' fer anuvver gel at the time an' then a little boy. Clara didn't know what 'appened ter Lucy afterwards – it was a long time ago. It doesn't 'elp us much, does it?'

'I asked Ellen, or Bubbles as she's known, if she'd seen anyfing o' Lucy after they were split up,' Jimmy told them. 'She said she'd 'eard that she got married to a businessman but that was all.'

'It seems strange that Thompson should call 'imself a builder if 'e wasn't,' Lana remarked. 'As a matter o' fact I found seven John Thompsons in the phone book but none of 'em 'ad a wife named Lucy.'

'You wanna be careful phonin' from work,' Ann warned her. 'You could get the sack fer makin' private calls.'

'Don't worry, I only do it durin' the lunch hour when all the bosses are out the office,' Lana told her.

Frank Johnson sauntered into the scullery. 'Any fear of a cuppa?' he asked, giving Jimmy a friendly wink.

'Put the kettle on an' I'll make it,' Ann said. 'We're busy gettin' nowhere at the moment.'

'What's the problem, maybe I could 'elp?' Frank said amiably.

'Not unless yer a magician,' Lana said smiling. 'We got a name, John Thompson, builder. But 'e ain't a builder, an' 'e's not in the phone book.'

''Ow d'yer know 'e was a builder?' Frank asked.

''Cos we went ter St Mary's Church an' looked frew the records,' Lana went on. 'It was on the marriage lines.'

'So why yer sayin' 'e ain't a builder?'

''Cos 'e's not registered wiv the Buildin' Federation fer a kick-off.'

'What about the phone book?'

'We've tried.'

'Well, yer've made a start,' Frank said encouragingly.

'Look, Frank, if yer can't be more 'elpful than that can yer just go back ter yer paper an' let us continue ter get nowhere,' Ann chided him.

Frank gave her a familiar smile. 'That's 'ow they caught George Brown.'

Ann looked at Jimmy and Lana in turn. 'What's 'e on about?' she appealed to them.

'Nah listen, luv, it's true,' he said with a serious face. 'George Brown lived in River Lane for years till they pulled them 'ouses down ter make room fer the new wharf. I was only a kid at the time but I remember 'im very well. Big man 'e was, wiv one o' those whiskery beards an' sideburns. 'E looked a bit like Farvver Christmas, 'cept 'e was dark. Anyway 'e 'ad five kids. As a matter o' fact I used ter play wiv the youngest boy. Tony 'is name was.'

'Is this story gonna take long?' Ann asked in exasperation.

'Nah, bear wiv me fer a minute,' he went on. 'George went missin' fer about a year an' in the meantime anuvver bloke 'ad got 'is feet under George's table. Beanpole of a bloke 'e was. 'E used ter frighten us kids, but George's missus must 'ave gone a bundle on 'im 'cos when George turned up again she wouldn't 'ave nuffing ter do wiv 'im. Told 'im ter piss orf she did.'

'I should bloody well fink so,' Ann cut in quickly. 'Disappear fer a year an' expect ter be taken in again, just like that? I'd 'a' done the same, Frank.'

'Well, I don't know the real strength of it,' Frank continued, 'but word 'ad it that George 'ad lost 'is memory. Anyway anuvver woman turns up an' claims ter be George's wife. She 'ad a marriage certificate ter prove it. George's first ole lady calls the police an' they charged 'im fer bigamy. Now when it comes ter trial George pleads loss o' memory, saying 'e didn't know 'e was already married, yer see.'

'Yeah, I got yer drift,' Ann said despairingly.

'So the prosecutor ses ter George, "What trade do you follow, Mr Brown?", an' George ses, "I'm a cordwainer".'

'A what?'

'A cordwainer, shoemaker.'

'Go on, Frank, for Gawdsake, the kettle's nearly boilin',' Ann implored him.

'Now listen, 'cos this is the bit that trapped George,' Frank chuckled. 'The prosecutor bloke 'eld up this bit o' paper an' said, "Are these your marriage lines?" an' when George nods the bloke ses, "It states here that you're a cordwainer." "Yeah, that's right so I am," George replied. "But you said on record that you were suffering a loss of memory at the time," the bloke goes on. Anyway ter cut a long story short, George got two years.'

'Well, fanks fer cuttin' the story short,' Ann said in the awkward silence that followed. 'Now p'raps you can make the tea while we're all busy finkin'.'

Chapter Thirty-Two

Moses was fifty years old but he had the mind of a child. Abandoned as a baby, he had been brought up by various relatives who it seemed had been glad to be rid of him. He had been to sea as a young man and had never learned to read and write. Strong as an ox but gentle and kind, Moses never had trouble making friends, but these tended to be of the kind who used him for their own ends. A bullied person would send for Moses; a group of young men feeling at a loss for some amusement might seek out Moses to entertain them with his inane answers to their loaded questions; young, flighty and empty-headed women would act appalled and frightened by the shuffling ox of a man, when in reality they had nothing to fear.

No one knew how Moses had got his name and no one knew his family name, but everyone who met the man was touched in some way by his very presence. Bubbles was no exception. She knew that he slept under the arches in Rotherhithe for most of the year and in the Surrey Docks during the winter months. As Moses told her, the timbeı gave off heat and the smell of resin put him off to sleep every bit as well as gas at the dentist. He told her too that getting into the docks was never a problem: he just followed the other tramps, who seemed to know where the loose fencing planks were situated.

Moses never used the services Bubbles and her colleagues provided but he would often stop to chat to them, and sometimes make himself available to dissuade a drunken seaman from pestering the girls. In return the good-natured women of the night made sure Moses had enough to get a meal or a cup of tea on a cold day, and for that he was grateful. Although of exceptional strength and endurance Moses was only human, and after a drenching that he got from sleeping under a leaking arch on a cold night he developed pneumonia. A spell in hospital returned Moses to the neighbourhood looking as daunting as ever, at about the time that Bubbles was toying with the idea of becoming a madam. Who better to look after the women's safety in return for a warm bed and regular meals, she thought. Still broad and muscular, with iron-grey hair closely cropped to his head and piercing dark eyes, Moses looked every bit the part of a minder. It quickly proved to be a sound idea on Bubbles's part, for his presence alone deterred many a liberty-taker.

Late on Saturday night Moses slept soundly in the basement flat set aside for his personal use. Beside him was an alarm bell which was connected to every room in the house. Trade had been busy and it was only when Bubbles gave him the nod that the minder took his leave and retired to his room. Outside the mist came in from the river and hung like a shroud in the cobbled street. It was a night to put the doormat up against the draught, huddle around a roaring fire and later sleep beneath mounds of warm blankets. On such nights the streets were left to the nocturnal, and to a tormented soul whose caged mind had become twisted and warped beyond redemption, gnawing itself to pieces in agony and anger. He walked the streets, feeling safe in the mist and able to pursue his holy quest to satisfy the Scriptures, the warning in the book of Ezekiel: 'Yet if thou warn the wicked, and he turn not from his wickedness, nor from his wicked way, to save his life; the same wicked man shall die in his iniquity; but his blood will I require at thine hand.'

Mad Jack the Preacher knew that the mist would vanish with the coming day and thus his excitement was high. What had to be done was only possible on such a night, and it was clear to behold that Providence had sent the mist to aid the messenger.

Bubbles leaned back in the armchair and put her slippered feet up on to a low stool. 'Get the bottle out, Trixie. No, not the alum, the Scotch, yer silly mare.'

'All right, all right, I know where the booze is,' Trixie replied with a tired smile. 'I know it's bin a bloody 'ectic night but I'm not ready fer the alum pot yet awhile, darlin'.'

'Nay, yer look pretty tidy ter me, luv,' Bubbles remarked.

Trixie fluttered her eyes mockingly then filled two glasses with the fiery spirit. Bubbles took the proffered glass and held it up. ''Ere's to us, darlin'. Long may we reign.'

Trixie felt the warmth of the whisky in her stomach and she sighed contentedly as she flopped down in the armchair facing the madam. 'That poor feller looked really frightened of us gels,' she giggled.

'Yeah, but what a turn-up,' Bubbles replied. 'Fancy me bein' invited ter Lottie Curtis's birfday party. The ole gel's eighty on Christmas Eve.'

''Ow did they come ter find out where yer were?' Trixie asked.

'Most likely it was that sister o' mine, though I don't know fer sure,' Bubbles told her. 'Irene was always the prim an' proper one. You know the sort, clean knickers an' a filfy tongue. She told me ter keep away from the street the last time I saw 'er. Mind you, though, the gel did 'ave a lot ter put up wiv when we was kids. She was the eldest, yer see. She was like a mum to us younger ones when our muvver was taken ill. That's 'ow I come ter be farmed out. Me bein' the youngest. They said Irene couldn't cope wiv us all.'

'Did yer get on OK at this Lottie woman's?' Trixie asked her.

'Yeah, she was smashin',' Bubbles went on. 'So was 'er ole man. Bill 'is name was. 'E always carried a camera about wiv 'im. Always takin' snaps of us kids 'e was. 'E used ter tell us fairy stories when it was time fer bed. Lottie would bring us a slice of 'er 'ome-made cake an' a glass o' warm milk an' then Bill would tell us those lovely stories while we sat all nice an' warm in front o' the fire. I remember those days wiv love an' affection. Shame on me I never went back ter see 'em, but yer know 'ow it is. We never 'ave the time for old people, never listen ter their chatter, an' never learn the lessons they could teach us. Well, at least I'm goin' ter Lottie's birfday party an' I'm gonna give that ole lady a great big smacker of a kiss, you mark my words.'

'Good fer you, Bubbles.'

'Yeah, an' I'm gonna see that sister o' mine too.'

'That'll make it all the better.'

Bubbles cocked her ear and then relaxed again. 'I thought I 'eard somefing,' she said.

'It's yer nerves. They've bin shook up somefing terrible since Mad Jack tried ter burn us down,' Trixie told her. 'That Scotch'll settle yer nerves.'

'Yeah, give us a top-up, will yer, luv?'

'I dunno why they don't lock 'em up in cells instead of 'ospitals,' Trixie went on. 'That's the second time Mad Jack's walked out o' that place.'

''E gives me the creeps,' Bubbles replied. 'I said ter the local copper I should be gettin' protection an' 'e just laughed. "We ain't got the men ter waste guardin' brothels," he told me.'

'Never mind, ole Moses won't let anyfing 'appen to us,' Trixie said encouragingly.

There was a clicking sound outside and Bubbles hurried over to the window. 'It's fick fog,' she remarked. 'I can't see a fing.'

'Don't concern yourself, it's only a cat scroungin' round the dustbin,' Trixie told her. 'C'mon an' sit down.'

Bubbles walked across the room and stood with her back to the fire. 'That loony bastard's given me the jitters,' she growled. 'I won't feel safe till 'e's locked up again.'

'D'yer want me ter sleep wiv yer ternight?' Trixie asked.

'No, you get off ter bed,' Bubbles replied, 'I'll be all right.'

Trixie drained her glass and then went over to plant a kiss on Bubbles's cheek. 'Sleep tight, an' don't let the bedbugs bite.'

As soon as the younger woman had left Bubbles placed a chair against the door with the back wedged below the handle and then glanced at the bell push beside her bed. It was silly to worry so, she told herself as a cold shiver ran down her back.

Jack the Preacher had passed the house many times and knew that the basement flat was where Moses slept. He had heard him coughing and on one occasion he had actually seen the man standing by the window in his nightshirt as he closed the curtains. There was no mistaking him.

The yellow fog hung like a giant cowl in Paradise Street as Mad Jack crept down the greasy stone steps to the basement area. The glass-panelled door had been boarded up and the preacher leaned his back against it as he glanced up anxiously to floor level. Not a sound disturbed the night as he reached into his coat pocket, took out a strip of tin and folded it in half between his fingers. It was the way he had managed to escape from the mental hospital and it would be the way into the house of evil, he grinned as he moved silently to the window. The catch offered little resistance and Mad Jack silently slid the bottom sash upwards. He could now hear heavy breathing as he climbed into the room. A floorboard creaked as the Preacher crept towards the bed and the sleeping figure turned on to his back and grunted. Mad Jack paused over the bed and withdrew a long double-edged knife from his coatsleeve, raising it slowly over his head with both hands clasped around the hilt. His wild eyes flared as he looked up at the knife.

'Vengeance is mine, sayeth the Lord,' he shouted as he brought the weapon down with force.

Vesta Friedland was nearing her sixtieth year and had never married. Hawk-faced and lean, she shunned her neighbours and was without friends. Vesta's only source of pleasure was her caged birds. Canaries, budgerigars and blue tits twittered and chirruped all day long in her drab parlour and she tended them with loving care. When night closed in, Vesta covered the cages and sat by the fire searching for the truth within the holy book. The Preacher had read to her from the Scriptures and he had taught her that the end of the world was nigh and only the chosen few would survive the floods and fire when the Lord pronounced the final Day of Judgement. If that was so then she would take her birds to the high ground and allow them to fly off into the sky.

Life had been simple and her living frugal, and Vesta had been happy in her own way, until the advent of Preacher Jack. He had come to her in the middle of the night, looming there in the doorway, shrouded in fog and pleading for shelter and sustenance. She could have sent him away, but blood cousins were as brothers and sisters and Vesta still bled for her family. Her father had worked in the Kent coalfields and died underground when she was only a child. Her mother had married again out of necessity, and the five children were able to eat regularly and grow sturdy. They had been happy days on the whole, for nearby, on a smallholding, her mother's brother William Dangerfield toiled nonstop to bring up his family, and the children of the two families were able to play together. Jack, the eldest of the Dangerfields, was Vesta's favourite cousin and she was saddened when he ran away from home at sixteen – she was to learn later that he had gone to Yarmouth and joined the fishing fleet there. It was many years before she saw him again, but by then he was a changed man.

When the Preacher came to her house in the middle of the

night he brought her religion and carnal knowledge, and Vesta was made happy for a time. With her parents dead and her siblings off in the wide world she understood the pain of loneliness and was grateful for his attention. He had come with a Bible tucked under his arm and she had been willing to learn from the Scriptures. Time passed and slowly she began to realise that what she had first seen as religious dedication and single-mindedness was in reality madness.

Now, in her autumn years, Vesta provided a safe haven for the Preacher whenever he came to her, but she barred him from her bed and forbade him to denigrate the Lord with his outpourings while under her roof. He was mad but harmless, she felt, and until such time that his madness became a threat to her she would feed and care for him.

Bubbles twisted and turned in her bed, unable to sleep and fearful of every sound. Her imagination began to play tricks with her and the shadows cast by the dying fire were demons rearing over her with fangs dripping blood and claws poised ready to tear her to pieces. She lay awake thinking of Trixie and wishing she had let her share the bed. Trixie was thoughtful and caring but thoroughly amoral; though the risk of seduction paled beside the thought of being eaten alive by the flickering monsters hovering over her.

The clatter of a dustbin lid made Bubbles jump out of bed and she quickly slid her feet into her slippers and reached for her flowered dressing gown. The passage was dark and she shivered as she eased her way along and tapped gently on the end door. 'Are you awake?' she called out softly.

A few seconds later the bolts were drawn and the door creaked open. Trixie was wearing a short nightgown and her short dark hair was tied back with a cloth band. She yawned widely as she took Bubbles by the hand and led her into the room. 'Let's get in bed, it's very cold,' she mumbled sleepily.

Bubbles removed her dressing gown and pulled up her long nightdress as she slipped in between the sheets. 'The bed's nice an' warm,' she remarked.

'Take yer nightie off,' Trixie told her as she slipped her own nightgown over her head.

'I'll do no such fing,' Bubbles said indignantly. 'I need yer company not anyfing else.'

'Don't be silly,' Trixie replied as she slipped in beside Bubbles. 'We'll be warmer cuddlin' in the nude.'

'I'm not takin' that chance,' Bubbles told her. 'Now you put that nightie on or I'll go back ter me own room.'

'Oh all right then, but you are a spoilsport,' Trixie said smiling.

The flimsy nightie had draped itself over the bedside table and as the young woman reached for it she cursed aloud.

'What's the matter?' Bubbles asked her.

'I accidentally pressed the bell,' she replied, looking worried.

'Don't worry about it,' Bubbles told her. 'When Moses knocks on the door just tell 'im yer must 'ave done it in yer sleep.'

The two women waited for footsteps on the stairs but it remained quiet, and after a few minutes Bubbles began to get worried. 'Are yer sure yer pressed the bell?' she asked.

'Yeah, sure I'm sure.'

'Well, Moses must be in a deep sleep.'

'P'raps the battery's run out,' Trixie offered.

'Moses changed it only last week an' it lasts for ages,' Bubbles replied.

'I'd better go take a look,' Trixie said sighing. ''E could be ill.'

Bubbles's face took on a frightened look. 'Don't leave me on me own.'

'Well, yer'll 'ave ter come wiv me then,' Trixie said testily.

The two women descended the steep flight of stairs to the basement and gently knocked on the bedroom door. 'Are yer OK, Moses?' Bubbles called out.

When they received no answer the women exchanged worried looks and Bubbles turned the doorknob. 'Oh my God!'

she gasped, her hand going up to her mouth as she fell against the doorpost.

Trixie's piercing scream woke up the rest of the household and the frightened women hurried down to gather by the bedroom door, sheer horror etched in their ashen faces as they peered into the room. There on the bed, with a knife embedded in his chest, was the body of Jack the Preacher.

Chapter Thirty-Three

On Monday morning Chief Inspector William Penrose passed the folder to the detective sergeant and leaned back in his chair. 'It's a strange one this,' he remarked. 'It could be the title of one of those old music hall melodramas. Murder at the Brothel.'

'We'll know the full story once we pull this Moses chap in,' Don Hallam replied. 'Funny name that. Strange character too, according to the girls at the brothel.'

'We've got a strange victim as well,' Penrose replied. 'Jack Dangerfield, alias Jack the Preacher. We've got a thick file on him.'

Hallam nodded. 'Charged with arson. Escaped from Moorlands Mental Hospital while undergoing tests. A lot of previous too.'

Penrose shook his head slowly as he pondered. 'How did the man stay free for so long?' he asked. 'Someone must have been taking care of him. According to the file, Dangerfield had no living relatives. What did we get from the local bobbie?'

'We drew a blank,' Hallam told him. 'None of the locals he spoke to knew where the Preacher disappeared to, and I believe them. They wouldn't cover for someone like him. None of the girls at the brothel was able to tell us much either. They heard nothing and they don't know where Moses could be hiding out. We've searched the dosshouses, checked with the local hospitals and we've got a bulletin out on him.'

'As long as he doesn't show up in the river. We don't want another unsolved crime to add to the list,' Penrose said pointedly.

'This woman Bubbles Madigan. She spoke highly of Moses,' Hallam remarked. 'She also said that Moses gave the Preacher a thumping over the arson attempt on the brothel.'

Penrose nodded. 'The basement door of the brothel is boarded up so it's safe to assume that the Preacher got in via the window and was tackled by this Moses character, and in the ensuing fight the Preacher was stabbed to death. Moses then realised the seriousness of what he'd done and bolted. All right, we could argue that he should have waited until the police came and then explained what had happened, but there we are.'

Don Hallam nodded. 'The questions remain though. Why did the Preacher break into the basement? Robbery? Was he after Moses to settle a score, or was he surprised by Moses?'

'Well, we do know that this Preacher character had a fixation about the place,' Penrose replied. 'What did he call it, a den of iniquity? The house of the devil?'

'He could have been after the girls. A modern Jack the Ripper,' Hallam suggested.

Penrose stroked his chin thoughtfully. 'It's quite possible.'

'Another question remains,' Hallam added. 'Whose knife was he killed with? Was it his, or did it belong to Moses?'

'You'd better get a team on this right away,' Penrose told him. 'I want Moses found, and fast. I'm sitting on the Baz Smithson case and it looks like there's trouble brewing on the manor. I can't afford any delay in putting this case to bed.'

On Monday morning Vesta Friedland fed her birds and then went to the market. Jack had not returned to her house and she feared the worst. He had been in a bad mood when he left and she had seen the wild look in his eyes. There was nowhere else for him to go and he was either lying ill somewhere, or the police had found him.

Vesta was soon to hear the news. While she was buying her weekly supply of vegetables the woman in the queue behind her was talking in a loud voice.

'Did yer see it in the mornin' paper?' she asked her friend.

'Yeah, I just read about it,' the woman replied. 'At least 'e won't be pesterin' us any more.'

'I saw 'im ranting off in Paradise Street only last week,' the loud-voiced woman went on. 'I thought ter meself at the time, Jack yer gettin' worse.'

''E used ter frighten the life out o' me,' her companion remarked. 'I was shocked when I see it in the paper, Jack the Preacher stabbed ter death.'

Vesta hurried home and stood for some time beside the canary cage, cooing softly and gently tapping her fingertips on the bars. Later that day she gathered together all of Jack's clothes, his papers, Bible and the bundle of Scripture tracts. In a drawer she found a few bits and pieces, including a strip of webbing that had a clip at one end fastened with a press stud. She put the whole lot together in a large suitcase that had belonged to him and carried it to Dockhead Police Station. One hour later she was allowed to go, leaving behind her a few answers in the brothel murder case.

'Well, at least we know now where Jack the Preacher hid out,' Penrose remarked.

'Look at this,' Hallam said as he examined the strip of webbing. 'It's a bayonet scabbard.'

Penrose took the murder weapon from his desk drawer and put it down on the leather top. 'And this is a bayonet,' he replied.

The sergeant clipped the weapon into the webbing. 'I think this would convince a jury that the murder weapon belonged to the Preacher,' he said smiling. 'Why do you think the old lady brought all this lot in, though?'

'The simple answer is because it belonged to Jack the

Preacher,' Penrose replied, 'but I think what she was actually doing was exorcising the devil.'

'Well, it's only a couple o' weeks ter Christmas,' Lottie remarked as she rocked to and fro.

'Are yer lookin' forward to it?' Lana asked her.

Lottie pulled a face. 'Christmas is nice, but it ain't the same wivout kids,' she replied. 'That's what makes Christmas, just ter see their little faces as they open their presents.'

Lana leaned forward in her armchair to shovel a live coal back into the fire. 'I wonder if the church carol singers'll be round this Christmas Eve,' she remarked.

'I 'ope so. I do love to 'ear those carols,' Lottie said. 'I shall be eighty on Christmas Eve, please Gawd I live as long.'

Lana patted her hand affectionately. 'Yer lookin' younger every day, Lottie,' she said smiling.

'Yeah, I gotta say the Lord's bin good ter me,' she replied. 'I 'ad me 'ands full at times wiv those kids, but I was guided, I'm sure I was. I 'ad a good 'usband too. My Bill was a brick. Never complained if 'is meal wasn't on the table when 'e walked in. It's more than I can say fer some ole men. If their food wasn't ready for 'em when they come in from work there'd be 'ell ter pay.'

'I bet all the children loved 'im,' Lana said.

'They did that,' Lottie replied. 'Mind yer 'e 'ad the patience of a saint at times. It was a good job wiv some of 'em.'

'Yer was sayin' that the last one you looked after was an 'andful,' Lana said casually.

Lottie smiled. ''E could be a cowson at times, but at ovver times 'e was like a little angel. Er, Joe, that's right, Joe 'is name was.'

'Tell me about 'im,' Lana probed.

The old lady stared down into the fire for a few moments and then when she looked up Lana could see the sadness in her eyes. 'John was twelve years old when they brought 'im ter me,' she began.

'Joe, yer mean?' Lana queried.

'Yeah, I mean Joe,' Lottie corrected herself. ''E was the oldest one I took in, an' p'raps it was a mistake. I was goin' on sixty at the time an' the boy really needed a younger woman ter look after 'im. I s'pose 'e looked on me as more like a gran'muvver than a muvver. 'E was very cantankerous at first an' I could understand it. 'E was 'alf-starved an' ill-treated, 'is muvver was on the streets an' no farvver be'ind 'im. Terrible start fer any lad, or gel fer that matter. Anyway, I did what I could an' it seemed that I was beginnin' ter win 'im over, but one day I left 'im on 'is own while I popped in next door wiv an errand I'd got fer ole Annie Shipley who was down wiv shingles. I was only gone a few minutes an' as I walked back in the room I saw 'im puttin' me purse back on the mantelshelf. I never said anyfing ter the lad. I give 'im the benefit o' the doubt, but later I found there was a florin short. Yer can imagine 'ow I felt. I never said anyfing ter my Bill at the time but I was really upset, after all the trouble I'd gone to fer that boy. From then on I never let me purse out o' me sight.'

'Did 'e ever take anyfing else?' Lana asked her.

'As a matter o' fact 'e did,' Lottie told her. 'It was a couple o' weeks after the florin went missin'. I used ter keep me brooches in a vase on the sideboard, an' there was one marcasite brooch that was shaped like a bow. Lovely fing it was, but the pin 'ad come off an' I was intendin' ter get it fixed. Anyway this day I was 'avin' a sort-out like yer do at times an' I couldn't find it. I knew I wouldn't 'ave put it anywhere else so I asked John, I mean Joe, if 'e'd seen it. 'E shook 'is head, but I could tell by the guilty look on 'is face that 'e 'ad. As a matter o' fact I found it a few weeks later in the boy's room an' it was only by chance. 'E'd 'idden it in one of 'is slippers. They was under the bed an' I pulled 'em out wiv the broom. I couldn't let it go, I 'ad ter speak to 'im about it. 'E just said 'e didn't fink I'd mind 'im 'aving it 'cos it was busted.'

'Was 'e cheeky?' Lana asked.

'Nah, that was the trouble,' Lottie replied. ''E 'ad a way of meltin' yer 'eart wiv those big blue eyes of 'is. I worried fer that boy. When 'e was out playin' 'e couldn't keep out o' trouble. A copper brought 'im 'ome once. 'E'd caught 'im stealin' apples off a stall. Then there was the time wiv ole Anne Shipley. Joe put a lighted sparkler frew 'er letterbox on Guy Fawkes Night an' set 'er mat alight. Anuvver time I caught 'im givin' out bars o' chocolate to all the kids in the street. 'E'd nicked 'em out o' the machine on London Bridge Station by stickin' a bit o' tin in the slot. Like I say, 'e was a cowson at times, but 'e wasn't all bad. That boy could be an angel when 'e wanted. 'E was the one who gave me the most trouble, but I couldn't 'elp lovin' 'im.'

'What 'appened to 'im?' Lana asked, almost holding her breath.

'Someone on 'is muvver's side took 'im in,' the old lady replied. 'I used ter see 'im from time ter time as 'e was growin' up an' occasionally 'e'd call in on me, but then 'e stopped comin'.'

''E wouldn't 'ave fergot yer, Lottie, I'm sure,' Lana said.

'Nah, 'e didn't ferget me, but there were fings that 'appened.'

'What fings?'

'I'd sooner not go inter that,' Lottie said quickly. 'Anyway, 'e's a man now an' please Gawd 'e's seen the error of 'is ways.'

Lana could see that the old lady was getting tired and she got up and stretched. 'Shall I make us a nice cup o' tea?'

'That'll be very welcome,' Lottie said smiling. 'I don't wanna keep yer though, 'specially if yer goin' out ternight.'

'Nah, I gotta wash me 'air an' do some ironin',' Lana told her, 'so Jimmy's gonna get an early night, or so 'e said.'

'Yer like that lad, don't yer?'

'Yeah, I do, very much.'

'I'm very pleased. 'E's a good boy,' Lottie replied with a smile. 'I've always reckoned 'e'd make someone a good 'usband.'

Lana took the teapot out to the scullery and lit the gas under the kettle. She was now beginning to build a picture of the last of Lottie's children. The old lady had taken him in when he was twelve years old, after Jimmy had left, which would be around nineteen twenty-four or twenty-five. That would put him in his mid-thirties. Lottie had also said that he had blue eyes. For some reason she was cagey about giving too much away. She had hesitated over naming him and got mixed up with the names, which was unlike her. Usually she was spot on. What had happened all those years ago to make her so upset?

Chapter Thirty-Four

Moses moved closer to the fire he had built in the punctured oil drum and held out his large gnarled hands to the flames. Steam began to rise from his sodden overcoat and he shivered uncontrollably as he listened to the rumble of a train overhead. That would be the milk train to London Bridge, he thought as he tossed another piece of wood on to the fire. There was a time, not so long ago, when he was able to identify all the night trains which passed overhead, but now the sounds were confusing. The slow rhythmic clatter of the freight train from Southampton Docks to the shunting yards at the Old Kent Road was noisier, and always seemed to last longer than the busy metallic clap of the chemical train from downriver to the sidings at South Bermondsey Station. Even the sound of the tenders tracking back and forth left him wondering. Were they upliners or downliners?

Moses let his tired eyes wander up to the wet, fungus-covered sweep of the arch and he sighed sadly. Once he could have survived here, left alone to savour the heat of the fire and eat a nightly meal of whatever he had managed to scrounge from the markets. Now though, the cold had got to him and there was nothing to eat, apart from a few green apples and a rock-hard crust of bread. Once he would have had a billy-can of tea brewing over the flames but now there was only cold water from the public drinking fountain near Surrey Docks

Station. He had grown too old and too soft with the good living.

A rat scampered along the base of the dripping wet wall to disappear under a bundle of rags and Moses shuddered. It had been a mistake to take up Bubbles's offer of a bed and food in return for his services as her protector, he told himself. Look where it had got him – a hunted man who could be looking at the rope, or at the very least a long term of imprisonment. Whatever the outcome he either had to face it, or surely die here, alone and unlamented. There was little choice: he would make his way back to the house at first light. But how was he to explain? Would they believe him when he told them how he had been woken by the Preacher breaking in and had feigned sleep as the man crept over to his bed and raised the long knife above his head. Would they believe him when he told them how he had grabbed his assailant's wrists as the knife plunged into the mattress and then killed him after a short struggle? At least Bubbles would believe him, and she would give him food and let him rest awhile before she called the police.

The rat appeared again, its eyes glinting in the light of the fire and Moses sent it scurrying away with a well-directed piece of wood. Yes, he had grown too old for all this. He would now have to retrieve the wood or the fire would die, something that must never be allowed to happen on a cold winter's night.

'Is that you, Moses?' a timorous voice suddenly called out.

The hunted man twisted his head quickly, his eyes squinting into the darkness. 'Bubbles?'

'Who else, yer silly ole sod,' the madam growled. 'C'mon out. Trixie's wiv me. We got a cab waitin'.'

Stanley Pressman had been driving cabs for a number of years and felt that he had seen it all, but two streetwalkers searching the Deptford arches for trade was something again, and he could not disguise his surprise and shock as the elderly man in his tattered overcoat emerged from under the arch. ''Ere, you ain't finkin' o' doin' it in my cab, are yer?' he said to Trixie in a disgusted tone of voice.

'Nah, we're gonna give 'im a good barf first,' she replied as she chewed on a stick of gum.

''Ere, I don't like the idea o' that ole tramp gettin' in my cab in that state,' he protested.

'Eivver that or yer'll 'ave ter whistle fer yer money,' Trixie told him.

Stanley drove back through the empty streets with a resigned scowl on his face, constantly shaking his head at the audaciousness of the women, but when he left Paradise Street he felt much better, and he smiled to himself as he tapped his top pocket and felt the folded five-pound note nestling there.

Chief Inspector William Penrose stood looking out into the fog and scratched his iron-grey hair thoughtfully. It now seemed likely that the River Thames would soon offer up another poor soul for examination, he thought. Where else could Moses be? Every beat policeman in the district had been out hunting and Deptford police too had been called in to help. A man like Moses was a Bermondsey native, not the sort of man who would take the first train out to invisibility. He had to be somewhere in the vicinity. Who would hide him anyway?

The phone ringing made him start and he grabbed up the receiver quickly. 'Chief Penrose. Yes. Yes, I know her. Show her in right away, sergeant.'

Bubbles looked dressed for action as she came into the office and took a seat without being invited. 'I ain't 'ere ter piss-ball about, guv,' she said without hesitation. 'I'm bringin' Moses in this mornin' an' I want your assurance that yer'll see 'im personally. The poor sod's in a bad way an' I've 'ad a good talk wiv 'im already. It's a clear case o' self-defence. Jack the Preacher was comin' for 'im an' 'e got 'is comeuppance. If Moses 'adn't stopped 'im when 'e did, me an' my gels would be lyin' on a slab by now.'

Penrose afforded himself a brief smile. 'Well, it's nice to

know that I've got the community behind me. Did you take a statement?'

'Now don't start takin' the piss, guv,' Bubbles replied quickly. 'Like I say, I'm bringin' 'im in as long as I got your guarantee.'

The inspector nodded. 'You've got it,' he told her. 'Where is he now?'

'The poor ole sod's soakin' in a nice barf,' she replied.

'Tell me. Where did you find him?'

'Under the arches.'

'What arches?'

'Railway arches.'

'Yeah, but which railway arches?'

'I dunno, is one different from anuvver?'

'Which area?' Penrose said in a flat tone of voice.

'Deptford arches.'

'Where in Deptford?'

'You coppers wanna know the ins an' outs of a nag's arse,' Bubbles growled. 'The ones be'ind the football ground.'

'I'm sorry but I have to be specific, you see I need the information for my report,' Penrose explained.

Bubbles stood up and gave her curls a pat or two. 'Promise me yer'll go easy on 'im,' she said quickly. 'I don't want none o' your dick'eads browbeatin' the poor ole sod.'

'You've got my word, Bubbles,' he told her, smiling benignly.

On a murky morning the *S.S. Empire Windrush* weighed anchor and slipped very slowly out of Southampton Harbour amid much handkerchief-waving and shouts of encouragement from the large group of people assembled on the quayside.

'I wonder if there's fog in Aussie,' a young man aboard remarked.

'I dunno, I shouldn't fink so,' his companion replied.

'Must be some fog, in the wintertime.'

'Yeah, but not like this stuff.'

'Gonna be strange, Christmas on the beach.'

'We won't need fires, that's fer sure.'

'Nice though, the ole coke fires in winter.'

'That's what causes 'alf yer fogs.'

'I wonder what the beer's like.'

'Gawd knows. Most likely a load o' crap.'

'Still, we can't complain. It's a new country.'

The two men walked away from the ship's rail as it sailed out into the Solent and their place was taken by a tall slim man wearing a fawn-coloured overcoat with rimless glasses on his pale face. For a while he stood staring out at the rapidly disappearing shoreline and then he too turned away for the warmth of the passenger lounge. No doubt there would soon be increasingly panic-stricken calls to his office, but they wouldn't affect him. There was a new life waiting for him on the other side of the world, and Frederick Barnfield was content.

Ben Ferris turned over in bed and the pounding in his head followed him. The card session had gone on late into the night and he could not remember much of anything. Had he come out on top? No, it was coming back. He had lost heavily and he suddenly recalled signing a slip. Well, they couldn't get blood from a stone, he told himself as he slipped his feet on to the cold floor. How did he come to let himself be drawn into the game? They were all strangers to him and it was never good practice to get into those sort of games. It was the drink. Sober, he would have declined the offer. What was happening to him? Why had he been so stupid?

At eleven o'clock that morning he took himself down to the cafe in River Lane and ordered a mug of coffee.

'You look bloody awful,' Joe Slavin remarked.

'I feel it too,' Ben growled as he picked up the brimming mug and walked unsteadily to a vacant table.

A few minutes later the cafe owner came over and sat down facing him. 'Are you back in the land o' the livin' yet?' he asked quietly.

Ben nodded. 'Just about.'

'Well then, pay attention,' Joe said in a serious voice. 'I got a call this mornin' from an ole pal o' mine.'

'Oh yeah?'

'Yeah, an' it ain't very good.'

'What d'yer mean?'

'Don't bring Gerry Knowland in 'ere any more,' Joe told him.

Ben blinked once or twice to focus his eyes properly while it sank in. 'Who's warned yer off?' he asked.

'It doesn't matter,' Joe said quickly. 'Just do yer chattin' somewhere else, not in 'ere. OK?'

'If that's the way you feel it's fine by me,' Ben replied abruptly.

The cafe owner leaned forward over the marble-topped table. 'Now listen, Ben,' he said quietly. 'You know as well as anyone that I don't get involved in what's goin' on round 'ere, an' that's what's kept me in business fer so long, but it seems Constantine's got 'is back up an' 'e's breavvin' fire an' brimstone. Like I say, I've bin warned. You know I wouldn't last more than five minutes if they thought I was lettin' Gerry Knowland use this cafe as a business base.'

'Yeah, yer right, Joe. I'll mark Gerry's card,' Ben told him. 'I wouldn't want anyfing to 'appen ter you. Yer've bin a good pal.'

'I 'ope I still am,' Joe replied, giving Ben a friendly punch on the arm.

Ben sipped his coffee disconsolately, watched closely by the cafe owner. 'I got suckered into a card school last night,' he remarked.

'Yer'll never learn, will yer?' Joe muttered, shaking his head in disgust. 'Where was it this time?'

'At the Dewdrop.'

'Did yer lose much?'

'Enough.'

'D'yer know somefing, yer gonna run out o' pubs if yer

go on like this,' Joe said grinning.

'It won't always be like this,' Ben replied quickly. 'I'm just goin' frew a bad patch. It'll come good, don't you worry. I just need a change o' luck that's all.'

''Ow long 'ave I bin 'earing that,' Joe said, smiling indulgently.

Ben finished his coffee and dragged himself from the seat. 'I got someone ter see,' he said. 'I'll catch yer later.'

Joe watched him leave, feeling saddened by his old friend's appearance. He was unkempt and pale-faced and there was a distinct look of desperation about him. There was no time to dwell on it, though. The lunch-time rush would be starting soon and there was much to do.

Saul Kosky put down the phone and stroked his temples in frustration. That was the latest of the Maltese accounts to cancel their standing order and there was nothing he could do about it. One or two cancellations could be taken on board with little or no effect on trade, but fifteen in one week was frightening. There were only three Maltese-owned shops left now and the day was young. Constantine would raise the roof when he arrived and Kosky knew that he would have to listen to him ranting off as though he was to blame. He should have joined Ira Greenbaum over in Tottenham: he had found a good post with a big grocery wholesaler and had phoned to say that there was another salesman's job going there. It would have meant a drop in salary and back to pounding the streets, but compared to this it would have seemed like heaven.

Saul Kosky picked up the phone and glanced anxiously through the glass-panelled door into the warehouse before dialling the number. 'Hello, Ira? Kosky speaking. The post you told me about. Is it still vacant? Good. Well now, listen. See if you can arrange to get me an interview for this afternoon. Yes, this afternoon. It's gone completely crazy here. It's totalled fifteen so far. I'm chewing milk of magnesia tablets by the dozen and I'm sleeping in the spare bedroom.

Mamie's threatened to go back to her mother with the kids. Yeah, that's right. She told me I'm frightening them. She actually called me a monster. Please Ira, do it. I can't take any more of this.'

Gerry Knowland stubbed out his Sobranie and drained his coffee cup. Mandy was late, he fretted. She should have been here an hour ago. Maybe something had come up. She had told him on the phone that Mick Constantine had been behaving like a bull with a sore head for the past few days and that she had to be constantly at his beck and call. It was to be expected. He would have realised by now that he had been duped into buying the Gold Star business and things were sure to hot up.

Mandy hurried into the Soho coffee house looking worried. 'I thought I'd never be able ter get 'ere,' she said breathlessly as she sat down facing him. 'Mick's ravin' mad. I've never seen 'im like this. 'E's bin tryin' ter locate Frederick Barnfield but no one seems ter know where 'e is. Mick said that Barnfield was the first one ter mention the Malt consortium.'

Gerry smiled to himself. Trying to find Barnfield would be like chasing shadows. The real danger would come when Constantine eventually weighed things up and put all the pieces together. 'Anyway, yer made it, finally,' he remarked. 'Coffee?'

Mandy nodded. 'There's somefing else too,' she said. 'Mick came in the room when I was on the phone ter you last night. I thought 'e was gonna be busy in 'is study.'

'Yer don't fink 'e suspects anyfing, do yer?' Gerry asked quickly.

Mandy shook her head as she accepted a cigarette from his silver case. 'I made out it was Brighton I was phonin'. Mick remarked that I looked all worried an' I told 'im me mum wasn't too good. I'm glad 'e was drunk, Gerry, or 'e might 'ave twigged somefing.'

'We've gotta be extra careful from now on,' Gerry stressed.

'I wanna see yer as much as possible, it goes wivout sayin', but we can't take chances.'

'I dunno 'ow long I can keep this up, Gerry,' she told him with a deep sigh.

'Just be patient, Mandy. It won't always be like this,' he replied encouragingly.

'Won't it? 'Ow's it gonna change, Gerry?' she said dejectedly.

'You listen ter me. Mick Constantine's livin' on borrowed time,' he told her in a low voice. ''E's made a lot of enemies, an' one day it's all gonna catch up wiv 'im. Someone's gonna stick 'im, or 'e'll be fitted up good an' proper, you'll see.'

The young woman squeezed his hand across the table. She realised that Gerry knew what he was talking about. She had realised it from the start and it had been her sole reason for marrying Constantine. One day he would suffer one of the fates others of his ilk had faced before: either a violent death or a long prison sentence. In any event she would at least have the security and comfort that his ill-gotten gains could provide. Never again would she be forced to earn her living on the streets with all their dangers. 'Take no notice o' me, I'm just a bit jumpy,' she said. 'I know, why don't we 'ave anuvver night out at the club? Maybe we could ask Ben an' Lana ter come too.'

Gerry shook his head sadly. 'Ben an' Lana split up a few weeks ago,' he told her. 'She's got a new feller in tow by all accounts.'

''Ow's Ben takin' it?' she asked.

''E's on the turps in a big way,' Gerry replied. 'Let's face it, Mandy, the man's a loser. Lana's a good kid an' she wants security, a home, kids.'

'Don't we all?' Mandy sighed.

Gerry shook his head sadly. 'Ben's gone down'ill fast. The last time I saw 'im 'e looked like a tramp. Apart from what the booze is doin' to 'im, 'e's up to 'is neck in debts.'

'Poor Ben. I really liked 'im,' Mandy said.

Gerry nodded. 'Yeah, it's sad when yer see a good pal go that way. Unfortunately there's nuffing I can do, nuffing anybody can do. It's all gotta come from 'im.'

Mandy squeezed his hand again. 'C'mon, Gerry, let's make a move. I'm gettin' depressed,' she sighed.

Chapter Thirty-Five

Madge Conroy was not feeling her usual self as she walked into the market on Monday morning. Her son's recent marriage had steered on to the rocks and her husband Charlie was his old obnoxious self now that Peter was back under their feet. Added to that, Sadie Pugh had ignored her when she walked by her front door and hadn't even passed the time of day. She had seen Sadie in earnest conversation with Irene Frost and it was more than likely that they were talking about her. Never mind, they could all go to hell. She didn't need to listen to their troubles, she had enough of her own to think about.

''Ello, gel, 'ow are you this mornin'?' the fish man asked her.

'Bloody well fed up,' Madge told him sharply.

'Is Charlie keepin' yer short – of money, I mean?' he ribbed her.

'Yeah, but that's nuffing new,' she replied. 'I got me boy back 'ome.'

'Did she chuck 'im out?'

'Nah, 'e walked out.'

'Good fer 'im. That muvver-in-law of 'is wants a good spankin',' the fish man remarked.

Madge had to admire the man's knowledge where neighbourhood problems were concerned. If he had been able to sell his snippets of information instead of fresh fish he would have been a millionaire by now. 'What d'yer fink o' that turn-out at Bubbles's place?' she asked, confident that he would have some tasty bits of news to pass on.

'I 'eard Moses is pleadin' self-defence,' he said as he expertly gutted a large cod. ''E'll get off, an' good luck to 'im. Preacher Jack got 'is comeuppance after all. At least 'e won't be pesterin' Bubbles an' 'er gels anymore. By the way, did yer know she's agreed ter go ter the ole lady's birfday party?'

Madge shook her head slowly in admiration. 'Is there anyfing yer don't know?' she asked.

The fish man smiled slyly. 'Let me tell yer somefing, luv,' he said in an assured tone of voice. 'I bin in this market for more years than I care ter remember, an' in that time I've listened patiently to all the chat, good an' bad. People respect that. They like ter know I'm a good listener an' they all know that I'm someone they can unburden themselves to. Yer'd be surprised the fings they tell me. In my time I've bin like a doctor, a solicitor, a vicar an' goodness knows what else. The day I ain't got time ter let 'em all bend me ear is the day I'll turn it all in.'

Madge Conroy had only intended to pass the time of day with the fish man but now she felt that maybe a piece of fresh cod would be preferable to a meat pie for the family's tea. ''Ere, while yer at it, slice that bit o' cod inter three pieces, will yer,' she told him.

The fishmonger quickly sharpened his long knife on a stone and then wiped it on his apron. 'Clara Buckman was tellin' me all about the birfday party that's planned,' he said as he sliced the fish. 'She told me the Johnsons were tryin' ter find out the whereabouts o' this gel called Lucy Rowley. Clara said that the gel's muvver walked wiv a limp. Well, I've bin makin' some inquiries an' I've found out that the ole lady's still alive. Apparently she's in the Medical Mission in Crimscott Street. D'yer know it?'

'Do I?' Madge replied quickly. 'I used ter take young Peter

up there all the time when 'e was a kid. Always somefing wrong wiv 'im there was. If it wasn't a cut 'ead it'd be a stye or a boil. I remember that they used to 'old services there durin' the afternoons.'

'Well, I ain't seen anyfing of Ann Johnson fer a few days, so yer might pass the info on. There's a good gel.'

Madge Conroy hurried back to Saddler Street with the three portions of fresh fish wrapped up in newspaper. Normally she learned the current news at second hand but today she had got it from the horse's mouth, and as she turned into the street she felt a little better.

The last of the fog had cleared by Monday evening and there was a distinct nip in the air as Lana and Jimmy strolled through Eastcheap. The wide City thoroughfare was lined with office buildings and it ran parallel to the Thames, linking Tower Bridge to the older London Bridge. Narrow cobbled lanes led down from Eastcheap to Billingsgate Fish Market, and already the penny-up-the-hill men were gathering around flaring braziers, hoping to earn the price of a hot pie and a mug of tea, as well as a bottle of beer or two, by hiring their muscle to the market porters who needed help pulling their laden barrows up the steep slippery slopes to the waiting transport.

Overhead the evening sky was clear and full of stars as the two young people walked hand in hand.

'I'm just 'opin' this business at Bubbles's place won't stop 'er comin' on Christmas Eve,' Lana remarked.

'Yeah, me too,' Jimmy replied. 'Do you realise I could 'ave bin attacked meself in that place? Those gels kept givin' me funny looks an' I was expecting ter get jumped at any minute.'

'I bet yer wouldn't 'ave screamed very loud,' Lana said smiling.

Jimmy's hand tightened over hers. 'Yes, I would, they weren't my type,' he said quietly.

'Am I your type?' Lana asked, a cheeky smile playing on her lips.

The young man nodded. 'I can't fink of anyone else I'd sooner be wiv,' he replied.

Lana looked straight ahead. 'I feel the same,' she said softly. 'I've never bin 'appier.'

Their conversation was interrupted by a scruffy-looking individual who stepped out of an alleyway directly into their path.

'Excuse me, mister, but 'ave yer got the price of a cuppa?' he asked.

Jimmy pulled some coppers from his pocket and gave them to the man. 'There you are,' he said cheerily.

'Gawd bless yer, sir, an' may 'E bless you too, lady,' the tramp said, touching his forehead with his first two fingers.

They watched him shuffle quickly down the cobbled lane and Lana sighed sadly. 'What a way ter live,' she remarked almost to herself.

'It's the way a lot of 'em choose to,' Jimmy said. 'Their needs are simple. All they want is a full belly an' a warm place ter lay their 'ead on a cold night.'

'Where do they stay at night?' Lana asked him.

'Some of 'em earn enough fer the doss'ouse an' ovvers spend almost every penny they earn on booze,' Jimmy told her. 'The ones wiv no money sleep in doorways an' down by the river in little encampments. They burn fish boxes ter keep warm an' sit around chattin' while they toast bread an' eat whatever they've bin able ter scrounge.'

'You seem ter know a lot about it,' Lana said, eyeing him curiously.

Jimmy smiled. 'Me dad used ter bring me over 'ere when 'e was 'ome from the sea. I couldn't 'ave bin very old but I remember a lot of what 'e said. 'E 'ad a way o' makin' everyfing sound so excitin'.'

They reached the end of Eastcheap and turned left towards London Bridge. Ahead they could see the avenue of wrought-iron gas lamps which spanned the bridge and the lights on the wharves arcing down on the quaysides.

'It's cold, but it's a beautiful night,' Lana remarked as she pulled the collar of her coat up around her ears.

Jimmy smiled and pointed towards the tall column in the sloping street to their left. 'That's where the Great Fire started, Puddin' Lane,' he said. 'It burned fer four days an' nights an' was s'posed to 'ave burned itself out in Pie Corner, but in fact it went on fer twenty more hours after Pie Corner was destroyed.'

'Very interestin',' Lana replied with a wicked smile. 'Did yer dad tell yer that as well?'

'Nah, I got it out of a library book.'

They strolled along to the middle of the almost deserted bridge and saw the white stone Tower Bridge looming out of the night downriver. When they stopped to lean on the cold stone parapet Jimmy slipped his arm around her waist.

'Are you really 'appy, Lana?' he asked her softly.

She let her head rest on his shoulder. 'Truly,' she whispered.

He could smell the scent of her golden hair and feel the warmth of her body as she nestled against him. 'I know we've only bin tergevver a short while but it seems a lot longer,' he told her.

Lana moved her chin along his shoulder and sighed. 'You've asked me twice ternight if I'm really 'appy, Jimmy,' she said quietly. 'Are yer worried about us?'

'Since I've met you it's like I'm walkin' on a cloud,' Jimmy replied, 'an' it scares me that it could all end.'

'Are yer worryin' about Ben?' she said, turning to face him. 'Well, don't. There's no reason even to give it a thought. It's all over. Finished wiv.'

He took her by the arms and pulled her to him. 'I've fallen in love wiv yer, Lana,' he said, his dark eyes gazing intently into hers.

She let her body relax, cherishing the closeness between them, and she rested her hands on his broad shoulders. 'I love you too, Jimmy,' she whispered, her lips parted slightly as she awaited his kiss.

His lips brushed hers for an instant and then he crushed her to him. The kiss was new and sensuous, as though a deep passion had been awakened in him and she savoured it. It told her of his love and desire for her as he held her tightly, and she felt herself answering him from the bottom of her heart. Footsteps passed, but they were in another world as burning love possessed them like a fierce flame.

Finally Jimmy held her arms and moved her away slightly to look into her eyes. 'I've not been able ter get yer out o' me mind fer a second,' he said in a husky voice. 'I fink about yer first fing in the mornin' an' last fing at night, an' all the hours in between you're there in me thoughts. I really love yer, Lana.'

The temperature had dropped and the cold wind was biting, but Lana glowed inside as they walked from the bridge and strolled down into Tooley Street. The kiss above the river had affected her in a strange way and she still tingled as they made their way home to Dockland. Jimmy's goodnight kisses, tender and soft, and his kisses in greeting made her feel wanted and cherished, but tonight had been different. He had shown her the profound, poignant nature of his need and desire for her, and as she held on to his arm along the deserted street she still felt the sparkle down her spine.

Joe Slavin was just about to slide the bolts over when Tommy Carberry walked up to the cafe. 'Am I too late for a cuppa?' the ex-wrestler asked.

'Nah, 'course yer not,' Joe told him. 'C'mon in an' I'll shut up shop. It looks a cold one ternight an' the boyos are gonna be congregatin' around 'ere very soon.'

Tommy sat down at a table and watched as Joe poured tea into a large mug. ''Ow's fings?' he asked.

'All very quiet,' Joe replied.

'I 'ope yer bin listenin' ter what I told yer,' Tommy said as he leaned his elbows on the table. 'I got a very disgruntled employer who's beginnin' ter run around like an 'eadless chicken.'

'Should that concern me?' Joe asked him as he put the giant mug down on the table.

'Not if yer took notice, Joe,' the huge man answered. 'From what I can gavver it seems Constantine's bin sold a pup an' 'e's ravin'. Anyone who's not wiv 'im is against 'im by 'is reckonin', so be careful who yer let in 'ere from now on.'

The cafe owner sat down at the table and clasped his hands on the marble surface. 'I'm grateful fer yer concern, Tommy,' he replied, 'but yer gotta realise that like Constantine I'm a businessman. I can't afford ter pick an' choose me customers. All right, I've warned Ben Ferris about meetin' wiv Gerry Knowland in 'ere, but Ben's an ole pal. What am I s'posed ter do, tell 'im 'e's not welcome any more?'

'It wouldn't be a bad idea,' Tommy said in a serious voice.

Joe's eyes narrowed. 'What's 'appenin', Tommy?'

When the minder finished explaining about the change of ownership in the Gold Star grocery business, Joe smiled. 'So the Malt shopkeepers 'ave all given 'im the elbow,' he laughed. 'Good fer them.'

Tommy's face remained serious. 'The trouble is, Mick's solicitor's gone missin' an' 'e was the one who Mick relied on more than anybody. There's nuffing ter link 'im wiv any double dealin's an' I was there when the geezer actually warned Mick against buyin' the business, but the big man's not convinced, an' now 'is trusted servant can't be found it throws a different light on the subject.'

Joe studied his thumbnails for a few moments. 'I would 'ave thought it was more sensible ter let fings settle down quietly,' he remarked. 'Mick knows that the Malts 'ave ganged up on 'im an' 'ave got financial backin'. They ain't the easy touch they once were. Surely the man knows if 'e goes against 'em now, 'e's likely ter get burned.'

'You know that, an' so do I, but we ain't Mick Constantine,' Tommy reminded him. ''E's bin 'oldin' the froat o' this manor fer a long time an' it galls 'im fer someone ter challenge 'is authority. So just you be on yer guard. I might not be able ter stop yer gettin' burned yerself, Joe.'

The cafe owner got up and went over to the counter, returning with a bottle of Scotch. ''Ere, let me stick some o' this in, pal,' he told him. 'It's a cold night out there.'

Ann Johnson was combing out her hair in the parlour when Lana returned from her walk with Jimmy. 'I've got some good news for yer,' she told her daughter. 'Madge Conroy called in earlier. She'd bin talkin' ter the fish man at the market. It seems that Lucy's muvver Lizzie Rowley is still alive an' kickin'. She's in the old people's ward at the Medical Mission in Crimscott Street.'

'That is good news,' Lana said brightly. ''Opefully she gets visits from Lucy. Even if not, she'll 'ave 'er address.'

'I shouldn't get too excited,' Ann warned her. 'The poor woman might be too ill to 'ave visitors, or she might not 'ave all 'er marbles. A lot o' sick old people get confused. They're not all like our Lottie.'

Lana sat down facing her mother and kicked off her shoes. 'I'm gonna try ter see 'er anyway,' she said. 'I'll go straight after work termorrer night.'

Ann smiled slyly. 'Well, did you an' Jimmy enjoy the stroll?'

Lana shrugged her shoulders. 'Yeah, it was all right,' she replied.

'Is it serious?'

'Is what serious?'

'Are you an' Jimmy goin' steady?'

'Yeah, we are,' Lana conceded, massaging her feet. ''E's nice ter be wiv an' 'e's got nice ways.'

'Well, I'm off ter bed,' Ann told her. 'That Madge Conroy was 'ere fer over an hour an' she didn't draw breath. She's left me wiv an 'eadache. I got all the news. 'Er son Peter's back 'ome. Apparently 'im an' 'is wife 'ave bin livin' wiv 'er muvver an' there's bin ructions. As I said ter Madge, they've only bin married a couple o' months. It could all sort itself out, but she said that the muvver was the domineerin' sort. She said 'er son couldn't even wear 'is boots in the 'ouse. 'E wasn't allowed ter use the parlour while she wasn't there. She sounds a right ole cow by all accounts.'

Lana smiled at her mother's pained grimace. 'Poor Mum,' she replied. 'Fancy 'avin' ter listen to all that. Never mind, at least she brought a bit o' good news. By the way, did yer go in ter see Lottie this evenin'?'

Ann nodded. 'Yeah, she's very chirpy.'

'I wish I could find out a bit more about that last young lad she fostered,' Lana said. 'It's certainly a mystery.'

'Well, if she won't say who 'e was there's nuffing can be done about it,' Ann replied. 'From what you told me, 'e was a little cowson anyway, an' I don't s'pose she'd want 'im there on the day.'

'I dunno,' Lana said, frowning. 'Lottie did say that 'e was the one she really thought a lot of.'

Ann stood up and stretched. 'Ole people often do talk about their black sheep in that fashion,' she replied. 'It's as if they've gotta make excuses for 'em, as if they've failed the kids in some way an' it's their fault.'

'Well, at least there'll be a few of 'er kids turnin' up,' Lana said positively, 'an' she'll be very pleased ter see 'em, that's fer sure.'

'Yeah, an' you an' Jimmy should take pride in what yer done,' Ann reminded her. 'It's bin no easy job.'

Lana sat staring into the dying embers of the fire for a while after her mother had gone to bed, her thoughts centred on Jimmy. She could still feel the kiss, still feel his arms around her and the delicious feelings that had welled up inside her as they stood locked in an embrace on London Bridge. It was different from anything she had ever experienced with Ben. Theirs had been a purely physical attraction and they had only ever been really happy together when making love. Just being with Jimmy, talking to him and sharing jokes, was wonderful.

The fire died and Lana raked out the ashes before going

up to bed. Tomorrow was another day, and with luck she and Jimmy might make some progress in bringing another of Lottie's children back to the fold on her special day.

Chapter Thirty-Six

Lana was eager to let Jimmy know the latest news, and after a rushed tea she hurried along to his house in Abbey Street. She found him ironing a shirt on the parlour table and her heart went out to him. The room was in a chaotic state, with washing piled on one of the armchairs and newspapers scattered about. She noticed that the curtains were in need of a good wash too, and there was a film of dust covering the sideboard and mantelshelf. Jimmy was doing his best, no doubt, but the house lacked a woman's touch, she thought. A day's work would transform the room.

'I'm sorry yer 'ave ter see it like this,' Jimmy said as he caught the look in her eye. 'This ironin's bin pilin' up an' there's anuvver wash in the yard all ready fer the mangle. I'm afraid me mind's bin on ovver fings lately.'

'If yer'll let me loose in 'ere this weekend I'll fix it all up for yer,' she told him.

'Nah, I wouldn't dream of it,' he replied quickly. 'I'll sort it all out. It's just that livin' alone allows me ter be a bit lapse.'

Lana watched as he picked up a heated flat-iron from the fire and ran it along the ironing blanket. As he pressed it on to the shirt collar she suddenly saw the cotton beginning to singe and she grabbed his hand. 'Jimmy, the iron's too 'ot,' she said quickly. 'Look, you get ready an' I'll finish the shirt.'

The young man nodded sheepishly. 'Normally I manage

the ironin' wivout any trouble. It's you. You're makin' me nervous.'

Lana stood the iron on its end and moved up close. 'You made me nervous last night,' she said softly. 'I could still feel that kiss when I got inter bed. As a matter o' fact I closed me eyes an' pretended you were kissin' me goodnight wiv yer arms wrapped around me. It was lovely.'

Jimmy pulled her to him and kissed her, feeling the softness of her body pressed to his as she ran her fingers through his hair. 'I do love yer, Lana,' he said gruffly.

'I love you too,' she whispered, not wanting him to stop caressing her.

It was Jimmy who broke free, a little embarrassed by his rising passion. 'I fink we'd better get goin',' he said with a grin.

They left the house and walked quickly through the cold evening air into Tower Bridge Road, passed John Feaver's tin factory and turned left again into Grange Road. It was dark now, with the moon hidden behind heavy cloud and the wind getting up. A few late workers hurried by and a bus pulled up at a deserted stop as they crossed the road and turned into Crimscott Street. The mission was situated just inside the turning, next to the huge Crosse and Blackwell's food factory, and Lana gave Jimmy a hopeful smile as they stepped out of the cold into the small hall. There were corridors running left and right and directly in front of them were glass-panelled doors. They could see some activity going on behind them and as they stood hesitating a tall, thin woman dressed in a blue uniform with a triangular headdress came along the corridor.

'Can I help you?' she asked.

Lana spoke first. 'I wonder if it's possible ter see a patient this evenin'?'

'It's Mrs Lizzie Rowley,' Jimmy added quickly.

'I'm afraid that visiting's over now,' the Sister told them. 'Is it important?'

'I s'pose we could come anuvver time, but we did 'ope ter get some information from Mrs Rowley,' Lana replied.

The Sister looked from one to the other. 'As a matter of fact we're just about to have evening service,' she said. 'If you'll just wait here for a few moments while we make the ladies comfortable I'll let you join us. Afterwards we serve them cocoa and biscuits. You may see Mrs Rowley then, but just for a few minutes.'

'We're very much obliged,' Jimmy replied.

The Sister motioned towards a long wooden bench in the left-hand corridor and then went through into the hall.

'So far so good,' Jimmy whispered as they sat down to wait.

In front of them was a long oak panel fixed to the wall, bearing a list of names in gold leaf beneath the heading, 'Roll of Honour'. Beside the names were dates and the two young people scanned the list.

'Look at that,' Jimmy said. 'Sister J. Forbes, China, nineteen ten.'

'Look at that one. Sister P. Moody, Tahiti, nineteen twelve,' Lana pointed out.

Jimmy quickly ran his eye down the list. 'There's twenty names there,' he said. 'They must be missionaries.'

'Yes, they were,' the Sister said, hearing his comment as she came back through the doors. 'They were all trained in nursing too. Our people have gone out to the far corners of the earth to spread the word of Christ and to help heal the sick. Some died out there and others returned broken in health. We're very proud of our roll of honour. Now if you'd care to join us . . .'

Jimmy and Lana followed the Sister into the hall and met a sea of faces staring at them as they took their seats at the rear.

An old lady with a patchwork blanket draped over her legs was sitting next to Jimmy and she nudged him in the ribs. 'Are you two visitin'?' she asked in a croaky voice.

He nodded and she looked him up and down for a few

moments. 'I don't s'pose yer've got any fags on yer,' she muttered.

'Only roll-ups,' he whispered as a priest appeared at the front of the assembly.

'Wouldn't like ter roll us one, would yer?' the old lady asked. 'They don't let us 'ave any fags in 'ere an' I'm gaspin' fer one.'

Jimmy showed her his tobacco tin. 'It's Golden Virginia, it's pretty strong,' he told her in a whisper.

'Don't worry, I used ter get me ole man ter roll me a fag now an' again, an' 'e smoked dark shag, Gawd rest 'is soul. It don't come stronger than dark shag,' she replied.

Lana smiled as he looked at her helplessly. 'Yer might as well roll 'er one or she'll keep on pesterin' yer,' she told him.

'Who is it yer've come ter see?' the old lady said in a loud voice.

'Mrs Rowley,' Jimmy whispered.

The Sister clapped her hands together once or twice. 'Now, ladies, quiet please. We're fortunate enough to have Father Beemish with us tonight and he'll take the service.'

The ruddy-faced priest held up his hands for silence. 'We'll begin with a prayer,' he said.

All the assembly lowered their heads, with the exception of the old lady next to Jimmy. 'Don't roll it too bleedin' thin,' she hissed.

The young man expertly twirled the cigarette paper around the tobacco and brought it up to his tongue.

'Don't wet it too much or it'll be all soggy,' she ordered him.

The congregation was now reciting the Lord's Prayer, and the old lady chose that moment to introduce herself. 'Me name's Emily Bartlett, but everyone calls me Emm fer short,' she said loudly. 'I bin a bit poorly lately so they brought me in 'ere. I ain't 'ere fer long though. They've got a nice place in the country an' they're waitin' fer a bed fer me.'

'That'll be nice,' an embarrassed Jimmy replied in a whisper.

'What yer say?'

'I said that'll be nice,' he replied in a slightly louder voice.

'It ain't bad 'ere really an' the food's very good,' Emm went on. 'As a matter o' fact they do all they can ter make us feel welcome, but it ain't like yer own 'ome. Mind you, my place ain't very nice in this weavver. The roof's leakin' an' the draught's somefing terrible, so I gotta be grateful. It's pleurisy. The pain was bloody awful. Ole Doctor Vine told me I shouldn't spend anuvver night in the place when 'e called round ter see me. It was 'im who got me in 'ere. Nice ole doctor 'e is. Very kind.'

Jimmy glanced at Lana in despair and she stifled a smile as the old lady's chatter went on after the Lord's Prayer ended. The Sister was standing by the door and she put her finger up to her mouth as she caught Emm's eye.

'I'm on me own, yer see,' she continued regardless. 'Bin on me own fer ten years now. All me kids are married off an' they can't get ter see me. I don't mind though, long as they're all 'appy. I mean ter say, they've got their own lives ter lead.'

The Sister was looking daggers at Emm as she went on, her voice rising above the musical introduction from the organist. 'I got a parcel last Christmas. There was a jar o' fish paste an' a tin o' pears. What else was there? Oh yes, I got a pair o' bed socks an' a bag o' nuts. Nice of 'em, wasn't it? They're good kids. They don't forget their ole mum. I expect I'll get anuvver parcel this year, please Gawd I live as long. My eldest is a good boy, really, but the coppers won't leave 'im alone. Anyfing 'appens in our street an' they're down on 'im. They done 'im fer burglary last time, but it wasn't 'im what done it. Someone else done it an' 'e only sold the stuff. They just won't leave 'im alone.'

The hymn singing was under way now but Emm Bartlett was not put off, straining her voice above the music. 'I did get a visit recently. It was just before I went down wiv pleurisy. Our Betsy came ter see me. She's the next eldest. She couldn't stop long 'cos the kids was comin' out o' school, but she brought me a nice bit o' fish an' chips. She was upset when she saw the state o' the place an' she said she's gonna get somefing done about it. She will an' all. She'll be round that council office an' she'll give 'em a piece of 'er mind, soon as she gets the chance.'

Jimmy saw that the Sister was edging round towards Emm and he touched the old lady's arm. 'The Sister's comin' over,' he warned her.

Emm saw the animated gestures from the Sister and she sat silently contemplating the cigarette Jimmy had made for her. The hymn finished and the priest began to read from the Scriptures. His strong voice carried throughout the hall and Emm nodded occasionally, picking her moment to comment just as the parable ended.

'That's a nice story,' she remarked to Jimmy, who by now was red with embarrassment. 'There's a lot o' trufe in it as well. 'Ow many people pass on the ovver side o' the street? You take me, where would I 'ave bin if it wasn't fer ole Doctor Vine? I'd be pushin' up the daisies by now, I'm sure I would. 'E was my good Samaritan.'

Jimmy continued to nod, feeling hot under the collar, but worse was to come.

'These bleedin' stays are cripplin' me,' Emm exclaimed. 'It's the bloody bones. They're stickin' in me ribs. I'll 'ave ter get anuvver pair soon as I can. I'll ask one o' the nurses ter get me a new pair fer when I go ter the country. I need a pair o' lisles from Custow's as well. Yer need a bit o' warmth on yer legs in this weavver.'

The hymn singing started again and Emm fell silent. Jimmy glanced at her and saw a faraway look in her rheumy eyes. Perhaps the hymn had some special meaning for her, he thought, or maybe she was just reflecting on her absent family; that caring, considerate brood who had left her to fend for herself but were moved enough to send a jar of fish paste, a tin of pears and a pair of bed socks, not to speak of the nuts to a toothless old lady. Jimmy suddenly sensed her loneliness and he reached out to squeeze the old lady's hand gently in his, a simple act that did not go unnoticed by Lana, who wanted to hug him as she saw the happy look that came over Emm's lined face.

The service ended and the Sister came over. 'You really must try to stop chattering during the service, Emily,' she said. 'It's very disrupting.' She turned to the young couple. 'If you'll kindly wait outside I'll take you up to see Mrs Rowley.'

As soon as the Sister left, Emm tugged on Jimmy's coatsleeve. 'Most of the people 'ere are all right, but that one's very bossy,' she grumbled. 'Still, I don't take no notice of 'er. Anyway, yer must both come an' see me again before I go in the country.'

'We will,' Jimmy said smiling. 'Bye, Emm.'

Lana fished into her purse and took out a half-crown. 'That'll get yer a nice pair o' lisles,' she said. 'Bye, Emm.'

A small lift carried them to the second floor and the Sister led the way to a small ward. There were only four beds, one in each corner, and as their escort pointed to the bed on the far left Lana caught her breath. The woman propped up against a mound of pillows was tiny, like a doll, and her face lit up as the young woman reached her bed. ''Ello, dear. I knew yer'd come,' she said in a squeaky voice.

The Sister touched Jimmy's arm. 'I'm afraid I can't let you stay very long. Mrs Rowley is very sick and she must get her sleep.'

Jimmy nodded, sharing Lana's disappointment as he sat down beside her. The old lady was obviously confused, mistaking Lana for someone else.

'Mrs Rowley, my name is Lana Johnson an' I live in Saddler Street,' she began in a soft voice.

'It's a nice place, dear. Mrs Simpkins lives there,' the old lady said. 'You know Mrs Simpkins. Four of 'em she lost. Two in the war an' two wiv the fever.'

'Mrs Rowley, can yer tell us where yer daughter lives?' Lana pressed her.

'Did 'e send the book in?' Lizzie Rowley asked her. 'I gotta sign the book or 'e won't be able ter draw the money.'

Jimmy and Lana exchanged glances and then Jimmy leaned forward, his hands clasped on top of the white bedspread. 'Lizzie, I'm Jimmy Bailey.'

'Mary Bailey's boy,' Lizzie said smiling. 'She was a nice lady.'

'It's 'opeless,' Lana sighed.

'Maybe we should come back anuvver time,' Jimmy replied.

They stood up to leave and saw that the old lady's eyes were already closed, and as they crept from the ward the Sister smiled sympathetically. 'I'm afraid she's been like this for a couple of weeks,' she told them. 'Her mind's wandering and she doesn't really know anyone. I was hoping that she might have rallied, having a visit.'

'Does 'er daughter never visit 'er?' Lana asked.

'Not for some time now,' the Sister replied. 'As a matter of fact we're trying to trace her. There seems to have been some kind of a slip-up in our procedures and we don't have her name and address listed for next of kin on our records. So I'm afraid that unless we do find the daughter's address the poor old lady will become a ward of this mission.'

Lana sighed sadly. 'Well, fanks fer everyfing, Sister. We're tryin' ter trace the daughter ourselves an' if we do I'll certainly pass the information on ter yer.'

As they reached the ground floor they saw the old patients being wheeled along the corridor and Jimmy spotted Emm. Her eyes lit up as he waved to her and she ordered the nurse to halt her wheelchair.

'I'm just gonna get 'er ter wheel me inter the carsey so I can 'ave a couple o' puffs,' she told him.

Jimmy smiled. 'You mind yer don't get giddy, it's strong stuff.'

''Ere, 'ow d'yer find Lizzie Rowley? Is she still ramblin'?' Emily asked him.

'Yeah, I'm afraid she is,' Jimmy replied.

'We wanted ter get 'er daughter's address from 'er,' Lana added.

'Yer should 'ave told me that before, it would 'ave saved yer time,' Emily replied.

'You mean you've got 'er daughter's address? Lucy Rowley?' Lana said quickly.

'Yeah, that's right,' Emm said nodding.

'Look, Mrs Bartlett, it's getting late and you should be tucked up in bed by now,' the nurse reminded her.

'Shut yer noise. Can't yer see I'm talkin',' Emm told her sharply.

The young nurse gave Lana a despairing glance. 'Well, don't be long, Emily. I'll be back in two minutes,' she sighed.

The old lady fished into her handbag and pulled out some cards. 'There we are,' she said triumphantly. 'Lucy sent me that one from Margate this summer. I've bin takin' care of 'er mum, yer see, an' we got sort o' friendly.'

''Ave yer got 'er 'ome address?' Lana asked, holding her breath in anticipation.

'Yeah, it's on this letter she sent me,' Emm replied. 'Travis Farm, Monks Felsham, Norfolk.'

'Emm, I love yer,' Lana said joyfully, planting a kiss on the surprised old lady's cheek.

We [illegible] for [illegible] [illegible] [illegible] from [illegible] [illegible] [illegible]

'[illegible] should have told me that before, it would have saved [illegible],' [illegible] replied.

'[illegible] you [illegible] [illegible] [illegible]?' Lucy [illegible] [illegible] [illegible]

'[illegible] [illegible] [illegible] [illegible] doing.'

'[illegible] Mrs [illegible] [illegible] [illegible] [illegible], you should be [illegible] [illegible] [illegible] [illegible] [illegible] [illegible] [illegible] [illegible]

[illegible] [illegible] [illegible] [illegible] [illegible] [illegible] [illegible] [illegible] [illegible]

The [illegible] [illegible] Lucy [illegible] [illegible] [illegible]. 'Well, [illegible] [illegible] [illegible] [illegible] [illegible] [illegible] [illegible] [illegible] [illegible] [illegible] [illegible] [illegible] and [illegible] out [illegible] friend.'

'[illegible] [illegible] [illegible] [illegible] [illegible]?' [illegible] [illegible] [illegible] [illegible] [illegible] [illegible].

'Well, [illegible] [illegible] [illegible] [illegible] [illegible] [illegible] [illegible] [illegible] [illegible] [illegible], Norfolk.'

[illegible] [illegible] [illegible] [illegible] [illegible] [illegible] [illegible] [illegible] [illegible] the [illegible] cheek.

Chapter Thirty-Seven

Ben Ferris slid his legs over the edge of the bed and sat with his head in his hands, waiting for the pounding to subside. It had been a long night and the cards had run more kindly for him. At least he would now be able to settle one of his previous gambling debts. Outside the wind was getting up and clouds scudded across a cold winter sky.

Ben dragged himself into the small kitchen and put the coffee pot over the gas. His head was still pounding and he felt nauseous as he flopped down at the table and pressed the heels of his hands against his eyes. He would have to go and see Gerry again. Perhaps he would be able to put a bit of business his way. He badly needed it, with his van broken down again and a month's rent due on the flat and yard.

The coffee pot started to boil and Ben pulled himself to his feet with a deep sigh. If Gerry couldn't help him it would have to be the Carmichaels. They were always good for a bit of dodgy gear, though with their prices it would only mean a few pounds profit at the most.

The black coffee tasted extra bitter and he scooped another large spoonful of sugar into it, downing it with distaste. He would have to see Toby at the garage this morning and find out if he could do the repair on tick. Gerry would no doubt be at the Dewdrop later or the Lord Nelson, and if not he could usually be contacted by phone.

Ben shaved with an unsteady hand and then dressed with much grunting and groaning. The nausea had lessened but the room kept spinning and the thumping was still there in his head. Maybe he should get some food inside him before he went to the pub, he thought as he slipped on his coat. Just then he heard the splintering of wood as the front door was barged open and footsteps dashing up the stairs. He dived for the carving knife by the sink but he was too late. Nipper Varley stuck out a foot and tripped him and as Ben hit the floor Sid Varley grabbed him by his hair and dragged him up on to his feet.

'We're gonna take a little trip,' Nipper said, grinning at Ben's discomfort.

Sid kept a tight hold of Ben's hair as he led the way down the stairs and into a waiting car.

'Just ter be on the safe side, we're gonna put the blinkers on,' Nipper said as the car moved off swiftly.

'What's goin' on? Where yer takin' me?' Ben asked anxiously.

'Just shut yer noise or I'll shut it for yer,' Sid growled at him.

Ben was squashed between the two brothers and could do nothing to resist as a large bag was pulled down over his head. He was aware of a strong smell of petrol as the car accelerated out into Jamaica Road and he tried to breathe slowly. The journey seemed to be going on for ever and all the time he could hear Sid humming tunelessly to himself. Were they out to finish the job they had started in the Crown, or were they taking him to Mick Constantine? The latter seemed the best bet, but why? What use could he be to the gang boss?

Finally the car squealed to a stop and he was hauled from the back seat, each brother taking an arm as they led him roughly up a short flight of stairs and into the warmth of a house. He could feel carpet under his feet and then he cracked his head as he was manhandled through a low doorway and down a steep flight of creaking stairs. It must be a cellar, he told himself. It felt cold and damp and he could tell that he was standing on a stone floor.

'Sit down,' Nipper ordered, pressing down on Ben's sagging shoulders.

The young man realised he was being tied down in the chair and when the hood was finally removed he blinked a few times before his eyes focused on the grinning Varley brothers. 'Where am I?' he asked fearfully.

'It don't matter where you are,' Nipper told him coldly. 'You just relax. Someone wants ter talk ter yer.'

A voice called out and the brothers hurried from the cellar, leaving Ben alone with his thoughts. He looked around and saw that he was sitting in the middle of a low, dank room. The brick walls had been whitewashed and there was a wooden workbench to his left. The place was lit by a single light bulb hanging from a frayed flex, and to his right was a tall metal cabinet. The only other item of furniture in the room was the padded chair he was sitting in and Ben cursed his misfortune as he strained against the ropes binding him. They had done a good job, he realised. Each of his legs was tethered by the ankle to a chair leg and his hands had been bound together behind the backrest. Even if he managed to free himself, which seemed very unlikely, there would be someone on guard at the top of the stairs. Better to do as he was told and try to relax. It might prove advantageous.

After what seemed like hours he heard footsteps on the stairs and Mick Constantine came into the cellar followed by a heavily built young man with a ring-scarred face. The man was a stranger to Ben but his presence could mean only one thing and he gulped hard as the gang boss walked over to him.

'I 'ope yer not feelin' too uncomfortable,' Mick said with a wicked smile. 'I need your 'elp, an' if yer co-operate everyfing'll be OK. If yer give me any grief, though, I'm gonna leave yer wiv Johnny-boy. 'E's got a very effective way of gettin' ter the trufe, painful though it may be. Johnny, introduce yerself.'

The big man ambled forward and suddenly brought his

hand sharply backwards across Ben's face. Lights seemed to explode in his head as it was knocked sideways and he felt a trickle of blood running down from his split lip on to his chin.

'Now, I'm sure we can dispense wiv this sort o' fing,' Mick said, smiling. 'First off, you an' Gerry Knowland are pals, right?'

Ben nodded. 'Yeah, that's right,' he replied coughing, his throat dry.

'What's the tie-up between 'im an' Darkie Samut?' Mick asked.

'I dunno what yer talkin' about,' Ben said quickly. 'There's no tie-up that I'm aware of.'

'Dear, oh dear,' Mick sighed, shaking his head. 'I thought we were gonna do this in a civilised fashion. I'll ask yer once more. What's the tie-up between Knowland an' Samut?'

Ben realised that he was in a desperate situation. Gerry was a good friend and linking him up with the Maltese boss could well put his life at risk. Better to try and bluff it out, he told himself, play the fool. 'Gerry knows everybody, but 'e don't sit round anyone's table 'cept 'is own,' he said as casually as he could.

'You're bein' evasive, Ben,' the gang boss replied, leaning down close to him. 'Gerry Knowland's ganged up against me an' I wanna 'ear it from you. I'm right, ain't I?'

Ben shook his head. 'The Malts don't take in outsiders. You know that as well as I do.'

Mick Constantine straightened up and glanced at his burly henchman. 'Johnny, I gotta make a phone call,' he said. 'I'll be ten minutes. Will you entertain our guest?'

Johnny nodded. 'A pleasure,' he growled as he wrapped a large handkerchief tightly round his right fist.

Luigi Comino was not a man to take Darkie's warning lightly. All the other Maltese bookies had been ousted from the area by Mick Constantine's mob and he himself would certainly be targeted, if the gang boss found out that he was using his house for betting purposes. He would have to be more careful in future. To that end Luigi stopped the casual comings and goings of his countrymen and took their bets via an agent. He allowed his wife Maria to collect bets from their neighbours and friends, not all of them Maltese. He also went to collect the council workmen's bets from the pub opposite the municipal yard, and felt that he had at least become less conspicuous.

On Tuesday morning Luigi collected the bets as usual from the workmen and then went on to meet his agent before going back home. Later Maria brought in her collection and the bookie gathered them all together on the table in his parlour. A few minutes later he heard a knock at the door.

'Are you there, Maria?' he called out.

'Yeah, I'll get it,' she replied.

'We've got some more bets fer Luigi,' one of the men at the door said, glancing quickly at his colleague.

'I'll get 'im,' Maria told him.

The two men pushed past her and dashed into the parlour. One shoved Luigi back down into the armchair and stood over him while the other intruder scooped up all the slips. 'Be warned. Next time we'll burn you as well,' he growled as he tossed the lot on to the fire.

Richard Carter had lodged in the little street behind the Old Kent Road for one week, and when he had first been shown the room he nodded agreeably and paid two weeks' rent in advance. The arrangement suited the Studleys. They felt that the man was clean, well mannered and educated, and what was more he had declined their offer to provide him with meals. Milly Studley preferred to eat in the privacy of her little tidy parlour and Len did shift work at the bus garage, which made it difficult to serve up regular meals anyway. The money came in handy too now that the last of their brood had left home to do National Service.

As for their lodger, he had been only too glad to pay the

rent in advance after looking round the clean and tidy room and then glancing through the curtains. Almost opposite was the Lord Nelson, and from his upstairs window he had an unlimited view through the net curtains.

He was proving to be a good lodger, Milly thought. Each morning he left at eight sharp and did not return until late evening, in a sober state, going straight to his room without intruding on her privacy, apart from a cheery 'Good evening'.

On Monday of the second week Richard Carter went out at the usual time but came back early in the afternoon saying that he felt a chill coming on and would rest in his room. On Tuesday morning he appeared downstairs briefly in his dressing gown and announced that he was staying in bed as he felt quite feverish. He accepted Milly's offer of a bowl of soup and some bread, and when she had taken it up to him he thanked her profusely and told her not to worry about him as he intended to go to bed and sweat the fever out, fortified by her delicious soup.

Milly felt gratified by his compliment and thought what a nice man he was: so considerate and polite. Had she been present in his room a little later that morning, however, her view of him would have changed drastically, for the supposedly sick lodger had quickly dressed and was in the process of assembling the high-powered hunting rifle which he had kept stored at the bottom of his suitcase.

The Maltese confederates were beginning to gather at the Lord Nelson. Today was a special day, during which a memorial service for Joseph Menotti was to be held at the nearby St Patrick's Catholic Church. It had been well publicised, and an article on the life and times of Joseph Menotti had appeared in the *Evening News* only last week.

Born in Malta, Menotti had come to England with his family at the turn of the century when he was twenty-five and had worked in their olive-oil business. He inherited the company in the twenties and promptly sold it, going into the fur trade, which was then flourishing in London. A millionaire by the time he was fifty, Joseph Menotti sought to alleviate some of the hardships suffered by immigrants from Malta, and to that end he bought properties in London's Cable Street and let them out at a low rent. He was inspirational in developing the Maltese community there, much in the way Little Italy had been founded in Clerkenwell. The benefactor had become involved south of the river too as the Maltese population increased there, and he was often seen walking the streets in his long astrakhan coat and fedora, the inevitable cigarette held in a gold-tipped holder. Always available to those of his countrymen who found themselves on hard times, and active in the Catholic Church, Menotti was revered. His death at the age of seventy from heart failure shocked and saddened the Maltese immigrants and in respect for his memory they had subscribed to a stained-glass window, which had been installed in time for his memorial service that day.

Darkie Samut wore a dark suit and white shirt with a black tie as he stood at the customer side of the counter. Beside him was Toni Rossi, a devoted lieutenant since the attempt on his life by Baz Smithson. Present too were Sam Castelano, whose barber shop had been burnt out, and Don Minto, whose grocery shop had been targeted by Mick Constantine's hoodlums. Other members of the Bermondsey Maltese community were present, as well as a large contingent from Cable Street.

Sam Castelano went over to the window at Darkie's request and peered out into the murky morning street. 'It's just arrived,' he called out.

Darkie banged his glass down hard on the counter for attention and looked round the packed bar. 'Right everyone, it's time,' he said in a loud voice. 'I'll see you at church.'

Led by Don Minto, the dark-suited men left the pub and set off along the small back street, turning into the Old Kent Road four abreast. Two of the men at the front of the procession carried a purple-coloured banner between them, strung between two brass poles, depicting the Knight's Cross of Malta in gold leaf. As the last of the contingent left the street Darkie turned to Toni Rossi and Castelano. 'We'd better get going,' he said, draining his whisky.

'Have you got your speech?' Toni asked.

Darkie tapped his breast pocket. 'Yeah, I got it but it's not a speech, it's an address,' he replied smiling.

'Speech, address, so what,' Sam Castelano said, shrugging his wide shoulders.

Darkie glanced quickly at the barber, saw that his face was flushed with drink and slipped his arm round his shoulders in a friendly gesture. Sam had not been the same man since his shop was burnt out and he had taken to drinking too much. 'C'mon, Sam, let's go,' he said quietly.

The three men left the pub and started across the pavement to the waiting car.

Richard Carter watched the procession leave the pub through a pair of binoculars as he crouched over the propped-up rifle. Each lunchtime for the past week he had gone into the Lord Nelson for a drink and now Darkie Samut's face was fixed in his mind. The arrival of the car had told him that the publican would most likely be driven to the church and he was ready as the three men came out of the saloon bar a few minutes later.

He bent over the rifle, squinting through the telescopic sight and moving the weapon until the small cross centred on Darkie's chest. Just as he reached the car Carter squeezed the trigger and the rifle recoiled with a dull thud.

Toni Rossi knew that he owed his life to Darkie Samut and he had become almost a fixture in the pub. Since that fateful night in Dockhead Toni had become very suspicious of strangers, especially the sort who sat around the Nelson alone and watchful. He had voiced his fears about a couple of individuals who had been coming in regularly at lunchtime for the past week but Darkie had made light of it. 'I can't go asking for their identity cards,' he joked.

Toni's suspicions had been aroused by the appearance of one of the strangers. He wore overalls and a reefer jacket with a scarf loosely tied round his neck, the ordinary garb of a workman, but the man's hands were white and soft-looking, his long slender fingers and manicured nails more in keeping with those of a musician or a surgeon. He could be watching their movements, accustoming himself to the surroundings and faces, Toni thought.

As they walked to the car Toni Rossi glanced to left and right, the way he had seen it done in the Hollywood gangster films *Little Caesar* and *Scarface*. The street looked clear and quiet and he raised his eyes to the windows opposite. Suddenly he noticed that one upstairs window was open slightly, unusual on such a cold day. Then he saw a slight movement and his heart missed a beat. With a shout he pulled on Darkie's arm a tiny fraction of a second before the bullet struck home.

The driver of the car was ashen-faced as he saw Darkie slump down on the back seat with blood beginning to stain his white shirt.

'Don't just sit there! Take us to the hospital!' Toni screamed at him.

Sam Castelano was traumatised by the suddenness of it all and he sat mute, his whole body shaking with shock as he held on to his injured boss.

'Don't fall asleep, Darkie! Stay awake!' Toni shouted at him as the car sped along the Old Kent Road.

It was done, and Carter worked urgently but calmly as he unscrewed the silencer, unclipped the telescopic sight and stock and put the components back into his suitcase. Milly Studley was dozing in her warm parlour and did not hear her lodger leave by way of the scullery, climb over the backyard wall and drop down into the alley behind. Five minutes later he was safely installed in a taxi cab on his way to New Cross Gate Station.

[illegible]ing for their apparently casual changes.

Tom's suspicion had been confirming the appearance of [illegible] of the stranger. [illegible] and [illegible] with [illegible] was [illegible] into his face, the ordinary garb of a workman. But the man's hand was white and soft-looking, with long slender fingers and manicured nails [illegible] [illegible]. He could be [illegible] [illegible], [illegible] to the [illegible], [illegible].

As they walked to the car Tom glanced to [illegible] and [illegible] the way he had seen it done in the [illegible] of the [illegible] and [illegible]. [illegible] looked clear and [illegible] and narrowed his eyes to the windows opposite. Suddenly he noticed that one of [illegible] windows was open slightly and through [illegible] a [illegible]. Then he saw a slight movement and the [illegible] moved a [illegible]. With a shout he pulled [illegible] [illegible] before the bullet struck home.

The driver of the car was [illegible] as he saw Castleford slump down on the back seat with blood beginning to stain his [illegible].

'Don't just sit there! Take us to the hospital!' Tom screamed at him.

Gary Castleford was [illegible] by the suddenness of [illegible] [illegible] his whole body shaking with shock as he [illegible] injured [illegible].

'Get to a hospital, [illegible]! Step on it!' Tom [illegible] at him as the car [illegible] along the Old Kent Road.

[illegible] and [illegible] but [illegible] of the [illegible] the [illegible], [illegible] the [illegible] and [illegible] the [illegible] into [illegible]. With [illegible] again [illegible] and [illegible] the [illegible] by way of the [illegible] [illegible] and [illegible]. [illegible] minutes later he was [illegible] in a taxi cab on his way to New Cross Gate Station.

Chapter Thirty-Eight

Ben Ferris was shivering and straining against the bonds, and he suddenly realised that he had been doused with a bucket of cold water. His lips felt like raw meat and he could only see out of one eye. He had been given a good battering and left to recover and he wondered how much he had told Constantine. It was all a blur from the first punch he had taken, and he sagged in the chair. It was hopeless. The ropes were biting into his ankles and he could no longer feel his feet. His hands too were numb and he stared agonisedly up at the low ceiling.

He could hear them coming down the stairs again and he gritted his teeth as he feared the worst.

'I see 'e's back wiv us,' Constantine said to the young boxer. He leaned over his victim. 'Now I'm sure yer've 'ad about enough o' this, Ben, so let's get it over wiv, shall we?'

'What more d'yer want from me?' Ben growled. 'I told yer all I know.'

'That's just it. Yer told us nuffing,' the gang boss said quietly. 'I've bin patient long enough, an' now I want some answers. What about Gerry Knowland an' Darkie Samut? 'Ave they teamed up?'

Ben found it painful to raise his head but he met Constantine's hard stare. 'I've told yer a dozen times I don't know,' he replied with a deep sigh. 'They wouldn't tell me if they 'ad.'

'Where do they meet?'

'I told yer I don't know.'

Constantine turned to the hefty young henchman. 'Yer gonna 'ave ter do a bit more persuadin', I'm afraid,' he told him.

Ben felt sick with terror as he saw the thug pull a cut-throat razor from his coat pocket. 'I've told yer all I know, fer Chrissake,' he groaned. 'D'yer fink I'd suffer all this if I knew any more?'

The gang boss grabbed Ben's hair in his large hand and yanked on it. 'Now listen, you little piss-arse,' he snarled. 'I don't like ter see blood spilled, so I'm gonna leave Johnny ter work on yer if yer don't come clean. Now fer the last time, what d'yer know about Knowland an' Samut?'

Ben knew that he couldn't hold out any longer. Gerry would understand. 'All right, I'll tell yer everyfing I know, but yer gotta take these ropes off. I can't feel me feet,' he groaned.

Constantine nodded to the boxer, who quickly slashed the ropes with the sharp razor. Ben leaned down and massaged his ankles and wrists for a few moments, then he looked up at his tormentor. 'Gerry an' Darkie 'ave teamed up. Darkie's got all the Malts be'ind 'im,' he said quietly.

'What about the consortium ter buy the Gold Star business?'

'There never was a consortium.'

'Did Knowland tell yer that?'

'Yeah.'

'Where do they meet, Knowland an' Samut?'

'Usually it's at the Lord Nelson.'

'Who was it who topped Baz Smithson?'

'That I don't know.'

Constantine leaned close to Ben's battered face. 'Yer don't want me ter leave yer wiv Johnny 'ere, do yer?' he growled.

'Look, I ain't never bin took inter their confidence an' that's the God's trufe,' Ben told him in an earnest voice. 'I'm sure Gerry don't know who done Smithson eivver. 'E just suspects it was Darkie's boys, same as we all do.'

'One more question,' the gang boss said. 'Sammy Goldbloom. Where's 'e fit in?'

'I didn't know 'e was in on the plan,' Ben replied. 'I flogged some gear to 'im a few weeks ago an' 'e told me 'e was sellin' out ter the Malts. It was Gerry who told me ovverwise. Sammy was just usin' me ter spread rumours, but I never said a word to anybody, I swear.'

'Did Goldbloom tell yer why 'e wanted ter sell up?'

Ben nodded. ''E told me 'e was just tired out an' was gonna spend 'is time workin' wiv this Zionist group.'

Constantine frowned. 'Zionist group? Who are they?'

'It's a powerful group who's got members all over the place,' he told him. 'They're after settin' up in Palestine, as far as I understand.'

'Did Knowland mention anybody by the name o' Frederick Barnfield?'

Ben shook his head. 'I've never 'eard the name mentioned.'

'Are yer sure?'

'I swear I've never 'eard the name.'

Constantine looked at the young thug. 'Tell the Varleys ter bring the car round an' take 'im back where they got 'im from,' he ordered.

Ben staggered to his feet and was suddenly grabbed by his coat collars. 'Now, listen carefully,' Constantine growled. 'Stay well away from Knowland an' Samut or yer'll find yerself in a lot o' trouble, is that understood?'

Ben nodded quickly. 'I got the message,' he gasped.

Lana was feeling optimistic as she hurried home from work that evening. She had sent the letter off to Lucy Thompson and now there was only the last of Lottie's kids to be traced. There was very little to go on at the moment but there was still time to get the old lady to open up a little about the lad. He might still be living locally or one of the old neighbours might be able to throw some light on him.

As soon as she arrived home Ann gave her a sealed envelope with the name Lana scrawled in large letters on it. 'This was put frew the letterbox this afternoon,' she told her. 'I went ter the door but I couldn't see who delivered it.'

Lana tore it open and her face became serious. 'It's Ben,' she said fearfully. ''E's bin 'urt. This is from Joe Slavin who owns the cafe in River Lane. 'E wants me ter call in an' see 'im soon as I can.'

Ann took the letter from her and quickly read it. 'I'd go an' see Jimmy first,' she advised her. 'Get 'im ter go wiv yer.'

'No, I can't involve 'im, Mum, it wouldn't be right,' she replied. 'Just put me tea in the oven. I'll 'ave ter go right away.'

The young woman hurried through the foggy street and turned into River Lane, her heart pounding. Was this some ploy on Ben's part to woo her back to him, or was he really badly hurt, she wondered. Her doubts were soon dispelled when Joe Slavin answered her knock and she saw the concern on his face.

'Ben staggered in 'ere late this afternoon in a bad way,' he told her as he led her up to his flat above the shop. ''E's bin beaten up. I cleaned 'im up as best I could, but 'e needs ter go ter the 'ospital. I fink 'e's got broken ribs.'

'Where is 'e now?' Lana asked quickly.

''E's at 'is flat as far as I know.'

'Who was it beat 'im up?'

''E wouldn't say, but it's gotta be Mick Constantine,' Joe replied. 'Ben's bin gettin' in dodgy company lately an' I fink this was a warnin'.'

'Did Ben ask fer me?' Lana inquired.

Joe shook his head. 'I didn't know who else ter turn to,' he said with a shrug. 'I know you two were goin' out tergevver till recently. Ben told me a lot about yer.'

'I'd better go to 'im,' she said quickly. 'Fanks fer what yer done, Joe.'

'Take this key,' Joe told her.

Lana hurried along the quiet lane and let herself into Ben's flat, climbing up the stairs anxiously and dreading what she might see.

'So Joe told yer,' Ben said, wincing as he held his hand against his ribs.

Lana was shocked by the state of him. Ben's face was cut and bruised and one eye was completely closed. His lips too were blue and there was a patch in his hair matted with dried blood.

'Joe reckons yer got busted ribs,' she told him. 'Yer'll need ter get 'em fixed.'

'I'll mend,' he said sharply.

'Don't be a fool, Ben,' she replied.

'It won't be nuffing new, will it?'

'Look, I've not come 'ere ter listen ter yer feelin' sorry fer yerself,' she told him firmly. 'I'm gettin' you ter Guy's straight away.'

Ben sighed deeply. 'Lana, I'll be OK. Don't worry about it. A few days' rest an' I'll be fine.'

'Who did it, Ben?' she asked him.

'It doesn't matter who did it,' he replied.

'Well, there's no way I'm leavin' yer like this,' she said adamantly. 'I'm goin' out ter get a cab. Be ready.'

Toni Rossi sat with Sam Castelano in the hospital corridor, both still in a state of shock. The medical team had been working on Darkie for some time and he had now been transferred to the operating theatre.

'I didn't have time to do anything,' Sam said. 'I just stood there.'

'It all happened too quickly,' Toni replied. 'I just caught a glimpse of something moving in the window opposite and I could only grab Darkie's arm. I've been expecting something like this to happen.'

'This can't be left,' Sam said. 'We've got to respond, and soon.'

'Now take it easy, Sam,' his friend told him. 'We need to

see how Darkie is first. A wrong move now could undo all that's been achieved. We'll get whoever's responsible, but we've got to be patient. It's what Darkie's always said.'

Sam leaned forward on the seat and cupped his chin in his hands. 'I warned Darkie what would happen if he let Constantine get away with it, but he wouldn't listen. We should have got him right at the start.'

'Talk sense, Sam,' Toni retorted. 'We were just a lot o' small shopkeepers fighting our own battles till Darkie sorted us out. Look at you, your shop was burned out and there was nothing you could do about it. Don Minto got cut and the bookies were chased out of the area, and what could we do to stop it? Nothing, that's what, not until we banded together. Just think for a minute. Where would I have been now if Darkie hadn't organised everybody? I'll tell you where, at the bottom of the river, that's where.'

They saw the surgeon coming towards them accompanied by a nurse and both men stood up quickly.

'Mr Samut was very lucky,' the man told them. 'The bullet entered his chest just below the collarbone and lodged behind the shoulder blade. We've managed to remove it but Mr Samut has lost a lot of blood. I'm afraid he'll be in hospital for at least a week.'

'Is he out of danger, Doctor?' Sam asked him.

'Well, it's early days yet, but yes, I think we can say that Mr Samut is out of immediate danger,' the surgeon replied. 'Of course we have to remember that there's always some element of risk after surgery, but Mr Samut has come out of the anaesthetic and he's resting comfortably.'

Mick Constantine smiled with satisfaction as he put the phone down. The biggest threat to his control of the area had been dealt with, and now there were only a few loose ends to be tied up. Then he would be in an ideal position to remove the last of his enemies without fear of reprisal. Gerry Knowland could safely be left to sweat it out for a while, he decided.

Mandy came into the room and put a tray of tea and sandwiches down on the table. 'The Varleys are back an' the ovver feller's still sittin' in the kitchen,' she said testily.

'Send 'em all in,' he said gruffly.

Nipper was smiling as he entered the large front room. 'We chucked 'im out in River Lane,' he reported.

'Right, I got anuvver little job for yer termorrer,' Constantine replied, a sly smile playing round his lips. 'Now this is what I want yer ter do . . .'

Mandy felt anxious as she busied herself in the kitchen. Things were happening and Mick was looking very pleased with himself. Who was the man they had dragged down into the cellar? Was Gerry all right? She would have to contact him as soon as possible.

'Mandy?'

The young woman hurried into the front room. 'Yeah, what is it?'

'I've bin finkin',' Mick said in an unusually pleasant voice. 'It's bin a bit frantic fer the past few days an' I fink me an' you should take a short little break away somewhere. We'll book in at an 'otel in Brighton. You can see yer muvver while yer there. 'Ow's that sound?'

'That'll be nice,' Mandy replied, feeling a sudden stab of fear that shot through her stomach.

'Yer'll be able ter do a bit o' Christmas shoppin' an' maybe introduce me ter yer muvver as well,' he said lightly.

'Mum's very ill. Yer wouldn't like ter see 'er in that condition, Mick,' she replied as casually as possible.

'Nonsense. I'll be pleased ter meet 'er,' he told her. 'After all, I am 'er son-in-law.'

'Mick, yer said fings 'ave bin frantic lately. What's bin goin' on?' she asked in an attempt to change the subject. 'Those Varley bruvvers put the fear o' God inter me the way they stare, an' then there was those noises comin' from the cellar.'

'It's nuffing fer you ter worry yer pretty little 'ead about,' he told her smiling. 'Now get on the phone ter Tommy Carberry. Tell 'im I'll be goin' out ternight an' I'll want 'im 'ere by eight o'clock.'

Chapter Thirty-Nine

Lucy Thompson had spent the morning repairing a gap in the dry-stone wall and feeding the pigs, and now there was time for a short break, she decided. Joel would be calling this evening and she wanted to look her best. Working the farm with his part-time help was not easy, however, and it was beginning to take its toll. Her hands were getting very rough and her skin too was becoming weatherworn. She would also have to do something about her hair and she sighed sadly to herself as she put the kettle on. Joel had told her that it was better for a young country woman to have a ruddy complexion than a pale city face that was over made-up, but then it was the sort of thing he would say. He had a vested interest, with her now owning the farm and the money that John had salted away.

Lucy leaned back in the rickety armchair and stretched out her stockinged feet to the fire while she waited for the kettle to boil. Joel would be a fine catch for any woman, she thought. He was young, good-looking, and he possessed a sound knowledge of farming. His help during the past few months had been invaluable and she knew only too well that she couldn't have managed without his help. He had given her the strength to keep up the pretence and play the deserted wife and she now felt much more confident when the village policeman paid his regular visit to the farm with a progress report.

The mystery of her husband's disappearance was the talk of the local countryside. To all intents and purposes John Thompson, builder and latterly farmer, had vanished from the face of the earth. PC Colman was always optimistic and supportive, however, and Lucy felt that his attitude had something to do with her personally. Like Joel, he was young and unattached, though without her secret lover's good looks. PC Colman was of the declared opinion that her husband had suffered a loss of memory during one of his business visits to Norwich and would one day reappear out of the blue. His true opinion he kept to himself, though she guessed that the policeman really suspected some harm had come to her devoted and hard-working husband.

The kettle started to boil and Lucy filled the small teapot. She realised that she had no choice but to play her part well. To the people of the local farming community John was a well-respected man. He had come from farming stock, gone to London and made quite a fair bit of money in the building trade, finally returning to his roots to farm the land. The truth was somewhat different, however. John Thompson had never laid a brick nor tiled a roof in his entire life. His money had been made from more devious dealings, and retiring to Norfolk to farm the land was in fact a way of distancing himself from those who were after his blood.

Lucy poured herself a mug of tea and cut a chunky slice of brown bread which she coated thickly with butter. A large knob of cheese completed her snack and she sat back to enjoy it. It had been a life of sheer hell until recently, she reflected. John Thompson had not only been a cheat and a fraud, he had been a wife-beater too, and she still carried the marks of his leather belt.

The shrill ring of a cycle bell made her glance through the window and she saw the postman enter the farm. Lucy quickly stood up and opened the window.

'Bills and more bills, I've no doubt,' the elderly man joked as he passed the batch of letters across the sill.

Lucy quickly shut out the cold and sat down again to flip through the mail. There was a letter from the Farmers' Association, a gas bill, and an invoice for the bags of fertiliser she had recently bought for the upper meadow. There was also a letter from the local tax office and a blue-coloured envelope which she paused over. It had a London postmark and Lucy frowned as she tore it open.

Joe Slavin had been kept busy as usual during most of the day and now in the late afternoon he found time to tidy up a little. There were only two lorry drivers in the cafe and they looked as though they were about to leave. He would be able to close early before the dossers came by and maybe slip out for a well-earned pint or two.

Joe's face dropped as the Varley brothers sauntered into the cafe and ordered mugs of tea.

'Anyfing else, gents?' Joe said, hiding his displeasure.

'Yeah, we'll 'ave a bacon sandwich each,' Nipper told him.

'I'm out o' bacon,' Joe replied.

'All right, make it cheese then,' Nipper said, grinning slyly at his hulking brother.

'Take yer teas an' I'll bring the sandwiches over,' Joe said, reaching for the sharp knife.

Nipper's eyes alighted on the knife and he made a mental note before picking up his tea. Sid followed him over to a bench seat and stared dumbly over at the two drivers.

Joe halved the two sandwiches and walked over to the table just as the lorry drivers got up to leave.

'See yer, Joe,' one called out.

'Yeah, see yer, Nick.'

Nipper Varley watched the men leave. 'What's this s'posed ter be?' he asked the cafe owner.

'What d'yer mean?' Joe replied, his eyes narrowing.

'I told yer I wanted a bacon sandwich,' Nipper said, turning to Sid. 'Didn't you 'ear me say I wanted a bacon sandwich?'

'Yeah, I did,' the older brother growled.

'An' I told you I was out o' bacon,' Joe said sharply.

'What sort of a place is this?' Nipper went on. 'I've never seen a more filfy place in all me life.'

'No, nor 'ave I,' Sid added.

'Right you two, get out,' Joe said, jerking his thumb towards the door.

Nipper slid out from the seat and stood facing the cafe owner. Suddenly he gave him a hard shove and sent him sprawling on the floor, then he rushed behind the counter and came back brandishing the carving knife. 'Make a move an' I'll open yer,' he hissed. 'Right, Sid, tidy up the place.'

The big man smiled inanely as he walked behind the counter and set to work. Joe Slavin sat hunched against the wall, able to do nothing as Sid Varley systematically destroyed his shop. Broken crockery, tea leaves and slices of bread littered the floor, and with a depraved grin Sid turned on the tap, letting the hot water pour out on to the mess. Next he took out a hammer and a knife from under his coat and turned his attention to the tables and padded benches. The marble tops were shattered and all the upholstered benches ripped beyond repair before he paused for breath.

'I got a little message for yer,' Nipper growled at a devastated Joe Slavin. 'In future be careful who you let in 'ere.'

The two thugs strutted out of the cafe without a backward glance as Joe dragged himself to his feet and stood there stunned, looking around him in despair.

A tramp popped his head in the door. 'Are yer still open, guv?' he asked blearily.

'What does it look like?' Joe replied sarcastically.

'Gawd Almighty!' the tramp exclaimed as he walked into the wrecked cafe. 'Whatever's 'appened?'

'I just 'ad a visit from a couple o' maniacs,' Joe told him.

The tramp scratched his matted hair with a mittened hand. 'It's a bloody mess. Want me ter give yer an 'and clearin' it up?'

Normally Joe gave the local tramps and dossers short shrift, but tonight he felt a strange affinity with his visitor. He had lost everything, his pride as well as his business, and in the middle of the depredation a natural feeling of brotherhood gave him some comfort. 'Nah, it's all right. Sit yerself down an' I'll see if they left me teapot in one piece,' he said, forcing a smile.

The tramp squeezed himself into a slashed bench and stared at the untouched sandwiches. 'Anyfing wrong wiv these?' he asked.

'Nah, they didn't want 'em so yer might as well get stuck in,' Joe replied.

'Me name's William Nugget,' the tramp said as he sipped his tea a few minutes later. 'I used ter be a French polisher. Good at me job too, even if I say so meself.'

'What made yer give it up?' Joe asked.

'Yer might well ask,' William replied. 'Ter be honest it was the curse o' John Barleycorn. There was me wiv a lovely little wife an' a nice little flat over in Stepney. 'Appy as a pig in shit I was, until I got the taste fer the 'ow's-yer-farvver. It was all very innocent at first. I used ter stop off fer a pint on me way 'ome from work, an' before long it was two, an' then it was more. After a while I couldn't face a day wivout a drink. Me work suffered an' I was given an ultimatum by me boss. Eivver stop the drinkin' or take me cards. 'E could see what I was gettin' up to. Yer use methylated spirits in the polishin' trade yer see, an' I was mixin' it wiv cider. That wasn't all. Me wife walked out on me one night after I gave 'er a spankin'. Ter be honest I can't even remember it. Anyway, I ended up goin' right down the pan, an' that's 'ow I come ter be on the streets. I can't drink much these days. I got ulcers, yer see.'

Joe pushed the other sandwich in front of the tramp. ''Ere, yer might as well eat this one too,' he told him.

'Gawd bless yer, me ole china,' William replied. 'Afterwards I'll give yer some 'elp. It won't take long.'

Joe laughed bitterly. 'It'll take about twenty years,' he said. Then he fished into his trouser pocket. ''Ere, take this two bob an' get yerself a bed at the 'ostel.'

William looked at the silver coin and his face lit up. 'Gawd bless yer, you're a toff,' he said with emphasis. 'Those geezers who did this better not come near me or I'll give 'em what for.'

Joe smiled affectionately. The tramp looked like a bag of bones and his hands were shaking as he held the mug. 'Yeah, I bet yer would at that,' he replied.

Lucy Thompson lit the candle in the bottle she had placed at the centre of the table and stepped back to admire her work. She had used her favourite green tablecloth and laid out the best china and cutlery. A joint of roast beef was finishing off in the oven and the log fire burned brightly, bathing the whole room in its orange glow. Lucy had added a few touches to make the night perfect. A vase of freshly picked winter heather stood on the old oaken sideboard and there was a small parcel beside Joel's plate. There was just time to slice the meat, she thought. Joel was a stickler about time and he could be relied upon to turn up on the dot. He would be pleased with his present. He had always wanted a square-faced wristwatch.

The sound of the latch made her start and the next instant she was swept up in Joel's arms. He was tall and broad, with unruly sandy hair and a ruddy complexion. His large white teeth gleamed in the light of the fire and Lucy melted in his arms. 'I've missed yer terday, Joel,' she sighed.

'I've missed you too, Lucy,' he replied. 'I've not been able to stop thinking about last night. Did I love you well?'

'It was sheer bliss,' she whispered, her pretty face flushed.

Joel released her and glanced down at the table. 'It looks fit for a king,' he remarked.

'That's fer you,' Lucy said, pointing to the package.

'Can I open it now?' he asked.

'If yer like.'

'It's beautiful,' he said, after he'd unwrapped the parcel.

'You're a beautiful man, an' I won't let yer go, ever,' she told him with smouldering eyes.

Joel sat down at the table and strapped the watch to his large wrist. 'There we are. What do you think?' he asked her.

'It's very elegant,' she replied with a wicked smile.

Joel watched while she served up the meal, noticing that she had gathered her dark locks behind her head with a large tortoiseshell comb, and then as she sat down facing him he looked at her over the flickering candle flame. 'Tell me, Lucy,' he said quietly. 'You don't regret what we did, do you?'

'Joel, yer must believe me,' she replied. ''E was a beast. I couldn't 'ave stood much more. Anyway, let's forget it an' enjoy the meal.'

The log in the hearth had burned to ashes now and the cold wind whistled around the old farmhouse as the two lovers lay naked in each other's arms beneath the patchwork eiderdown.

'I can't get enough of yer, Joel,' she whispered, her lips brushing his thick neck.

'You're insatiable,' he said smiling.

'I never ever thought that lovin' could be so good,' she sighed. 'It won't ever end, will it?'

Joel moved on top of her, supporting himself on his arms. 'Now, listen to me,' he began. 'No one will ever find out, as long as we're patient. In time you'll be able to apply for a divorce for desertion and then we can marry. Until then we have to keep calm and sensible.'

'Yes, I know,' she replied.

The young man bent his head and kissed the tip of her nose. 'In the meantime we can still be lovers.'

Lucy raised her hand to stroke his face. 'Joel, will yer take me ter London on Christmas Eve?'

'Whatever for?'

'I want ter see an old lady.'

'A relative?'

'She was me mum fer a short time, an' I owe 'er so much.'

'What about yer real mum?'

'I can visit 'er too while we're there, although she won't recognise me, she's too ill,' Lucy said sadly.

'I think it'll be all right, as long as we don't publicise it,' he replied. 'We have to remember that this is a small community and people will be sure to gossip.'

Lucy pulled him down on to her, feeling his growing passion as she tormented him with the tip of her tongue. 'Oh, Joel,' she gasped, 'take me now.'

The night grew hostile as rain battered the roof and lashed against the windows. The iron gate creaked on its hinges and rainwater gurgled down from the leaking drainpipe on to the soft, saturated earth. Lucy lay on her back, listening to Joel's slow, deep breathing. He was right, she realised. Nothing could touch them. All John's clothes had been burned, along with his suitcase and personal belongings. Of the man himself, no trace would ever be found: Joel had seen to that. John Thompson, builder and con man, self-opinionated, vain and violent, had been strangled while he slept, and then fed to the pigs.

Chapter Forty

Chief Inspector Penrose looked around at the detectives assembled in the office, his face dark with anger. 'I'm not having my patch turned into a little Chicago, do you hear me?' he growled. 'There's the Baz Smithson killing still on file and now we've got an attempted assassination to deal with, not to mention the beatings and unwarranted damaging of property. What's going on out there?'

The policemen looked uneasy, not wanting to state the obvious: that the violence had had the effect of shutting people's mouths. No one was willing to say anything, not even to pass an opinion, and so they themselves had nothing to say.

'Well? Are you all struck dumb, or is there anyone who wants to enlighten me a little?' Penrose asked sarcastically, his eyes going from one to another.

Sergeant Hallam shuffled uneasily. 'With due respect, sir, we've done the best we could,' he replied. 'We've linked in with the beat constables and done the rounds. The very fact that people are not talking says one thing, that it's a gangland feud coming up to the boil.'

'I don't need you to tell me that,' Penrose retorted. 'I want to know what we're going to do about it.'

Hallam met the hard gaze of his superior officer. 'We're up against a wall of silence, sir,' he replied.

'Well, we'll just have to break it down,' Penrose said sharply, 'even if we have to lean on a few people. Which reminds me, see if any of the local Maltese community are waiting for immigration clearance. In the meantime I'll get on to Camberwell and see if they'll co-operate in putting the screws on Constantine's club. I don't care if it's only a petty infringement of the gambling or drinking laws. I want him to know we're still in business.'

'If I could add something, sir,' a young detective piped up. 'It seems to me that our best bet is the beat bobbies. They can use their rapport with the local housewives and traders to wheedle information out of them if they're properly briefed beforehand. My opinion is that they're too often kept in the dark.'

The rest of the gathering cringed, waiting for the inevitable explosion. To their surprise the inspector nodded his head slowly. 'That's a good point, Grant. Has anyone got any other ideas?' he said looking around. 'Right then, get to work.'

Bella Wickstead, Nell Moseley, Sadie Pugh and Madge Conroy stood together outside Bella's front door on that cold morning discussing the recent events.

'The bloody place ain't safe ter walk about in,' Sadie was going on. 'People gettin' shot goin' ter church. It's downright wicked.'

'It always was a rough 'ole, that Ole Kent Road,' Madge cut in. 'I remember when I was a kid. There was always a fight outside the pub on Saturday nights.'

'What about ole Joe Slavin?' Nell said, bringing her hand up to her mouth. 'They made a right ole mess of 'is cafe by all accounts.'

'Who's they?' Madge queried.

'Why, them ole tramps what use the doss'ouse,' Nell told her. 'My ole man said they're always 'angin' around there.'

'They should lock 'em all up,' Bella said firmly. 'Lazy ole gits.'

'I fink there was a bit more to it, if yer ask me,' Madge Conroy remarked. 'My bloke reckons that Joe Slavin must 'ave upset one o' the villains. 'E reckons it could be over protection money.'

'Good Gawd, what's it all comin' to?' Sadie said, shaking her head slowly.

Clara Buckman came along the turning carrying a laden shopping bag. 'What's this, a muvvers' meetin'?' she said grinning as she rested her bag down on the pavement.

'We've just bin talkin' about 'ow rough it's got round 'ere lately,' Bella told her.

'Yeah, I know,' Clara replied. 'I was only sayin' ter my Albert the ovver night, it makes yer frightened ter go outside the door. I 'ad nightmares over that Preacher Jack turn of events.'

'Oh, that reminds me,' Sadie said quickly. 'I was chattin' ter the fish man yesterday an' 'e told me Irene Frost got a letter from that sister of 'ers.'

'Who? Bubbles?' Bella asked.

'Yeah. Apparently she wants ter come round ter see 'er.'

'Whatever for? They ain't bin speakin' fer years.'

'Well, accordin' ter what Irene told the fish man, Bubbles said she's comin' round ter Lottie's birfday party an' she can't face walkin' past 'er own sister's front door, so she thought it'd be nice ter break the ice before then, so ter speak.'

'She's got a point there,' Bella remarked. 'It's terrible fer sisters ter fall out.'

'Don't I know it?' Madge said, digging her hands deeper into her tatty winter coat. 'Me an' my sister didn't speak fer years. It was over this feller who I was sweet on. My Rene fancied 'im too an' she was the cause o' me an' 'im splittin' up. Anyway she ended up marryin' the two-faced git an' I was really upset at the time. In fact I never went ter their weddin'. I just couldn't face it. Mind you, though, I didn't realise it at the time but she done me a favour. 'E turned out ter be a right royal bastard. Knocked 'er about somefing terrible 'e did. I come out best in the end. My bloke's good as gold. 'E wouldn't dream of raisin' 'is 'and ter me. Mind yer, I did warn 'im right at the start. I told 'im if 'e as much as laid a finger on me I'd slice 'is onions.'

A little way along the street the lace curtains at number seven moved slightly as Irene Frost monitored the group. 'They're still rabbitin',' she announced.

'So what?' Wally growled as he tried to ease his aching back.

'I bet they're talkin' about Bubbles,' she said. 'I bet the fish man's told 'em about the letter.'

'Well, it's yer own stupid fault,' Wally told her. 'Why yer tell 'im everyfing, I'll never know.'

'I wasn't finkin'. It just come out,' Irene replied. 'Sometimes it's better ter get fings off yer chest.'

'Yeah, but not ter that dopey git,' Wally went on. ''E's like a bloody ole Mary Anne. I've seen 'im meself. Rabbit rabbit rabbit. 'E only wants an apron on an' 'e'd be the real fing.'

'I fink I'll go out an' 'ave a chat wiv 'em,' Irene told him.

'Yeah, way yer go,' he said sarcastically. 'Don't ferget ter warn 'em ter keep their 'usbands off the street when Bubbles comes round.'

'Don't go makin' light of it, Wally,' she said sharply. 'I'll be the talk o' the street. They all know what she is.'

Irene's long-suffering husband shook his head slowly. 'I just can't understand why yer get yerself so screwed up over it,' he growled. 'All right, Bubbles is on the game, but so's fousands more like 'er. Anyway, you ain't 'er keeper. She's a big gel now, an' I mean big.'

Irene looked at him in disgust. 'You men are all the same. Yer only interested in one fing.'

'Right now, I'm only interested in gettin' some peace, so will yer eivver go out an' join the party or get away from that poxy winder,' he grated.

Irene decided to venture out to face the scandal and she slipped on her coat. 'Don't ferget ter turn that oven off in ten minutes or yer'll be 'avin' burnt offerin's for tea,' she warned him.

The women were generally sympathetic to Irene's problem and Madge Conroy meant well as she took her by the arm. 'Yer shouldn't worry so much, luv,' she said kindly. 'I bet we've all got skeletons in the closet if we stopped ter consider. It don't do no 'arm ter let 'em rattle now an' then. What yer gotta remember is, if people are talkin' about you they're leavin' someone else alone.'

'Trouble is, all that stuff that's bin in the paper about Mad Jack don't 'elp none,' Bella remarked. 'Bubbles 'as got ter be quite a celebrity these days.'

As Irene was beginning to wish she had stayed indoors, PC Walker turned the corner of the street. 'I ain't gonna be seen talkin' to 'im,' Bella said quickly as she picked up her shopping bag. 'See yer, gels.'

Irene made her excuses and hurried off, as did Nell, leaving Sadie, Madge and Clara to face the rotund constable.

''Ello, ladies. Cold day,' he said in greeting. 'What's the news?'

'About what?' Madge asked.

'About anyfing,' he replied, grinning.

'It's all bin very quiet round 'ere,' Sadie remarked.

'Yeah, I'm sure it 'as,' Joe Walker replied. 'There's bin a shootin', a beatin', an' a bloke gets 'is shop smashed up, all on the same day. Nice an' quiet, like yer say?'

'Well, it ain't nuffing ter do wiv us,' Clara told him quickly.

The constable smiled judiciously. 'I bin on this beat fer a few years now, as yer know,' he said with a grandiose furrowing of the eyebrows. 'I was walkin' these streets all frew the war, an' what strikes me is 'ow yer've all changed. When the Blitz was on yer couldn't do enough to 'elp each ovver. Now it's all over, yer close yer eyes to everyfing. This was a good place ter live at one time, but look at it now. The villains are takin' over. They rule by fear, an' until yer get tergevver an' say enough's enough then they'll only get stronger an' more dangerous.'

'Yer right,' Clara declared. 'I fink it was a bad fing Joe Slavin gettin' 'is cafe all busted up, an' I 'eard that Ben Ferris got beat up too. But like you, we can only guess who done it. Believe me, if I knew who was responsible you'd be the first one I'd tell.'

'Well, that's refreshin' to 'ear,' the policeman replied. 'You ladies can 'elp us by keepin' yer eyes an' ears open. Let me know anyfing yer find out, no matter 'ow insignificant it seems. Will yer do that fer me?'

'Yeah, I will,' Clara told him.

'Yeah, so will I,' Madge added.

'Yer can count on me too,' Sadie told him.

PC Walker strolled away feeling a little less frustrated, while the women went home to reflect on his unexpected homily.

Lana had been worried all day about how Jimmy was going to react to her seeing Ben and as soon as tea was over she hurried along to Abbey Street.

'I'm sorry about last night, Jimmy,' she said quietly as he let her into the tidied-up parlour.

The young man looked angry. 'When I called round yer mum said yer got a message ter see Ben.'

'Yeah, that's right,' she replied. 'It was from Joe Slavin. 'E's the feller that owns the cafe in River Lane an' 'e's a friend o' Ben's. Someone beat Ben up an' 'e was in a bad way. Joe reckoned 'e 'ad some broken ribs an' 'e couldn't get 'im ter go ter the 'ospital. That's why 'e sent the message.'

'So yer went round there ter persuade 'im,' Jimmy said coldly.

'Yeah, I did. What else could I do?'

He lowered his head for a few moments. 'Did yer get 'im ter go ter the 'ospital?' he asked.

'I got a cab an' forced 'im ter go,' she replied. 'As it 'appened it was only bad bruisin' but I wasn't ter know.'

'Yeah, an' I gotta know about you,' he said sharply. 'Are yer still carryin' a torch fer the guy?'

'Don't be silly, Jimmy, yer know it's all over between us.'

'Do I? Yer get a message an' can't wait ter get round there.'

'What else was I s'posed ter do, just leave 'im?'

'No, I'm not sayin' that, but yer could 'ave come round ter me first. I could 'ave gone wiv yer,' he said in an angry voice.

'Oh, I see. It'd 'ave bin all right if you were there. Just ter see that I wasn't gettin' up to anyfing,' Lana flared.

'I gotta know once an' fer all, Lana. Are yer sure yer got Ben out o' yer system. I gotta know.'

'I've just told yer,' she said, raising her voice.

'No, yer didn't,' he countered. 'Yer just said I know it's over between yer. I want you ter tell me what you really feel.'

Lana was finding the heat of the room oppressive and she unbuttoned her coat as she walked round the table, sinking down into an armchair dejectedly. 'I would 'ave thought it was obvious 'ow I feel about yer,' she sighed. 'Since our first date I've never given Ben a thought. I've told yer 'ow I feel about yer but it seems yer wasn't listenin'.'

'Oh, I was listenin' all right,' he replied sharply. 'An' I believed yer.'

'But now yer don't?'

'What am I s'posed ter believe?' he shouted. 'Ben coughs an' yer drop everyfing.'

'Jimmy, yer bein' unreasonable,' she replied, her eyes filling with tears of anger. 'It was just the shock o' gettin' the message. I didn't know what to expect. I couldn't leave 'im; even though we're finished I couldn't ignore it, could I?'

Jimmy sighed deeply. 'I can't 'elp me feelin's, Lana,' he said quietly. 'Yer've never bin out o' me mind since we first spoke at Lottie's. I just get scared that Ben Ferris is gonna come between us.'

Lana bit back her tears and stood up. 'There's no contest,' she said. 'Ben Ferris is an 'opeless drunk an' 'e's gone down'ill so fast it frightened me when I saw 'im. I could only feel pity, the way I would fer anyone who looked the way 'e did. It was pity, not feelin's o' love, that made me get the cab an' force 'im ter get some treatment. Yer gotta understand that, 'cos if yer don't then Ben Ferris is gonna haunt us for ever an' split us up fer sure.'

Jimmy had moved closer to her while she was speaking and suddenly he reached out and took her in his arms. 'I'm sorry, Lana. I'm sorry fer ever doubtin' yer,' he said. 'I love yer in a way I've never loved before. Yer must believe me.'

In answer she kissed him, her hands around his neck, her body pressed tightly to his. He slipped his hands inside her coat and clasped her to him, his arms encircling her slim waist, his lips pressed tightly to hers, feeling her salt tears.

'I want yer, Lana,' he gasped.

'I want you too,' she replied. 'Make love to me, Jimmy.'

He reached down and took her hand, leading her out of the room and up the dark stairs to the cold bedroom. Her breath came quickly as he caressed her in the darkness and she slipped out of her coat and let it fall to the floor. He kissed her quickly and urgently as he found the zip fastener of her skirt, undressing her with shaking hands as she fumbled with the buttons on his shirt. They did not feel the cold as they stripped and fell back on to the bed, their bodies burning with desire. He lay on top of her, nibbling her ear sensuously and she reached her hands down to clasp his swollen manhood. He groaned with pleasure as she guided him into her, wrapping her long slim legs around his waist. The urgency left no time for extended pleasure. It was forceful lovemaking, brief and energetic as they raced to a climax, and Lana's nails bit into his shoulders as she shuddered with pleasure.

They lay together beneath the bedclothes, her head resting on his chest, his protective arm holding her firmly to him.

'I'm yours, Jimmy, fer ever and ever,' she whispered.

'I won't let yer leave me, darlin', not ever,' he replied, his lips brushing her forehead.

Outside the wind had dropped and the first snow of the year started to fall from a leaden sky.

Chapter Forty-One

Mick Constantine paid off the taxi driver outside the seafront Regent Hotel and passed over a one-pound note to the doorman. 'Get someone ter see ter them cases, will yer?' he asked.

Trade was quiet at the hotel and the doorman pocketed the money with relish. He considered himself to be very astute and would have been willing to wager that these were important guests. The man was expensively dressed in a camel-hair overcoat and fedora, and from what he could see of his suit and shoes they were quality ware. The woman was wearing an expensive silver-fox fur coat with a matching cossack hat. He would have bet too that she wore some expensive rings under her chamois-leather gloves, if the necklace she had on was anything to go by. He was most likely a film director and she was his 'protégée'. They did not strike him as being man and wife: most wealthy women fussed over the luggage and bullied their husbands; this woman looked nervous and subservient, and she was far too young.

The gang boss strolled up to the desk with Mandy walking behind him and the porter following in their wake carrying the two large matching suitcases.

'I've got a reservation fer four nights. The name's Constantine,' he said.

The porter put the cases down by the desk and stood

waiting for instructions. The man was a villain no doubt, and the woman was probably his moll, he told himself. All the villains seemed to come to Brighton these days.

'Yes, sir, we have the reservation. A suite, first floor, sea view,' the receptionist said. 'The porter will show you the way.'

As soon as they went into the tastefully furnished suite Mandy hurried over to look at the bathroom and Constantine tipped the porter. 'What's yer name, pal?' he asked him.

'Billy Kenny, sir.'

'Well, Billy, I might be wantin' some information on the area.'

'In that case I should see the doorman, sir,' the porter replied. 'There's not much he doesn't know about Brighton.'

Mandy walked out from the bathroom looking pleased. 'It's lovely,' she gushed.

'Billy, can yer get a bottle o' Scotch an' a bottle o' gin sent up?' Constantine asked.

The porter pointed to the telephone by the bed. 'It'll be quicker if you phone reception, sir,' he replied.

Constantine sat down on the edge of the bed, dismissing the porter with a nod as he picked up the phone. Billy closed the door behind him and his face set hard. 'Bloody jumped-up ponce,' he mumbled. A porter was employed to transport luggage to and from rooms, not to be a skivvy, he fumed.

When he had placed the order Constantine turned to Mandy. 'Why don't yer phone yer muvver?' he suggested.

The young woman shook her head and gave him a smile, hiding the sudden fear that stabbed at her insides. Mick was probing. She would have to be on her guard and think of something . . . quickly.

Gerry Knowland walked into the side room of the ward and found Darkie Samut propped up with pillows. His face looked ashen and he gave his visitor a wan smile.

''Ow yer feelin', Darkie?' Gerry asked.

'The shoulder's sore and stiff, but otherwise I'm fine,' he replied.

'You were a lucky man, that's fer sure,' Gerry remarked. 'Anuvver inch or so the ovver way an' it'd 'ave bin curtains.'

'It was all so quick,' Darkie said. 'I was just about to get in the car when I felt this thud in my chest. Toni Rossi told me the shot was fired from a house opposite. He's been to see the couple who live there and they told him that the police had already called and taken statements from both of them. Apparently they'd let the upstairs room to a middle-aged man a week ago. They told Toni the same as they told the police. Their lodger looked a respectable bloke who kept himself to himself. After the shooting he just disappeared.'

'Constantine got 'im from out o' town, it's a stone certainty,' Gerry replied.

'Mick's not going to be very pleased with the result,' Darkie said, smiling.

'What's our next move?' Gerry asked.

Darkie winced as he eased his position in the bed. 'Toni and Sam Castelano both wanted to take some of the men along and torch Mick's club, but I warned them off,' he replied. 'There's bound to be a round-the-clock guard on the place and they could get captured in the process.'

'Darkie, I 'ave ter tell yer,' Gerry said. 'About the same time that yer got shot, Ben Ferris got nabbed by the Varley boys. They took 'im to a cellar, most likely at Constantine's place, an' worked 'im over. Joe Slavin got 'is shop smashed up as well. 'E phoned me late last night.'

'Why?' Darkie asked quickly.

'It's Constantine's way of tellin' 'em both ter stay clear of us,' Gerry explained.

'Does he know about us going in together?' Darkie queried.

'Yeah, it was forced out o' Ben,' Gerry replied. 'I went ter see 'im last night an' 'e looks as though 'e's bin run over by a steamroller.'

'We need ter set up a meet,' Darkie said quietly.

'I don't agree,' Gerry answered quickly. 'It could be misconstrued. I wouldn't want that no-good whoreson ter fink we've got no bottle fer a fight.'

'Gerry, what we need more than anything else is time,' the Malt told him. 'I can't look after things while I'm stuck in this bed, and the danger is that the boys might decide to act on their own. Constantine would welcome that.'

Gerry leaned back in his chair and folded his arms. 'I got a call from Mandy last night,' he said. 'She told me that 'er an' Constantine were leavin' for Brighton terday fer four days, so we got a bit o' time. I don't fink there'll be any moves made till 'e comes back. By the way, 'ave you 'ad a visit from the law?'

'Yeah, the gaffer at Dockhead came to see me,' Darkie replied. 'There wasn't much I could tell him. He gave me the usual advice about letting the police handle this and not making any reprisals.'

'What about some protection while yer in 'ere? Didn't 'e mention that?' Gerry asked. 'I walked in wivout bein' challenged. I could 'ave bin one o' Constantine's men.'

Darkie shook his head. 'Penrose was straight about it. He told me they couldn't spare a round-the-clock guard, unless I was due to go to court as a witness. To be honest, I think he'd be quite happy for me and Constantine to rub each other out. But don't worry,' he added with a glint in his eye. 'You were checked as you came past the last bench in the corridor, though I don't suppose you noticed.'

Gerry smiled. 'Yeah, I should 'ave given yer more credit, Darkie.'

The older man studied his friend with some concern. 'You look a bit worried,' he remarked.

'Yeah, I've bin finkin' about Constantine suddenly decidin' ter take Mandy ter Brighton,' Gerry replied. 'I'm terrified 'e's sussed somefing. It's where me an' 'er go when she can get away. She told Mick she goes down there ter see 'er muvver who's in a nursin' 'ome.'

'Did Mandy say anything about it?' Darkie inquired.

Gerry shook his head. 'I didn't get the chance to ask 'er. 'E came in an' she 'ad ter ring off quick.'

'I wouldn't worry,' Darkie replied, 'she'll bluff it out, I'm sure.'

After much soul searching and swallowing of pride, Bubbles Madigan had decided to take the bull by the horns. Her sister's letter had made it clear that she would not be welcome at the Frost home and it would be better if she stayed away from Mrs Curtis's party as well. Bubbles had shed a few angry tears at the intransigence of her elder sister, but she soon recovered. Her time on the streets had hardened her to the knocks of life, and she had been ably supported by her good friend Trixie, who reminded her, 'If the mountain would not go to Mohammed . . .'

Bubbles stepped down from the late afternoon tram wearing a brown fur coat which had seen better days, her face made up with bright-red glossy lipstick. However cold it was she would never cover her crowning glory, and the tight blond curls were shaped around her head with expert care. A silk scarf was tied high on the neck and she carried a large leather handbag over her arm. Her feet were squeezed into high-heeled shoes, protected by galoshes, and in case of any further snow an umbrella was swinging from her wrist.

When Bubbles walked into Saddler Street she immediately saw Bella Wickstead who was busy sweeping snow away from her front door. 'Poxy weavver, ain't it, luv,' she said.

'Seasonal though,' Bella replied, looking her up and down. 'I must admit I like ter see snow at Christmas.'

'I prefer it on Christmas cards,' the buxom blonde remarked. 'Me name's Bubbles Madigan an' I've come round ter see our Irene.'

'That'd be Mrs Frost.'

'Yer right first time.'

'She lives at number seven.'

'Yeah, I know where she lives, dearie.'

'Is she expectin' yer?'

'I shouldn't fink so.'

Bella started sweeping once more. 'Well, I wish yer luck,' she said.

Bubbles frowned. ''Ere, she ain't bin sayin' anyfing about me, 'as she?'

Bella stopped and leaned on the broom. 'Well, ter be honest she did say yer wouldn't be welcome.'

'Oh she did, did she?'

'S'right.'

'Do you realise I'm 'er sister, 'er baby sister, an' she's got the gall ter deny 'er own sister a chance to talk to 'er,' Bubbles growled. 'Where's 'er Christmas spirit?'

'Well, like I say, that's what she told me, an' Sadie, an' Madge, an' I fink Clara was there too at the time,' Bella replied.

'So she's told the 'ole poxy street then.'

'Nah, only us few,' Bella answered with a smile playing around her lips.

'Well, I'm gonna 'ave it out wiv 'er shit or bust,' the big blonde said with passion.

Bella stood watching as Irene's sinful younger sister used the doorknocker with a vengeance. There was no answer and she hammered on the door once more.

'She must 'ave slipped out,' Bella told her.

'Well, I ain't leavin' till I've fronted 'er, that's fer sure,' Bubbles said determinedly.

Clara Buckman came into the street carrying the evening paper. 'What's goin' on there?' she asked.

'That's Bubbles,' Bella whispered.

'So that's 'er. She looks a right trollop, don't she?' Clara remarked.

Bubbles knocked again and Clara smiled at her neighbour. 'She won't get any answer. I just seen Irene walkin' down terwards the market. She told me she was goin' fer some saveloys an' pease puddin'.'

Bella's soft heart took over. 'When yer fink of it, it is a bloody shame,' she remarked. 'Never mind what she is, she's still 'er sister.'

'That's what I said ter you the ovver day,' Clara replied. 'Blood's ficker than water.'

Sadie Pugh had been adjusting her clean net curtains which she had just hung in her parlour when Bubbles came by and she was now riveted to the window. She could see Clara and Bella talking together and she searched frantically for some excuse to join them.

'Well, I don't care if I do get a bad name, I'm gonna invite 'er in fer a cuppa,' Bella said stoutly. 'You're welcome too, Clara.'

'I bet she's in an' won't answer,' Bubbles called out to the two women. 'Well, I ain't leavin' wivout talkin' to 'er.'

'Excuse me, but Clara 'ere's just seen yer sister down the market,' Bella told her. 'Yer welcome ter wait in my place if yer like. I got the kettle on. It's better than freezin' out 'ere.'

'Well, I'm very much obliged,' Bubbles said, smiling broadly. 'It's nice ter see someone wiv the Christmas spirit.'

Sadie came trudging through the snow. ''Ere, Bella, you ain't got five tanners fer this 'alf-a-crown, 'ave yer?' she asked. 'Me bleedin' gas 'as just run out.'

'Sadie, this is Irene's sister, Bubbles,' the good Samaritan said, cutting through the waffle.

'Pleased ter meet yer,' Sadie said smiling. 'Is Irene out?'

'She's gone down the market,' Clara informed her.

'Come in, luv, come in, gels,' Bella said cheerfully.

Madge Conroy came into the turning and was immediately stopped by Nell Moseley. ''Ere, that Bubbles woman's showed up,' she told her. 'She's gone in to Bella's. Sadie an' Clara are in there too. I saw 'em all chattin' tergevver from me upstairs winder. I wonder what's goin' on?'

'Search me,' Madge replied.

'Irene's obviously not in. That woman was fair layin' inter

that street door,' Nell went on. 'I wish I knew what they were all talkin' about.'

'C'mon, let's find out,' Madge said grinning.

'Yer can't go knockin', they'll fink yer nosy,' Nell told her.

'Well, it wouldn't be no lie.'

Madge led the way to number one and knocked on the door. 'Nell just told me you all come in 'ere an' I was wonderin' if everyfing's all right,' she said winsomely. 'After all, we gotta stick tergevver, gels.'

Bella gave her an indulgent smile. 'Yer might as well all come in. I've just made a pot o' tea.'

Outside the snow was starting to fall again, while in the warm parlour the Saddler Street women sipped their tea and listened as they became acquainted with the local brothel madam.

'Well, ter be honest we do get the odd strange geezer,' Bubbles was saying. 'You take the ovver week. Me an' my friend Trixie was tidyin' up the rooms an' changin' the curtains an' suddenly she said ter me, "'Ere, Bubbles, come an' take a look at this." Well I couldn't believe me eyes. It was one o' those – what do they call 'em? – mortarboards, that's right. The sort o' fings the teachers wear in those posh schools. It was tucked down by the bed, an' then we found this cane as well. Now, I 'ave ter tell yer I don't encourage my gels ter play funny games wiv the punters. I like the ole crash, bang, wallop an' straight out the door. The trouble wiv playin' funny games is that it attracts the wrong sort. All right, most of 'em are 'armless but there's always the chance o' gettin' one loony who'll end up slicin' the gel or even worse. Anyway, I told Trixie ter send the gel in ter see me as soon as she came inter work that night. Sandra 'er name was. Pretty little fing. "Now what's all this, luv?" I asked 'er as I put the fings down on the table. "It's fer Bernard," she said coyly. "An' what d'you an' Bernard do wiv these?" I asked 'er. "We play 'eadmasters," she said. Well, I really 'it the roof. "You know the rules in this establishment," I shouted at 'er. "I've told yer time an' time again I want no 'anky panky." "Bernard's different," she said, sheddin' a few tears. "I just wear the mortarboard an' I 'ave ter give 'im a few easy sums ter do. Bernard always gets 'em wrong, an' then I tell 'im ter drop 'is trousers so I can give 'im a few strokes wiv the cane. I don't do it very 'ard."'

The women were wide-eyed as they listened. 'Go on, Bubbles,' they chorused.

'Well, there's not much more ter tell really. That's 'ow 'e got 'is kicks,' Bubbles explained. 'Anyway I told Sandra that it 'ad ter stop, an' a few days later she comes in ter me an' says she's leavin' at the end o' the week 'cos she's got a nice young man who wants ter marry 'er. 'Course I wished 'er luck an' I got 'er a nice card from me an' the gels. "What's yer feller's name?" I asks 'er. "Bernard," she replies.'

Irene Frost had a few errands to do before the market closed and then she went to Kellerman's the butcher. During the day the shop sold meat and poultry, but then in the late afternoon customers saw a sudden transformation. In place of the pork chops, lamb cutlets and various other cuts of meat there were trays of pease pudding, saveloys, tripe and onions, as well as sheeps' heads, black pudding and breakfast sausage. Irene bought a large portion of pease pudding and two saveloys, then she made her way home.

On the corner of Dockhead she paused for a short while to listen to the St Mary's church choir who were standing in the churchyard singing 'Hark the Herald Angels Sing', and as her eyes travelled along the lines of singers Irene spotted two of the younger members who were holding lighted candles. They were obviously sisters, she thought, her mind going back to her own childhood days. It was her, with her baby sister, singing merrily as they walked through the backstreets on Christmas Eve, proud members of St Agnes Church choir.

A large tear dropped on to the newspaper wrapping and Irene set off home, cursing her sentimentality. It was a long time ago and people grow up, she told herself as she stepped into Saddler Street. As she reached her front door she saw the note tucked under her doorknocker.

'Please knock at number one, Bella.'

Irene frowned to herself and bit on her lip as she hurried back to the first house. Something must have happened to Wally, she thought, or one of the kids.

''Ello, gel, come on in,' Bella bade her cheerfully. 'Merry Christmas.'

Irene stepped into the parlour and looked around in surprise at the unusually large gathering. Suddenly she caught sight of her sister, and for a few short moments the sisters' eyes locked together. Bubbles stood up, her arms outstretched. 'Merry Christmas, Irene,' she said, her voice breaking.

The older sister went over to her and they embraced tightly. Irene could see the children singing in her mind's eye. She could smell the scent of her baby sister's soft skin when they cuddled at the foot of the dark stairs after the Saturday night bath. Everything had changed, but nothing had changed.

'Merry Christmas, Ellen,' she said.

Chapter Forty-Two

Lottie Curtis was almost purring with pleasure as she sat in her old rocking chair by the banked-up fire. The two young people looked so much in love as they sat there holding hands, she thought. It was how she had been with Bill, though they never dared hold hands in her parents' house. They were never left without a chaperone either. But times were different now, Lottie reminded herself. These days the young people openly showed their affection for each other, and not a bad thing either.

'So what you two bin doin' wiv yerselves lately?' she asked.

Lana felt a sudden little squeeze of her hand and she quickly suppressed a smile. 'Not a lot, really. We've bin ter the pictures an' we like goin' fer walks,' she replied.

'Not the weavver now though fer walks,' Lottie said. 'I fink there's a lot more snow ter come down yet.'

'Are yer lookin' forward ter yer birfday, Lottie?' Jimmy asked.

She shrugged her shoulders. 'I s'pose I'll just take it like any ovver day,' she remarked. 'Mind you, though, I shall 'ave a little drop o' tiddly. After all, eighty years is a milestone.'

Lana was eager to get her talking about the last of her children who remained the only one still to be traced, now that Lucy Thompson had written promising to be there on the day. She had to be careful though, since Lottie tended to feign tiredness and steer away from discussing the young lad whenever she brought him up. 'You're right, Lottie,' she replied. 'It's a lot o' years ter go back over. I bet yer do though.'

The old lady nodded. 'I s'pose I'll get me album out an' go frew it, an' look at all those little smilin' faces. I'll wonder what they're doin' now an' then I'll get all sad fer a while. I always get sad when I look at those photos.'

'I'm sorry, Lottie, I thought yer liked lookin' frew the album,' Lana said with concern. 'That's why we've bin encouragin' yer ter show it to us.'

'No, don't get me wrong,' she replied. 'I do like showin' yer the pictures an' talkin' about the kids, but when I'm on me own, wiv me thoughts, I get a bit upset.'

'Yeah, but we asked yer lots o' questions about that little boy yer looked after, the last one I mean, an' that upset yer,' Lana reminded her.

'I must 'ave bin feelin' a little down at the time,' Lottie replied. 'Anyway, I done what I could while 'e was wiv me, an' I'm sure 'e's realised by now that I only 'ad 'is best interests at 'eart when I went off at 'im so.'

'Look, yer don't 'ave ter say any more if it upsets yer, luv,' Lana said quickly, hoping that Lottie would indeed go on.

'Nah, yer might as well know the full story,' the old lady replied. 'Like I said, 'e used ter come an' see me from time ter time. It wasn't all that regular, I 'ave ter say, but when 'e did come it was nice at first. We'd sit wiv a cup o' tea an' 'e'd make me laugh. I was gettin' worried about 'im though, 'cos there was talk round 'ere about what 'e was gettin' up to. 'E got in trouble wiv the police a few times, over the black market, an' I told 'im 'e was wrong in what 'e was doin'. Now yer gotta remember that the war was on an' there was lots o' ships gettin' sunk an' lots o' seamen getting killed on them convoys that was bringin' the food ter this country. A young friend o' mine, Minnie Coffley, Gawd rest 'er soul, 'ad lost 'er 'usband when 'is ship went down, an' there was 'im braggin' about what 'e was up to. I told 'im it was wrong, but 'e just laughed an' shrugged it off. Anyway, a few weeks later 'e came ter see me an' 'e was goin' on about this load o' tinned fruit 'e'd got 'old of. I was very upset that day about somefing I'd just 'eard an' I really let 'im 'ave it. I took me anger out on 'im an' I'm afraid I said more than I should 'ave. I told 'im 'e was a disgrace an' a parasite an' 'e wasn't welcome 'ere any more.'

'But you was right,' Jimmy told her. 'Those black marketeers were exactly that, parasites.'

'Yeah, but I shouldn't 'ave let me anger spill over on to 'im,' Lottie went on. ''E was like me own son, an' there I was tellin' 'im ter get out an' stay out. As bad as they are yer don't do that wiv yer own, do yer? As it 'appens that was the last time I saw 'im, but I've never fergot 'im an' I still love the lad, whatever 'e's done. If it 'ad bin any ovver day fings might not 'ave turned out the way they did, but like I say I'd just 'eard some bad news an' I'm afraid I took it out on 'im.'

'No one can blame you fer what 'appened, Lottie. Anyone would 'ave acted in the same way,' Lana told her.

She nodded her head slowly. 'P'raps yer right, but anyway it's over an' done wiv now an' we can't take the fings back that we say in anger, more's the pity.'

'What was 'is name, Lottie? Does 'e still live round 'ere?' Lana asked gingerly.

The old lady stared into the fire, choosing not to hear the question, and the two young people glanced despairingly at each other.

'I fink it's time I put the kettle on,' Jimmy said quickly.

Lana attempted to revive the conversation. 'Yer was sayin' you 'eard some bad news that day, Lottie,' she prompted her.

Lottie nodded her head slowly. 'I didn't say what it was 'cos I thought it might upset young Jimmy,' she explained. 'Minnie Coffley 'ad put 'er 'ead in the gas oven that same mornin'. She'd left a note sayin' that she couldn't go on livin' wivout 'er feller.'

''Ow terrible,' Lana murmured.

'I often wonder about that poor cow,' Lottie said in a quiet voice. 'Was we all ter blame fer what she done? Did all 'er neighbours leave 'er ter suffer in 'er grief, leave 'er ter get on wiv 'er life when we should 'ave bin there for 'er? I've asked meself that question a fousand times, an' it still comes out the same way. Yes, we was ter blame, all of us.'

Lana realised with sadness that the mystery of the last of Lottie's charges was now a closed book. It would serve no purpose to pursue it. There were too many painful memories involved, too much self-recrimination for the old lady. Better to leave him in the past where he belonged. There would be others to make Lottie's day: Charlie Smedley, the union man; Samuel Selby, now a successful barrister; Bubbles Madigan and Lucy Thompson; Alice and Morgan Jones too, if he was well enough to travel; and there was Jimmy Bailey, reliable Jimmy, the man she loved. They would all contribute to making it a day for Lottie to savour and cherish for the rest of her life. Lana's only regret was that Phoebe Francis had chosen to deny her past, forget where she had come from and discard her principles for the sake of fame and fortune. She would have to live with herself over it, and good riddance.

Lottie rubbed the backs of her hands. 'I fink we could do wiv a bit more coal on the fire too,' she remarked, and a smile creased her old face. 'Talk about Christmas Day in the work'ouse when the snow was fallin' fast.'

Mick Constantine was deep in thought as he sat alone in the spacious lounge at the Regent Hotel. Mandy had not wanted to join him, saying that she had a headache coming on, and it irked him. She had not been very responsive towards him of late and when he had spoken to her about it she had put it down to the worry of her mother, but now they were in Brighton she had been evasive when he suggested that they paid the old lady a visit. Did she feel ashamed of him? Was she worried about letting him see her mother, or was there some other, more devious reason for her evasiveness?

For a while Mick toyed with his glass of Scotch, his mind

racing, then suddenly he spotted the doorman talking to the receptionist. As the man left the counter he beckoned him over.

'I understand you're quite knowledgeable about Brighton,' he said.

'I do have some knowledge, sir,' the doorman replied cheerfully.

'Could you put me in touch with a good private inquiry agent?' Mick asked.

'I'm sure I could,' the man replied. 'As a matter of fact I'm going off duty in about an hour. I could have a recommendation for you tomorrow. I come back on duty at ten o'clock.'

The gang boss fished into his waistcoat pocket and took out a pound note. 'There we are,' he said, slipping it into the doorman's hand. 'I'll double that if yer get me a good one.'

Up in the seaview suite above the lounge Mandy had been trying to sleep but found it impossible. She sat clad only in her flimsy nightdress, disconsolately looking out at the twinkling lights of the deserted promenade and the pier. She could hear the sound of the waves as they rolled ceaselessly up to break upon the dark stone beach, and the sound of the slipping shingle. She could see the fitful moon riding high over the cloudy Channel and the occasional star, and her heart was heavy. Gerry was far away and she needed him. She wanted to feel his arms around her and taste his kisses. She wanted to experience once more the sense of security and safety that he gave her. Here in Brighton she felt cold fear. Mick had been probing, and it wouldn't be long before the truth came out. How was she to deal with his questioning? How was she going to satisfy his curiosity? It was hopeless. What options did she have? She could leave him, run away in the night, but she would be running from Gerry too. In any case Mick would find her and punish her severely.

The moon was hidden away again and Mandy heard the key in the lock. She scampered across the bedroom and dived under the bedcovers just in time. Mick went straight into the bathroom and she curled herself up as though sleeping. At least it would delay the inevitable, she thought.

Joe Slavin had grown to like the dockland borough and it hurt having to admit to himself that he was now forced to leave. There was no point in spending every penny he had saved on refurbishing the cafe only to have the same thing happen again. He had to accept it. He had inadvertently upset Constantine and the man would make sure that he never forgot it.

'What the bloody 'ell's 'appened?' Del Brady said as he looked in the cafe.

'I 'ad visitors,' Joe said simply.

'Where did they come from, a demolition firm?'

'Yer could say that.'

'I was lookin' forward to a nice cup o' tea an' a bacon sandwich,' Del remarked.

'Well, I'm sorry I can't oblige yer, Del, but yer can see the problem,' Joe told him.

'So what yer gonna do?'

'Well, there's not much I can do.'

'It's a bloody shame,' the big docker said, shaking his head in disgust. 'I 'ave ter tell yer, Joe, this is the best little cafe in Bermondsey as far as me an' me mates are concerned. Now we'll 'ave ter use that soapy git Norman's cafe in Jamaica Road.'

Joe watched the big friendly docker amble away. All day he had been turning his customers away and it hurt.

Charlie Smedley had been very busy in his capacity as convenor. There had been a dispute at Chamber's Wharf and then there was a stoppage at Mark Brown's Wharf over manning levels. Now a potentially serious situation had arisen at Libby's Wharf after a docker had been badly hurt in an accident on the quayside. As far as the labour force was concerned the accident could have been avoided, had the management heeded their demands to review the standard safety procedures.

The harassed convenor had been shuttling back and forth between Tooley Street and Rotherhithe organising a full meeting to seek support for a new safety code, which would then be put forward to the management. During his travels he called at Joe's cafe in River Lane only to find a notice on the door. He hurried off to the nearby cafe in Jamaica Road, and there he was put in the picture by Del Brady.

'I was choked fer the poor bastard,' Del went on. 'I told 'im straight it was the best cafe in Bermondsey.'

'Who's it down to?' Charlie asked.

'Why, that Constantine mob. They're gettin' right out of 'and.'

Two more dockers joined Del. 'What a bloody shame,' one said. ''Ow does that no-good whoreson get away wiv takin' a man's livin' away from 'im?'

'Cold bloody fear, that's 'ow,' Del told him.

'Whoever done it should be sorted out,' the newcomer's companion declared.

'It was those Varley slags, yer can bet yer life on it,' the first docker remarked. 'It was them who done that pub in the Borough last month.'

'Look, lads, it's nice talkin' ter yer but I've gotta shoot off,' Charlie told them. 'Don't ferget the mass meetin' termorrer mornin'.'

''Ere, before yer go, I got an idea,' Del said. ''Ow about you askin' fer a levy from everyone to 'elp Joe Slavin? Most o' the lads know 'im an' they'd be only too glad ter dip their 'ands in their pockets.'

'Del, I got a serious problem on me 'ands,' Charlie said quickly. 'I won't 'ave time ter talk about Joe's problems, much as I sympathise wiv 'im. Besides, I'd be goin' outside me mandate. I could get kicked off the committee.'

'Over our dead bodies,' Del growled.

'Too bloody true,' the other dockers chorused.

After the convenor left the cafe Del Brady and his two mates sat in a huddle.

'I'm playin' darts at the club ternight,' Flossy Harris said. 'I'll put the word about.'

'Good fer you, Flossy,' his friend Albert replied. 'I'll 'ave a few words ter say at the Bell ternight. By the time we 'ave that meetin' termorrer a lot o' the lads'll be primed up.'

'You bet,' Del said. 'I'm gonna make sure all the lads at Chamber's Wharf get ter know about it before that meetin' starts.'

Unaware of the intrigue going on not too far away, Joe Slavin worked to salvage what was left of his business. Almost every bit of crockery was smashed. The tea urn was ruined and all the seats and tables were slashed and shattered beyond repair. The Varley brothers had done a good job, he conceded with a heavy sigh. The cutlery would fetch a few bob, and some of the cooking utensils had survived the vandalism. They too were saleable. Not much to show for nearly twenty years of hard work, he thought.

Chapter Forty-Three

Mandy pulled the collar of her fur coat tighter round her ears as she pretended to stare into the shop window. He was still there, she realised, biting on her lip. She had first spotted the tall man in the High Street when she had hesitated over which direction to take. He had been strolling along behind her and her attention was attracted by the way he suddenly stopped and looked into a women's clothes shop window. She had met his kind before. He had policeman written all over him. During her time on the streets she had learned to sniff them out, but this was no policeman out to make a pinch; he was following her.

Mandy walked into the shop and casually strolled between the rows of garments on display, furtively glancing out through the large window. He had crossed the road and was now buying a newspaper. She had purposely chosen a route which left her in no doubt that he was definitely tailing her and she now understood Mick's words this morning. He had casually suggested that they visit her mother that morning, and when she had made the excuse that the old lady would be too ill to meet him he had shrugged his shoulders and gone on to say that perhaps she should go alone initially, and arrange a later visit for both of them.

Mandy realised now that she had made a mistake in agreeing with him. She should have held out and made some excuse or other for not going to see her mother. Mick had expected her to agree with him and had planned to have her followed, it was the only answer. Was that his reason for wanting to come to Brighton? Had she given him enough cause to suspect that she was seeing someone else?

'The dress is new in, madam,' the young shop assistant said with a smile. 'It's only twenty coupons but I'm sure we can come to some arrangement.'

Mandy felt the quality of the material, one eye on the tall stranger across the road. 'Tell me, do you 'ave a fire exit?' she asked suddenly.

The shop assistant looked shocked. 'Are you from the council?' she inquired.

'No, of course not,' Mandy replied, touching her arm reassuringly. 'As a matter o' fact there's a man across the street who's bin followin' me an' I'm a bit scared.'

'I could call the police, if you like,' the young woman told her.

'No, yer'd better not. The man's a debt collector an' I can't pay 'im this week, but yer know what they're like,' Mandy said smiling.

The shop assistant looked aggrieved. She had never run up debts, and what was more there would not be much hope of selling the dress or anything else to a woman who was trying to avoid a debt collector. 'Just as you like,' she replied haughtily.

'Is there anuvver way out?' Mandy asked again.

'Yes, there's a service entrance.'

'Lead on then, luv.'

The assistant showed her to the door which led out into an alleyway. 'Sorry you didn't like the dress,' she said with sarcasm.

Mandy ignored the comment, more concerned with giving her pursuer the slip, and as she hurried along into a side turning she glanced fearfully behind her. She had to have time to think, to plan her course of action. A cruising taxi came past and she hailed it. Ten minutes later she was sitting in a small seafront cafe with a cup of coffee in front of her, becoming more distressed as she thought of the options left to her. She could go back and bluff it out with Mick. She could tell him that she had had a change of heart, not wanting to get upset by seeing her mother suffer while they were enjoying the break. It would not work, she told herself. He was already suspicious and the excuse would only compound it. He would most likely call her bluff and force her to show him the nursing home. Another idea was to admit that she had lied over her mother and say that she went to Brighton whenever she was feeling depressed and below par. It might work, but Mick would be furious at the deception and it would only serve to reinforce his suspicion that she was carrying on with somebody. He was not the sort of man who could let it rest. He would force the truth out of her, and the prospect terrified her.

Mandy sipped her coffee. What else was there to do, she sighed, already knowing the answer as she searched her handbag for coppers to make a phone call.

Ben Ferris was still feeling the pain of his bruised ribs as he left the flat at lunchtime and strolled dejectedly along River Lane. His life was a mess and he had no one to blame but himself. Lana had urged him to change his ways, and now she had left him for someone else. Joe Slavin had tried to warn him too but he had chosen not to listen. The Carmichaels had given him the elbow and no doubt it was down to Mick Constantine. He was asserting his grip on the manor and it spelled trouble for anyone who got in his way.

When he reached the cafe Ben was surprised to see that it was closed. He rang the bell and heard the upstairs window open.

''Ang on, I'll come down,' Joe called out.

Ben shook his head as he stepped inside. 'I don't believe it,' he said, with anger welling up inside him.

'Yer better believe it,' Joe replied bitterly. 'We've both got the message now. Constantine 'as spoken.'

Ben followed Joe up to the flat above the shop and sat down heavily in the armchair. 'I'm gonna swing fer that whoreson one day,' he growled.

'No, yer not. Yer gonna do like me an' stay well clear o' the geezer, an' I'll tell yer why,' Joe said quietly. 'Darkie Samut's bin shot, Gerry Knowland's gone ter ground an' word 'as it that the Malts are runnin' around like 'eadless chickens. All 'ell's breakin' out round 'ere, so do yerself a favour an' keep yer 'ead down.'

Ben stared hard at the cafe owner. 'Darkie's bin shot, yer say?'

'Yeah, someone took a pot at 'im as 'e was goin' ter church, but 'e was lucky by all accounts,' Joe went on. 'The bullet went into 'is shoulder an' 'e's recoverin' in Guy's. It's gotta be down ter Constantine.'

'What you gonna do now, Joe?' Ben asked him.

The cafe owner shrugged his shoulders. 'I dunno,' he sighed. 'I'm not stayin' round 'ere, that's fer sure.'

'Well, I'm not lettin' Mick Constantine frighten me off,' Ben growled. 'I'm gonna get even if it's the last fing I do.'

'It prob'ly will be,' Joe said sardonically. 'See sense, pal. Yer'd be out o' yer league.'

Ben afforded himself a brief smile. 'I've bin stuck in that flat o' mine fer two days wivout seein' a soul, but it's given me time ter fink, Joe,' he said quietly. 'I've bin scratchin' around, doin' tuppenny'a'penny deals wiv no-good scum like the Carmichaels an' suckin' up ter that evil bastard Constantine. I've 'ad ter go on the tap fer money, an' worst of all, I've lost Lana. I've sunk as low as I'm gonna go, ole pal. From now on yer gonna see a new Ben Ferris. I'm gonna make people round 'ere sit up an' take notice.'

'That sounds suicidal ter me,' Joe admonished him.

Ben's eyes burned with hatred as he shifted painfully in the armchair. 'I'm gonna get Constantine fer what 'e did ter me. One way or anuvver I'll get 'im,' he said with passion.

Joe gazed at his friend's face and noticed the hollowness of his pale cheeks. ''Ere, when was the last time you 'ad somefing to eat?' he asked.

'I dunno,' Ben said shrugging.

'I've got a meat pie in the oven an' there's some spuds on the boil,' Joe told him. 'Yer gonna join me fer tea, an' no arguin', OK?'

Gerry Knowland put down the phone and cursed to himself. Mandy had decided to leave Mick and she was coming to him. She wouldn't be able to stay here, he thought. It would be too risky. He would have to find her a flat out of the area. The timing was all wrong. Constantine had shown his hand and in a few days' time the manor was going to get hotter than an oven, without Mandy complicating things further. From what she had told him Mick had become suspicious, and her leaving him in such a way would only serve to convince him that he was right.

The phone rang again and Gerry jumped nervously. The message from Darkie Samut came as a surprise.

'Gerry, this hospital is going to the dogs.'

'What yer talkin' about?'

'They're taking in anybody these days.'

Gerry did not feel in the mood for jokes. 'What you on about, Darkie?' he said irritably.

'Sid and Nipper Varley have been admitted, so I've been told,' the Malt went on. 'They're in the ward below. In a bad way too, I've been told. Nipper's got a suspected fractured skull and apparently Sid looks like an army's walked over him.'

'Your boys?'

'Not mine,' Darkie replied. 'It seems that they got waylaid as they came out of the Crown.'

'Dockers?'

'Yeah.'

'It figures,' Gerry replied. 'Joe Slavin's got a lot o' docker friends. I don't s'pose they were too 'appy about 'is cafe bein' smashed up an' they decided ter do somefing about it.'

'It's come at the wrong time, to be honest,' Darkie said in a serious voice. 'We needed a few days' grace to get organised again.'

Gerry replaced the receiver and stood thinking hard. Constantine would soon replace the two thugs, but more worryingly, he would no doubt assume that the Malts were behind the attack. Darkie had been calm about it but he knew that the man was as worried as he was.

Mandy walked back into the hotel, her heart pounding. She was praying that Mick would be in the bar, which would give her time to pack her things quickly. As she hurried through the carpeted lounge, she saw him through the open door sitting with his back to her in conversation with another male guest. She swallowed hard as she waited for the lift to arrive, fearing that at any second he would spot her. As the lift doors closed Mandy breathed a huge sigh of relief. So far so good, she thought.

Five minutes later she snapped her suitcase shut and hurried from the suite.

'Here, let me carry that for you,' Billy Kenny the porter said as he came along the corridor. 'I didn't know you were leaving.'

'We're not. I am,' Mandy told him, slipping a pound note into his hand.

'I'm sorry, madam,' Billy said.

''E's a beast,' Mandy growled. ''E'll kill me if 'e spots me goin'.'

'You leave it to me,' the porter said, giving her a huge wink. 'I'll take you out through the service area. You'll be able to get a cab easily enough.'

'You're a dear,' she replied sweetly.

Suddenly Mick Constantine stepped out of the lift, his face dark with anger. 'Put 'er case back in the room, Billy, an' make yerself scarce,' he growled.

Mandy stood shaking in the corridor as the porter did as he was told; then when he had gone away the villain gripped her arm tightly. 'Goin' somewhere, was we?' he asked in a silky tone as he pulled her into the suite.

'You 'ad me follered, Mick, an' it upset me,' she replied. 'I don't fink yer trust me. I wouldn't two-time yer, surely yer know that?'

'I fink yer've got a guilty conscience. I never accused yer o' two-timin',' Mick said, pushing her down into the settee. 'You was just gonna up and leave wiv not a goodbye or a kiss-me-arse. Well, I don't go a lot on that. I would 'ave preferred yer ter be up front. Where was yer goin' anyway?'

'Just back 'ome,' Mandy told him. 'That man you 'ad foller me gave me the creeps. Why did yer do it, Mick?'

He leaned down over her menacingly. 'You thought yer gave my man the slip, didn't yer?' he growled. 'Well, I can tell you that when yer slipped out the back o' that shop 'e was still on yer tail. Yer went to a cafe on the seafront an' stayed there fer a while, then yer got a cab an' came straight back. So 'ow's yer muvver?'

Mandy burst into tears, fearing for her life. 'I was gonna see 'er but I changed me mind,' she spluttered.

'Why?'

'I dunno why. I just did.'

Mick suddenly yanked her out of the settee, his face inches from hers, his eyes flaring. 'You're lyin', yer little whore. Tell me the trufe,' he shouted.

'Yes, I am if yer must know,' she yelled back with spirit. 'Me mum's dead. I come ter Brighton ter get away from you.'

'Who is it yer meet 'ere?' he hissed.

'Nobody,' she gulped.

Mick slapped her hard across the face. 'Don't lie ter me, yer little toe-rag.'

'There's nobody else,' she cried.

The gang boss brought his hand back sharply across her

face and blood ran down from her lip. 'Who is it yer seein'?' he shouted.

Billy Kenny had seen the hard menacing look in Constantine's eyes and he crept back along the corridor and put his ear to the door. When he had heard enough he hurried down to the reception desk.

'Look, Billy, I can't interfere in every family squabble that takes place in this hotel,' the manager told him.

'I sussed that man out as soon as I set eyes on him,' Billy said firmly. 'He's a London villain. If you don't do something to stop him you could have a murder on your hands. Just think what the papers'll make of that. I can see the headlines now.'

'All right, all right, don't get all melodramatic,' the manager replied quickly.

Billy followed him to the Constantine suite and stood back while he knocked on the door. 'Mr Constantine, this is the manager,' he announced. 'Is anything wrong?'

Mandy rushed past Mick and pulled open the door. 'I'm leavin' right away,' she said tearfully, dabbing at her cut lip. 'Can you take my bag down?'

Billy picked up the case with a satisfied smile on his face. 'I told the manager something was wrong,' he said as they went into the lift.

As it jerked to a stop, Mandy quickly kissed him on the cheek. 'Fanks fer everyfing,' she said.

The young man looked happy as he carried the case to the entrance. 'Mrs Constantine wants a taxi immediately,' he told the doorman.

Later that day the private detective went to Mick Constantine's suite looking pleased with what he had accomplished. 'Being on the force once has its merits,' he said smiling. 'I managed to trace that call she made. It was to London and the operator logged the number. Here it is. Rodney 1467, and it was to a Mr G. Knowland.'

Chapter Forty-Four

Charlie Smedley stood on an improvised dais to address the mass meeting, his strong voice carrying to the back of the crowd. The men stamped their feet on the freezing cobblestones, their breath condensing in the winter air while they listened. Charlie's impassioned plea to return to work while discussions on safety procedures took place with the management was received with the usual moans and cynical quips, but the men knew the convenor's track record and raised their hands in support.

'That Charlie's got a sweet tongue,' Del Brady growled. ''E'd charm the poxy birds orf the trees.'

The dockers were about to drift away and report back to work but Charlie held up his hand. 'Before yer go, lads, I got somefing important ter say,' he announced. 'Most of us 'ere know Joe Slavin. We've all used 'is cafe in River Lane at one time or anuvver and I gotta tell yer that a couple o' no-good whoresons walked in there a few days ago an' wrecked the place. They've effectively put Joe out o' business, an' they've deprived us of a decent cafe. Now I'm not askin' yer ter take sides, but when the feudin' affects us we gotta do somefing about it.'

'It's bin sorted, Chas,' a burly stevedore shouted out.

'Well, I'm pleased to 'ear it,' the convenor went on, 'but we still gotta remember that Joe's out o' business. What I'm askin' for is a levy. I want every man jack o' yer ter dip inter yer pay packet this week an' put a few bob in the tank. Now don't forget, it's fer Joe Slavin. Let's show 'im that the Bermondsey dockers look after their own. Fank yer, lads.'

As the men began to disperse the burly stevedore grabbed hold of Del's arm. 'Our lads from Tooley Street sorted out those flash-bastard Varleys last night,' he said. 'Apparently they were in the Crown braggin' about turnin' Joe's cafe over an' Bonzo Merriman over'eard 'em spoutin' off. 'E was playin' in a darts match wiv the team from the 'Orseshoe in Tower Bridge Road. They all use Joe's place an' Bonzo 'ad ter stop 'em steamin' there an' then. Anyway, they got 'em as they come out the pub. Bonzo was like a madman. That Sid Varley can fight but 'e was no match fer Big Bonzo. The lads 'ad ter pull 'im off. 'E'd 'a' killed 'im fer sure.'

Frank Johnson strolled up accompanied by his sons Alan and Derek, the latter sporting a black eye. 'I can't keep 'im out o' trouble,' he joked to Del.

''Ow'd 'e get that?' Del asked.

Frank pulled a face. 'Playin' darts, so 'e told me.'

A light fall of snow covered the evening streets and smoke from banked-up fires drifted up into the sky. An icy wind rattled the windows as the Johnson family sat chatting together around the parlour tea table.

'I've made some mince pies an' I've got a Dundee cake,' Ann told them. 'I don't s'pose Lottie'll eat much, but we've gotta lay a spread on fer those that's comin'.'

Lana looked apprehensive. 'I just 'ope they don't all ferget,' she replied. 'Wouldn't it be terrible if no one showed up, after all the 'ard work.'

'Well, I can tell yer that Charlie Smedley'll be there fer one,' Frank assured her. 'I was speakin' to 'im only this mornin' after the meetin'.'

'Lucy Thompson promised in 'er letter that she wouldn't miss it fer the world,' Lana said. 'I dunno about Samuel Selby, though. 'E's one o' those top barristers an' 'e might be too busy.'

'What – on Christmas Eve?' Ann replied. 'I don't fink trials go on that near ter Christmas.'

'It's a shame about Phoebe What's-er-name,' Derek remarked. 'She looks a real cracker, goin' by those pictures of 'er in the *People* last Sunday.'

'Lottie can do wivout 'er,' Lana said quickly. 'She's 'orrible.'

'I wouldn't worry over it,' Ann told her. 'You an' Jimmy done all yer could an' we're gonna give the ole lady a day ter remember.'

Frank pushed back his chair and rubbed his stomach. 'Any more apple pie left?' he asked.

'I've a good mind ter cut yer rations,' Ann joked as she got up. 'All those stoppages don't 'elp put bread on the table.'

'We don't want bread, muvver,' Derek piped up. 'We only want some o' yer luvverly apple pie.'

Ann smiled as she glanced over at her son. 'I dunno about apple pie. Yer look like yer could do wiv a steak on that shiner,' she replied.

'It was all in a good cause,' Derek told her. 'Those Varleys were gettin' a bit too stroppy. They won't be usin' the Crown again, that's fer certain.'

'Yer wanna be careful, though,' Frank warned him. 'Mick Constantine's got a lot o' muscle. 'E'll be after puttin' some of 'is scrappers in the pub from now on.'

'Don't yer worry about that,' Derek said dismissively. 'Even Mick Constantine knows 'e can't mess wiv us dockers. If 'e takes one on, 'e'll 'ave ter take the lot on. We've got fifty like Bonzo Merriman.'

Ann came back into the room carrying a large plate with what was left of the apple pie. 'There we are, share it between yer,' she told them, 'an' when yer finished yer can do the washin' up fer a change. Me an' Lana's got fings ter talk about.'

The folk of the small riverside street had their usual problems this coming Christmas, but they all spared a thought for their elderly neighbour. Madge Conroy had knitted Lottie a pair of bed socks and a matching woolly hat, braving her husband's ridicule.

'I bet she won't wear those,' he remarked. 'No one wears a woolly 'at in bed these days.'

'Shut yer stupid noise,' Madge told him sharply. 'Anyway, 'ow many ole ladies 'ave you slept wiv?'

'Yer'd 'ave done better knittin' 'er a bed coat,' he went on regardless.

'Bed coat, me arse. Stop criticisin' an' stick the kettle on,' she growled.

At number seven Irene Frost hummed contentedly as she wrapped up a pair of carpet slippers. Most of her presents had been wrapped already and she was looking forward to Bubbles calling later that evening. They had been estranged for some considerable time and it would be nice to chat over a cup of tea the way they used to, she thought.

Sadie Pugh and Nell Moseley had seen a pink candlewick bedspread in a market shop and they had agreed to share the cost and make it a joint present. Clara Buckman had thought about giving a cushion for Lottie's rocking chair, but after consulting with Ann Johnson she had decided against it. 'I dunno what ter get 'er then, I'm sure,' she sighed.

'I've got 'er a pair o' linen sheets fer 'er bed,' Ann told her. 'I usually change 'er sheets an' the ones she's got 'ave gone all threadbare.'

'P'raps I should get 'er a pair o' towels,' Clara suggested.

'Lana's bought 'er towels,' Ann said smiling sympathetically.

'Well, I just dunno what ter get 'er.'

'What about a nice tablecloth?'

'That's a good idea,' Clara replied, her face brightening. 'I've seen some nice ones down the market.'

With her neighbour's problem solved, Ann concentrated on her own part to play in Lottie's special day. It was going to be a bit tricky, she thought. The house had to be thoroughly cleaned and a fresh tablecloth put on, the curtains would need changing, and there were the presents to smuggle in. The seating arrangements were going to pose a problem too. Lottie only had two fireside chairs and four dining chairs. Maybe Frank and Derek could pop round to the church hall and borrow a bench.

All Ann's initial problems paled into insignificance later that evening when Lana came back into the house after popping next door with a bag of coke.

'I don't believe it. I just don't believe it,' she said, looking very dejected.

'What's the matter?' Ann asked her.

'Those interferin' busybodies from the Women's Guild 'ave bin in ter see Lottie terday,' she groaned. 'They've invited 'er to a Christmas party at the church 'all on Christmas Eve.'

'Lottie's not accepted, 'as she?' Ann said quickly.

'She 'as.'

'What time's it takin' place?'

'All day.'

'Oh no,' Ann sighed.

Lana leaned on the table, her chin cupped in her hands. 'They told Lottie that they'd collect 'er in the mornin' an' bring 'er back in the evenin',' she reported. 'They said that there'd be a lot o' pensioners goin' an' there was gonna be plays put on by the schoolkids an' carol-singin'. Then there's ter be raffles an' a sit-down party. They made it sound so good that Lottie's all for it.'

'They'd do more good comin' round durin' the year instead o' just makin' a fuss at Christmas time,' Ann said angrily.

'What we gonna do, Mum?' Lana puffed.

Ann thought for a while then a smile suddenly appeared on her face. 'Leave it ter me,' she said.

Mandy lugged her suitcase out of the taxi and tottered up the few steps to the house in New Kent Road. She looked around her fearfully as she rang the bell, willing Gerry to be in.

When he opened the door she almost fell into his arms. 'Gerry, I'm so frightened,' she gasped. 'I 'ad ter come, there's nowhere else I can go.'

The young man took her case and followed her up to his comfortable flat on the first floor. 'I didn't understand what yer was tryin' ter tell me on the phone,' he said, taking her coat.

Mandy flopped down thankfully into the settee by the fire. 'I couldn't stay on the phone too long,' she replied. 'I thought I'd given that private detective the slip, but 'e followed me ter the cafe where I phoned yer from. Mick told me.'

Gerry bent down and took her chin gently between his thumb and forefinger. 'Did 'e do this?' he asked angrily.

Mandy nodded. ''E knows I'm seein' someone an' if the manager 'adn't knocked on the door 'e would 'ave beat it out o' me. I'm scared, Gerry.'

'All right, calm down,' he told her, going over to the sideboard.

'I was finkin' about it all while I was comin' 'ome on the train,' she went on. 'That 'tec must 'ave seen me make the phone call. S'posin' 'e's managed ter trace it?'

Gerry came over with a large brandy. 'Get that down yer,' he said firmly. 'I've managed ter fix yer up wiv a flat fer the time bein'. It's in Streatham an' yer'll be safe there fer a while. We'll leave after it gets dark.'

'What about that phone call? Could 'e 'ave traced it?' she asked again anxiously.

'It's possible,' Gerry replied.

'I've put you at risk now,' she said. 'I'm so sorry, Gerry, but there was no one else I could turn to.'

'It's all right. Just drink that up an' try ter calm down,' he said quietly.

Mandy did as she was bid, feeling the sudden warmth in her stomach. 'Mick won't find us, will 'e?' she asked fearfully.

'No, of course 'e won't,' Gerry replied. 'That no-good whoreson'll 'ave 'is 'ands full when 'e does get back. There's bin a lot goin' on an' there's people after settlin' scores.'

'Don't underestimate 'im, Gerry, 'e's very powerful,' Mandy warned him.

The young man squeezed her shoulder reassuringly. 'You just relax fer a while,' he told her. 'I won't be a minute.'

He went into the bedroom and pulled open the top drawer of the tallboy, searching beneath some folded shirts until he found his service revolver. He quickly checked it, knowing already that the gun was fully loaded, then he slipped it into a leather shoulder holster and laid it on top of the bed before returning to Mandy. Later that evening, as the moon rose up over the rooftops, the two lovers left New Kent Road in a taxi, and only then did Mandy begin to breathe more easily.

William Nugget lined up with the rest of the tramps and drifters, hoping for a bed at the dosshouse. The queue looked extra long to him and he cursed his luck. On most days he couldn't scrounge the one shilling and sixpence needed for a bed and breakfast but today had been a good day and now tonight, when he had the money, there seemed little chance of reaching the front of the queue before the full-up sign was displayed.

'What's 'oldin' 'em up?' William growled to the man standing in front of him.

'It's that poxy Percy,' the tramp replied. ''E does this on purpose 'opin' we'll walk away. Well, I fer one ain't sleepin' under no bleedin' arches in this weavver.'

'Me neivver,' William said with spirit.

The queue moved slowly forward, and with only a few shivering men left the dosshouse keeper brought out the sign. 'Sorry, gents,' he said. 'The place is full. I ain't even got room in the coal cupboard.'

William turned to the tramp in front. 'I got an idea,' he said quietly. 'Foller me.'

Four other drifters tailed along for want of anything better to do and the six scruffy-looking down-and-outs wended their way to the cafe in River Lane.

'Now be quiet while I sort this lock out,' William told them. 'I used ter be a dab 'and at this at one time.'

One of the tramps looked up at the flat above. 'There's no light up there. Is anyone livin' 'ere?' he asked.

'Yeah, the geezer's a pal o' mine, so don't go makin' a mess when I get yer in,' William warned them.

At ten o'clock Joe Slavin left the Horseshoe public house and walked back through Abbey Street to his cafe by the river. As he was about to let himself in by the side door he heard the sounds of snoring, and looking through the window of the cafe he saw the various shapes sprawled out on the slashed benches. He tried the cafe door and found it to be locked. With a sigh of resignation he let himself in to his flat and went to bed. Next morning when he went to investigate his visitors had already left, but on the counter there was a small pile of coins.

Chapter Forty-Five

Ann Johnson finished changing Lottie's bed linen and then made a pot of tea. It was going to be tricky, she thought. The old lady was not in any way senile. In fact she was in fine fettle and as sharp as a button.

'I really appreciate what yer do fer me, Ann,' she said as she sipped her tea noisily.

'There's no need ter fank me,' Ann told her. 'You've done enough fer ovver people in yer time. It's just a little bit back.'

'Well, yer a good gel anyway, an' so's yer daughter,' Lottie went on. 'I'm very lucky to 'ave such neighbours.'

'It's no more than you deserve,' Ann replied. 'By the way, I understand yer goin' to a party on Christmas Eve.'

'Yeah, some ladies from the Women's Guild came round ter see me terday,' Lottie told her. 'Very nice they was.'

'Mrs Arnold from West Lane went ter their Christmas party last year,' Ann remarked. 'She was talkin' ter me about it only yesterday. She's disappointed they've not asked 'er ter go this year, 'specially after she bought a new coat fer the occasion.'

'That's a shame,' Lottie said. 'I wonder why they didn't ask 'er.'

'Mrs Arnold said she reckons it's ter do wiv Farvver O'Shaunessy,' Ann went on. 'She said 'e gets drunk an' wants ter dance wiv all the ladies. Not only that but 'e's not too careful about what 'e comes out wiv when 'e's on the turps.

Yer know what I mean, dirty jokes an' smutty remarks about some o' the women. Mrs Arnold pulled 'im up about it last year an' she reckons 'e's crossed 'er name off the list.'

'Some o' those priests are like that,' Lottie replied. 'Mind you, Farvver McCarfy never misbe'aved 'imself. I'm not a prude, never 'ave bin, but I draw the line at that sort o' carryin' on.'

'Still, yer don't 'ave ter dance wiv 'im, nor listen to 'is snide remarks,' Ann told her. ''Ere, what yer gonna do about a coat?'

'I'm goin' in that one be'ind the door,' the old lady said quickly. 'I certainly ain't buyin' anuvver one, not at my age.'

'Far be it from me ter criticise what yer wear, Lottie, but it is a bit dowdy fer that sort o' do,' Ann commented. 'Mrs Arnold was tellin' me that they all dress up ter the nines. She went an' got 'er 'air permed last year.'

'Well, I ain't tartin' meself up just fer a party,' Lottie said with spirit. 'They can take me or leave me. I don't care.'

'Good fer you. I'm sure yer'll look fine,' Ann said reassuringly. 'I'll make yer up a bit. 'Ere, you can borrer me brown coat. It's quite smart an' it'll fit yer, I'm sure. I can't get into it since I put on all this weight.'

'Nah, that one'll do,' Lottie replied.

'Well, please yerself, but yer'll need to 'ave yer 'air tonged at least. Lana'll do it for yer.'

'I dunno what yer fussin' over. I ain't said I'm definitely goin' yet.'

'I thought yer said yer was.'

'Yeah, but it's not definite.'

'I'm sure yer'll enjoy it, though it's a long day,' Ann went on. 'Mrs Arnold said it got a bit tirin' last year. She said she didn't like the band very much, but the games was good.'

'What band? What games?' Lottie queried.

'Well, the boys brigade band put on a bit of a show. They march up an' down the church 'all playin' their bugles an' drums,' Ann explained, trying to keep a straight face, 'an' then the women who run it split yer up inter two groups, accordin' ter Mrs Arnold. Yer play musical chairs an' pass the parcel. Mind yer, they don't expect you ter join in the musical chairs, not at your age, but you can join in the parcel bit. Yer'll like that.'

'Sounds a bit childish ter me,' Lottie said, making a face.

'I dunno, Mrs Arnold said it was all right.'

'Yeah, well Mrs Arnold ain't me.'

'Oh dear, I 'ope I ain't put yer off,' Ann sighed, 'but I wouldn't want yer ter go an' be disappointed. Yer could just as well sit 'ere an' enjoy yer birfday 'avin' a nice cuppa wiv me an' Lana, not fergettin' Jimmy of course.'

Lottie put down her empty cup. 'I wonder why those women called on me?' she said almost to herself. 'They've not done it ovver years.'

'I dunno really,' Ann replied. 'Maybe it 'as somefing ter do wiv what Mrs Arnold was tellin' me.'

'What was she tellin' yer?' Lottie asked.

'Well, she said that they 'ave ter get so many ter go, an' a lot o' the people round 'ere won't 'ave nuffing ter do wiv 'em.'

'Whyever not?'

'Look, I don't wanna put yer off from goin', luv,' Ann said quickly.

'Nah, yer won't, but I should know what I'm lettin' meself in for,' Lottie told her.

Ann put down her empty cup and folded her arms over her ample bosom. 'As a matter o' fact those Guild women ain't yer everyday Catholics or Protestants, they're more yer inter-denominationals.'

'Inter what?'

'They're sort of bits an' pieces really, so Mrs Arnold was sayin'.'

'What, from all different churches?'

'Yeah, that's right. Some are Jehovah's Witnesses an' some are Pentecostal,' Ann explained. 'They try an' get yer ter join their particular church. Mrs Arnold said she made the mistake o' takin' some tracts from one o' the Guild women an' they kept callin' on 'er afterwards. She said it made 'er fair ill, what wiv all the pesterin'. Anyway, yer don't wanna let that stop yer goin'. Just don't take any o' those tracts if they offer yer any, an' don't let 'em browbeat yer inter joinin' their church, whichever one it might be.'

'Poor ole Mrs Walsh used ter get pestered wiv them Jonah's Witnesses,' the old lady said in a severe tone of voice. 'Nearly drove 'er mad they did. In the finish she put 'er dog on 'em.'

'Well, if yer take my advice yer'll 'ave a good fink about it before yer decide,' Ann told her.

Lottie stroked her chin for a few moments. 'What I'd like ter know is, why is that Mrs Arnold so disappointed about not bein' invited after all the bad fings she told yer about 'em?'

'That's exactly what I asked 'er,' Ann replied quickly. 'She said she wasn't really looking forward ter goin' but she'd resigned 'erself to it, an' now after tellin' all 'er neighbours she was goin' the Guildwomen 'aven't sent 'er an invite.'

Lottie still looked bemused. 'I thought they called round.'

'Only the first time.'

'Oh, I see.'

Ann felt that she was rapidly getting out of her depth and decided to change the subject. ''Ere, while I fink of it, Lottie. Is there anyfing special yer'll want from the market fer Christmas? There's only a few days ter go.'

'Yeah, I know. Ain't it come round quick,' the old lady remarked.

'Well, if yer do, let me know termorrer, OK?'

Gerry Knowland had stayed the night with Mandy at Streatham and returned to Bermondsey the following afternoon. His first visit that evening was to the Lord Nelson pub, and he sensed the tense atmosphere as soon as he set foot in the door. Hard-looking characters sat about the bar alert for strangers, andToni Rossi was busy behind the counter alongside a stern-faced Sam Castelano.

Gerry guessed that there were not only glasses stored beneath the counter and he dreaded to think of what might happen, should Constantine or any of his cronies venture into the pub.

'Darkie's expecting you. Come round the counter,' Toni said, lifting the flap.

Gerry climbed the stairs to the room above and found his friend resting in a large armchair. His arm was in a sling and he looked pale and heavy-eyed.

'Nice to see you, Gerry.'

The two shook hands warmly and the young man sat down facing Darkie. ''Ow yer feelin'?' he asked.

'The shoulder's stiff but I'll live,' Darkie replied smiling. 'What's the news?'

'I've bin a bit out of it lately,' Gerry told him. 'Mandy's done a runner from Mick. I've managed ter get 'er a flat in Streatham.'

'Does he know about you and her?' Darkie asked.

Gerry shrugged his shoulders. 'Mick 'ad Mandy follered. The silly little mare phoned me from a cafe in Brighton an' it's on the cards that whoever was tailin' 'er saw 'er make the call. Yer can bet yer life it's bin traced.'

'So it figures that Mick Constantine is going to be looking for you.'

'Yeah, it seems that way.'

'Take my advice and stay here for a few days,' Darkie told him. 'I've got this pub well sewn up.'

Gerry nodded. 'It seems a good idea, under the circumstances. What's the news wiv you?'

'Gold Star Groceries is in a bad way,' he replied. 'I heard from one of the shopkeepers that the sales manager has left and two of the reps as well. All our shopkeepers are trading elsewhere and you can bet that those salesmen who left would have taken a few accounts with them. And now on top of that there's this Mandy business. Constantine's going to be like a raving bull. There's no way we'll get him round the table collectively. One look at you and he'll be going for your jugular.'

'What's the alternative?' Gerry asked.

'I might be able to persuade him to sit down and talk,' Darkie replied. 'That's if I can convince him that you're off the scene. The idea would be to offer him back all the Maltese accounts in exchange for our bookies being allowed to set up their pitches again. Our lads would go along with it, I'm certain.'

'S'posin' Constantine agreed,' Gerry queried. ''Ow long would it all last before 'e starts puttin' the squeeze on the shopkeepers an' the bookies again? An' what if 'e decides ter take you off the manor prop'ly this time?'

'Don't worry, I'm not an idealist,' Darkie said quickly. 'I know there'll never be any real peace between us and them, but if we can get a deal we'll gain time. The Maltese community in Bermondsey is growing steadily but we need to draw closer together, become strong and united. Then, when I deem the time ripe, I'm going to personally cut Constantine's throat from ear to ear.'

Lana was working an extra half an hour in the evenings during the Christmas period, and today as she prepared to leave for home she cursed to herself as she straightened her stocking seam. There was a ladder running from ankle to above her knee. It was her only pair too and the shops would be closed. As she neared Saddler Street she saw that the corner shop was still open and decided to try there. The Nolans sold many other items apart from groceries, but Lana discovered that stockings were not amongst them.

'Nah, I'm sorry, luv,' Fred Nolan told her. 'We used to, but there's so many shades an' makes ter contend wiv I just ain't got the room ter put 'em all on show.'

Lana was turning to leave when Fred called her back. 'I've 'eard all about ole Lottie's birfday party an' what yer've bin doin',' he said. 'I fink it's very good of yer. It'll certainly make 'er day. She's a lovely ole gel.'

'Yeah, she is,' Lana replied. 'Most o' the kids she fostered'll be there. I bet she'll recognise 'em all, even after all those years.'

Lily Nolan walked out from the back room. ''Ello, gel. I could 'ear what yer was sayin'. I fink it's a very nice fing too,' she remarked. 'I was only sayin' so to Albert Robey this mornin'. Albert was goin' on about 'ow 'e remembered some o' those kids Lottie used ter look after. Little bleeders some of 'em, but the ole gel loved 'em all. Albert said she was an angel.'

'Albert Robey? 'E wasn't 'ere all that time ago,' Lana said quickly. 'The shop was owned by the Goodrich family. We found that out when we went frew the pollin' lists at the town 'all. As a matter o' fact we were lookin' fer neighbours who lived in the street at the time Lottie Curtis was fosterin'.'

'Yeah, that's right, the Goodriches did own the shop,' Lily replied. 'Albert Robey's muvver died when 'e was a little tot an' 'is farvver moved in wiv Sara Goodrich a couple o' years later. They never got married but when Sara died she left the shop to Albert's farvver. 'E passed away just before the outbreak o' war an' that's 'ow Albert come ter get it. Albert Robey's lived in this street most of 'is life an' 'e's knockin' on sixty now.'

Lana left the shop with a flutter of excitement. Would Albert Robey know the identity of the last of Lottie's children, she wondered, the one who had meant so much to her? Should she pursue it now after having decided not to? It seemed that fate had led her into the shop at a time when trade was slack and the Nolans were in a chatty mood. Was Lottie meant to meet her favourite son once more? As she had said herself, she had lived to regret her harsh words, and Lana knew in her heart that a reunion would make the old lady very happy.

She hesitated for a few moments then hurried across to the other corner shop. Albert Robey was busy polishing the brass scales which he used for weighing snuff. ''Ello, gel. If yer want snuff yer'll 'ave ter wait,' he said grinning.

'As a matter o' fact I need some info, Albert,' she replied.

Ten minutes later Lana left the newsagent's and hurried out of the turning towards River Lane. It had to be done now, she thought as she reached Ben Ferris's house and rang the bell.

Chapter Forty-Six

Lottie sat beside the fire, her gnarled hands resting on the arms of her rocking chair as she moved rhythmically backwards and forwards. 'I was 'avin' a nice chat wiv yer muvver earlier,' she said. 'We was talkin' about that party.'

'At the church 'all?' Lana queried.

'I told 'er I ain't goin' after all,' Lottie went on. 'It ain't my cup o' tea. Bloody pass the parcel an' musical chairs at my age. I got better fings ter do wiv me time.'

Lana had been told by her mother that Lottie was thinking it over, and her decision not to go was a huge relief. 'I fink yer've made the right decision, Lottie,' she said. 'Those Guild women are a lot o' biddies.'

The old lady nodded. 'I've bin a Catholic all me life an' I don't want the likes o' them tryin' ter convert me,' she replied indignantly. 'Mind you, I ain't bin ter church fer years, but I still say me prayers.'

Jimmy came into the room carrying the hot teapot. 'I 'eard that, Aunt Lottie. I say my prayers every night,' he quipped, winking at Lana.

'Yer don't 'ave ter go ter church ter be God-fearin',' Lottie remarked. 'Anyway, I couldn't sit on them 'ard benches fer long. They'd play me back up terrible. Mind you though, I do miss the church, 'specially at times like Easter an' Christmas. The children used ter get so excited. I remember those times very well. It was durin' the month of Mary – that's the month o' May – that one o' the children was chosen ter do the crownin'.'

'What's the crownin'?' Lana asked.

Lottie stopped rocking and folded her arms, which told Jimmy that this was going to be a lengthy explanation, and he reached for the teapot.

'It's when they crown the statue of the Virgin Mary at the altar wiv a garland o' flowers,' Lottie went on. 'One child, a young boy, carries the flowers on a velvet cushion an' all the children follow on in the procession, an' they're all singin'. Durin' the time Phoebe was wiv me she was picked ter do the crownin'. She was such a pretty child, an' when she marched in that procession she looked beautiful. She 'ad 'er 'air in ringlets an' she was wearin' a lovely white dress.' Lottie smiled as she recalled the time. 'The little madam 'ad a tantrum as I was gettin' 'er ready. She 'ad this little strawberry birfmark just above 'er wrist an' she danced the polka 'cos the dress 'ad three-quarter sleeves an' it didn't cover the mark. She was quite a little actress even then when she didn't get 'er own way. Anyway, I managed ter cover the mark wiv borax powder, an' if yer could 'ave seen 'er in that procession. She looked like a little angel. I could 'ear 'er voice above all the rest as they sung.

"'Oh Mary we crown thee with blossoms today.
Queen of the angels and Queen of the May."

'It used ter make me cry when I watched the crownin'.'

Jimmy handed the tea over to Lottie with a sideways glance at Lana. 'There we are, Aunt Lottie,' he said smiling.

The old lady sipped her tea gratefully, dwelling in silence on the bygone days, while Lana thought about what they had achieved so far. Of the ten fostered children, one had been killed in the war but the rest had now all been contacted. Only the 'Queen of the May', little Miss Prim and Proper, had openly refused to attend on the day and it riled her.

'My mum came from a Catholic family, but me dad was a Protestant,' Jimmy announced, breaking the silence. 'I s'pose the Catholic Church would say she committed a mortal sin, killin' 'erself.'

'It doesn't matter what they say or what they fink, son,' Lottie said firmly. 'She was taken wiv open arms, yer can rely on it.'

Lana reached out and laid her hand on Jimmy's. 'I'm sure Lottie's right,' she said quietly.

The old lady saw the sad look in the young man's eyes and Lana's spontaneous gesture, and she stopped her rocking. 'I fink it's nice that you two get on so well,' she remarked. 'It does an ole lady good ter see two young people so 'appy tergevver. You are, ain't yer?'

Jimmy slipped his arm around Lana's shoulders. 'Yes, we are, Aunt Lottie,' he replied.

'Does that mean yer'll be gettin' engaged soon?' she asked.

'I've not asked 'er yet,' Jimmy said, feeling Lana's grip tighten on his hand.

'Well, don't leave it too long or she might get fed up o' waitin',' Lottie said chuckling.

'We've got a lot o' savin' ter do,' Lana told her. 'Jimmy wants ter start up a business.'

'Oh, an' what business might that be?' Lottie asked.

'I wanna be a blacksmith,' he replied.

'D'yer mean yer'd be shoein' 'orses like a farrier?' she queried.

'Yeah, but I'd also work wiv iron, like fittin' cartwheel rims an' makin' fings such as iron gates an' railin's,' he explained. 'It's a dream I've 'ad fer a long time.'

'I seem ter remember yer workin' fer a blacksmith when yer was a kid,' Lottie told him. 'Please Gawd it'll all work out for yer.'

Lana could see that the old lady was getting tired. 'Well, we'd better be off if we're ter catch the big picture,' she said.

Lottie raised her hand wearily, her eyelids beginning to droop. 'G'night, me ducklin's,' she mumbled.

William Nugget had learned his lesson and tonight he was at the front of the queue for the dosshouse. His new-found friends were with him and they stood rubbing their hands together as the cold wind whipped through the cobbled lane.

'It was a good kip-down at yer pal's place, Will,' one said.

William rolled his shoulders, feeling rather important. 'Yeah, well I got a few friends in Bermon'sey,' he said. 'Mind yer, I don't take advantage, but now an' then I ask a favour.'

Vic Snelling was impressed. 'Good idea ter get 'ere early ternight,' he remarked. 'There's a bloody great queue be'ind us.'

A short, slightly built man wearing a filthy raincoat shuffled his feet and kicked on the closed door of the dosshouse. 'Come on, Percy, it's bleedin' cold out 'ere,' he shouted.

'I wouldn't upset 'im, Dodger, or 'e'll only keep us waitin' longer,' Vic warned him.

'Yer right, Vic. Percy likes ter see us suffer,' William cut in. 'That woggly eyed bastard would 'a' done well runnin' a concentration camp.'

A wino came staggering along past the queue, ignoring the unfriendly comments. His overcoat was held together with string and he carried a quart bottle of cider in his gloved hand. As he reached the entrance he broke into song.

> 'Standin' on the bridge at midnight,
> chuckin' snowballs at the moon.
> She said "Jack, I've never 'ad it,"
> but she spoke too bloody soon.'

'Go on, yer drunken ole bastard, give us anuvver one,' one of the tramps shouted at him.

'It's the same the 'ole world over.
It's the poor what gets the blame.
It's the rich what gets the pleasures.
Ain't it all a bloody shame?'

Suddenly the door of the dosshouse was thrown open and the towering figure of Percy Pocknell appeared. 'Right, you,' he growled, pointing at the drunken tramp. 'You're pissed. On yer way.'

The inebriate ignored the command and took a swig from his bottle.

'There's a yeller, green-eyed idol,
ter the north o' Kathmandu.
There's a little wooden cross above the town . . .'

'If yer don't piss orf yer'll get a bucket o' water,' Percy snarled at him.

The mention of water, and on such a cold night, was enough to send the drunk scurrying off, and the queue started to move slowly forward.

William and his friends sat at the long trestle table, their hands cupped round bowls of hot tomato soup. Men were still arriving and the large dining hall was filling up quickly.

Nosher King slumped down next to William. 'I got a bit o' good news,' he said, dipping a chunk of bread into his soup. 'Percy Plonker's goin'.'

'When?'

'Next week,' Nosher told him. 'I 'eard 'e's bin sacked. 'E's workin' 'is week's notice.'

'I wonder what ovver treasure they're gonna dig up ter take Percy Plonker's place,' Vic remarked.

'I don't fink they've got anyone yet, accordin' ter the cook,' Nosher replied. 'Bein' a doss'ouse manager ain't everyone's cup o' tea.'

'Nah, I s'spect yer right,' William said, looking a little distracted.

Vic nudged his friend Dodger. ''Ere, look. The drunk's slipped in.'

'Bloody 'ell! I 'ope Plonker don't spot 'im. Well, not till 'e's finished 'is soup anyway,' Dodger whispered.

A huge vagrant sitting opposite the drunk pushed his empty bowl away from him and belched loudly. 'Who called the cook a bastard?' he suddenly shouted at the top of his voice.

Immediately the whole of the hall responded as one: 'Who said the bastard can cook?'

Percy Pocknell came storming along between the tables, his large flat face dark with anger. 'Who's the clown?' he growled.

The huge vagrant belched again. ''E is,' he said grinning, pointing to the innocent drunk.

Percy grabbed the unfortunate by his coat collar and manhandled him from the dining hall to a mixture of cheers and obscenities.

William shook his head in disgust. 'That wasn't a very nice fing ter do,' he said.

'I already owe that ugly great git one,' Dodger growled. 'I'm gonna get 'im ternight.'

Later that night William and his friends sat together on Vic's bed passing a cigarette between them. In the bed opposite the big vagrant snored loudly. 'When they turn the lights out I'm gonna nick 'is boots an' chuck 'em out the winder,' Dodger declared.

The December moon climbed high above the wharves and lit up the fresh carpet of snow. Inside the dosshouse the noise of varied snoring drifted out from the broken window as William Nugget and his friends slept soundly, their boots safely pinned down with the legs of their beds inside them.

Dawn arrived, and the sound of the biting wind was not conducive to early rising, but the big vagrant made sure that every man jack of the dossers would rise early that morning when he fished down for the tobacco tin and matches which he had hidden in his boots. 'What no-good whoreson's nicked me poxy boots?' he boomed out at the top of his voice.

After an extra early breakfast of toast and a boiled egg William Nugget and his friends marched out of the dosshouse like an army squad.

'Well, lads, I've got a job ter do that won't keep,' William said, touching the side of his nose mysteriously.

For want of something better to do, William's friends followed in his wake.

'Mornin', Mr Slavin.'

'Mornin', Mr Nugget.'

'Got a minute, Mr Slavin?'

'I should fink so, Mr Nugget.'

'You lads move on while I talk ter Mr Slavin,' William told his contingent. 'I'll catch yer ternight, front o' the queue.'

'What can I do fer yer, Mr Nugget?'

'I got a proposition ter put ter yer, Mr Slavin.'

Charlie Smedley rolled a cigarette while he waited for the management to return to the meeting. 'They'll agree,' he said confidently. 'I could tell by the antics of ole Groombridge. 'E always scratches the tip of 'is nose when 'e's on a loser.'

'That's not all 'e scratches,' one of the shop stewards remarked. ''E couldn't keep still this mornin'.'

Charlie turned to another steward. ''Ere, Bert, will you be seein' Del Brady later?' he asked.

'Yeah, why?'

'Can yer ask 'im ter take the levy money ter Joe Slavin?'

'Sure fing.'

When the working day ended Del Brady made his way to River Lane. 'The lads 'ad a little collection, Joe,' he said as he made himself comfortable by the fire. 'We miss yer tea an' bacon sandwiches, an' the chat, so we wanted ter make sure yer don't stay closed fer ever. 'Ere you are, wiv the lads' good wishes.'

Joe took the bulky envelope and stared down at it, his eyes misting. 'I dunno what ter say, Del,' he replied.

'There's nuffing ter say,' Del said smiling.

'As a matter o' fact, I'm in an embarrassin' situation really,' Joe told him. 'Yer see, I've 'ad this offer ter manage the doss'ouse in Dock'ead. The wages are good an' it's a job I fink I'd like.'

'What, lookin' after all those no-good ole bastards?' Del said disbelievingly.

'Yer don't really know 'em,' Joe replied quietly. 'There's a lot o' decent 'earts beatin' under those scruffy overcoats. After all, yer don't just decide ter become a tramp when yer leave school. It's the cards yer dealt frew yer life, an' most o' them 'ave bin dealt poxy 'ands.'

Del nodded slowly. 'I make yer right, ole mate,' he concurred. 'Anyway the money's yours. Take it.'

Joe shook his head. 'No, Del, I couldn't,' he replied. 'But I know what can be done wiv it. Give it ter that poor sod who got 'urt on the quay last week. Better still, give it to 'is wife. She could do wiv it, I've no doubt.'

Del Brady took the envelope and slipped it back into his coat pocket as he stood up. 'Well good luck, Joe, an' tell the dossers that our loss is their gain,' he said as he held out his hand.

'I'll tell William Nugget ter pass yer message on,' Joe said, grinning.

Chapter Forty-Seven

There was a frosty chill in the air and lines of footsteps criss-crossed the bright snow as Lana stepped out of the insurance building on Friday evening. She saw Jimmy standing a few yards away, hands in his pockets, the collar of his reefer jacket turned up and a scarf tied around his neck. He walked over to her with a big smile on his face. 'I managed ter get away in time,' he said.

'I was 'opin yer would,' Lana replied, smiling back at him as she slipped her arm through his. 'I'll feel better if yer wiv me.'

They crossed the wide approach to London Bridge Station, passing parked buses and taxis, and hurried into the concourse. Tired workers with blank faces scurried towards the platforms and City gents with bowler hats and rolled umbrellas marched along beside them at a military pace with the evening paper tucked under their arms.

The train to Charing Cross was packed but the two young people managed to squeeze into a seat, their bodies pressed together, their eyes occasionally meeting and eliciting shy smiles from each other. They saw the medieval Southwark Cathedral rising up beside them as the train arced westwards, and it was not long before they trundled on to the lattice bridge and gazed down at the River Thames, the oily surface of its treacherous waters illuminated by the elegant Embankment gas lamps.

The fat lady sitting opposite looked uncomfortable squeezed between two elderly men and she stared over unblinkingly, her eyes flitting from Lana to Jimmy, which began to irritate the young man. He puckered his lips suggestively at Lana and winked slowly, and was rewarded with an embarrassed smile from her and an even more intense stare from the fat lady.

The train shuddered to a stop and as soon as Lana stepped on to the platform she turned to Jimmy. ''Ave I got a smudge on me face?' she asked. 'That woman didn't take 'er eyes off me once.'

'Actually she was taken by yer beauty, an' my good looks,' he joked. 'I bet she was finkin' to 'erself what a nice couple we make.'

Lana gripped his arm tightly, nestling against him in the cold air as they hurried out into the Strand. 'Look, Jimmy, I really do appreciate yer comin' wiv me,' she said. 'I know yer fink it's a waste o' time, but I gotta try an' see 'er once more. After what Lottie was sayin' I feel I owe it to 'er.'

'I know,' he said quietly. 'It's just that I got the impression last time she's not the sort o' woman ter bend. She seemed really 'ard.'

'Well, at least I'm gonna give 'er somefing ter fink about,' Lana replied resolutely.

They reached the Royal Theatre and saw a small group of people standing by the stage door, eagerly watching the passing traffic.

'They must be waitin' fer the star to arrive,' Lana said with a note of sarcasm in her voice.

'I s'pose we'd better wait 'ere wiv 'em,' Jimmy suggested.

They stood together a few yards away from the group, Lana leaning against him, holding on to his arm with both hands, feeling his warmth and recalling how he had made love to her so tenderly yet so passionately. She thought about the harsh words they had exchanged that evening before they made love and she understood his fears. She would have felt the same way if he had gone off alone to see an old flame. She knew that she was hopelessly in love with him, and she saw her future clearly now, like a warm blue sky, with no clouds of doubt or mistrust on the horizon.

As though reading her thoughts, he bent his head and quickly kissed her on the tip of her pert nose. 'I love you,' he whispered.

'I love you madly,' she said, her eyes flashing fire.

A sudden squeal from the group of waiting fans brought the two young lovers down to earth and they turned to see a shiny black car with whitewall tyres pulling up at the kerb. A uniformed chauffeur stepped out and quickly opened the passenger door as the fans hurried over.

'Cor, look! It's really her!'

'Can you sign my book, Miss Francis?'

'It's a wonderful show, Miss Francis.'

'I've seen it four times.'

The star had climbed from the car with practised elegance, her long blue dress reaching below her ankles, its rhinestones and sequins sparkling in the light of the huge illuminations above the theatre. Her calf-length silver-fox fur was draped over her shoulders and her blonde ringlets were piled high on her head. She smiled indulgently, and almost glided to the stage door, signing the autograph books with a flourish.

Lana watched the spectacle with distaste, pulling Jimmy by the hand as she stepped into the path of the star. 'Do yer remember me, Miss Francis?' she said in a firm voice.

For a brief moment the star looked puzzled, then as the realisation dawned on her she tried to sidestep but Lana moved in front of her again.

'Please stand aside,' the star said haughtily.

The fans were still milling around but Lana ignored them as she eyed Phoebe Francis coldly. 'I'd like ter talk ter yer fer a minute,' she said.

'I've already told you I've nothing more to say,' the woman replied coldly.

Lana's eyes narrowed. 'But I 'ave,' she retorted quickly. 'Shall I say what I've come ter say out 'ere or can we go inside?'

The determined look in the young woman's eyes was enough to convince the star that she wouldn't be put off. 'Follow me,' she ordered.

Jimmy squeezed Lana's hand and gave her a wink of encouragement as they hurried through the long corridor, past the many ropes, spotlights, props and paraphernalia of the show. Phoebe Francis led the way, hips swaying and shoulders thrown back, and when they reached her dressing room they saw her briefly touch the silver star that was stuck to the door.

'I can give you four minutes,' she announced as they entered. 'I've got a performance to do.'

Lana drew a deep breath as she watched Phoebe sit herself at the dressing table and study her hair. 'Yer'll remember when we first came ter see yer we wanted ter give yer an invite ter Lottie Curtis's birfday party on Christmas Eve,' she began. 'But you chose ter deny ever knowin' the old lady. I can understand why, what wiv you bein' a star an' writin' in yer book about bein' brought up in India, but you know the trufe. You know very well that it was Lottie who took you in an' cared for yer when yer was a snotty-nosed kid from Bermon'sey . . .'

'I don't care to hear any more,' Phoebe cut in sharply. 'Will you please leave now.'

'Yeah, we'll leave, but not till I've said what I've come ter say,' Lana replied quickly. 'You can deny yer origins as much as yer like, but we know the trufe. We know the debt you owe that ole lady an' I fink it's despicable that yer won't agree ter see 'er, even fer a few minutes.'

Phoebe swung round in her chair, her eyes flaring. 'I'm saying nothing more. Will you please leave?'

'D'you remember the month of Mary?' Lana asked, as if not hearing her. 'Lottie does. She told us about the beautiful little child who did the crownin'. The little child who sang the crownin' song above all the rest. The little child who 'ad a tantrum over the strawberry mark on 'er arm. Yer do 'ave a birfmark on yer arm, don't yer, Miss Francis?'

'That doesn't prove anything,' Phoebe replied with a wave of her hand. 'You could have seen the mark last time you came here and decided to make up a story about it. Now please go.'

Lana looked at Jimmy, her face flushed with anger, then she turned once more to face the star. 'Lottie Curtis 'as follered your rise ter fame an' fortune but I don't fink she'd be 'appy ter know just 'ow selfish an' smug yer've turned out,' she said in a measured voice. 'So when yer takin' yer bows an' milkin' all that applause, just give fanks fer what yer've got, an' then try ter spare a thought fer one old lady who's not sittin' out there in the audience. An' last of all, just take a look at yerself in that poxy mirror when yer come off stage. Just ask yerself if yer like what yer see. Come on Jimmy, we're not welcome 'ere. Let's go.'

They walked out into the cold night air and Jimmy noticed the tears welling up in Lana's eyes. 'You were great,' he said with feeling. 'I wanted ter hug yer.'

'Take me 'ome, Jimmy,' she said, her voice full of emotion. 'Let's go back ter your place.'

Ben Ferris walked into the Lord Nelson and was immediately aware of the hostile looks as he ordered a drink.

Toni Rossi eyed him closely as he put the pint of beer down in front of him. 'I'm trying to place your face,' he said. 'Have you been in here before?'

'The name's Ferris, Ben Ferris. I'm a mate o' Gerry Knowland,' he answered. 'As a matter o' fact I'm lookin' for 'im.'

'Do you know who owns this pub?' Toni asked suspiciously.

'Yeah, Darkie Samut,' Ben replied. 'Gerry introduced me to 'im in 'ere a couple o' weeks ago.'

'You know the score then,' Toni remarked.

'I know that Darkie got a bullet in 'im, about the same time as I was gettin' six buckets o' shit knocked out o' me by the dirty bastard it's down to, Constantine,' Ben said angrily.

Toni slipped into the back room and emerged a few seconds later. 'Come through 'ere, it's the room at the top of the stairs,' he said.

Ben hurried up to the flat above the bar to find Gerry and Darkie chatting together. 'Gerry, I need a favour,' he said quickly, nodding to Darkie. ''Ello there, mate, 'ow yer gettin' on?'

Darkie motioned towards a seat and looked inquiringly at Gerry.

'You remember Ben Ferris,' Gerry reminded him.

'Yes, of course,' Darkie replied, nodding.

'What is it, Ben?'

'Yer know Joe Slavin got turned over by the Varley bruvvers?' Ben queried.

'Yeah, I know,' Gerry replied. 'An' did you know that Nipper Varley an' that idiot bruvver of 'is got sorted out by some o' Joe's docker pals?'

Ben looked surprised. 'No, I never.'

'I don't fink they'll be troublin' anybody else fer quite some time,' Gerry remarked with a wicked smile. 'So what's the favour?'

'Sell me that gun o' yours, Gerry.'

'Now just a minute, ole pal. What would you be wantin' wiv a gun?'

'It's no big secret,' Ben replied, his eyes burning into his friend's. 'I'm gonna blow that bastard Constantine away.'

'Whoa now! Let's calm down,' Gerry said, his hands out in front of him. 'I know 'ow you feel, but . . .'

'You don't know 'ow I feel. No one does,' Ben growled. 'I've took a beatin', Joe's 'ad 'is cafe wrecked, Darkie 'ere's bin shot, an' it's all down ter that evil git Constantine. It's about time someone did somefing about it.'

'So you're after puttin' yerself in the frame,' Gerry said

with a cold smile. 'Yer wanna blow 'im away, an' wiv my gun.'

'Don't worry, I'd drop it in the river,' Ben replied. 'They'd never find it.'

'Talk sense, Ben. You'd never get the chance ter shoot 'im,' Gerry said calmly. 'Constantine never goes anywhere wivout Tommy Carberry. Are yer intendin' ter shoot 'im as well?'

'I'd bide me time,' Ben told him. 'I could do it.'

Darkie raised a hand for attention. 'I'd like to say something. If I thought it was the answer I'd find you a gun myself, but it's not. There's a better way of dealing with Mick Constantine. To start with we have to be patient.'

'Patient? I've run out o' patience,' Ben said with disgust.

'Now you listen to me,' Darkie said sternly. 'All right you've taken a beating, but some of my countrymen have had their shops burned down, others their faces slashed, and I was shot on the way to a church service. You're not the only one who wants to get even. When the time comes I'm going to be the one who settles with Constantine, make no mistake about it, but in the meantime we're going to play it cool. Is that understood?'

'So what've yer got in mind?' Ben asked quickly.

Gerry raised his hand a little to interrupt Darkie. 'Could you get close enough ter Constantine ter deliver a message?' he asked Ben.

'Yeah, I fink so.'

'Would yer be prepared to do it?'

'Yeah, why not?'

Darkie eased his position in the chair. 'Gerry, get that bottle of Scotch out of the sideboard,' he said. 'I think we could all do with a snort.'

Mal Lawrence had had a distinguished career in the Sussex Police Force, rising through the ranks to become a chief inspector. His capacity for work and hard drinking finally took its toll, however, and one evening he came home to find a note from his wife saying that she was leaving him. Mal sought solace in the bottle, and it wasn't long before his drinking caught up with him. A catalogue of errors and mismanagement finally forced his superior officer's hand and he was offered early retirement on medical grounds.

Life had reached an all-time low for the once-proud police officer and in desperation he sought the help of Alcoholics Anonymous. His rehabilitation was furthered by an ex-police colleague who had supplemented his retirement pension with part-time work as an inquiry agent. He spoke for Lawrence, and now life for the ex-chief inspector was a little rosier. His standing at the agency was high, and after his successful surveillance of Mandy Constantine he had been engaged by the Bermondsey gang boss once more.

The private detective was given the London address of Gerry Knowland and his inquiries began there. An inquisitive soul told him that the tenant of the flat had left in a taxi after dark a few nights ago, in the company of an attractive blonde. Mal Lawrence took a few taxis in the New Kent Road and found out that when they were empty the drivers tended to head for either the cab rank at the Elephant and Castle or the one at Borough Road, which led to London Bridge Station. His inquiries at both ranks were painstaking, and with a police badge as authority, a plausible story and a concerned attitude, he was able to make progress.

'She's done nothing wrong. It's merely a question of finding her in time,' the detective explained. 'The young woman's been treated for a dog bite but the animal concerned was later found to be rabid. She has to be found and treated as soon as possible if she's to survive. Pass this number on. I can be contacted night or day.'

Word spread through the taxi ranks, in the cafes and at the coffee stalls, and finally the driver who had taken Mandy and Gerry from New Kent Road to Streatham came forward.

Alf Barlow had driven taxis for years. In his fifties and with an astute mind, he was suspicious of the story as he heard it. Why had he not heard an SOS for the young woman to come forward broadcast over the wireless, he wondered. Why wasn't the case in the newspapers? His doubts were tempered by the fear of withholding information which might save the woman's life, however, and he phoned the number which had been passed on to him.

The man on the other end of the line sounded plausible enough, but he was at pains to point out that there was a very good reason for keeping the operation and search low key. Alf remained suspicious, and he decided to call in at his local police station at Dockhead.

Chief Inspector William Penrose was now faced with a puzzling problem. There was a bogus policeman operating on the manor searching for an unnamed young woman. From Alf Barlow's detailed description of the couple he had taken to Streatham the inspector was able to brief his team, who in turn immediately sought out their own informers. All the incoming information was sifted carefully and the case file grew. The woman's description, a very smart young blonde wearing a long fur coat, fitted at least half a dozen local women, according to one reliable source, and one of the names submitted was that of Mandy Constantine. Gerry Knowland was identified as the occupant of the house from which the taxi driver had collected the couple and he fitted the description supplied by the observant Alf Barlow. Knowland had a police record and was rumoured to be in league with the Maltese, who were at loggerheads with the Constantine mob. What did it all mean?

With the distinct possibility of a liaison between Mandy Constantine and Gerry Knowland, and its investigation by a private detective, the prospect of utter mayhem erupting was more likely than ever. Penrose quickly picked up the phone and dialled Streatham Police Station.

forward pundits over the witness, he wondered. Why wasn't the case in the newspapers? His doubts were tempered by the fear of withholding information which might save the woman's life, however, and he phoned the number which had been passed on to him.

The man on the other end of the line sounded plausible enough, but he was at pains to point out that there was very good reason for keeping the operation and search low key. Alf remained suspicious, and he decided to call in at his local police station at Dockhead.

Chief Inspector William Penrose was now faced with a puzzling problem. There was a bogus policeman operating in the manor searching for an unnamed young woman. From Alf Pardoe's detailed descriptions of the couple he had taken to Streatham the inspector was able to brief his team, who in turn immediately sought out their own informants. All the incoming information was sifted carefully and the case file grew. The woman's description, a very smart young blonde wearing a long fur coat, fitted at least half a dozen local women, according to one reliable source, and out of the names submitted was that of Mandy Constantine. Gerry Knowland was identified as the occupant of the house from which the taxi driver had collected the couple and he fitted the description supplied by the observant Alf Pardoe. Knowland had a police record and was rumoured to be in league with the Maltese, who were at loggerheads with the [illegible] mob. What did it all mean?

With the distinct possibility of a link between Mandy Constantine and Gerry Knowland, and an investigation by a private detective, the prospect of further mayhem was more likely than ever. Penrose quickly picked up the phone and called Streatham Police Station.

Chapter Forty-Eight

It was the week of Christmas, a bitterly cold Monday with snow hard-packed on the pavements and a seasonal atmosphere in the air. Women hurried to and from the market, children squealed excitedly as they played together on the street and here and there the sound of carols rang out as the carol singers did their rounds. Coloured paper chains hung in shops and on market stalls, and overhead the leaden sky threatened to deliver another carpet of snow as soon as the northerly wind dropped.

Ben Ferris had neither the time nor the inclination to dwell on Christmas as he made his way to the Crown and Anchor at Dockhead. His mission filled him with trepidation and beneath his grim exterior a strange feeling of dread gripped his innards. He had not been inside the pub since his abduction and subsequent beating and he wondered about the reception he would receive.

As he entered the saloon bar that lunchtime Ben was immediately aware of people's eyes on him and he saw Mick Constantine standing in the far corner along with Tommy Carberry and the young thug who had administered the beating. He gritted his teeth, cold fury welling up inside him as he reached the counter and ordered a drink. He realised that they were all looking over at him and he clenched his fists into tight knots. 'I've got an important message fer Mick

Constantine,' he said to the smirking barman.

The man went over to the gang boss and after exchanging a few words he came back. 'Come frew,' he said, still wearing the smirk.

Mick Constantine came into the back room, his eyes full of menace as he glared at Ben. 'I'm surprised yer've showed yer face in 'ere again,' he said icily. 'What's the message?'

'I got a visit from Darkie Samut late last night,' Ben told him. ''E wants a meet.'

'Why should 'e get you ter be the messenger boy?' Mick asked him.

'I dunno,' Ben said, shrugging his shoulders. 'P'raps someone told 'im I used the pub an' I knew yer.'

'What else did 'e say?'

'Just that if you agreed ter meet 'im, 'e'd set the time an' place an' I'd relay it ter yer.'

'Just me an' Samut?'

'That's what 'e said.'

The gang boss stared hard at Ben, his mind racing. 'I 'ope yer not still associatin' wiv that mob, after the warnin' I gave yer,' he growled.

'I told yer that Darkie just called on me, an' that's the trufe,' Ben replied. 'I know the score, I'm not exactly stupid.'

Mick took out a cigar from his coat pocket and bit off the end, spitting it down at Ben's feet. 'Tell 'im I'll meet 'im, providin' the venue's right. But warn 'im against tryin' anyfing, Ferris.'

Ben nodded. 'Where can I contact yer?'

'Right 'ere.'

'OK, I'll tell 'im what yer said.'

Ben left his beer untouched and hurried out of the pub, still feeling that Darkie was being naive. Constantine was never going to agree to anything that Malt proposed. He would assume that Gerry Knowland was still involved and planning against him. There was also the business with the private detective. As Gerry said, Mick would have already found out about him and Mandy and would be coming for him sooner or later. It seemed to Ben that Constantine's only reason for agreeing to the meet was to find out where Gerry was. He might well ask Darkie to serve him up on a plate.

As he hurried back to the little pub behind the Old Kent Road Ben saw a group of Salvationists singing carols on the wide pavement, and on the way past he dropped a few coppers into the collecting box.

'May the Good Lord bless you, my son,' the elderly soldier of Christ said, smiling.

Ben returned the smile and turned off the thoroughfare into the backstreet. It was going to be a long day, he realised.

Tommy Carberry was turning things over in his mind as he sat in the back room of the Crown early that evening. He glanced across at the thick-set young boxer who sat facing him with his head buried in a newspaper and sighed irritably. The man seemed incapable of conversation and any attempt to draw him out only resulted in unintelligible grunts. Tommy rued the day he had agreed to act as Constantine's minder. It had seemed an easy enough job at the time. His bulk and reputation were enough to deter any young villain who might decide to cause some aggravation, and the pay was good. Things had not turned out as he imagined though and he realised now that if he was not very careful he could end up doing a long stretch or even worse. Constantine seemed to have become crazed by recent events and his reasoning had gone out of the window. He had recruited a ruthless thug in Johnny Bryan and it worried the ex-wrestler. He was concerned too about the arrangements made for that evening. Constantine had said that he had to see someone urgently and they should bring Ferris along to Wakeman's Wharf in Rotherhithe as soon as he arrived.

The tap on the saloon bar door caused Johnny Bryan to drop his newspaper and he eased himself out of the chair. Tommy watched him amble across the bar and noticed the sway of his broad shoulders. He would be a dangerous adversary, he thought.

'We're gonna take yer ter Mick,' the boxer told Ben. 'Get in the car.'

Ben looked surprised. 'Ain't 'e 'ere'?' he asked.

Tommy walked up behind the boxer and motioned towards the waiting Morris saloon. 'Get in, son,' he said quietly.

The cold night had kept all but the hardy off the streets, and as Johnny Bryan drove the vehicle along the deserted Jamaica Road Ben turned to glance at Carberry. 'Where we goin'?' he asked anxiously.

'Take it easy,' Tommy replied, feeling anxious himself.

The car swung into a narrow turning by the Rotherhithe Tunnel and carried on down a riverside lane. The place seemed devoid of life as the boxer steered the car on to a stretch of wasteground between two wharves and pulled up facing a low wall overlooking the river. Ben spotted the gang boss's Bentley parked some distance away and he felt a sudden twinge of fear strike at his stomach.

'Get out the car,' Johnny ordered.

Ben did as he was bid and stood shivering despite his thick overcoat and scarf. He watched Mick Constantine get out of his car and walk over to the wasteground towards him.

'I couldn't meet yer at the Crown,' Mick said in a surprisingly amiable voice. 'I 'ad some urgent business ter take care of. Well, son, where's the meetin' ter be?'

Ben considered not telling him and insisting on taking him to the venue, but he knew that Mick's two thugs would only knock it out of him. 'Darkie wants yer ter meet 'im at St Patrick's Church in the Old Kent Road,' he said. 'It's ter be just the two of yer. Go in the church at ten minutes ter nine. The service'll be endin' about that time. Sit in the last but one row o' the pews and wait till the priest approaches yer.'

'Is that all?'

'That's all 'e said,' Ben replied with a shrug of his shoulders.

Constantine stared at him for a few moments, then suddenly

his face contorted and he reached inside his overcoat. Ben Ferris stepped back a pace, his hands spread out in front of him as he saw the gun. 'Now wait a minute,' he gasped. 'I only did as I was told.'

'Yer never learn, do yer?' Mick growled. 'Yer in this as much as that whoreson of a Malt Darkie Samut an' that fornicatin' bastard Knowland. You 'ad yer chance an' yer didn't take it. Yer time's up, Ferris.'

Tommy Carberry was standing next to Johnny Bryan and he glanced quickly at him, seeing nothing but blankness in the boxer's eyes. He turned and saw Constantine thrust the gun forward. The revolver jerked with a sharp report and Ben spun sideways as the bullet hit him, his eyes wide with surprise as he clasped his hands to his stomach, and he fell face down on to the snow.

'Christ Almighty!' Tommy gasped. 'Yer've killed 'im!'

The gang boss held the smoking revolver down at his side as he walked the few paces to stand over Ben's inert body. Tommy expected him to put another bullet into Ben's head, but instead Constantine smiled coldly as he saw the growing circle of blood colouring the snow. 'It seems I'm goin' ter church,' he remarked.

Johnny Bryan nodded towards the body. 'What do we do wiv 'im, leave 'im 'ere?'

'Chuck 'im in the river,' Constantine scowled.

Tommy watched disbelievingly as the gang boss climbed into his car and sped off, then he stared down at Ben.

'C'mon then, let's get it over wiv,' the boxer said.

Tommy saw a slight movement from Ben and heard the low groan. ''E's still alive!' he exclaimed.

'So what?' Bryan said, bending over to grab the young man.

Tommy Carberry pulled the boxer away from him. 'We gotta get 'im ter the 'ospital,' he said quickly. ''E's still alive, I tell yer.'

Bryan tore free from the older man. 'Mick said 'e's ter go in the river,' he growled.

Tommy straddled the prone figure, his eyes flaring. 'If yer touch 'im I'll kill yer, so 'elp me, Bryan.'

The young boxer crouched like a panther waiting to spring and then suddenly lunged forward throwing a looping punch, but years in the ring had taught Tommy Carberry what to expect. He parried the blow to one side and dived inside it, clasping Bryan in a bear hug and pressing upwards under the man's chin. He gritted his teeth, squeezing as hard as he could, and he felt the boxer suddenly go limp. When he slowly released his grip Bryan collapsed in a heap.

Ben felt no pain, only a floating sensation as he lay on the snow. He heard the car speed away and then turned his head slightly, shocked at seeing the dark blood draining from his side. He heard a crunching sound and then Tommy's voice. 'Let's take a look, son.'

Ben shook his head slowly as the big wrestler turned him on to his back. He could see the Salvationists standing in a circle and remembered the soldier's words. 'The Lord must 'ave fergot,' he mumbled and then he closed his eyes.

Tommy cursed loudly as he tore open Ben's overcoat and tried to stem the flowing blood with his handkerchief. His worst fears had been realised. What had possessed him to get involved with a man like Constantine? He must be getting old and stupid. Ben groaned and moved slightly, spurring Tommy into action. He dragged Ben up against the wall and let him fall forward over his shoulder, gasping with the exertion as he staggered off the wasteland.

A meeting on holy ground meant nothing to Mick Constantine. He was taking no chances, and it was a packed car which pulled up in the churchyard. The heavily built passengers watched warily as their boss climbed out into the cold night and pulled up his coat collar. They could hear hymn singing, and as two figures appeared out of the shadows one of the men sitting in the rear seat pointed a sawn-off shotgun through the window.

'Just a second,' Toni Rossi said as he stepped in front of Mick. 'We need to check you out.'

Constantine raised his arms without saying anything and allowed the Malt to frisk him, looking unconcerned as his gun was taken from the shoulder holster.

Sam Castelano eyed Mick with distaste as Toni handed him the revolver. 'I'll mind this till you come back out,' he growled. 'You won't be needing it there. This is a church, in case you've forgotten.'

Darkie Samut had been sitting at the front of the large congregation throughout the late Mass, and as the benediction finished he slipped quietly from the pew and into the vestry. Father Mancini watched him go and glanced up towards the back of the church. He knew all of his flock, if only by sight, and he easily picked out the heavily built stranger sitting in the last but one pew.

'It's time we met,' Darkie said quietly as Mick Constantine was shown into the room.

'Yer picked a good place,' Mick replied as he took a seat.

'It's a good place to talk, and a good time,' Darkie told him. 'There's been enough blood spilt.'

'What 'appened ter the arm?' Mick asked, a ghost of a smile playing on his wide face.

Darkie adjusted the sling. 'A slight accident. It's mending well,' he said lightly.

'I'm glad to 'ear it.'

'I want a truce,' Darkie said, leaning back in his chair. 'We want to be able to live and trade in peace. We want a say in what goes on.'

'Yer ferget, this is my manor,' Mick replied sharply.

'Not any more. We share it. We control it. You in your area, me in mine,' Darkie said calmly. 'What's more, I want our bookies back on their original patches.'

'An what 'ave yer got ter bargain wiv?' Mick asked.

'We get the bookies back, an' you get the shopkeepers' business once more. Fifteen accounts at my reckoning.'

The villain took out a cigar and rolled it between his fingers thoughtfully, then his eyes came up to fix on Darkie Samut. 'I don't need 'em,' he said quietly. 'I'm pickin' up trade over the water.'

'I don't believe it,' Darkie replied. 'You bought the Gold Star Groceries because you saw it as a way of squeezing the Maltese shopkeepers. You wanted to put them all out of business. It didn't work, and now the business is suffering. I hear that your senior sales team has left you in the lurch and you're running into the red.'

'A couple o' the sales team 'ave left, that I won't deny,' Mick told him. 'But then when a business changes 'ands that sort o' fing is ter be expected. As fer bein' in the red, that's not true. There's somefing else you should know while we're talkin' business. A good businessman never rushes in ter buy something before 'e susses it out. I knew when I made the offer ter Sammy Goldbloom that a big grocery concern 'ad recently made 'im an offer fer the business. If I chose I could sell out ter them termorrer an' make a nice profit.'

'Well, I'm sure that's comforting,' Darkie said sarcastically.

'If you wanna do a deal yer'll do it on my terms,' Mick growled. 'You can 'ave yer bookies back in exchange fer Gerry Knowland. I want 'im trussed an' delivered. I got a big score ter settle wiv that son-of-a-bitch.'

'I'm sorry, but it's out of the question,' Darkie replied.

Mick Constantine stood up and flipped up the collar of his overcoat. 'Termorrer's Christmas Eve,' he said in a measured tone. 'I want Knowland gift-wrapped by five o'clock. Then yer can tell yer bookies the good news.'

'You know I can't agree to that,' Darkie said contemptuously.

'Well then, it's gonna be a cold, bleak New Year for some,' the gang boss replied as he walked to the door.

Sam Castelano was waiting on the steps of the church and he stepped forward and handed the gang boss back his revolver. 'Merry Christmas,' he said with a blank face.

Constantine took the gun and slipped it into his shoulder holster before climbing into the car, and then with a withering look at the Malt he drove out into the Old Kent Road.

Chief Inspector Penrose hurried into St Olave's Hospital after being informed at home of the shooting in Rotherhithe, and the attending police constable showed him into the room put aside by the matron. 'I've taken a statement, sir,' he said. 'Mr Ferris is still in the operating theatre.'

Tommy Carberry was white-faced as he stood up from his chair. 'What's the news?' he asked anxiously.

'We won't know for a while yet,' Penrose told him, studying the notepad the officer had passed to him. 'You stated that Constantine was going to St Patrick's Church to meet Darkie Samut.'

'Yeah, that's right,' Tommy replied. 'An' like I told the officer, 'e said 'e was goin' over ter Streatham afterwards. I dunno whereabouts in Streatham though.'

'I do,' Penrose muttered. 'This Johnny Bryan. Where is he now?'

'I dunno. 'E might still be on the wasteground where I left 'im,' Tommy replied, 'or 'e might 'ave gone 'ome by now.'

Penrose looked hard at the ex-wrestler. 'In your opinion, would he testify against Mick Constantine?'

'I'll find 'im, and' 'e'll testify,' Tommy growled.

'Well, I want you to find him and get him to come in first thing tomorrow,' Penrose replied. 'You tell him from me that if he doesn't show by nine-fifteen I'm putting out a warrant for his arrest. Another thing. You tell him that if he doesn't agree to testify I'm going to charge him with being an accessory to attempted murder.' He turned to the police officer. 'Phone Streatham Police Station. Tell them to locate Inspector Morris and let him know I'm on my way over.'

Mick Constantine drove his henchmen back to the Crown, and stood at the bar talking with them for a while. He had expected Carberry and Johnny Bryan to report back to the pub by now but there was no time to concern himself with them. He had another urgent matter to take care of.

At ten o'clock he left the pub and drove alone to Streatham. This was personal, and he didn't need any backup.

The cold northerly was dropping and flakes of snow started to fall, dancing in the headlights of Mick Constantine's car as it cruised past the house for a second time. Two policemen had just turned into a side street and strolled off slowly, and the gang boss calculated that if they did the same circuit they would pass the house again in ten minutes' time. On the third drive past he saw the two policemen walk along and turn off the street once more. He had worked it out right. He swung the car into a side turning opposite the house and pulled up, taking a tyre lever from the glove compartment. The residential road was quiet as he hurried over and climbed the few steps to the front door. He saw that there were six separate bells, five with names beneath them. The bell beside number four was blank and Constantine smiled to himself as he slipped the thin end of the lever into the small gap between the door and the frame and forced it open. Pushing the door to behind him he hurried up to the flat on the first floor.

'Who's there?' a woman's voice called out.

'Telegram for Miss Gregson.'

'Miss Gregson doesn't live 'ere any more.'

'Can yer sign me board please, miss?'

Mandy sighed with irritation as she slipped the bolts and opened the door. Mick Constantine charged through the opening and grabbed her, stifling her scream of terror by clapping his hand over her mouth. 'I'm gonna blow the top of your 'ead off if yer don't do as yer told,' he hissed.

Mandy felt the cold barrel of the revolver pressed up hard under her chin and she gulped in terror.

'Yer gonna make a phone call,' he told her. 'Get yer coat on.'

She looked at him pleadingly. 'No, Mick! Please!'

'I want that no-good whoreson Knowland an' I'm gonna finish 'im. Get yer coat on!' he shouted.

Inspector Penrose turned to his colleague from Streatham as they reached the top of the steps. 'This door's been forced,' he remarked.

They hurried up the flight of stairs, their footsteps silenced by the thick carpet, and as they reached the first floor they heard Constantine's raised voice. Without a second's hesitation Penrose barged into the flat in front of Inspector Morris, only to stop dead in his tracks as he found himself looking down the barrel of a revolver.

'Put that gun down before you do anything you'll regret,' Morris called out over his colleague's shoulder.

'It's all over, Constantine,' Penrose said, taking a step forward.

'Take one more step an' I'll kill the pair of yer,' the gang boss snarled.

Mandy recoiled in terror as Constantine moved back to her and grabbed her round the throat. 'Give 'em the gun, Mick, yer'll only make it worse fer yerself,' she told him.

In answer he pressed the muzzle of the revolver to her temple. 'Shut yer noise or I'll finish yer,' he growled.

Penrose was edging forward. 'Do as she says, Mick,' he said calmly.

Suddenly a uniformed policeman appeared in the doorway and as Constantine swung round to face him Penrose leapt. The gang boss was a fraction faster and he smashed the butt of the gun against the police inspector's head. Inspector Morris saw his colleague crumple, and as he rushed forward to grab the revolver Constantine pointed the weapon at his head and pulled the trigger.

For an endless moment time seemed frozen, and the metallic click of the hammer on an empty chamber echoed like the clank of a bell. Then in a second the policeman had pounced and bundled Constantine to the floor.

'Michael Constantine, I'm arresting you for the attempted murder of Benjamin Ferris and a police officer,' a dazed Penrose said as he slapped on the handcuffs.

The gang boss was dragged to his feet and he hung his head as his rights were read out to him, then as he was led to the door he turned and glared at Mandy. 'I took you off the streets, you little whore, an' that's 'ow you repay me,' he growled.

'C'mon, let's go,' Penrose told him.

As they made their way to the waiting police car Inspector Morris looked across at his colleague. 'Do you realise it's almost Christmas Eve, William?' he said quietly, his face still white with shock. 'For an instant there I thought I was going to miss it.'

Sam Castelano sat down on a bar stool in the Lord Nelson and smiled at his friend Toni Rossi as he slid five bullets from the palm of his hand on to the counter. 'I thought it made good sense to take these out of the gun I was minding,' he remarked. 'Loaded guns frighten me.'

'Only five? Shouldn't there be six?' Toni queried.

'That was all there was,' Sam replied.

'I dread to think where the other bullet ended up,' Toni said with a shudder.

Chapter Forty-Nine

The women of Saddler Street were out early on the morning of Christmas Eve sweeping the previous night's snow from their doorsteps. Bella Wickstead wore her old coat and a scarf as she cleared the pavement along as far as Lottie Curtis's front door. The rest of the pavement as far as Clara Buckman's had already been cleared and Bella stood up and pressed a hand to her aching back for effect as she saw Sadie Pugh come out of her house with a stiff yard broom. 'Well, we certainly got a white Christmas,' she called over.

'I asked my Phil ter do this before 'e went off ter work,' Sadie called back. 'The lazy git won't lift a finger to 'elp.'

Clara came out carrying a shopping bag. 'I'm gonna queue up at the bread shop before it all goes,' she announced.

'I got mine soon as the shop opened,' Bella told her.

Madge Conroy came hurrying along the street with an envelope which she slipped through Lottie's letterbox. 'I got 'er a religious card, I fink she'll appreciate it,' she said.

'I put mine in first fing,' Bella replied, not wanting her neighbour to think she had forgotten. 'I got it off the card stall. They 'ad some really nice ones.'

'It's a nice age when yer come to fink of it,' Clara remarked, ready for a chat before she faced the bread queue.

'She's still very sprightly,' Madge said. 'Please Gawd she'll live long enough ter get a telegram from the King.'

Irene Frost popped her head out of her front door to see what was going on. 'I got my Wally out 'ere early this mornin' ter sweep the snow away,' she informed her neighbours. 'I told 'im ter go right ter the end. Wait till that lazy cowson gets 'ome.'

Sadie was not going to be left out of the conversation and she came over carrying her broom. ''Ow's yer sister, Irene?' she asked.

'Still as brassy as ever,' Irene replied. 'She said she's gonna pop in when she comes round.'

'What's 'appened about that Moses feller?' Sadie asked her.

'The case comes up in January.'

'D'yer fink 'e'll get off?'

'I should fink so. Bubbles reckons he will.'

'I fink 'e done us all favour,' Sadie remarked. 'We could 'ave all bin killed in our beds wiv a maniac like that runnin' around loose.'

'I don't fink we 'ad anyfing ter worry about,' Bella laughed. 'Preacher Jack was only after wicked women – no disrespect, Irene.'

Clara reluctantly left to get to the bread queue and Irene made her excuses to leave before she got embroiled in an argument over her sister. Bella stood by the front door leaning on her broom. 'Wouldn't yer 'ave thought 'er Wally could 'ave swept right along 'ere,' she remarked to Sadie.

''E's a lazy git. 'Im an' my ole man make a fine pair,' Sadie growled.

The street was coming to life as women went off on their last-minute shopping trips to the market, and when Bob Ashley drove his coal cart into the turning everyone stood at their front doors ready to take their Christmas delivery of nutty slack.

Jimmy Bailey had only a few local deliveries to do that morning and at lunchtime the firm closed for Christmas. The young man excused himself from going to the pub with the rest of the drivers by saying that something urgent had come up, and he hurried off to the Crown and Anchor. The public bar was packed by the time he arrived and he immediately spotted Frank and Derek chatting to some other dockers. Reinforced with a drink he managed to get Frank to one side, and an hour later, feeling a little bit lightheaded, he strolled along to Saddler Street.

Lana was at the market when he arrived but Ann was busy cutting sandwiches for the party, and Jimmy was grateful for the opportunity to talk to her in private.

Lana looked mystified and she glanced at Jimmy quizzically as they walked into Jamaica Road early that afternoon. 'Where are we goin'?' she asked.

He led her into the church gardens, their feet making deep holes in the virgin snow, and he pointed to a bench facing the church steps. 'When me mum was feelin' well enough an' the weavver was nice I used ter bring 'er 'ere,' he said quietly. 'She used ter sit on that bench. It was always that one. Sometimes she'd chat away, an' ovver times I couldn't get a word out of 'er, but I knew she was at peace 'ere.'

Lana squeezed his arm as they walked on. 'Are you feelin' all right?' she asked with concern.

He nodded, still serious-faced. 'Lana, would yer say we were good tergevver?' he asked.

'Of course I would.'

'Are yer really 'appy?'

'Yes, I really am.'

'Would yer . . . I mean could yer . . . ?'

'Jimmy, what are yer tryin' to say?' she asked, suddenly feeling anxious.

He sighed deeply then he stopped and turned towards her. 'I 'ad it all worked out,' he said in a quiet voice as he took her hands in his, 'but the words I'd planned ter say seem trivial now. So I'll just say, Lana, will yer marry me?'

She felt a lump in her throat and a stinging sensation in

her eyes as she stepped closer to him. 'Darlin', of course I will,' she said.

In the secluded gardens their lips met in a soft, sensuous kiss and Jimmy looked down into her eyes. 'I love you very much,' he whispered.

'I love you too,' she said.

He took her by the hand. 'C'mon.'

'Where are we goin' now?' she asked smiling.

'To get the ring.'

Lottie Curtis tutted as Ann took the last of the curlers out of her hair. 'I dunno what all the fuss is about,' she moaned. 'It's only me birfday, an' I've 'ad a few in me time.'

'People'll be callin' in soon ter wish yer many 'appy returns,' Ann told her. 'Now keep still.'

'I dunno why yer got all that food in,' Lottie went on. 'Who's gonna eat it all?'

'Lottie, I can't fix yer 'air prop'ly unless yer keep still,' Ann sighed.

'I got a nice lot o' cards.'

'Yeah, yer did.'

'I reckon 'alf the street sent me a card.'

'It seems like it.'

'I never got one from 'er next door ter you.'

'Mrs Frost? Yes, yer did. That's the one wiv bells on the front.'

'Oh yeah, that's right. Mrs Cleg'orn never sent me one though.'

'Mrs Cleg'orn's bed-ridden, luv. I don't s'pose she even knew it was yer birfday,' Ann told her.

Lottie sat impatiently in her rocking chair while Ann put the finishing touches to her hair. 'There we are. Yer look very nice, even if I say so meself,' she said smiling.

'Can yer shake me cushion up a bit, Ann?' the old lady asked as she eased herself out of the chair.

Ann did as she was bid. 'Let me take that bottom cushion

away,' she urged her. 'That cover could do wiv a good wash.'

Lottie shook her head adamantly. 'No, leave it. It's nice an' comfortable.'

The younger woman sighed in exasperation. The cushion was flattened with wear but Lottie seemed to have a profound attachment to it. Even when she had been given the new cushion she would not part with it. 'All right, luv, keep yer shirt on,' she said, 'I was only suggestin'.'

Once Ann had made her a cup of strong tea Lottie settled down to enjoy the rest of her day, and when Jimmy and Lana came in a little later she beamed when they told her the good news. 'I got a confession ter make,' she told them. 'Yer remember that night I sent yer round ter get Jimmy ter fix me tap? Well, there was nuffing wrong wiv it. I just wanted ter get you two tergevver. Wasn't that clever of me?'

Lana bent over and kissed the old lady on her cheek. 'I'll never fergive yer, Lottie,' she said smiling broadly. 'D'yer really like me engagement ring?'

'It's lovely,' Lottie replied. 'It matches yer eyes.'

A knock at the door made Ann glance quickly at Lana. 'This'll be the first of 'em, I should fink,' she said quickly.

Charlie Smedley walked into the room carrying a small parcel and grinned at the old lady. ''Ello, me love. Remember me?'

For a few moments Lottie stared at him, then her hand came up to her mouth. 'Gawd! It's me little Charlie!' she gasped.

The bulky shop steward kissed her warmly and then handed her the parcel. 'I 'ope yer like it,' he said, hardly able to take his eyes off her.

'Cor! Look, Ann, it's a pair o' drop earrin's,' she said breathlessly. 'I always used ter wear drop earrin's at one time.'

Jimmy answered another call a few minutes later, and as the tall, gaunt figure of Morgan Jones walked into the parlour on the arm of his wife Alice, Lottie was overcome with emotion. 'Morgan an' Alice? Well, I'll be blowed. I knew in me 'eart you two would get tergevver one day,' she said, beginning to weep. 'Come an' sit down next ter me. I wanna know all about what yer bin up to.'

Ann made a pot of tea while Lana passed round the sandwiches and homemade cakes. Lottie chatted happily with her surprise guests, stopping to wave her fist at Ann in feigned anger. 'So that's why yer was so concerned about makin' me look presentable,' she growled.

'I wonder where Dad an' Derek 'ave got to wiv that bench,' Lana said.

'If I know them they've fergot ter get it,' Ann replied. 'I warned 'em not ter ferget.'

Jimmy came into the room and whispered to Lana. 'There's a posh car just pulled up outside.'

Samuel Selby walked in wearing a navy-blue overcoat trimmed with astrakhan and a homburg, which he doffed smartly. 'Lottie, you haven't changed a bit,' he said cheerfully. 'You're just as I remember you.'

The old lady held out her arms. 'It's me little Sammy,' she cried. 'I can't believe it. All me children are comin' ter see me. All me little children.'

Samuel handed her a gaily coloured package. 'Merry Christmas and a very happy birthday, dear Aunt Lottie,' he said, planting a kiss on the old lady's forehead.

The next guest arrived with a flourish. 'Where's that naughty Aunt Lottie 'idin' 'erself?' she called out from the passage.

Once again the old lady brought her hand up to her mouth in surprise. 'I remember that voice. We used ter play that game togevver. It's me little Ellen!'

Bubbles stepped into the parlour and shook her hips, to the delight of everyone. 'Not so little now, Auntie!' she laughed.

Lottie held out her arms and Bubbles cuddled her long and tightly.

'Fank yer, darlin'. Fank yer fer everyfing,' she said, her voice faltering with emotion.

Ann and Lana stood in the background, allowing the old lady to revel in her happiness as she chatted excitedly with her long-lost children.

'If those fellers don't bring that bench soon I'll kill 'em,' Ann growled to Lana.

A few minutes later Jimmy called Ann to the window and she turned away with her hand over her eyes. Frank and Derek were staggering along the street carrying a large wooden bench between them. They were making ridiculously slow progress, with a backward step for every two forward ones.

'I'll kill 'em both, I will, so 'elp me,' Ann muttered.

The drunken pair staggered into the parlour singing 'Happy Birthday' and Jimmy and Charlie Smedley quickly took the bench from them before any damage was done.

'A very 'appy birfday to yer. Give us a kiss, my love,' Frank slurred.

'You two 'ad better go indoors an' 'ave a kip,' Ann hissed at them, her eyes flashing.

'A good idea,' Derek said staggering back a pace. 'We wish you all a Merry Christmas.'

Ann ushered them out, trying to keep an angry face. 'Don't they show yer up,' she growled to Lana.

'I remember you an' Lucy 'idin' in that coal cupboard an' I was worried somefing terrible,' Lottie was saying to Bubbles. 'Did yer ever see anyfing o' Lucy after yer left?'

'No, but I fink we might do, please Gawd,' Bubbles chuckled.

'Are yer workin'?' Lottie asked her.

'Not at the moment,' she replied, giving Ann a wink.

'What is it yer do exactly?' the old lady pressed.

'As a matter o' fact I run an 'ome fer wayward gels,' Bubbles told her, hiding a smile.

'That must be rewardin' work.'

'It 'as its moments, Aunt Lottie.'

The initial excitement had subsided somewhat and the guests were sitting around the room chatting together and reliving old memories when Lucy Thompson was shown in. Bubbles screamed with delight as she jumped up and the two women hugged each other tightly.

'What did I tell yer?' Bubbles said grinning at Lottie.

The old lady sat holding Lucy's hand in hers as they chatted joyfully together and Ann felt a glow of happiness welling up inside her. 'You two certainly made 'er day,' she told Bubbles.

Jimmy slipped his arm around Lana's shoulders. 'It's lovely ter see 'er so 'appy,' he remarked. 'Just look at all those presents lyin' there at 'er feet.'

The jubilant old lady was holding court, gently rocking as she eyed them all in turn, passing a word here and there and reliving an old memory or two. Her fosterlings all felt humble in her presence, and everyone savoured this brief interlude in their busy lives when they could pay their respects to the old lady to whom they all owed so much.

At six o'clock a taxi drew up outside number three and a tall, elegant woman stepped out wearing a raincoat with the collar turned up around her ears. She had dark glasses on and her hair was covered with a silk scarf tied under her chin. She knocked at the door, looking left and right nervously. 'Does Mrs Curtis live here?' she said as Jimmy opened the door to her.

'You decided ter come after all?' he said, his eyes wide with surprise.

Phoebe Francis stepped into the passage and removed her scarf and glasses, a smile forming on her face as she saw Lana emerge from the parlour. 'I hope you realise you have a very persuasive way about you, Miss, er . . .'

'Johnson. Lana Johnson.'

'Well, Miss Johnson, or should I say Lana. I hope you'll forgive me.'

'Of course, Miss Francis. It's lovely of yer ter spare the time.'

'I thought about what you said,' Phoebe told her. 'As you know, I have a very large mirror in my dressing room and I have to spend quite a lot of time staring into it when I'm making up. I've always liked what I saw and I want it to remain so.'

Lana took her by the arm. 'Come an' meet your Aunt Lottie,' she said, smiling warmly.

All eyes were riveted on the star as she glided into the room, and when the old lady saw her she beamed. 'Come an' give us a kiss, me little songbird,' she crowed.

Another present joined the pile and a very happy old lady began to reminisce over one particular month of Mary with her latest guest.

The magical hours slipped by all too quickly, and as night drew on the snow began to fall again. One by one Lottie's guests said their goodbyes, each promising to call again before very long. The old lady felt a weariness descending over her and she set the rocking chair slowly in motion. 'What a lovely day,' she sighed. 'It was all your doin' an' I'm very grateful.'

Ann smiled as she got up to make some fresh tea and Lana joined her in the scullery, while Jimmy gathered up the parcels into a tidy pile.

'Yer'll enjoy yerself termorrer openin' this lot,' he told her.

Lottie nodded, and then her face suddenly took on a serious look. 'Do you believe in the 'ereafter?' she asked.

'That's a strange question to ask, Aunt Lottie,' he replied.

'Do yer?'

'Yeah, I do as it 'appens.'

'So do I,' she said, nodding her head slowly. 'I believe people we've loved an' lost visit us sometimes. I felt it terday. Just fer a few minutes.'

Jimmy looked at her questioningly. 'Yer mean Uncle Bill?'

'No, not yer Uncle Bill. I'm sure young Freddie Williams dropped in just ter wish me a Merry Christmas,' she said quietly.

Another knock startled the old lady and then her face broke into a lovely smile. 'I believe I know who that'll be,' she said.

Jimmy went to the door with a puzzled look on his face.

'Is that young Gerry?' Lottie called out.

He stepped into the room. 'Yeah, it's me, Aunt Lottie. Yer prodigal son, come ter wish yer a very 'appy birfday an' a Merry Christmas.'

The old lady rose from her chair, dwarfed by the tall, handsome young man. 'Come 'ere,' she said, the tears beginning to flow. 'I some'ow knew yer'd come.'

Gerry Knowland enveloped her in his arms, and for a few moments they stood together in the centre of the quiet room. Jimmy left them alone, going out to join Lana and Ann. 'So that's the one,' he said. 'I wonder 'ow 'e found out?'

'Someone must 'ave told 'im, I expect,' Lana replied, catching her mother's eye.

Gerry helped the old lady down into her chair and sat facing her, holding her hands in his. 'I couldn't stay away terday, Aunt Lottie,' he said quietly.

'Of course yer couldn't,' Lottie replied, smiling shyly. 'It's bin a bit too long anyway, Gerry.'

'Am I forgiven then?' he said, smiling back at her.

'There's nuffing fer me ter fergive,' she told him. 'Rantin's of a silly old lady. Harsh words said in a moment an' then years o' regret. You was always special ter me, an' nuffing's changed.'

'No, Lottie, you was right,' Gerry replied. 'I let yer down, you an' Uncle Bill. You two taught me right from wrong an' I turned out a bad 'un.'

Lottie pulled a hand away to wipe a tear from the corner of her eye. 'You ain't such a bad 'un, son,' she said. 'There's a lot o' good in yer. I can see it in yer eyes. I saw it the day you arrived on me doorstep. There's a lot o' yer farvver in yer.'

Gerry frowned. 'My ole man was a bad lot, Aunt Lottie,' he replied quickly. ''E was a drunken waster who constantly knocked me muvver about an' then finally left 'er ter fend fer 'erself.'

The old lady nodded her head slowly, a sad smile forming on her lined face. 'I know all about that,' she said softly. 'Yer see, I knew yer muvver very well. We were very close. Despite the life she led Winnie was a good woman. When she was very young she fell in love wiv a man who broke 'er 'eart. No, not Len Knowland. It was before she met 'im. The man she loved chose the cloth. I'm sure 'e never realised at the time just 'ow much Winnie loved 'im. Anyway it broke 'er 'eart an' she turned ter Knowland. She was soon ter find out what a big mistake she'd made. 'E started knockin' 'er about an' then 'e forced 'er ter go on the streets. Yer muvver 'ad no option. She was terrified of 'im. One night she met 'er first an' only love again. By that time 'e was a fully fledged priest an' she turned to 'im out of need. It all began innocently enough, but it wasn't long before 'e realised that 'e loved 'er as much as she 'ad always loved 'im an' it just 'appened.'

'What are yer tryin' ter tell me, Lottie?' Gerry asked quickly.

The old lady took a deep breath before she went on. 'The priest I'm talkin' about is Farvver McCarfy, an' the love 'im an' yer muvver shared brought you into the world. I know it sounds unlikely that a Catholic priest would fall fer someone, what wiv the oath o'celibacy they 'ave ter take, but it's true. Yer muvver confided in me terwards the end of 'er life. She told me that she 'ad to let 'im go, back to 'is callin', an' fer 'is sake she never told 'im she was pregnant wiv 'is child.'

Gerry swallowed hard. 'So 'e never knew?'

Lottie smiled. ''E knew, I'm sure 'e did. It was 'im who brought yer ter me doorstep that night an' I could see the worry in 'is eyes. 'E knew right enough.'

'Didn't me farvver – I mean, didn't Len Knowland suspect anyfing?' Gerry asked her.

'Farvver McCarfy was dark 'aired an' you was born fair, just like yer muvver,' she told him. 'Len used ter swagger about, tellin' everyone 'ow much yer resembled 'im, but the trufe was there in yer eyes. They're as deep blue as Farvver McCarfy's were. There was no mistakin'.'

The young man shook his head slowly as he tried to take it in, and a smile creased his handsome face. 'The son of a priest, eh?'

Lottie nodded. 'That was why I was so upset when I saw the road you was goin' down, Gerry,' she replied. 'I s'pose if the trufe was known I wanted yer ter foller in 'is footsteps.'

'Be a priest, yer mean?'

'No not really. I just wanted yer ter lead an honest life.'

'Well, Aunt Lottie, I'm goin' to from now on,' Gerry told her, smiling broadly. 'I've got plans, honest plans, so yer've no need ter worry ever again.'

She smiled. 'Wherever yer farvver is 'e'll be watchin' over yer, I feel sure. Don't let 'im down, son.'

'I won't, Lottie, yer can take that as gospel,' he replied, then his eyes narrowed. 'Does my Aunt Sadie know about all this?'

Lottie shook her head. 'We're the only two.'

Gerry made to leave. 'I'll be callin' round again very soon,' he said, adding with a big grin, 'yer never know what I might find out next time.'

The old lady looked up at him. 'I'll look forward ter that,' she replied. 'By the way, I never used that money yer gave me. Yer knew that though, didn't yer?'

'Yeah, I guess I knew all along,' he said, smiling. 'But it was meant fer you, Aunt Lottie. It ain't tainted, believe me. I wanted ter make fings a little easier for yer.'

'I've bin very lucky all frew me life,' she told him. 'I've got good neighbours an' all you children. What more could a woman ask for?'

'I won't take it back, yer know.'

'No I don't s'pose yer will. You always was an awkward little bleeder,' she said smiling.

'Use it, Lottie. Yer'll find a good use fer it,' he said, resting his hand on hers.

The fire burned low and outside the sound of 'Good King Wenceslas' carried through the quiet street as carollers from St Mary's Church turned the corner. They had all gone, all her grown-up children; adults now, but still babies in her eyes.

'Jimmy? Lana? Come 'ere a minute. Ann? Bring the scissors.'

'What is it?' Ann asked as she came into the parlour.

'Take this cushion from under me,' Lottie bade her. 'Not that one, the old one. That's right, now slit it open.'

Ann stared at her in disbelief. 'Yer want me ter slit it?'

'You 'eard me. Slit it open.'

Ann did as she was told and the old lady smiled mysteriously. 'Give it me,' she ordered.

They all watched while Lottie delved inside the cushion and removed a flat package.

'I'm in the winter o' my life, but you two are in the spring of yours,' she said, eyeing Lana and Jimmy in turn. 'This'll do you more good than me. Take it.'

Lana hesitated but the old lady pushed it into her hands. 'Go on, do as I say an' take it,' she insisted. 'Yer'll be gettin' married soon an' Jimmy's always wanted ter be a blacksmith. This'll 'elp.'

'I dunno what ter say,' Lana murmured.

'There's nuffing to say,' Lottie replied smiling. 'Now, if yer don't mind it's bin a tirin' day, what wiv all me kids bein' under me feet. I need ter get some shut-eye. Bank me fire up an' then close this door on yer way out. Oh, an' by the way. A Merry Christmas to all of yer.'

Epilogue

On New Year's Eve Ben Ferris sat propped up in bed, making eyes at the young dark-haired nurse as she straightened his bedclothes. She gave him a coy smile and then moved on to the next bed.

'I'm gettin' first-class treatment in 'ere. I fink I'll book anuvver week,' he joked.

Lana smiled, catching the nurse's backward glance as she fussed over the other patient. She was obviously smitten by him, she thought.

'Yeah, I can see the attraction,' Jimmy replied with a lopsided smile.

Ben eased himself up against the pillows. 'It was nice of yer both ter pop in,' he said. 'An' I s'pose congratulations are in order. Well, I wish yer both all the very best. Take good care of 'er, Jimmy, she's a good 'un.'

The young man nodded in reply and Lana smiled. 'You take care too, an' get well soon,' she told him.

The nurse was coming back along the ward and Ben watched her as she moved. 'I certainly will,' he answered.

'I'll just take this water jug and fill it for you,' the nurse said, her eyes smiling.

The bell sounded and Ben suddenly felt an old yearning as his visitors walked away from the bed. A chapter in his life was closing, silently and irrevocably, and he still felt a certain sadness about it all. Life moves on though, he sighed, bringing with it new challenges and new temptations.

'There we are, Mr Ferris. I've put some ice in it,' the nurse said. 'Anything else you'd like?'

'There is, but yer'd have ter draw the screens,' he replied with a saucy wink.

In January 1947 Frank and Ann Johnson became grandparents for the first time, when Beth presented them with healthy twin daughters after a long and tiring birth and warned her husband that she would never let him near her again. That same month Moses walked away from Bermondsey Crown Court a free man, with Bubbles Madigan and her good friend Trixie there to greet him. Photograph bulbs flashed and a picture of the happy, smiling trio made the front pages of the local newspapers.

Mick Constantine was not so fortunate when he appeared at the Old Bailey later that same year. Both Tommy Carberry and a very subdued Johnny Bryan gave evidence for the prosecution, and the Bermondsey gang boss was sentenced to twelve years' imprisonment for attempted murder.

Constantine refused to divorce Mandy and six months later they were reconciled. He ran his affairs from his prison cell, with Mandy acting as proxy. The club in Camberwell was sold, along with the Crown and Anchor, and the money ploughed into the ailing Gold Star Groceries. Saul Kosky was persuaded to return with a free hand to run things his way, and inside two years the business was once again showing a healthy profit.

In the winter of '49 Mick Constantine died of a massive heart attack while exercising in the prison yard, and the following summer Mandy Constantine was married to Gerry Knowland. The Gold Star Groceries went from strength to strength, and in return for his loyalty and business acumen Saul Kosky was given a seat on the board of directors by the Knowlands.

Ben Ferris had married the nurse who had cared for him after he had been shot and was taken on as a sales representative by the company. Shortly after the birth of his second child he was promoted to the vacant sales manager's post.

In 1948 Johnny Bryan was killed in a car accident while drunk at the wheel, and shortly afterwards Tommy Carberry was fatally stabbed outside a Bermondsey backstreet pub. The Carberry investigation file eventually joined the Baz Smithson file at Dockhead Police Station in the section marked unsolved murders.

Darkie Samut moved into the political arena, and in the local elections of '48 he took his place as a Labour member for the Ashley ward on the Bermondsey Borough Council.

Jimmy and Lana were married in the spring of '47 and their union was blessed with three children. Their modest blacksmith's business in Dockhead flourished, and in 1951 they opened the Bailey Engineering Works.

Lottie Curtis survived five more winters, but in December 1952 she developed pneumonia and died in her sleep on Christmas Eve at the good old age of eighty-six. Beside her on her bed was the tattered album of her children, opened at the last page, which now displayed a recent photograph of the last of her brood.

In the summer of 1975, the eminent sociologist Professor Patrick McCarthy undertook an extensive lecture tour on 'Today's diminishing community spirit and its causes'.

'. . . and in conclusion I have to turn once again to the notes of my great uncle Father McCarthy. To quote: "A common people, the working-class, are proud. Joined inseparably by their common enemies: disease, poverty and exploitation. Large families, living for the most part in dark, unsanitary accommodation, not only in London but in all cities and towns throughout the length and breadth of our proud nation. A common people with an indomitable community spirit that cannot be extinguished. Represented and epitomised by the people from the backstreets in my riverside parish. Proud, uncompliant and contumacious, yes, but never too haughty or proud to take another to them. It is my understanding and belief, that in their eyes and in their hearts, there was always room for one more."

Father Shamus P McCarthy,
Bermondsey 1931.'

More Enchanting Fiction from Headline

PEDLAR'S ROW

HARRY BOWLING

In 1946 Pedlar's Row in Bermondsey is home to a close-knit community counting its blessings to have survived the war intact – and full of curiosity about the new family moving into number three. And the Fosters' move into the Row is not without incident

Laura Foster, who's unmarried, having had to care for her invalid father, enjoys the excitement of her new home – not least because of her growing attraction to docker Billy Cassidy. But her sister Lucy finds life harder with rationing, a shortage of homes, having to contend with a husband who is emotionally scarred from his internment in a Japanese POW camp, and her guilt about a war-time affair, it isn't easy to settle down to normal married life. So the situation isn't helped when Lucy finds herself and her family embroiled in local villain Archie Westlake's shady dealings. And when a body is discovered on a bombsite behind the Row, no one is beyond suspicion of murder.

'What makes Harry's novels work is their warmth and authenticity. Their spirit comes from the author himself and his abiding memories of family life as it was once lived in the back streets of southeast London' *Today*

FICTION / SAGA 0 7472 4520 7

More Enchanting Fiction from Headline

PEDLAR'S ROW

HARRY BOWLING

In 1946, Pedlar's Row in Bermondsey is home to a close-knit community counting its blessings to have survived the war intact – and full of curiosity about the new family moving into number three. And the Priors' move into the Row is not without incident.

Laura Prior, who's unmarried, having had to care for her invalid father, enjoys the excitement of her new home – not least because of her growing attraction to docker Billy Cassidy. But her sister Lucy finds life harder; with rationing, a shortage of homes, having to contend with a husband who's emotionally scarred from his internment in a Japanese POW camp, and her guilt about a war-time affair, it isn't easy to settle down to normal married life. So the situation isn't helped when Lucy finds herself and her family embroiled in local villain Archie Westlake's shady dealings. And when a body is discovered on a bombsite behind the Row, no one is beyond suspicion of murder.

'What makes Harry's novels work is their warmth and authenticity. Their spirit comes from the author himself and his abiding memories of family life as it was once lived in the slums of southeast London'
Today

FICTION / SAGA 0 7472 4520 7

More Enchanting Fiction from Headline

The Farrans of Fellmonger Street

FROM THE BESTSELLING KING OF COCKNEY SAGAS

HARRY BOWLING

When widowed Ida Farran runs off with a bus inspector in 1949, she leaves her five children to fend for themselves. Preoccupied with the day-to-day task of earning enough money to keep the family together, eighteen-year-old Rose battles bravely on, thankful for the mysterious benefactor who pays the rent on their flat in Imperial Buildings on Fellmonger Street, a little backwater off the Tower Bridge Road.

Life isn't easy but between them Rose and her younger brother Don just about manage to make ends meet – though the welfare would soon put the three young ones into foster homes if they believed Rose couldn't cope. Recently, however, Don has become rather too friendly with the Morgan boys. Everyone knows the small-time Bermondsey villains are a bad lot and Rose is desperately worried Don might end up in trouble. But even this concern pales into insignificance when Rose finds herself pregnant. Now it'll need a miracle to keep the Farrans of Fellmonger Street together.

FICTION / SAGA 0 7472 4795 1